PRAISE FOR MIKE NICOL

'Compelling . . . like its predecessors in the trilogy, *Black Heart* paints a vivid portrait of post-apartheid society'

MARCEL BERLINS, THE TIMES

'*Black Heart* has a crime fiction duo worthy to be spoken of in the same breath as the late Robert Parker's Spenser and Hawk or Robert Crais' Cole and Pike; plus one of the best – and scariest – female villains I have had nightmares about'

MIKE RIPLEY, SHOTS MAGAZINE

'Mike Nicol's novels have everything I love about the genre in just the right amount: shady characters, twists, turns, murder, mayhem, humour, wonderful dialogue, white-knuckle pace and lots of authentic Cape Town colour'

DEON MEYER

'Mike Nicol is one of the brightest thriller writing talents to have emerged in the last decade, and the Mace and Pylon novels are as good as any being written in the field today. They prove that the thriller, at its best, can both entertain and provoke, while tackling serious issues with the lightest of touches'

JOHN CONNOLLY

'Watch out Elmore Leonard; here comes Mike Nicol'

SOUTHERN MAIL

'South Africa joins the hard-boiled stakes, and in a wondrous, dazzling, humorous novel.'

KEN BRUEN (on OUT TO SCORE)

'I
Nicol's   ecalls
th   '

BLACK HEART

First published in Great Britain in 2011 by Old Street Publishing Ltd
Yowlestone House, Puddington, Tiverton, Devon EX16 8LN
www.oldstreetpublishing.co.uk

This paperback edition published 2012.

ISBN 978-1-906964-99-3

A CIP catalogue record for this title is available from the British Library.

Typeset by Old Street Publishing Ltd.

Printed and bound in Great Britain.

BLACK HEART

MIKE NICOL

Also by Mike Nicol:

PAYBACK
KILLER COUNTRY

BLACK HEART

Wednesday, 27 July

Grainy black-and-white CCTV footage: a man, tallish, bulked out in an anorak, a beanie covering his hair, face down, walking towards the camera along a corridor. Upmarket corridor: marble tiles on the walls and floor, three large photographs of wild beaches hanging on the right-hand side. The photographs in wall-mounted aluminium frames. On the left, two doors. On each the apartment number stencilled in black filling most of the door: 7, 8. A funky touch. At number eight, the man stops, keeping his back to the camera. His head bent forward like he was listening for movement inside the flat, except from the tremor in his shoulders he has to be working something with his hands. Forty seconds spool by, the door pops open. The man rolls down his beanie that becomes a balaclava covering his face. Looks up at the CCTV camera.

'Nice touch,' said the woman watching the footage on her laptop. Speaking aloud, smiling. She tapped the keyboard with her gloved hand to pause the image. Caught her own face reflecting on the screen: her high cheekbones, pencilled eyebrows, the plum richness of her lips. Her latte face ghosting over that of the balaclavaed man. She puckered her lips in a kiss. Putsch.

He was good, the balaclavaed man. Only one or two people she knew could've done it faster. She smiled. Raised her gloved hand to touch theface. 'Mace Bishop,' she said. 'Welcome to my world.'

She clicked play. The man was in. The CCTV footage running on, showing the now empty corridor, the two closed doors. After a minute the automatic timer kicked in, switched off the lights. She waited: three minutes later the lights clicked on. There was the man closing the apartment door, not rushing, keeping his back to the camera. Walking down the corridor to the lift at the far end. Going past the lift to the stairwell, reaching up to take off the balaclava as he disappeared from the screen.

He'd behaved exactly as she'd wanted. Couldn't resist sniffing out her lair.

She ejected the DVD with the CCTV footage from her laptop, the DVD a little favour courtesy of the block's security company. She'd told them it was a friend playing the fool.

'Some friend, some fool,' the boss man at the security company had said, not making too much effort to keep his eyes off her cleavage. 'You know people with interesting skills, Miss February.'

'You better believe it,' she'd said, sashaying out of his office in her long coat, her black hair floating above the collar.

Sheemina February slotted another DVD into the laptop. Footage from her own surveillance system. There was the balaclavaed man in her apartment, picked up on infrared, the colours muted blues and blacks. The balaclava dark blue, the anorak black, the man wearing gloves, jeans, trainers. The uniform of anybody. Standing there, dead still, listening.

No visible gun.

Meant he wasn't expecting her to be home. He was scoping the terrain. Cautious Mace. Predictable Mace. Curious Mace. Exactly what she'd anticipated. Lure him in for the kill shot. It was almost too easy.

On screen the man moving into her open plan lounge by torchlight. Running his fingers along the back of her white sofa, walking across her white flokatis to her desk, opening drawers, fidgeting among her papers, moving on, sliding the beam too quickly over the pictures on the walls to take them in. But stopping at the box of cut-throat razors mounted above her desk.

Blades that had once shaved famous men. Blades she'd tracked down, paid top dollar for. A blade that'd belonged to Cecil Rhodes. Another to a killer called Joe Silver. Had his name engraved on it. A man some historian had fingered as Jack the Ripper. She liked that, the posthumous fame of the gold rush pimp and trafficker, Joe Silver.

Each of the six blades she'd collected had a story. Except there were only five there now. The missing one, her grandfather's, had been used to cut the throat of Mace Bishop's wife. Before that, quarter of a century before that, her grandfather had used it to slit his wrists. Rather die than be turfed out of his house. In a way, Sheemina believed, that particular cut-throat was an instrument of history: destiny manifest. Pity to lose a family heirloom but it couldn't be helped. The razor probably lying in some evidence box waiting for the autopsy hearing. No worries. There were ways she reckoned she could get it back.

She snapped again on Mace Bishop, Mace Bishop focusing on the empty space in her cut-throat collection. Realising that the blade used to kill his wife had once been an ornament on her wall. How'd that make him feel? Rise the rage in him? Bring up the red pulse? What was he thinking, this man, Mace Bishop? This man in her white lair, among her things. This man intent on killing her. Fired by revenge. Did he even begin to figure out why she wanted to hurt him? Why she wanted to ruin him? Wreck his life? He would. By the time she'd finished, he would.

She watched him, as she'd done so many times since he'd broken in, watched him leave the lounge, enter her bedroom. This was the part that got her agitated, excited. Brought up her heart rate. Sent a tingle through the fingers of her broken hand. The hand he'd smashed with a mallet. Back in the day. She crossed her legs.

There he was in her bedroom. Shining the torch over her bed, the bedside table with the digital clock, 04:20, the landline phone on its recharger, the photograph in a silver frame. The only photograph in the apartment. A photograph of Mace Bishop in his Speedo after a swimming session at the gym pool. One of a number she'd taken on the sly. Put it there hoping it would push him over the top.

But he didn't look closely, swept the beam to her built-in cupboards, the light reflecting off her mirror, for a moment whiting out the image. Then he was visible again, reaching to open the doors on her dresses, slacks, jackets, glancing at the racks of shoes stacked at the bottom. She watched him run his hand over one of her evening dresses. Imagined she was wearing it, his hand gliding down her back. Sometimes she thought of him like that. His hands hard against her breasts, hard on her buttocks pulling her into him. She shook her head to throw the thought. Flushed by the thrill of it.

There was the man she wanted to kill with his hands in her underwear, coming out with one of her thongs, satin, red, holding it up, crushing it into his fist. He threw it back into the drawer. Sat on the edge of her bed, bounced like he was testing the comfort factor. Fell backwards against the pillows, his hand sliding underneath, finding a black negligee. Holding it up. Silky. His torch beam sliding from it to the photograph on her bedside table. Pity she couldn't see his expression.

He dropped the negligee, grabbed the photograph for a closer look. Brought the torch up to the glass. Stared at himself: that strong body dripping water, that small costume. Then put the photograph back on the table, carefully. Shot off the bed fast, closed the drawers in the cupboard, shut the doors. Buried the negligee in his anorak pocket, heading out the apartment. The screen darkened, the camera switched off.

Sheemina February fetched a white wine from the fridge, took her time drawing the cork, thinking, he'd aroused her taking the underwear. Something secretive about it. Exciting. Lustful. Sex and death.

She poured a glass: De Grendel sauvignon blanc, tasted it, let the wine lie in the bowl of her mouth before she swallowed. Got herself settled. Thing was, why had he treated the photograph like it didn't matter? She'd expected some violence. Wanted some violence, the glass smashed, the picture ripped out. Which was why she'd set it up. Instead he went Mr Ice. She sat again at her desk, replayed the disc.

Halfway through, her cellphone rang.

'Mart,' she said.

'Just checking in,' said Mart Velaze against a background of music, voices. Mart the government man. National Intelligence Agency.

Who'd called her out of the blue, given her the heads-up on a deal that'd gone down even better than she'd hoped. A deal that'd done for Mace Bishop. Mart who'd handled matters in recent days like he couldn't put a foot wrong. Efficient Mart, looking after her interests. The man with the wide white smile. Except you never knew, was it a smile as in friendly, or a smile as in deadly? The only black man Sheemina February had encountered who'd never pulled a move on her. Which made her wonder: why not? 'Keeping an eye out,' he said.

'There's no need.'

'Part of the service.'

'Not on this score.' Giving him the back-off but holding her voice light all the same. 'Where're you?'

'Not far away. In a cafe opposite the beach. I can come over.'

'Best if you don't.'

'In case something goes wrong.'

'Nothing'll go wrong.'

'You can't be sure in a situation like this.'

'You can't be sure ever, Mart, but you can load the dice.'

'He's going to be focused. In the kill zone.'

'You think I'm not?'

Sheemina February waited for his answer. Heard the cafe music, Tina Turner doing the only Tina Turner anyone played, Simply the Best.

'I'll call you,' she said. 'As we agreed.'

'Yeah,' he said. 'Just get in first, okay. Don't give him a chance.'

'I'm a big girl, Mart. I've been waiting for this for a long time. I'm not going to freak out.'

A pause while Tina Turner had her say.

'Till later.'

Mart said, 'Right.'

She thumbed him off. Useful guy.

He'd got her the gun. The .38 Smith & Wesson. The revolver lying beside the laptop. The gun that would be within reach every moment of the next six, seven, eight hours, however long it was before Mace Bishop rocked up.

Sheemina February took her wine onto the balcony. Stared out over the ocean, a flat glassy sea sliding against the rocks below to break with a crack. The sun lowering, its warmth gone. Tomorrow when it came up everything would be different.

Between then and now all she had to do was wait for him. Mace Bishop. But she was good at waiting.

Tuesday, 12 July

I

No one knew where he was.

He'd been careful.

He was in a pension in Berlin, on Knesebeckstrasse, off the Kurfurstendamm, registered under a false name, J Richter. One of those family hotels.

Pension Savigny. Entered through an unpretentious door on the street, up a flight of stairs. No lift.

The proprietor apologised for the room. If Herr Richter had phoned earlier to make a reservation he could have had a better room. In the summer the hotel was always full. Would have been full had it not been for a cancellation. Herr Richter was very fortunate.

The room was long and narrow. A window into the branches of a plane tree. He couldn't see the street.

He stood at the window. Over the city a thunderstorm crashed, jags of lightning revealing the buildings in white relief. He closed the curtains, eased off his shoes, lay down.

He was on the run. A pity. Another two days he would've been away, off the radar again. What had tipped them off? His mother's death. Of course. He should've been more careful. Should've anticipated that they'd find out. He was careful. Had been careful.

Aka J Richter rubbed his eyes. He needed sleep. Nor was there any point to working out what he'd done wrong. It didn't matter. They'd found him, he was on the run. At worst an inconvenience that required a plan. Tomorrow he'd come up with a plan. A way of getting away. He had time on his side.

He could feel the drowsiness dragging behind his eyes. Being on the run had never troubled his sleep. Not then, not now. He closed his eyes. Fully clothed he drifted off.

Fourteen hours earlier, the man, aka Herr J Richter, had returned from his morning jog to be attacked at the entrance to his mother's apartment block. Two men trying to hustle him into a white Audi. Except a neighbour with a broom came to his rescue, beating at the men. A wild violence that brought others out. The men gave up and drove off. To Richter's surprise they hadn't waved guns around. Usually the Albanians weren't so polite.

'Criminals,' said his neighbour. 'Russians most probably. They want ransom money. Anything. Even a few hundred euros.' He offered tea. Said they should call the police.

The man, aka Herr J Richter, said, no, it wasn't necessary. He would go later to report it. Right now he needed to calm down. Get his breath back. Steady his shaking hands.

'Tea with three sugars,' said the neighbour. 'And some schnapps.'

Upstairs aka Richter found the apartment trashed. At first wandered around in the chaos panting from the shock, the attack, the hour's jogging. Control, he kept telling himself. Stay alert. Clear-headed. Think about this carefully. They want you to run.

He didn't, wouldn't run blindly. Next time they'd be brutal.

He cleared up the mess, put everything to rights. Packed his suitcase and an overnight bag. Decided he would wait till dark. Do not panic, he told himself.

The hours of the morning passed minute by minute, sometimes he watched the second hand go round on the grandfather clock, thuk, thuk, thuk in the quiet. The chimes on the quarter hour. Sitting there waiting. He tried to read. Fetched the book beside his bed, settled in his mother's armchair. Found his place: chapter thirty-one. 'He knew he was dreaming, knew he couldn't stop.' Carried on to the end of the chapter: 'Ed changed and taped his spare key to the door. He left a light burning.' What had happened in between he couldn't say. His eyes sliding over the words like there wasn't a story in them. He put the book aside. He needed activity.

Richter sat down at the piano. His fingers flat on the keys. The deformed little finger of his left hand, too short to touch the ivory. But he'd learnt to compensate. He could play a jazz tune and fool most everyone. He started in on Gershwin, Summertime. Only it'd been a long while since he'd played. Too long. The notes cracking, off-key. The phrases impossible, taunting him, out of reach. He kept running through the phrases again and again until he slammed the lid down. Sat there staring at the blur of his body in the varnished wood. For half an hour he didn't move. Eventually he got up, went to the window, checked the street. The car hadn't moved. Throughout the afternoon he checked the street.

The white Audi parked a hundred metres down towards the river didn't leave all day.

They wanted him to make a move. Run scared. Make their job easier to pluck him off the street. To have him disappear.

On a Thursday like any other in Frankfurt an der Oder.

He watched the street: pedestrians, pensioners pulling shopping baskets, boys on skateboards, girls in skimpy clothes with cellphones. Traffic. A van offloaded vegetables, fruit, crates of milk at the supermarket. Municipal men repaired a water main. At the small cafe opposite, the pavement tables filled during lunchtime. Come four-thirty the owner shut up shop.

He thought about making a phone call. Throughout the day he'd thought about making a phone call. The landline would be tapped. His cellphone too. There was his mother's cellphone, he could use that. An old model. A brick. Pay as you go. But it would be unexpected. Short and sweet might be too fast for them.

He hoped there was airtime.

He put through the call. In English said, 'Quickly. They have found me. I will need help later.' He disconnected. Switched off the phone.

He doubted the men in the Audi were scanning the building but you never knew. It didn't take much equipment. If they picked up the call they would pick up the destination too. Not a happy thought. Perhaps it had been a mistake to phone. But he'd needed to. Needed to talk. Even a few words.

He told himself to calm down. He walked around the apartment touching objects. The brass candlesticks. The carriage clock. Ornamental art deco figurines. Small busts of composers. His father's pipes on a wooden stand. The cushions his mother embroidered. The family photographs in silver frames on a silver tray with bone handles. His father, aged twenty-five, twenty-six, holding a bunch of fish. His mother, about the same age, wearing a nurse's uniform. The young family on a beach when he and his sister were children in the 1960s. His graduation day.

He poured himself a short vodka, wished his mother had kept whisky. Forced himself to sit down and drink it slowly.

July's long light was a downside. But the man Richter sat it out. With the twilight, switched on lights in the apartment for the benefit of the two men in the Audi. Ensured they saw his shadow pass across the windows.

In the dying day, fifteen minutes before the train was due, he left the apartment. Paused once in the doorway to look into the sitting room, a sentimental moment. Quickly he pulled the door closed, locked it.

He left the block by a back exit through a park. Only groups of teenagers still on the grass. Drinking beer. Smoking. Listening to loud rap music. He came out three streets from the station. Quiet streets where a man could hurry past the open doors unnoticed. He took the last train to Berlin. Easy as that. From the train's phone made the hotel reservation.

Heard the proprietor's bluster, 'This is very late for a reservation.'

'I'm sorry. Can you help me?'

The tutting. 'Ja, gut, we have one room only. A single room.'

'That is all I need.'

At Berlin Zoo the man Richter left the suitcase in a locker, walked up the Kurfurstendamm while the storm rumbled nearer. No reason to think anyone knew where he was.

He went for a run early the next morning. Along Knesebeck to Ku'damm, up the slow rise to Halensee. Running easily, sweating in the hot and humid dawn, the city unrelieved by the rain storm. At the lake he watched the swimmers, pale flesh in the brown water, couldn't see what pleasure they took. Most of them naked. Older people, impossible to tell the genders apart.

By now the men in the Audi would be hunting him again. They would know he'd caught the Berlin train. They would be here watching the airports. And the stations, Haupt, Zoo. Richter decided he would take buses, then regional trains to a big city, Leipzig maybe, hire a car there. Keep moving. It was best to keep moving. Drive to Vienna. They would not be watching that airport. Get a flight to Dubai. A link to Johannesburg. Ja, gut, to quote the pension proprietor. Why not? By Wednesday he would be home in Cape Town. A different man.

Smiling, Richter left the swimmers of Halensee, jogged easily up the hill to the interchange, crossed the railway bridge, loped down the wide pavements. Antsy to be on the stir again.

At the pension he showered, changed into a golf shirt, brown chinos, moccasins, no socks. Stuck his sunglasses in the neck of his shirt. A man with casual business in the city. Perhaps in tourism. Or sports accessories. An unpretentious man who preferred quaint pensions to the big hotels. A man relaxed in the breakfast room, admiring the high moulded ceilings, photographs of old Berlin on the walls.

In English he advised a young American couple to take a booze cruise along the Spree. They looked like kids, early twenties at best. 'Not long ago there were gunships on the canal,' he told them, 'now it is a tourist pleasure. The world changes.'

The couple laughed. The boy-man said, 'Great, hey thanks, man.' The girl-wife doing a full teeth display.

The couple went off.

Richter smiled. What was great? The world changing? The gunships? The outing? Perhaps it was George Bush-land made them peculiar.

The proprietor approached, offered a coffee refill. Asked if mein Herr would like the room for another night?

Richter said, unfortunately, no. A lovely hotel – made an expansive gesture round the room – but he was on his way to Hamburg. To spend the weekend with family. A sister's brood.

Ja, gut, said the proprietor, he would make out the bill.

An hour later aka Richter sauntered along Knesebeck towards Zoo. A man seemingly at leisure, except the man wasn't. The man watched ahead. Checked in shop windows at those behind him. Stopped suddenly to search in his bag, took time to scan the street. Ten paces on did it again. And at the railway bridge. You couldn't be too careful.

Not in this heat. Not when you sweated just walking fifty metres. The heat made you fuzzy. Inattentive. Likely to make mistakes. Better to be on a bus, minimise the risk. But first there was his suitcase in the locker. His laptop. The files.

On the corner of Kant a man grabbed his overnight bag, wrenched it from him, threw it into the back of a white Audi. The man shoving him after it. Richter sprawled onto the seat. The man ducked in behind him, pushed a gun into his kidneys.

The car pulled off slowly. A pedestrian running alongside, knocking on the window. Shouting, 'Halt, halt.'

'Polizei,' the driver shouted back. The citizen stopped, stood watching the car merge into the traffic.

'We are going somewhere quiet,' said the man in the back seat, speaking Albanian. 'And no more Herr Richter, okay.' Pinching Richter's cheek. 'What do you like to call yourself these days? Max Roland, isn't it? We have a lot to talk about, not so, Max?'

'Tricky Max,' said the driver, grinning at him in the rearview mirror. Playing with him, reaching over to grab his left hand. 'Ah, there we are, Max.' Holding up Max Roland's small finger. 'Only one knuckle. This's how they told us we would recognise you.' He held up a photograph. 'In case you were in disguise. But you're too cocksure for that.' He flipped the photograph onto the passenger seat. 'Come, Max, don't be so disappointed. Be happy it is us. If it wasn't, you would be in the shit with the guys from The Hague.'

'Locked away forever,' said the man beside him. 'What a sad life that would be.'

The two men laughed.

Max Roland swallowed hard, wanted to puke.

Saturday, 23 July

2

'Mr Oosthuizen,' the voice said. 'I think you need my help.'

Magnus Oosthuizen glanced at his cellphone screen: private number.

'Who is this?' he said.

'Right now who I am doesn't matter,' said the voice.

A woman's voice, clear, bold. Slight accent on the vowels, made them too full, over elaborate. Cape Town. Probably coloured, he reckoned. One of the educated ones straining to overcome the nasal flatness of her kind.

'What matters is that I know about your weapons system and that I know you need fathering – or should I say mothering. Seriously, I'm surprised you've managed this long without anyone to smooth your way with the government people, but as you know that time has ended.'

'I don't know who you are,' said Oosthuizen. 'Goodbye.'

'If I were you,' said the caller, 'I would be curious. I would want to know how this mysterious person got my cell number. How she knew about the weapons system. How she knew that once I had the ear of the right government men. And I would want to know what was meant by "that time has ended." With so much money at stake, I would be anxious. Like you I would huff and bluff, but I wouldn't let this unexpected conversation end, shall we say, inconclusively.'

Magnus Oosthuizen closed his eyes, pinched the bridge of his nose. Released his fingers. Shivered, turned up the temperature on the heater. Damp Cape Town winters got into your bones.

'Who are you?'

'One thing you will have to learn about me, Mr Oosthuizen, is I'm not big on repetition.'

Oosthuizen rose from the couch to stand at the window looking into the garden: long bright lawn edged with lavender bushes, at the far end the gardener skimming leaves from the pool. Might have been poling a gondola down a Venice canal with that action. John the Malawian. Probably got the motion growing up on the lake, Oosthuizen liked to joke to his cronies.

'Shall I help you out, Mr Oosthuizen? Shall I answer some of those niggling questions for you?'

Niggling. Truly a jumped-up lady.

'Ja,' said Oosthuizen. 'Okay.' He sat down again. Chin-chin his Chihuahua in a tartan jacket pawed to be picked up. Stared at him goggle-eyed, whining. 'Ag, no, man,' he whispered at the dog, brushing it away. Chin-chin came back, snapping at his fingers.

'Let me give you the name Mo Siq.'

'What about him?'

The dog yapped, high-pitched, insistent. Oosthuizen bent over to scoop him up, settled the animal on his lap.

'Is that a Chihuahua?' said the woman.

'It is.'

'Horrible dogs,' she said. 'Very northern suburbs.'

'Mrs,' said Oosthuizen 'I …'

'Ms. But we'll get to my name. Back to Mo Siq. Government front man on the arms deal, till he was assassinated. Before that your advisor. Proposer. Guardian angel. Inside man. How you've managed these last few years without him, I don't know. Congratulations, Mr Oosthuizen. You survived the vipers. That took some doing. And fancy footwork. Perhaps you are a ballroom dancer. Any questions so far?'

'How did you get my phone number?'

The woman laughed. A light gentle laugh. 'That's an easy one. It is right here in Mo's laptop. Let me put it this way: Mo's laptop was one of the things I inherited on his death.'

'You stole it.'

'Inherited, Mr Oosthuizen. There are circumstances you are not aware of. Now ...' – she paused, he heard the splash of a drink being poured – '*prost*, Mr Oosthuizen ...' – he heard her sip – 'nothing to beat the sauvignon blanc, when it's good.' Another sip. Oosthuizen checked his watch. Wine at eleven-forty on a Tuesday morning! 'Now, Mr Oosthuizen, what you should want to know' – her voice more liquid, oiled – 'is what do I know that you don't?'

'Listen, Ms ...'

'No, you listen, Mr Oosthuizen, this will be worth your while. You see I know that the Europeans have an offset budget as part of their tender for the weapons system.'

'That is no secret.'

'By offset, I mean, not to be prissy about it, bribes. Not promises of stainless steel plants. Not aluminium smelters. Not condom factories. Bribes, Mr Oosthuizen. Money in the back pockets of the government men. In Cayman accounts. Or Channel Islands, Iceland, Barbados, wherever their back pocket happens to be. The sort of back pockets you cannot fill, Mr Oosthuizen, which is why you need me.'

'And what can you do?' Oosthuizen snorted, squirmed to resettle the dog from squashing his balls. Chin-chin grizzled.

'A lot,' said the voice. 'Believe me. Keep your scientist Max Roland alive for one thing. Get him freed for another. Even help you bring him home.'

'Where are you?' said Oosthuizen.

'In the same city as you, Mr Oosthuizen. How about a drink this afternoon at the Waterfront? Den Anker. We have much to discuss. Why don't you join me?'

'How will I recognise you? I don't even know your name.'

'You won't. And admittedly, you don't. Much better you don't know my name until we meet. All very mysterious, I realise, but that's my style, Mr Oosthuizen. Shall we say at five? I'll be the blonde with the rosebud. But don't worry, I'll recognise you.'

<h1 style="text-align:center">3</h1>

Sheemina February switched off the handset.

Mr Magnus Oosthuizen, one of the world's survivors. Like her. Like her, an operator working the system, except he didn't know how the system was about to work him. And the attractive Max Roland. The ladies' man.

She put down the phone, went to stand on the balcony with her glass of wine. Rested her rigid left hand on the stainless steel railing. Looked down at the sea, still wild from the last storm, still lathered with brown foam, still pounding on the rocks three storeys below. She could have bought that apartment, the lowest one: had seen it on a calm day with the sea a slow gurgle along the rockline. Very beguiling. Seductive. To sit on the balcony so close to the water, like being on a boat. But she knew the Cape Town seas, knew they could rise up with power and destroy. Hadn't happened yet but the chances were it would one day.

She took a sip of the wine, held it in her mouth to absorb the flavours.

The pity of it was she would have to leave her lair. Her white lair, this cave in the cliff face. A luxurious cave in a cliff of expensive caves owned by film stars, rich business machers, trust babies, high-flying models with too much money too soon.

But for her plans to succeed she had to leave the flat and wait. Ever the black widow under the eaves, waiting for the fly, Mace Bishop.

For years she had treasured the apartment. Allowed no one into it. Not even casual lovers. Lair and sanctuary was how she saw it. All that was ended now, now it was a web.

She turned to face the room: the white couches between white flokatis on ash flooring. On most surfaces, white votive candles that she lit at night. Limewashed dining-room table and chairs.

Her haven. Her large, open-plan ritual of white.

Except she wore black: boots, slacks, a roll-neck top. A black leather glove on her tormented hand when she went out. A long black coat against the cold. Sometimes a pashmina under the collars hanging down. For flair. For her tall elegance. Black to sharpen the ice-blue of her eyes. Black in this bright white world. Apart from her short blond hair. But that was temporary, a disguise of sorts. Not her colour or her style, just an expediency. Times would change she'd go back to the black bob.

She sipped again at the wine. What a wonder was life?

Sheemina February smiled at her reflection in the plate-glass picture windows. Gave a flick to her blond hair. Sometimes life played into your hands. Hand. Magnus Oosthuizen and Max Roland were prime candidates for Mace Bishop's services. How convenient. And at a time when Mr Bishop was staggering with grief, mourning for his lovely Oumou, and slowly losing his daughter. Poor man, this couldn't come at a worse time for him. If she could swing it his way which she was sure she could. Magnus Oosthuizen would be clay. Like the clay Mace's lovely wife Oumou had used to make her little pots.

'What're you but a matchmaker, Sheemina,' she said aloud. 'You should get a commission.'

She went inside, drew closed the sliding door. On her laptop were pictures from Mart Velaze, pictures of Max Roland, a completely naked Max Roland. The background was a white tiled wall, his hands were raised above his head, tied with plastic straps to a shower nozzle. The position gave excellent definition to his body: the line of his arms, chest, flat stomach, strong thighs, although his calves were too small. A well-toned body that needed more work on the calves. A runner, they said. Sometimes runners had surprisingly small calves. Swimmers, too. Like Mace Bishop. For a long-distance swimmer he had thin calves. The longer she stared at the body of Max Roland the more his physique reminded her of Mace Bishop. Perhaps that was the attraction.

She sat down at the dining-room table, pulled the laptop closer.

A series of four photographs, taken over some hours, she imagined. In the first there was still strength in Max Roland's body. Resignation on his face, his feet planted apart. In the second: his right leg bent at the knee to prop himself against the wall. Something starting in his face: a tightening at the eyes, his lips slightly parted. The next showed his hand clasping the showerhead as if he were trying to hold himself upright. His mouth open. She imagined he was panting. Sheemina February zoomed in on his nostrils. Examined how they flared wider in each of the pictures. Also his lips were dry. She could see the tip of his tongue in the third photograph. And his eyes had gone feral: tiny black pupils staring off to the left. In the fourth he was wet, his blond hair plastered against his scalp. Droplets on his chest hair. His eyes were closed, his mouth gaping. They'd opened the shower to revive him but it hadn't: he dangled from the nozzle, his full weight dragging on his arms, his body arching forward, his feet buckled under him. He would be hurting. Sheemina February reckoned twenty-four, thirty hours maximum to get him to that state. Probably with some help that was invisible in the photographs. A couple of jabs with a taser worked wonders.

Imagine having Mace Bishop in that condition? In that position?

She zoomed in on the genitals. In number one the scrotum tight, the penis withdrawn into its bush. Reminded her of a moray eel. Number two was different: his sac fallen, his cock thrust forward by the posture. Drooping in the third photograph, thin and useless. Lastly, fallen forward like old fruit left too long on the tree, purpled, stung by wasps and flies.

Sheemina February closed the file, opened the document that contained the other information about Max Roland. For an hour she read through it, too absorbed even to refill her glass of wine.

Afterwards she made a salad for lunch, took another glass of the sauvignon blanc. Undoubtedly Max Roland and Magnus Oosthuizen would make excellent clients for Mace Bishop. How strangely the world worked. How conveniently sometimes.

She fished from her handbag the photograph of Mace Bishop she kept in a plastic sleeve. Mace wearing a black Speedo about to dive into the gym swimming pool where three times a week he put in the laps. Where she'd go to watch, if the urge took her. Watch without his knowing. Just like she'd snapped the photo surreptitiously. He had a good figure for the most part, perhaps a thickening at the waist, but otherwise trim enough. She held the picture in the fingers of her rigid hand.

At four-fifteen Sheemina February left her apartment. From the marble corridor she activated the alarm system by remote. Took the lift up two flights to the foyer, the stairs to the rooftop parking. Three cars in the visitors' bays, other than that her neighbour's Merc, the BMW of the widow below her. Next to it her big BMW X5. The breeze pulled at her coat, a cold viciousness off the sea that made her shiver. She drew closed the coat with her gloved hand. Breathed in deeply the strong tang of the sea.

Twenty-five minutes later Sheemina February took a table in the restaurant facing the door, laid a rosebud across the tablecloth. She was well ahead of time. She had no doubt that Magnus Oosthuizen would be early too. He was that sort of man. Wary. Suspicious.

Sunday, 24 July

4

Mace Bishop, an empty coffee mug in his hand, sat on the deck of his house staring over the city. Cape Town on a cold afternoon, daylight fading, rain still in the air. Solid Gold Sunday on the radio. Thought of how it was seven or eight weeks back. How it was before Oumou was killed. Her lovely presence. Her calm. Her quiet. The touch of her. Their daughter Christa standing with an arm around them both for a photograph. Before Oumou was slashed to death downstairs in her own pottery studio, the blood, the blood pouring from her, her body heavy in his arms, on a Sunday like this. Except earlier they'd been laughing. Happy times then.

Now he was alone. Christa with her friend Pumla. Rather there than at home. Yesterday's music playing. A Rolling Stones number about a line of cars painted black.

Mace hurled the mug against the house wall. One of Oumou's mugs. The mug exploded, shards ricocheting at him.

He'd have cried if he could.

The thing with grief, Mace thought, was the pain. You couldn't get rid of the ache. It lodged in your chest heavy and throbbing. Every waking moment. One kind of relief was to sleep. A double whisky. One, two, three Ambiens. Go blank on the blood that had pumped out of her.

Or keep on the move. Work. Swim. Those long distances, length on length through the pool down the white lane without a thought, without the hurt. Just the mechanics of it, arm after arm coming up and out and down, bubbles streaming away. Until his arms couldn't take any more. His lungs were good, but his arms slowed first. Got so he could hardly pull himself out of the pool at the rungs. No strength to hold on.

Then the trembling. The muscle spasms. More like shaking than trembling. Only a hot shower could stop it. Afterwards he'd dress slowly. Distracted, remembering the blood. With no reason to go home.

Except there was Christa. When Christa was home. Mostly she seemed to be at school, with Pumla, anywhere but home. And when she was, she was locked behind her bedroom door into her iPod and her novels. She and Mace moving around one another like ghosts. Oumou's murder pushing them apart.

Earlier, in the morning, he'd swum for hours until his arms gave in. Come back, mooned about the house. Christa on a sleepover. He'd watched movies. Sat in Oumou's studio with the big clean patch on the floor, staring at the items she'd made arranged along the shelves. The plates, bowls, vases that would never be fired.

Most days he sat there. Sat staring, hurting for her.

Remembered coming down the stairs, seeing the blood first. The smear of it across the floor. Then Oumou's feet. Then her body, the barber's razor in her back, her dress soaked red, the blade slashes across her hands, arms, throat. Her face turned to him. Her eyes losing their light.

He had watched more movies. Eventually taken a mug of coffee on to the deck. The mountain behind, grey cliffs rising into mist. Cape Town below wet and glistening, a hard light on the sea.

He thought of Christa. Of being father to a daughter without a mother. Could it be more difficult? Her hurt that she kept silent. Except her nagging insistence: teach me to shoot.

'I do that,' Mace'd said, 'you have to be okay about killing someone.'

'I'm just learning to aim straight.'

'No you're not.'

'I'm not going to shoot anyone.' She'd turned her back on him, stood staring out the window at the city. Mace'd put his hands on her shoulders but she'd shrugged away. 'I have to protect myself.'

The unspoken criticism: because you can't. Or my mother wouldn't be dead.

Mace'd said, 'You're prepared to shoot a human being?'

She'd snapped back. 'Yes.'

'Even if they don't have a gun?'

'A man threatens me, yes.'

'The law doesn't allow it.'

'Papa,' Christa'd said, 'my Maman was killed.'

More unspoken criticism: what's the use of the law?

Good question, Mace figured. Obvious answer. He'd agreed, yes, alright, he'd teach her to shoot.

Not a thank you. Not a hug. Not a kiss of reconciliation. Just: 'When?'

'Can't be this weekend,' he'd said.

'You see. That's what you always say.'

'I've got a business to run, C. Clients. I can't go dashing out whenever I want to. I can't leave Pylon to manage everything.'

'I'm your daughter,' she'd said. Plugged in her iPod, picked up her book, refused to look at him, to answer him, turned away when he'd sat down opposite her to beg, yes, beg for her not to be like that.

That'd been Friday night.

What Mace didn't know was that she'd cut herself later. Taken one of his three-bladed razor heads, held it between her thumb and index finger, ran the blades gently along her inner thigh for a couple of centimetres, high up just below her panty line. Pain that burnt. Made her suck in her breath, bite on her teeth, ball her free hand into a fist. But for the long moment the blades sliced in, the cut was all she felt.

A longer score than the first one. The old scabs crusted, brushed off, leaving pale stripes. Three parallel lines. The new blood below, beading, rivering down her thigh. She dabbed at the flow with toilet paper, let the cuts bleed until the blood coagulated.

Saturday morning Treasure had called round to pick up Christa. Pregnant Treasure and her daughter, Pumla. Pylon driving his wife and step-daughter. He'd stayed out of it. Treasure hadn't. When Christa wouldn't kiss her father goodbye, Treasure'd got out of the car, waddled over to Mace, took him aside.

'Get your act together, okay. She's hurting, Mace. Let Pylon run the business. Be with her. Go away with her like you've been threatening. She needs closure. Go to Malitia. Let her see where her mother grew up. Scatter Oumou's ashes, give the girl something. Some emotion. Some memories. You close up. You think it's macho holding it all together. It's not. It's not doing her any good. She thinks you're cold. That you don't care. She wants to see you cry, Mace. Be like her, so heartsore her chest wants to burst.'

'I am,' said Mace..

'You could fool me.'

She got into the car. Mace, his hands in his pockets, stood looking at them: the happy family and his daughter. Pylon shrugged in sympathy, fired the car, reversed into the street. Only Treasure waved as they drove off.

Mace gazed up at the mountain's heights: above the ridge patches of blue opening in the clouds. He needed to do something: swim or climb the mountain. Maybe up there a thug bastard would be kind enough to mug him. He could vent a little. Like bash the dipshit's brains out with a rock.

The emptiness of the house when he went back in was chilling. A physical cold. And silence. Silence like being in a glass cube: you could see the outside, you just couldn't hear it.

Cat2 rubbed against his legs, made her strangled cry. As a kitten she'd been hung on the wall of a rave club. Mace stroked her, could feel the lump of scar tissue at the back of her neck where the nail had gone through. Lifted her up, said, 'This is crappy, Cat2. Crappy as hell.' Cat2 opened her mouth, gave a soundless pink yowl.

He fed her smoked pilchards, grabbed his kitbag, headed for the Alfa Spider. A swim, long and hard, was the best option. Only thing, the Spider wouldn't start. Great idea as a car, only it was acting up. Had become unreliable. Temperamental. Then again it was old. Thirty-five, thirty-six years. Except back in the day it hadn't been as bad.

He had no choice but to take Oumou's station wagon. He'd driven it a couple of times since. Meant to sell it but couldn't place the advert. If it wasn't there, the car in the garage, her absence would be worse. Yet another gap, yet another reminder of the hole in his life.

The car still smelt of her. Of clay and perfume. Even these weeks later. Still had memories of her everywhere. Dry knobs of clay in the boot. In the cubby hole hairclips and sunglasses. Under the front seat a pair of canvas shoes he'd found while trying to stow his gun. Oumou. Put a hand into a seat pocket and there'd be a strand of hair, long, black. Her long black silky hair that she'd waft across his chest. Sitting on him, her breasts pushed through the cloud of hair, stroking it across him until he had to pull her down, close on her lips. Kiss her, get lost in her.

He snapped away from the memory. Fumbled the key into the ignition, started the engine. Revved the motor harder than he had to.

For the rest of the weekend Mace watched movies, slept, again went swimming to keep the blood from seeping into his mind. Thing was he could've taken Christa to the range in the quarry. Done something for her.

Instead sat flopped before the flat screen: Once Upon a Time in the West, episodes of Deadwood, The Outlaw Josey Wales.

Slept. Swam. Ended up on Sunday afternoon, Cat2 in his lap, watching the beginning of Once Upon a Time over and over again. The first six minutes with the three shooters at the station. The rhythmic screech of the windmill, the buzz of a fly. The guy on the bench trapping the fly in the barrel of his gun. Holding the gun against his cheek, smiling at the angry buzz. Until the train's whistle cut the quiet. The piston thunder of the train coming across the flats. And the gunmen checking their hardware, walking out onto the platform as the train pulled in. A man got off. Not their man. The men relaxing, moving away while the train draws out. Then the harp, the loud strong call of the harp and the men turning to face the Bronson character – Harmonica.

The long wail gave Mace chills down his spine. Thrilling. The sort of signature tune you needed.

Harmonica drawing it out, unhurried. Eventually letting the mouth organ dangle on the lanyard round his neck.

'Where's Frank?'

'Frank sent us.'

Harmonica's stare, eyes shifting to the three horses roped to a railing. 'Didn't bring a horse for me?'

'Looks like we're shy one horse,' says fly catcher, the men laughing.

Harmonica slowly, barely shaking his head. 'You brought two too many.' The flat no-nonsense: 'You brought two too many.'

Mace loved it. Legendary. The tight moment before the gunfight, and after the bullets only the creak of the windmill turning. Then Harmonica slowly sitting up.

Five times he watched those six minutes. Afterwards he'd sat in Oumou's studio, then gone upstairs, switched on Solid Gold Sunday, made coffee, taken it outside. Sat there in dark self-pity while the Stones sang Paint it Black. Hurled the mug against the wall. An overwhelming sadness filled his chest.

He phoned Christa.

Her reluctant, 'Papa.'

'What'ja doing?'

'Nothing. Watching movies.'

'Yeah, what?'

'Scream 3.'

'Again?'

'It's cool.'

He could hear how cool the screams were in the background. What was it with teens and slasher films?

'You haven't been out anywhere?'

'It's been raining.'

'Not all the time.'

'Most of the time.'

A pause. Mace gripping the cellphone tighter.

'You've done your homework?'

She sighed.

'Have you?'

'Friday night, Papa. You saw me.'

'Just checking.'

'You don't have to.'

'I know, C.' He wanted to say, 'I miss you not being here' but didn't.

If he'd said that, she'd have said, 'Why? We don't do anything together.'

And there was no answer to that.

Instead he said, 'Has Pylon left yet?'

Christa said, 'I think so. Hang on.' Then: 'Not long ago.'

'We're picking up clients from the airport,' said Mace. 'Should be finished by eight, then I'll fetch you.'

'Can't I stay here?'

'It's school tomorrow.'

'I can go through with Pumla.'

'I don't think so, C.'

'Why not?'

'I don't want it that way. We've got to be together on this.'

A silence. Long enough to make Mace edgy but he held off breaking it.

Then: 'Pylon's got hair clippers. Electric ones. Pumla can shave my head.'

Mace frowned. 'What for?'

'For Maman. It's like tradition for people in mourning.'

'Whose tradition?'

'Pumla says people do it.'

Mace thought, Jesus Christ! Said, 'No, C. It's not something we do.'

Silence again. He could imagine the sulkiness in her mouth.

Then: 'Take me shooting.'

This was something he could relate to. 'Next Saturday.'

'Promise.'

'Of course.'

'Promise.'

'Promise, C.'

'I'm going now,' she said.

Mace nodded. Couldn't get any words out to say goodbye before she disconnected.

He put down his cellphone, let the wallow engulf him. In the midst of it thought of Sheemina February. Like she was standing nearby in her long black coat, black gloves, holding out to him a red rosebud. A smile on her lips showing the tips of perfect teeth. Her eyes ice blue. He got out the photograph the German woman had taken: he and Christa on the mountain at the cable station, not long after Oumou's killing. Despite the grief, a good picture of them. Except there in the background, the figure of Sheemina February, watching them.

5

The first morning Max Roland thought God was calling. He woke to a voice. Loud. Insistent. Booming out from speakers. Filling his hotel room. An amplified God. A voice joined by other voices.

Max Roland lay on a single bed covered by a sheet. His arms hurt. The weals around his wrists were livid. Otherwise he was okay. Over the ordeal.

Except now there was God.

He propped himself up, groaned at the ache in his arm muscles, collapsed back on the bed.

There was light at the open windows. Dawn with the heat pressing down.

Not God but the mullahs calling the faithful to prayer. He listened. Wondered why they needed loudspeakers? Why their voices were no longer enough?

Max Roland could see a blood-red dawn behind the far hills. At any moment expected the sky to crack, God's mouth to appear. This was how the world would end. Fire in the morning, a voice across the sky. Angry. Demanding obedience. Obeisance.

He'd quickly got used to the dawn chorus. There was no sleeping through it, but afterwards the city rested. Stasis in the moments between the prayers and the traffic.

He would read. A thriller he'd bought at the airport. He would soon finish the book. He would have to start it again.

Before breakfast each morning, Max Roland jogged into the souk, quiet and shut, jogged up to the Great Mosque. At first the alleys had been confusing but he soon figured them out. Enjoyed this time in the praying city before the sun set fire to the heat. With every morning his mind running away from the room of white tiles, the patient, insistent men.

Now, on the fifth night, he phoned Magnus Oosthuizen from the hotel phone in reception. What passed as a reception. A counter with a registration book on it. A languid young man in attendance. Men chewing qat lay about the room on cushions. Sometimes they talked. Mostly they chewed with a slow concentration. Watched scenes from a war on television, the sound turned down. Listened to a pop singer wailing the anguish of love on a portable radio.

'Max,' said Magnus Oosthuizen, 'for God's sake.'

'I thought so,' said Max Roland. 'On the first morning definitely that is what I thought.'

'What?' said Oosthuizen. 'What are you talking about?'

Max Roland told him about the voices of God.

Oosthuizen said, 'Where are you?'

'Sana'a,' said Max Roland. 'Yemen.'

'Yemen. How the hell did you get there?'

'By plane, of course.'

'I thought … I thought you'd been caught.'

'Yes, that is true. But then I got away. They were careless. These Albanians think they are too clever but they make mistakes. So I walked out.'

'With money to buy an air ticket?'

'With my suitcase, yes.'

Max Roland heard long distance telephone crackle, one of Oosthuizen's silences. He waited.

'Just like that?'

'I told you. They are stupid.'

'Maybe they let you go,' said Oosthuizen. 'Maybe they followed you.'

'Bah!' Max Roland pinched some fresh leaves off the qat twigs, stuffed them in his mouth. Chewed.. 'That is why I am in Yemen. To make sure they did not. It is the last place on the earth they would think of.'

'I'll send someone,' said Oosthuizen, Max Roland smiling to himself at how Oosthuizen had lowered his tone, calmed his voice. 'Are you alright?'

'Oh ja,' said Max Roland. 'I like it very much here.'

'And you haven't been followed.'

'No, no. But now it is time to move again.'

'Give me a day,' said Oosthuizen. 'I'll get back to you. On this phone.'

'Of course,' said Max Roland, tasted the bitter qat in his mouth. Five days is too long in one place.'

'I'll get you home,' said Oosthuizen. 'Believe me, we have to move quickly.'

'You can call me in the afternoons. I am in the garden then. Reading. In the afternoons.'

Magnus Oosthuizen didn't respond. Max Roland said, 'I am getting anxious.'

'Are you eating?' Oosthuizen asked. 'What time is it there?'

Max Roland looked at his wrist watch. Frowned. Said, 'Eleven twenty.'

'You're eating supper?'

'Leaves. Qat,' said Max Roland. 'Everyone does from lunch time into the night to slow down the city. A most wonderful habit. We all have green teeth.' He laughed.

'Stay there, in the hotel,' said Magnus Oosthuizen. 'I will phone you tomorrow afternoon.'

'Please,' said Max Roland. He smiled at the languid young man. Replaced the phone in its docking station, took his branch of qat into the garden.

A small garden lit by candles. A garden lush with trees and shrubs, protected by high walls from the street. An oasis in a desert city. Yet as hot here, even at this time of night, as anywhere in the crumbling hotel. He sat on a bench. Wondered why the Albanians had been so careless. Wondered how close they were to tracking him down. By now they would have made the links. Definitely it was time to be on the move again. He tore off more qat leaves, stuffed them into his mouth. Chewed. Sometimes in transit was the safest place to be. Sometimes in transit felt like prison.

6

Mace's cellphone rang. 'Old son, Dave here,' the voice said. 'I've got something for you.'

What he had was an address.

'I'm not saying it's her, my son. I'm saying it could be.'

A Bantry Bay address.

'Very nice apartment. Very nice block. On the rocks. You stand on your balcony you could be on a ship. Know what I mean? Ocean, my son. Miles and miles of ocean. All the way to the horizon. Pad like that's worth a mint. Sort of place the rich Jews buy. As a summer hangout. They come back for Christmas from Tel Aviv, Toronto, Sydney, wherever the hell they've buggered off to. Well, not exactly for Christmas. Though I've known some celebrate it on account of the presents.'

Mace said, 'How'd you know it's hers?'

'That's it, my son. I don't. I'm guessing. On account of there's no title deeds, no transfers, no paperwork. Deeds office's got zilch. Everything misfiled I reckon. Nudge, nudge, wink, wink. Only thing, my son, Dave's an estate agent with connections. Turns out I know the agent who sold the flat. Asked her if the buyer was a coloured lady, a lawyer, black hair, startling blue eyes. Bingo. Number one ID. Except the agent says she's a blondie now. Got rid of that black bob a few weeks ago, got it short like what d'you call that style, pageboy.'

'All the same, no doubts?'

'Not a one, son.'

Mace took down the address in ballpoint on the palm of his hand.

'I get any thanks for this?' Dave said.

'Sure,' said Mace. 'Thanks.'

'Make it Johnnie Walker, Black.'

'Don't push it.'

'What you want her for anyhow? This Sheemina February.'

'For killing my wife.'

A pause. Then Dave hesitant: 'I thought …'

'What?'

'The papers ran it as a robbery. That she'd surprised the bugger. Your wife.'

'Was a hit, Dave. Ordered up by one Sheemina February.'

'Why?'

'Call it history.'

The house bell rang.

'Got to go,' said Mace. 'Pylon's here. Celebs flying in we have to collect.'

'Wait, my son, hold on …' said Dave. 'Listen, if you wanna sell your house I'm your man.'

'Why'd I do that?'

'You know … On account of your wife's murder. Still living there. It's weird, my son.'

'Happens I don't think so.' Mace disconnected. In his head a refrain from the Stones' song on a loop: 'hmmm, humm, until my darkness goes.'

7

Four men in a shack, drinking Blackie quarts. A corrugated iron shack, the walls papered in magazine covers, mostly of cars. Two men sitting on an car bench seat, one in a wingback chair, the short-arse propped on the bed. Keeping them warm a paraffin heater up full. On the table at the door, four guns, neatly arranged side by side.

The men dressed in black tracksuits, red stripes down the sides. Black anoraks. All wearing beanies. On their feet, black Hi-Tec trainers that might've come out of the box that day.

The men relaxed. Kicking back. Chilling. Smoking. A wet Sunday afternoon in the township. Zola on the Sony ghetto blaster. Soccer on the TV, the sound turned low. The brother in the wingback half watching the action on the box.

A cellphone rang. The man in the wingback answered. All he said was, 'Ja.' Listened, disconnected. Set down his quart. 'Okay,' he said. 'We have the address.'

'My brus,' said one of the men on the bench, 'quick picture.' The four of them going into a huddle, the brother holding his cellphone at arm's length to get in their heads. 'For the record.' The men grinning, gung-ho for the show.

Short-arse turned off the paraffin heater, waited while the men each took a gun from the table, ducked out of the door into the rain. The cameraman took the Beretta. Short-arse about to say something, then didn't. That left an H&K. He could live with it. Was a good gun to have in your hands. People saw any gun they took you seriously. He switched off the Sony, the TV, the single light, grabbed two quarts, ran out to the Citi Golf he'd jacked earlier in the day. Sort of car no one was going to notice.

8

In the big Merc going down Molteno Road, Mace's first words to Pylon: 'I've got her address. Dave came through.'

Pylon glanced at him. 'You can't take his word.'

'An agent friend of his sold Sheemina February a Bantry Bay flat. Confirmed. Dave describes Sheemina February, the agent says, that's her. What more do I want?'

'And you're going to do what? Stake out the place? Break in?'

'Confirm it first,' said Mace. 'Then I don't know. Disappear her like we should've done all those years ago. In the camp. We knew she was bad news. A spy. We'd shot her then, I would have Oumou now. Christa would have a mother. This's because we let her walk.'

'We weren't sure, Mace.'

'We bloody were.'

'Not as I remember it.'

They'd smashed her left hand trying to get the truth out of her.

Broken every bone in it with a mallet. 'She's a government spy,' their commander insisted. 'We know. Make her confess.' They couldn't. Even through all the pain she kept her story: I want to join MK, be a guerrilla fighter. Mace had watched her taken away to the Membesh camp. Nights of rape ahead of her as the big boys had their way. The big boys now MPs, government men, oligarchs. Was hardly a wonder he and Pylon went off to run guns. The camps weren't a picnic.

'What I recall is someone knew her handler.'

'So they said.'

Mace turned sideways. 'Shit, Pylon what's it matter? The bitch is a killer. Had a go at killing me. You and me both. That doesn't work, she kills Oumou. I don't need any more reasons. She's history. Dead.'

They drove not talking, Mace hearing Paint it Black looping through his head, looked down on the city buildings shining white as whale bones on a beach. City of the dead. And the blood seeping across his mind. Thought, why're we arguing about this? This's not about the past, this's about now. Just get out there and do it. Move on.

The silence holding between the men down hospital straight, under the railway bridge, over the Black River before Pylon broke it.

'Okay. What I'm going to say is this: you don't go alone. I go with you. Maybe she's been after you. Maybe she's got a thing about you. But we started this together. We finish it that way.'

Mace considered the option. 'I'm fine with that. First though I get the details. Confirm the address.'

'Without funny stuff.'

'Sure.'

'I mean it.'

'Sure you do.'

The partners going quiet again to a love song on the radio and the hiss of tyres on the wet surface. Mace kept away from the words, staring maudlin at the decommissioned cooling towers, the squatter camp, the shacks strung with washing. In the gloom, Pylon switched on the headlights, muttered about the winter dark.

Said, 'Time we thought about the Cayman money again. I am so sick of this.'

'No kidding. Let me tell you about my overdraft.'

'Overdraft? You're on overdraft again! Shit, Mace. That's what I mean? How long've we been doing this? Nine years. Ten years. Forever. You're on overdraft. That's bullshit. There's got to be a way to bring it in, that money. Without the tax guys jumping us.'

Mace shrugged. 'I'm the one that's broke. You're the finance man.'

'Who's out of ideas. Out of tolerance. Not sure how many more of the bright and beautiful he can take. That's what we are, Mace. Goons for the rich and famous. Where's the advantage in that?'

'No advantage. Only bucks.'

'Scrape-along bucks. This isn't money. This isn't making us rich. Treasure's going to pop soon. This week I'm a father. Probably. Most likely. Almost certain. Then we have to get the Aids orphan. Not forgetting young Pumla or me. That's five mouths I must feed. What I call a big deal for one bread-winner.'

'Treasure not going back to work?'

'Nurses earn shit, Mace. And how's she going to work with two babies? Next we're employing staff. More of my earnings blowing away. This's rubbing my face in it because we're rich on paper. Government men, all the old strugglistas, get fatter by the minute with their deals and schemes. But us, who earned it the hard way in hard times, we're penalised.'

'I suppose,' said Mace. His cellphone vibrated in his hand. A no number advice showing on the screen. Mace connected, pressed the phone to his ear, turned down the heartache duet on the radio. 'Talk to me.'

'Mr Bishop?'

'Sure.'

Silence. Except the wheel drums of the big Merc on the highway.

The highway surface at this section rutted and torn up, stones clattering against the chassis. Pylon clucked at the noise.

'Mr Bishop of Complete Security.' The voice of an Afrikaner, deep toned. A voice of earth.

'Exactly.'

'Your Colindictor gave me this number.'

Colindictor? Who used the word any longer? Mace wondered. Only a dinosaur.

'Interesting name for an answering machine,' said Mace. 'Haven't heard anyone call it that since 1985.'

Again the silence. Like the guy didn't know which way to go with this.

'You talking?' said Pylon, glancing at Mace, keeping the speed steady onto the airport slip road. 'Ring him back.'

Mace shook his hand, no. Gravel voice saying, 'My name's Oosthuizen. Magnus Oosthuizen. That mean anything to you?'

It did. To Mace a name that came up alongside the name of Dr Death, the chemical-warfare scientist. Mace paused, said, 'Can't say so. Any particular reason?'

'If it doesn't, it doesn't,' said Magnus Oosthuizen. 'That's good. I like a clean slate.'

More unused airtime. Mace thinking, what's with the man he can't get to the point? But holding off. Not making it easier for Magnus Oosthuizen.

'You were recommended. You and the darkie, your sidekick.'

Mace said, 'Goodbye, Mr Oosthuizen,' – thumbed him off.

'And now?' said Pylon.

'Magnus Oosthuizen,' said Mace. 'Recall the name? Linked into the germ warfare unit. Cholera, anthrax experiments in Angola. Tied up with Wouter Basson.'

'Dr Death.'

'The very one. Dr Only-Following-Orders Basson. This's his chommie. Got the manners of an arsehole.'

'And he wants what? … Our protection?' Pylon laughed. 'There's a thing. Like we're gonna do that!' He smiled at Mace. 'On the other hand, why not for the right tom? Make a change from the botoxed.'

Mace's cellphone rang. 'Persistent bugger. Called you a darkie.'

'I am,' said Pylon.

'Not in that sense.'

Pylon held up his hand. 'Pink one side, black the other. Take your pick. Talk to him. Like we can turn down a job.'

Mace answered. 'I'm listening.'

'I don't like being cut off, Mr Bishop.'

'No, don't suppose so,' said Mace. 'It's bad form.'

The Oosthuizen silence. Mace broke it as Pylon stopped the Merc at the entry boom to the parking lot. Reached out, took the ticket, cursing at the rain sluicing down.

Mace said, 'You want to set up a meeting, name the time and place? I can't hang on longer. Can hardly hear you in this downpour.'

'Your place,' said Magnus Oosthuizen. 'Tomorrow. Ten o'clock. I want to see what kind of outfit you run. Big time or small fry. Need to know you've got the balls for this, Mr Bishop. You and your pellie. How big're his nigger balls, huh?' He laughed. Not a laugh so much as a rasp without mirth. Put Mace in mind of waves sucking at a pebble beach. He cut the connection. It was dead already.

'What a gentleman.'

'You get them,' said Pylon.

They found parking at the back of the lot. He and Mace hurrying off through the rain towards international arrivals.

9

Four men in a Citi Golf, streaming along the highway in the rain at sixty. Sixty-five tops, anything faster the wheel-shudder was disturbing. Short-arse in the back with the H&K at his feet, an open quart in his hand. The other quart with the brother in the passenger seat. The driver pissed off with short-arse, pissed off that the wipers didn't work properly. Pissed off with the car. Calling it a skorokoro. A rustbucket. A crock. A heap of shit.

Number four doubled up with laughter.

The driver swearing in Xhosa. Cursing short-arse for a fool. Wanting to know did he get the car from a scrap yard?

Short-arse looked hurt. Said high-voiced, 'Outside a church, my bra. A Pentecostal. To get their blessings.'

Number Four beside himself, smacking his knees at the expression on short-arse's face.

Short-arse: 'Wena, my brother, what kind of moegoe you think I am?'

The man in the passenger seat also shaking with laughter.

The driver reached back, slapped at short-arse. 'You went to church?'

'No, man. When they came out I asked them for the keys. Nicely. Not even showing them the knife. The old man says, It's all we have. I tell him not a problem. When I'm finished the emergency the police will call him to come and fetch his car. His wife says, thank you my son. The Lord will bless you.'

The driver going into Xhosa about the blessings that would rain on short-arse's head if the car broke down.

The laughter died, the men passing the quarts between them. They didn't speak again, listened to a man on the radio talking about the reincarnation of the Dalai Lama.

The driver said, 'That's crap. When you die, you're dead.'

'You go to the ancestors.' Short-arse squirmed on the back seat, could feel the springs through the plastic.

The driver snorted. 'Wake up. You think somewhere there's ancestors herding cattle?'

'The ancestors are close.'

'Watching now.'

'They watch for us.'

The driver banged his head on the steering wheel. 'Moegoe. A moegoe fulla shit.'

The men went quiet again, the man on the radio saying it was the Dalai Lama's fourteenth reincarnation. That in Tibet he was a sacred man.

The driver said, 'This car goes any slower we'll be late.' Going past the airport, squatter settlement, the cooling towers, Black River, up Hospital Bend, taking the Eastern Boulevard into Woodstock.

'This's the place?' said short-arse.

'For some more beers,' said the driver, turning left into a narrow street, cars parked against the kerb. He cruised slowly, checking out the lighted windows, every one barred. Stopped at a dark house, two straggly trees in the front yard, thick beds of cannas beneath the windows. Kept the engine running.

'No one's there,' said short-arse.

'Always someone here,' said the driver. He got out walked up to the door, a metal door, pressed a button on the buzz box. A voice said, 'Hoezit?' Queer tone, a coloured moffie to the driver's ear. The driver said, 'Two Blackie quarts, four white pipes.' The voice said, 'Bottleneck or finger?' – drawing out the 'er' like a long 'a'. The driver said bottleneck. The voice told him how much.

The driver said, 'No, man, that's double.'

'Sunday night prices,' said the voice. 'Okay, my sweetie. You want it still?'

The driver said yes.

The voice told him to pull out the tray at his feet, put the money in it. The driver bent down, dropped the notes in the tray, pushed it back in.

The voice said, 'Wait, sweetie.'

He could hear them other side of the door putting his order into the tray.

'Okay, now,' said the voice.

The driver pulled out the tray: two quarts rolling about, in a plastic bag four bottlenecks stuffed with dagga and mandrax. Even a plug of tape over the broken ends to stop the mixture spilling out.

The voice said, 'Enjoy.'

The driver picked up the items went back to the car.

They drove out of Woodstock along Main Road, came into the city at the Castle. Only people in the rain were the vagrants: bergies in the doorway of the City Hall, some street children outside a fish-and-chips takeaway. No traffic in Adderley, the lights in their favour up past the Slave Lodge into Wale, left into Queen Victoria.

'Where's the job?' said short-arse.

'Not far.' The driver reached forward to wipe condensation from the windscreen. Cursed in Xhosa the car's failings – no heating, no power, no lights in the dashboard. He tried to wind down the window, the handle came off in his hand.

'Not my fault,' said short-arse. 'You must be careful with old cars.'

The driver hurled the handle over his shoulder, short-arse ducked.

'Just a joke, my bra. Just a joke.' He used his sleeve to clear his side window, peered out. Said, 'This's Nigeria-town. Those brothers catch you in the street, they're cannibals, they eat your heart while it's still beating.' He fished for the H&K at his feet, placed it in his lap.

The driver clucked his tongue. Told short-arse he was missing out. 'Nigerian women,' he turned round, wagging his tongue at short-arse, 'hey la la, you taste that flesh you want more. Those ones with the stuff cut away. The best.' He kissed the tips of his fingers. 'Tight, my brother.'

The men laughed, uncapped one of the beers.

They drove off into the Gardens backstreets: Victorian rows, gracious homes behind high walls. The driver stopped in a street hung with dripping trees, pointed at a gate up ahead.

'How long?' said one of the men.

'One hour. Two hours. We are here,' said the driver. 'We can wait.'

The men lit one of the pipes, handed it round, each taking two hits.

On the radio the man from Tibet said the Dalai Lama was the living Buddha. His words were powerful. He said the Buddha says, 'The purpose of our life is to feel happiness, joy, satisfaction and peace.'

Short-arse let the smoke trickle from his nostrils. Said, 'I can feel the satisfaction, my bra.'

10

Mace and Pylon were late. Passengers streaming out of customs, off to the side their celeb clients marooned among suitcases. More suitcases than would fit in the Merc's boot. Enough suitcases to fill a small van.

Pylon groaned. 'Would you look at that? What're we supposed to do with them?'

The woman, seeing the two dudes dressed in black, shouted, 'Yo, you guys, over here.'

'We've got to stop dressing like this,' Mace said to Pylon, giving the clients a once-over: the woman in a dark suit, a necklace of small bone beads; the man in a coat looked like it might once have been a bear. Underneath that a suit, his shirt fastened with a turquoise-inset bolo tie.

'It's the image, remember,' said Pylon. 'It's why we do it. Snappy dressers.'

Mace unsure who the last referred to. The woman standing pert before him, her hand outstretched.

'I'm Dancing Rabbit,' she said, bright smile, lovely face. 'Right here's my husband, Silas Dinsmor – Dinsmor without an e. You're Complete Security, right? Mace and Pylon?'

'We are,' said Pylon. 'Didn't know you were Red Indians.'

'Choctaws,' said the woman. 'We don't use that term anymore.' She looked Mace in the eye, not letting go of his hand. 'There's a hurt in you,' she said. 'And anger. You need to de-stress, my friend.'

Before Mace could respond she'd released his hand, was shaking Pylon's. Mace stood hesitant, not sure what to say. Heard Pylon asking, 'That's your name? I call you Dancing Rabbit?'

'That's what I answer to. Also Veronica. But I prefer the other.' She glanced from Pylon to Mace. 'Which one of you's Pylon, which Mace?'

'I'm Pylon,' said Pylon. 'After the electricity pylons. He's Mace. After the ornamental staff, not the chemical.'

'You know the movie, Bandolero?' said Silas Dinsmor, talking to Mace.

Mace shook his head, looked up at the big man, a good head taller, broad shouldered. One thing: outsize ears. You couldn't help notice.

'James Stewart played a hangman name of Mace Bishop. Not a good Western. Funny to start with then goes foolish. But you got Stewart and Dean Martin playing the heroes it's not gonna work. You like Westerns?'

'Some of them,' said Mace.

'Give me three.'

Mace frowned. Gave it a few seconds thought. 'Probably Unforgiven first off. Then Tombstone. Maybe Peckinpah's Wild Bunch a close third. Also the first six minutes of Leone's Once Upon a Time …'

'I could live with that,' said Silas Dinsmor, folding his arms over his stomach. A stomach as large as a Zulu belly. 'Thing about Unforgiven I most appreciated was the sheriff saying his life shouldn't of ended that way because he was building a house. Spoke of the complexities in the world.'

Mace nodded. Like the complexity of Oumou being cut to death. Just when she'd won an award. Not the way her life should have ended at all. Mace could imagine being Unforgiven's William Munny though, standing over Sheemina February, taking her out with a face shot. Put blood into her ice blue eyes.

'Perhaps,' said Pylon, 'we could talk movies in the car. Not sensible to be standing here. Except we have a problem.' He pulled out his cellphone. 'We need to call the cavalry to help with the suitcases.'

Ten minutes later Pylon had the luggage delivery sorted with a courier company. He brought the big Merc round to pick up the couple and Mace outside the terminal. The rain drumming down.

'See the black guy still does the work,' said Silas Dinsmor.

Mace held the door open for Dancing Rabbit, the woman winking at him. Said, 'Some things never change.' Whupped the door closed, taking his position shotgun beside Pylon.

The big Merc set off, the courier van following through the traffic lights down the straight towards the highway.

On the overpass Silas Dinsmor gestured at the shackland below lit up by mast lights. 'About as pretty as a reservation.'

'Reservations I've seen were a lot prettier,' said Mace.

'Government started clearing it up,' said Pylon, catching the eyes of his passengers in the rearview mirror. 'Wants to build a project called Gateway in a place we'll pass down the highway. Trouble is, soon as the shacks are cleared off, other squatters move in. Holds up proper housing schemes.'

'Story of the poor,' said Silas Dinsmor.

'We have the same problems,' said Dancing Rabbit.

Silas Dinsmor reached forward, tapped Mace on the shoulder. 'Your movie choice,' he said, 'goes for a lot of wild justice.'

'I suppose,' said Mace, shifting sideways in his seat to look back at the couple.

'Honour and revenge.'

Mace nodded. 'You should think of it another way, the kind of official justice we get these days isn't worth talking about. Also, security's what we do. Cos the cops can't. We're keeping you safe, sometimes that means being the law.'

'With all due respect,' said Dancing Rabbit, 'you could call it vigilantism.'

'You could,' said Mace. 'We like to think of it more as being proactive.'

'Talking about honour and revenge,' said Silas Dinsmor, 'there was another Bishop in those movies. Called Pike.'

'In The Wild Bunch.'

'Sells out his buddies.'

'No relation,' said Mace.

They all laughed.

Pylon said, 'Hasn't sold me out yet.' He caught the couple's eyes again. 'Can I ask you something?'

They answered sure.

'We do a lot of celebrities, our line of work. Can't see that you fit the profile.'

The two laughed.

'Celebrities, we ain't,' said Dancing Rabbit.

'That's what your PA said.'

'Her opinion. Pumps up her job.'

'So what're you then?' said Mace. 'To need us.'

'Casinos.' Dancing Rabbit, fidgeted in her handbag, pulled out a leaflet, handed it across. 'Our experience, when you're talking casinos, you're talking about tough people. Ourselves excluded.' She giggled. 'Most of the time.'

'What we're here for,' said Silas Dinsmor, 'is an investment opportunity. We've heard some folks aren't pleased about this. Folks don't like foreign money coming in. They feel they're not getting their slice of the pie when the dollars flow. Some folks told us, stay away.'

'Told you how?'

'Phoned us.'

'Death threats?' Mace turned so he could see Silas Dinsmor. The expression on the man's face impassive.

'Sounded like that.'

Mace heard Pylon mutter, 'Save me Jesus.' Said, 'Maybe you should have told us. Sort of thing puts you in a different category for us.' He faced forward. 'In our books you weren't high risk.'

'In our books,' said Pylon, 'you were rich and famous coming here for a good time. Just needed the edge taken off the street life. No big deal.'

'Still not,' said Dancing Rabbit. 'In our experience people say they're going to scalp you, they're generally blustering.'

'Not here,' said Mace. 'People here say that's their intention, most often it is exactly.'

'We have this problem,' said Pylon, 'called xenophobia. You might've seen clips on the news. People being necklaced. Burnt to death with car tyres round their necks. Makes good TV footage.'

'We've seen that,' said Silas Dinsmor.

'Then you understand the type of situation we might have going here,' said Mace.

'What we understood,' said Dancing Rabbit, 'was you had rule of law. A constitution. Bill of Rights. A democracy.'

'We've got all those, ma'am. On paper. Just doesn't mean squat in reality. What we've got in reality is another way of conducting ourselves.'

Pylon broke in. 'You're looking at a two-tier society: what we aspire to, and what we are. What we are can be ugly.'

The couple in the back took this in without comment. Mace glanced over his shoulder, saw them staring out at the lighted suburbs either side. Said, 'Where's your appointment tomorrow?'

'Place called Grand West,' said Dancing Rabbit.

'You're buying in there?'

'No. No shares on offer,' said Silas Dinsmor. 'Our interest is new ventures. Development ventures. That's our expertise.'

'Back home, you see,' said his wife, 'on the reservations there're casinos. Some profitable, some not so. We're in the first category. We got experience situating these sort of ventures in unusual areas.'

'It's a two-way thing,' said Silas Dinsmor, 'you got to know how to trickle down some money, upgrade the locals. Win-win, all round.'

Pylon took the car into the fast lane, said softly to Mace, 'I've got the courier van in the rearview all the time. Can't see what's behind them.'

'You think there's a tracker?'

'Could be.'

'See anything?'

'Only far back. Too far to tell. We'd of known about this, we'd of done it differently.'

Mace didn't respond, said to the two in the back, 'Your PA didn't say anything about your business. She should have.'

'Ain't no stress,' said Silas Dinsmor. 'We get this all the time.'

'This's under our watch, that's the difference,' said Mace. 'You need us for the meeting?'

'We do. What our PA was supposed to contract you for,' said Silas Dinsmor, 'was twenty-four/seven guarding. Don't say it's not so.'

'It's so,' said Mace, although it wasn't. 'What we need's an updated schedule. Where you've got to be, when.'

'You got it,' said Dancing Rabbit.

She spoke to her husband in a low tone, though Mace couldn't make out a thing she said. He glanced at Pylon. The glance that said, suckered.

Silas Dinsmor answered his wife in the same language. Then said, 'Our first appointment is noon tomorrow. Like I said, at Grand West.'

Mace and Pylon said, 'No problem' – Mace thinking plenty of time to handle Magnus Oosthuizen first. A silence settling while the Merc powered up the rise, Devil's Peak above, the road going into the snake curves of De Waal Drive, the city below.

'That's the city?' said Dancing Rabbit, leaning over her husband.

Pylon launching his history spiel about a town built by slaves, their bones still part of the foundations, saying the disadvantage of coming in by night you didn't get to see the drama of the mountain, the city, the ocean. Dancing Rabbit saying the lights were pretty though in the valley.

'We call it the city bowl,' said Pylon, his eyes flicking onto the rearview mirror.

'Anything?' said Mace.

'Not as I can tell.' Pylon cursing the courier van for sticking so close behind.

For the rest of the ride along De Waal, Mace and Pylon shut up, the Dinsmor couple talking in their own language like fluttering doves. No cars overtook them, the rain eased off to a drizzle which Mace liked. In the dip Pylon accelerated up onto Jutland, came off at the slip road to zigzag into the suburb. Deep in they stopped at a security gate, waited for it to roll back, the van tight behind them.

'These gates,' said Pylon, 'are the worst. They take forever to open, eternity to close.' They drove in up a short drive to a cottage back among trees and high shrubbery.

'Looks cute,' said Dancing Rabbit.

'Cute alright,' said Mace. 'Has a heated pool if that takes your fancy in winter. Quiet, secure. Close to the Gardens Mall. You want to go there we can make arrangements.'

'I'll open the house,' said Pylon, heading up the stairs to a wide stoep. Mace going round the van to help with the luggage, noticed the gate hadn't closed. He walked down, pressing the remote to activate the mechanism. Could hear the motor whining. At first thinking, damn it, before the realisation clicked in, the gate was jammed. Mace stopped. Scanned the darkness. Listened to the whisper and drip of wet trees, the distant drone of the city. From where he stood he couldn't see into the street. Behind him could hear the van driver asking where to leave the luggage, Silas Dinsmor's response, Pylon calling from inside the house for the couple to come in out of the rain. Then a shout, and the high pitched scream of Dancing Rabbit cut off. Mace stepped sideways into the shadows, wet foliage slapping at him. And stopped. Drew the Ruger from under his arm. Racked the slide.

How many? he wondered. Two or three? More likely three. Three's what it usually took. One to keep everyone under the gun. The others to pull off the robbery. Supposing it was robbery. He crouched. Went slowly forward, thankful that the damp had soaked the fallen leaves, made the ground spongy. He circled to the left, away from the street towards the side of the house. From there he reckoned he could look on them unseen. Still puzzled: was this a syndicate job? Cherry pick the victims at the airport. And the Dinsmors were easy targets. All that luggage. A syndicate looking for a pushover, these two were it, and stuff the security. Track them back to the accommodation. Maybe even know their destination in advance.

If they had someone inside trolling through the landing cards, no need to even set up a following vehicle then. All you've got to do is send round the welcoming committee, wait for everyone to arrive. Walk up, wave some hardware, drive off with the cars and the bounty in the boot. Couldn't be easier.

Mace kept to the shrubbery, thick either side of the driveway. Ideal for a waylay. Could hear Pylon saying, 'Okay, guys, let's stay cool. You take the cars, no problem. Release the people.' The hijackers responding in Xhosa, calm, assured. So it wasn't a coloured gang. Coloured gang the issue was robbery. Black fellas it could be anything. One thing it wasn't was a hit. A hit there'd be no messing about. Pop, pop, the screech of getaway tyres. Though Mace knew sometimes the hitmen got greedy. The amateur jacks. Went for a little search and seizure on the side. But this wasn't one of those. This, Mace believed, was a scare job. Bit of rough stuff. Fire a clip into the trees. Whisper a few words in the large waxy ears of Silas Dinsmor. Enough said. Have the Dinsmors checking into international departures toot sweet. Complete Security's rep in tatters.

The van's engine fired. Then the Merc's.

Pylon said, 'You don't need them. Leave the people here. You don't want to get involved in hostage-taking.' Not speaking vernacular, keeping to English for the Dinsmors' sake.

Mace thought, shit. Kidnapping. Maybe weren't three but four men. One each for the Dinsmors, one to drive the van, another to take the Merc. From the garden had no clear view of the driveway. No idea of the positioning except of Pylon on the stoep. Could see him standing backlit. An easy target for anyone wanting to up the ante. No chance of getting to the side of the house either without the kidnappers seeing him. Mace looked round. Didn't want anyone surprising him. Nothing moved.

Heard Pylon saying, 'Wait, wait.' Saw him start forward. The crack of a Magnum, saw Pylon hurled backwards. Mace went into instinct, fought the urge to rush out. Crept forward. Doors slammed. The van reversed, tyres skidding before they gripped on the cobbled drive. The Merc's engine revved. Mace stepped onto the driveway, put a nine-mil hollow-point through the passenger window into the driver's head. The Merc roared back, left the driveway smashing up against a tree. A rattle of Beretta fire in there too. Mace circled towards the car through the garden's darkness. Stopped metres away. The back windows sprayed with blood. He peered forward. Unsure. If the shooter popped out with the Beretta on auto, he was going to take at least one smack. Mace moved behind the car. Waited.

The far passenger door opened, Silas Dinsmor heaved himself out. 'Poor bastard shot himself,' he said. 'The other one, you killed him.'

'I've always been lucky that way,' said Mace. 'You okay?'

'Full of his gore,' said Silas Dinsmor. 'Where's Veronica?'

'They got her.' Mace backed off towards Pylon, digging out his cellphone. 'And the van. And your luggage.'

Heard Dinsmor groan, say something in his strange language.

Pylon had taken a shoulder hit, was lying propped against the stoep wall, gun in hand. Said, 'Just my luck, the arsehole can shoot.'

Mace bent down to his friend, a lot of blood, but nothing life-threatening. 'Don't move. Let me get the emergencies.'

Ten minutes they had to wait before a cop van pitched. Another few minutes for the ambulance. In Mace's estimation not a bad response time. He called Captain Gonsalves too. Always best to have a friend on the scene.

11

Captain Gonsalves, in a plastic mac, hands in the pockets, spat a tobacco plug into the shrubbery below the stoep. He and Mace standing out of the rain. The cop scrimmaged deeply in a pocket for his cigarettes, drew out a crumpled packet. The two of them looking down on the crime scene activity. Men and women in jumpsuits getting the bodies out of the car.

'Trouble with rain,' said the captain, 'washes everything away. The evidence.'

'Doesn't matter,' said Mace. 'You got my statement, Pylon's statement, the American's. What more evidence d'you want?'

From behind them in the house came the loud voice of Silas Dinsmor demanding action.

Gonsalves said, 'Sounds like your Yankee doodle's raising merry hell.'

'Can't blame him.'

The captain shook out a cigarette, stripped it, rolled the tobacco in the palm of his hand. 'I was in a foreign country my wife got abducted I'd be calling on the embassy.' He popped the pellet into his mouth. Sucked hard on it. 'Then again, maybe not.'

Said, 'Ja, your statement. This's a difficulty, Mr Bishop. You might've used too much force here, in the eyes of the law. Know what I mean, you weren't under threat. Technically. Nobody about to shoot you.'

'My client was,' said Mace, 'under threat. Was being kidnapped by two armed men. That piece of shit' – he pointed at the body being zipped into a bag – 'had already shot Pylon. Killing him wasn't using too much force. Was the only way to go.'

'I tell them,' said Gonsalves, working the pellet round his mouth, 'our legal eagles that is, I tell them that they've gotta change the law. Maybe not back to the good old days when we used to tell the crims run 'n shoot them in the back, end of story. Suspect died attempting to escape, your honour. If it ever got that far. Often saved the justice system, saved a forest of paperwork too.

'No, what I mean is, we've gotta stop hounding the good guys. See, we're going to have to charge you. Manslaughter. Sort of as a matter of course. Nothing personal. Usually in the end prosecution drops the charge. Calls it self-defence before it gets to court.

'Though,' he chewed, 'I heard of this case, a businessman gets hijacked. Senior executive type. Also fancies himself on the shooting range. Steps out of his car like the darkies tell him, only in his hand's a fancy target-shooting pistol. Three monkeys facing him. A Z88. A .38 S&W. A niner Browning. Dot, dot, dot, goes the executive type, takes them out one by one. The action boys don't get a look in. Three to us, nil to them. Except the law pulls rank, hey, buddy, nobody shot at you. Two years on, two hundred grand down in legal fees, our hero is finally let off a three times manslaughter.

'Get the picture, here's this happy camper driving off to golf on a sunny day, a family man, responsible citizen not thinking of harming anyone, out of the proverbial he gets jumped, the good man does us a favour, for which the law skins him. That's our justice, hey.'

A man in a yellow jacket shouted up that they were taking off the bodies. Captain Gonsalves raised an arm in response. He and Mace watching the ambulance reverse down the drive, following two cop vans. The scene suddenly quiet. Only Silas Dinsmor ranting in the house. Gonsalves pointed at the Merc slammed into the tree. 'Got a bit graunched. Like your reputation.'

Mace sighed. 'Like we needed either.'

'Word's going to get around. After the last time with the German guy taking a hit in your car, this'll wag tongues.'

'I suppose. We'll ride it.' Mace leant against a column at the top of the steps. 'I need that gun back.'

'You know the scene.'

'Which is why I'm asking,' said Mace. 'For some leeway.'

'Ja, Mr Bish, Mr Bish.' Captain Gonsalves chewed vigorously, saliva glistening in the corners of his mouth. 'Listen, man, what's the real story with the other chappie?'

'What Mr Dinsmor said. The stupid shot himself up.'

'Serious?'

'Serious.' Mace brushed distemper from his jacket sleeve. 'I told you, I'm ducked down round the back of the car figuring an angle, the next thing there's brains all over the rear window. Moment later Mr Silas Dinsmor emerges, picking the grey stuff off his lapels.'

'No, man.'

'Yes, man.'

'That's how it went?'

'Scout's honour.'

Gonsalves spat out shreds of tobacco. 'Amazing.' Touched Mace on the arm. 'You want me to shepherd this?'

'What else?'

'For the usual. Say a grand.'

'Jesus, Gonz.'

'You heard about inflation? Rampant, I tell you.'

Mace shook his head. 'Give me a break. All this shit hitting the fan, what I need's stress release. I don't need extortion.'

'Come on,' said Gonsalves. 'Look at the sunny side, you shot one of the baddies.'

12

Mace checked Silas Dinsmor into a small hotel lost in a horse-and-hound suburb. A safe haven he and Pylon used for clients wanting peace and quiet. Good perimeter security, tight in-room systems. Not that Mace was taking chances, had called Tami to babysit. Tami the receptionist at Complete Security.

'What?' she'd said. 'I don't do guarding. What's wrong with the boys?'

'I don't want one of the boys,' said Mace. 'I want you. Someone discreet.'

'Very nice.'

'It's a compliment.'

'On a Sunday night. When I'm home in my flat, warm, relaxed, cuddled up. I don't need compliments.'

He'd begged.

She'd said, 'You owe me one, big time.'

Mace grinned at himself in the foyer mirror. Pocketed his cellphone, steered Silas Dinsmor into the hotel's sitting room where a log fire crackled. No one else in the room. Mace ordered brandies. The two men sinking into leather armchairs before the fire.

'Prime fools, our consulate,' said Silas Dinsmor, accepting a snifter, a good measure of fine amber in it. 'We're doing all we can, Mr Dinsmor. The South African police are doing everything possible. Huh! Does it look like it? Do you see a US presence? Do you see cops?'

'You're safe here,' said Mace. 'We know this place. Use it often.'

'I'm not talking my security. I'm saying is this the way people take it seriously? My wife's kidnapped. No one cares.'

Silas Dinsmor swallowed a hefty slug of brandy. Serious ten-year-old KWV, matured in French oak. He placed the glass on a side-table, stared at Mace.

'This happen often here, these kidnappings?'

'Not that much,' said Mace. 'Usually it's straight robbery. The planes come in, a gang selects a tourist going through customs, follows to the hotel, gets you in the car park, even in your room. That's what I thought this was. Standard procedure.'

'Except it's not.'

'No,' Mace signalled a waiter to refill their glasses. 'I would say you're not going to hear a word till after your meeting.'

'Wondered about that,' said Silas Dinsmor. 'You're telling me the casino people snatched her?'

'Most probably,' said Mace.

Silas Dinsmor frowned. 'It has a logic.'

'Depends how they want to play it.'

The big man rolled the brandy round the glass, sniffed the aroma. Said, 'Mmmmmm.' Drank off a mouthful. 'Damn good.' He cradled the glass in the bowl of his hands. 'On the phone, these people I spoke to didn't strike me as doing business that way.'

'The problem,' said Mace, 'was we didn't get the right info about you. We'd got that we'd have handled things differently. Could have advised you.'

'I acknowledge,' said Silas Dinsmor. 'My fault. Veronica's low-profile demands.'

'Issue is, Silas,' said Mace, 'doing business here has complications. Lots of people want in on the act. People who maybe won't add value, but you've got to have them because they're related, you know, to government people.'

'You talking bribes?'

'We got another name. Here it's black economic empowerment.'

'No problem there.'

'Except mostly it's the ones that're rich already that get the deals.'

'This happens.'

'They're fronts, Silas. Stooges. Dished out shares for a buy-in. Except it isn't a buy-in. Not a proper one with incoming cash. Instead, the company issues paper IOUs, the old directors strip out the cash assets as payment. But hallelujah, the company's compliant with legislation.'

'The black fellas get a hand-out just like that?'

'Payback time. For centuries of suffering.'

'We been through the same, didn't get diddly.'

'You need to write the rules.'

'That's a point.' Silas Dinsmor sniffed at his snifter, took a swallow. They sat not talking, listening to the fire snap and pop, and outside, against the shutters, the tick of rain. Silas Dinsmor turned to Mace. 'So what's going on here?'

Mace pursed his lips. 'My guess, you're up against a local consortium who believe history owes them recompense and your dollars are foreign interference.'

Silas Dinsmor blew out his cheeks. 'I'm Choctaw. Native American. Redskin if they want it that way.'

'Doesn't matter which way you put it. Maybe they've figured you're fronting for white men in suits sitting in boardrooms high up a New York skyscraper. To their way of thinking you've come to plunder.'

'You're kidding me?'

Mace thought the strange thing about Silas Dinsmor was that apart from what he called hollering at the consul he didn't seem overly cut up about Veronica's situation. Not agitated or anxious, sitting there knocking back vintage brandy like Veronica was upstairs waiting to put out. When Christa was kidnapped, Mace recalled, the world went brittle. He'd been almost too smacked to act. He and Oumou both immobilised. Dazed. Dry mouthed. Staring wall-eyed at nothing. Not talking, not even able to hold one another. Silas Dinsmor wasn't in that space. Mace wondered why not.

Said, 'These sort of situations, kidnapping situations, generally they work out. Nobody gets hurt.'

'Sure,' said Silas Dinsmor. 'We've been here before.'

Mace glanced at the man, nothing moving in his face. You wouldn't want to play poker against such a face. 'That so? You have?'

Silas Dinsmor leant towards the fire, rested his elbows on his knees. 'About five, six years ago Veronica was kidnapped. In Bogota. Same scenario. We're negotiating a deal with a casino, so happened some locals aren't impressed. That time they lifted her off the street. Wanted a million bucks for her release. Myself I thought she was dead. In that country no one plays soft. In a kidnapping in Colombia, most times, the hostage dies. Also, how'm I going to rustle up a million? In two days? Or they send me her fingers, one at a time. Not original but not nice. I'm up the creek. Can't get the money, have no way to contact them, nothing I can do. Soon they'll send me her pretty little digits. Couple of hours before the horror show starts, I'm sweating, panting, can't sit still, she walks into the hotel, says she couldn't have been hosted by a nicer bunch of people. Her word, hosted. Didn't hurt her, gave her good food, talked to her. Trusted her. We did what they wanted, cut them into the deal.'

Silas Dinsmor stared at the fire.

'What I'm thinking this is the same play. Poker without cards.' He stood up, turned his back to the fire. 'You play poker, Mace?'

Mace shook his head.

'In poker you need four things: the will and the patience, up front. The face thirdly. What you don't need is a tell. You got that, you're not a player.'

'The fourth thing?'

'Luck, Mace. Blind luck. The cards don't fall for you, nothing else matters.'

'The cards fall for you, Silas?'

'Usually,' he said. Smiled at Mace. 'That's why I'm not concerned. Also it's Veronica they've got. Veronica has a way with these sort of people. With incidents like this. Veronica's not somebody you want to kidnap.' He forced a chuckle. 'What'd she say to you? You got too much anger bottled up?'

'Something like that.'

'She reads people. Pushes their buttons. She looks at you sees a bundle of pain and rage. Damn right. Got to have anger to shoot someone in the head. Whup. Hey, toast' – he clinked glasses with Mace – 'when you said "I've always been lucky that way" that was the line William Munny used?'

'It was.'

'You had occasion to quote him before?'

'No,' said Mace. 'Never anyone around who'd recognise it.'

Silas Dinsmor sat down again. Mace heard his colleague Tami making her entrance.

'Come,' he said, 'meet Tami, she'll be staying with you.'

Before they could move Tami was there. Hands on her hips glaring at them. Small package of dynamite.

'This's nice,' she said, 'on a Sunday evening.'

'Emergency,' said Mace.

'Emergency! Pylon's shot up. The client kidnapped. Fancy service we're offering.'

'Shit happens sometimes.'

She stuck her hand out at Silas Dinsmor. 'I'm Tami. Usually the receptionist.'

'You've been promoted,' said Mace, hauled out Pylon's gun, gave it to her.

'What's this? Acceptance into the club? One up for the sistas?'

'However you want to think of it,' said Mace.

'Never been guarded by a receptionist,' said Silas Dinsmor.

Tami slipped the pistol into her belt, snapped the American a smile. 'Don't think I'm gonna answer your phone.'

'Be warned,' said Mace. 'She bites sore.'

13

'Hit her. Hit her. Shut the bitch up.'

The driver ducking, fists slamming the side of his head.

'Get her off me.' Losing his beanie in the fray, pulling the woman's hands off the steering wheel.

The driver turned the minivan into the industrial estate, drove slowly to a warehouse at the end of a street, stopped. Beyond was darkness, rain, vlei, bush, rapists.

The bitch, Veronica Dinsmor, Dancing Rabbit, kicking out, flailing her arms, bouncing all over the back of the minivan as the short-arse attacked her.

Short-arse showing his crack as he leant over the woman, pounding her with the butt of his gun. Didn't seem to alter her attitude.

The driver shook his head. Went up the ramp to open the warehouse doors. He got back the woman was quiet, lying between the seats. Short-arse panting.

'She's dead, bru, you're mincemeat.'

Short-arse glared at him. 'She's not dead.'

'Better not be.'

Short-arse came out of the van. 'This's up to shit.'

'Yeah, how?'

'The others, my bru, we can't leave them.' He grabbed at the sleeve of the driver's cammo jacket.

'No?'

'No.'

The driver shook free his arm. 'Here. This place' – he stamped his foot – 'is where we must wait. This is the address she told me.

Drive here, into the warehouse, lock the doors, wait. That's what she said. That's what's happened.'

'It's up to shit.'

'I heard you.'

The driver drove the minivan into the warehouse. Short-arse dragging his feet up the ramp, pulled the doors closed, locked them. Looked around. A shithole. Some crates stacked near the doors. Empty pallets. At the back end a cupboard, a gas heater, desk and chairs, small fridge, on top of it a kettle. A door onto a toilet. Piss and a cigarette butt in the bowl.

'What's this place?'

'Storage.'

'Doesn't look like storage.'

'Hey, man.' The driver swore in Xhosa. 'I don't know. It's what it is. This is where we are. Okay?' Advancing on short-arse. 'Okay?'

Short-arse holding up his hands, backing off. 'Okay.'

The driver said, 'You with me, my brother? I don't want kak.'

'Okay, my bru,' said short-arse. 'No problem.'

The driver told him in the cupboard was duct tape, plastic ties with grips.

'You've been here?'

The driver held up his cellphone. 'Hey, wena. What is this?' Pointed at the phone. 'She told me, okay. Is that clever?'

Short-arse turned away. Mumbled again: 'This is up to shit.'

They lifted the woman out of the minivan, tied her to one of the chairs. Taped her mouth. Her face streaked with blood. Bruised. A cut in her cheek. Another, still oozing in her scalp. Blood stains on her jacket.

'I'm gonna phone the lady,' said the driver.

Short-arse didn't respond.

14

Mace drove away from the hotel through empty streets. Wet, dark roads overhung with trees. Puddles glistening in the headlights. Paint it Black still in his head. Almost midnight but he felt no fatigue. At the intersection to the highway stopped on the red, checked the approach, accelerated across. This time of a Sunday night only the innocent and the optimistic waited at red robots.

He thought of Silas Dinsmor. Brandy quaffer. Victim of a botched kidnapping. One man shot in front of him; another beside him. His wife abducted. Three hours later Silas Dinsmor could drink vintage brandy beside a fire. Like an untroubled businessman.

He thought of Veronica Dinsmor. Dancing Rabbit. Snatched away as if he and Pylon were not a consideration. Pictured her tied to a chair in an empty factory. Pictured her ordering room service in a fine hotel.

He thought of Pylon. A bullet hole in his arm.

He thought of the dead men. Tags on their toes in the Salt River mortuary.

He thought this wasn't a job he wanted to do much longer.

Mace Bishop, disgruntled, drove into the hospital parking lot. Rain drummed on the car. He killed the headlights, the ignition, rested his forehead against the steering wheel. Closed his eyes. In that moment he smelt the perfume. Her perfume. Oumou's. He groaned. Deeply. Sadly.

Pylon was in a private ward, sitting up in bed, his arm bandaged in a sling, a drip leaking into the back of his good hand. Pregnant Treasure preparing to leave. Mace came in frowning concern.

Pylon took a look at his face said, 'I'm not dying. Or dead.'

Treasure said, 'It's not a joking matter.' She put her glare on Mace. 'And you're not to stay long.' Went up on her toes, leant forward over her stomach to kiss Pylon goodbye. Pylon turning it into a smooch. Treasure pulled back. 'Where you think you are?' she said. 'Our bedroom?'

'Ah, baby,' said Pylon.

'Ah baby nothing.' Treasure rounded on Mace. 'Up to you to get Christa and Pumla to school tomorrow, mister.'

Mace shook his head. 'No ways. How'm I supposed to manage that? Come'n Treasure, help me out. We've got a situation.'

'I am,' she said. 'I have been all weekend, trying to help you out. Trying to get your daughter to ease up on her father.' She headed for the door. 'They'll be ready, Mace, seven-thirty. Don't be late. Situation or no situation.' Blew kisses at them both.

'There's a gal,' said Pylon. 'Fulla goodness and joy.'

Mace slid a chair to the side of the bed. 'What's it with black women? First I have to take Tami's lip. Now Treasure gives me a hard time.'

Pylon shrugged. 'Don't let it get to you.'

Mace gave him the frown. 'Huh! What're you on?' Gestured at the drip. 'Morphine?'

'Smells like you're on brandy.'

'Had one or two with Silas Dinsmor. To settle him.'

'How's he?'

'Settled. Never was unsettled really.'

Pylon grimaced at a sudden pain flash. 'That wasn't a set-up. Couldn't have been. Not a chance.'

'Except it looks like it,' said Mace. 'Our clients pitch up without a full brief so we walk straight into it. We don't even know who these people are we're supposed to be protecting. We think they're celebs. But, no brother, they're casino hustlers. Big difference.'

'Why I don't think it was a set-up,' said Pylon, 'is because of my wound. You know what made it, the bullet?' Not waiting for Mace's response. 'Magnum .45. That's not play-play. Person with a gun like that means business. Could shoot straight enough to hit me, too. Those guys were for real. Absolutely.'

'He's dead,' said Mace.

Pylon toyed with the drip line. 'Thought he might be.'

'So's the one with the Beretta. My take on that, you want to hear it?'

'Tell me.'

'My take: Big Silas leaned on the chappie, pressed his finger and viola, ran most of the clip into the guy's face. By useful accident. All in a day's living.'

'You reckon?'

'I do.'

'Mr Silas Dinsmor's up for these kind of events?'

'Mr Silas Dinsmor and his spouse Dancing Rabbit.'

'Interesting,' said Pylon.

'Like a hole in the head.'

'Or one in the arm.'

Mace crossed his legs, shifted on the hard-back chair. 'What's the damage?'

'Missed the bone. Took out some muscle tissue. Not so much a hole, more a gouge.' He stretched his neck to get an angle on his wound. 'What's that? Ten, twelve centimetres to the right it would've been a heart shot?'

'It isn't,' said Mace.

'Isn't what?'

'Isn't twelve centimetres to the right.'

'Could have been. That's the point. For Treasure.'

'Shit,' said Mace. 'What if this? What if that?'

Pylon laughed. 'You said it.'

'So?'

'So I'm stitched up. Can't drive for a while. Can't shoot a gun. Stitched up.'

Mace thought, lovely. A wrecked car. A kidnap. A weird redskin. A pissed-off daughter. A murdered wife. A pain in his chest like he was suffocating. How grand was his life?

'Have to get one of the boys or Tami to help you out,' said Pylon. 'For tomorrow at least.'

'Then what? Tuesday you're going to be back 'n up to speed? Play receptionist.'

'I can answer a phone.'

'And make coffee.'

Pylon snorted. 'When last did Tami make coffee for you?'

'Friday.'

'Not her job description, she told me.'

'Depends on how you ask.' Mace grinned. 'Know what I mean?'

'You mean I ask her, I'm a black dude playing the patriarch. You ask her, you're the white boss.'

'Something like that.'

'In this day 'n age? Bullshit.'

Mace stood. 'Call you tomorrow.' As he turned, said, 'Oh, yeah, I gave her your gun.'

'What?' Pylon sat up from the pillows, gasped at the movement.

'Gave her your gun.'

'Save me Jesus. No. No, tell me you didn't.'

'For the night. While she's babysitting the Red Indian. Isn't a big deal. And she needed something.' Mace stuck both hands into the pockets of his jacket. 'Couldn't lend her mine, could I? The cops have it.'

'She gives it back,' said Pylon. 'Tomorrow. I'm not having her wandering around with my gun. It's special, Mace. You know that. The sort of item you don't dish out to anyone.'

'Tami's not anyone.'

'She's twenty-three. People that young haven't got zip in their heads. Especially Tami.'

'Thought you said she could hang out with me.'

Pylon groaned. 'No, no, no. Save me Jesus.'

Smiling, Mace held up his hand, goodbye.

'You bring it to me,' said Pylon. 'To my house.'

Mace headed down the dim corridor, the wards in darkness either side. At the nurses' station, said goodnight to a nurse stuffing soiled sheets into a plastic bag. Someone had to do the job. Always best that it was people who felt inner reward.

Outside the rain had eased off to a fine drizzle. You stopped to listen, you heard frogs everywhere. Mace didn't stop to listen. Got into his car, was about to turn the ignition, saw a rosebud held by the wiper straight up on the windscreen. A blood-red rosebud. The sort of rosebud Sheemina February used to send from time to time. Except there hadn't been one since Oumou's funeral. And now again. The night he gets to know her address. Coincidence? Coincidence, hell. Mace didn't stop to think about it. Shot out of the car, scanned the parking lot.

At the hospital reception desk he asked if anyone'd seen a woman walk through, long black coat, black gloves. A striking woman. Very elegant. Impossible not to notice her. The duty staff shook their heads.

Mace went back to his car, pulled the rosebud free. He smacked it on the palm of his hand, felt the thorns bite. No ways she could've been following him. Yet she must've been. And he didn't notice. Mace snapped the stem. Jesus! Step it up, brother, get her. He threw the flower into the shrubs. Quietened the frogs for a moment.

15

On the day after Oumou's killing Mace'd gone quietly into the offices of Fortune, Dadoo & Moosa. Dressed in black but then black was usual. His Ruger in his belt. No clear plan of action in mind. He'd approached the receptionist, asked to see Ms Sheemina February.

Who shall I say's calling?

Had given a false name: Holden. Bill Holden.

One moment, Mr Holden.

Watched her buzz through, say, I have a Mr Holden for Sheemina. Be told something, glance at him. An okay. She'd clicked off, smiled at him. I'm afraid Ms February isn't in. She has an office here but with all her other commitments, her other companies, we don't see her often these days.

Mace asked if she had an assistant?

Got a nod and a smile.

Could he see her?

A young woman came through, said she was Ms February's assistant, what could she help him with. Mace told her it was urgent that he contact Ms February. Got a bright reassurance that messages would be forwarded, Mr Holden.

Look, Mace'd said, perhaps you don't understand. I need to contact her, speak to her myself. Urgently. Mace earnest, stressing the importance, keeping everything cool, calm and collected. Which of her companies should I contact?

You could try Zimisela Mining.

They're out of town?

Johannesburg.

She gave him the phone number. Also that of West Coast Dev, a property company developing a golf estate on the West Coast. The young assistant smiling at him, glistening purple lips. Perhaps if you could tell me what it's about, Mr Holden?

Sure, said Mace, my wife's death.

The assistant shook her head, puzzled. I'm sorry.

Mace saying, My wife was murdered. Stabbed to death.

The assistant slapping her hand over her mouth, staring wide-eyed.

Yes, said Mace. Ugly. Tell Ms February I called. Give her this. Holding out a business card. Ask her to phone me. Urgently.

He left it there, the assistant's latte face gone a whiter shade.

He'd walked out of the office reception. Waited at the bank of lifts. Watching them watching him. Before he got into the lift he phoned Zimisela Mining. A receptionist told him Ms Sheemina February was not expected. He could leave a message. Mace left his name and number.

The same at West Coast Dev.

What'd happened was nothing less than he'd anticipated. But Mace reckoned one thing: Sheemina February was probably in town. She'd want to be, to watch his pain.

Since then he'd shaken down the city. Rattled a long list of florists. Rattled some of her known associates. Staked out her townhouse.

Staked out her legal office. Driven the streets day and night on the off chance of a sight of her.

Niks.

Yet he could feel her. Sense her. He walked the city's pavements. Imagined she lurked behind him. Sometimes he spun to surprise her but she was gone. A figure disappearing into the crowd. He chased ghosts. Apologised to strange women. Believed he saw Sheemina February everywhere.

Might be no evidence that she'd ordered the hit on Oumou but Mace knew it in his gut. Was convinced. Certain he had to kill her because she was hunting him.

Whenever Christa was elsewhere, Mace was on the prowl, in the Spider mostly, hoping it wouldn't cause any grief. Once it broke down, he had to call a vulture to get him home. The tow-truck driver giving him endless jokes about the Spider. Mace got the car fixed, went back on the scour.

Niks.

He knew she had another apartment, he just didn't know where. He put Dave the estate agent onto finding out.

And Dave came through.

Now, on the way back from the hospital, he hit that address. Victoria Road, Bantry Bay. In Mace's book, the cliffhanger's paradise. One side, block after block of apartments fastened to the cliff going down to the sea. Other side, block after block of apartments fastened to the cliff going up the mountain. In Mace's opinion, owned by rich merchants mostly. Mining executives. Industrialists. Old politicians. Foreign celebrities. Foreign trash with cash. He cruised slowly, side window down so he could see the numbers. Here people fancied names rather than numbers. Rain spattered his shoulder, cold against his face. A strong smell of the sea came up on the gusts, kelp, salt spume, red bait, the tang of ozone.

The address was a seaside block. Roof parking ramped one level up from the street, entered through a security boom. Probably room for twenty cars on the deck. Only cars there now four German makes and one Swedish. All the latest models. Had to be one of the cars was hers. Assuming she'd delivered the rosebud. The thought clenched Mace's fists on the steering wheel. Nothing he could do about it. He could wait. He could come back. He relaxed, eased his fingers. Took another look at the situation.

From the deck you entered the building down a flight of stairs into a street-level foyer. In this weather all the moneyed classes getting soaked between their cars and the foyer. Mace wondered how come they enjoyed paying millions for the pleasure. Door there was probably opened by a smart card or buzz-through for guests.

The foyer gave onto the street through glass doors. Armour-plated glass doors. A buzz phone or keypad got you in. No guard on duty but Mace reckoned the security company would be working this angle. Raising the residents' paranoia levels. Not difficult to do in this sort of setting. Couple of flyers detailing break-ins involving rape and murder convinced most. Trade up the neurosis, offer twenty-four/seven guarding as the solution. Usually your client said where do I sign? Standard industry strategy. One Mace and Pylon had laid out a couple of times.

He stopped opposite the apartment block, kept the engine running. Wondered if somewhere in the block Sheemina February was asleep. Not that there was anything to be done if she was. He wasn't prepared. No gun being a major drawback.

When it came to it though, the obvious problem was getting in. The random buzz claiming to be maintenance, cops, estate agents, door-to-door couriers, a florist, worked most of the time but no guarantee. Sometimes the one you hit on was a cynic. Not often but sometimes.

An issue too would be internal security. Ms Sheemina February's alarm code. Then again that was easily solved. Get her code from the security company. He had leverage there, could grease it with a grand or two. Dealing with the locks on the apartment door Mace didn't see as too hectic. Even double cylinders weren't the end of the world, you knew what you were doing.

Best thing was not to go in balls out, get the lay of the land, a sense of her schedule. Then, wop, wop, two .22s to the head. Classic. Exit Sheemina February. Brought a twitch to his lips that was half smile, half sneer.

'Got yer, bitch.'

Mace left the car idling, jogged over to the parking deck, snapped each of the cars on his cellphone camera. Checked for CCTV cameras: only one in the entrance that could be easily blocked. Back in the warmth of Oumou's station wagon, he checked the pictures. The number plates all legible. Some admin work for Tami later.

He drove off, a Grim Reaper cast to his face. Played out scenarios in his mind: trap her in the apartment, no need to say anything. Give her a moment to adjust to the gun. A moment to know terror. Then: overs-cadovers. Over cadaver more like it. Brought a smile to Mace's lips. He eased back in the seat, wondering which of the cars was hers.

The picture-taking triggered a thought: a nag that'd been at the back of his mind over the hours. As he'd left the kidnap scene, the sight of a sad red Golf in the street. Parked way down in the deep shadow of the trees. Almost unnoticeable on a wet night. Suppose there hadn't been a fifth man to drive off their car. Suppose that was it. Then the car'd still be there. Cops hadn't checked out the street. It was worth a look. Was on his way home anyhow.

Mace drove out of Clifton along the twisty Victoria Drive, took the Round House road through the stone pines up to Kloof Nek. Not another motorist to be seen. Going down Kloof the same: the city quiet, glistening under the rain. He threaded his way into Gardens, found the red Golf still there beneath the trees, about fifty metres down from the crime scene tape. Mace opened a door, stuck his head into the car, coughed at the stench of white pipes and beer. Had to be theirs. He took a picture of this car too.

At home 2:10 on his kitchen clock. Cat2 pleased to see him, mewing soundlessly. Mace talked to the cat to fill the silence of his house. His angry grieving house.

'We've got her, pussy cat, got her at last. End of story.' He flopped down on a sofa. 'Ms Sheemina February's had her day.' Lifted up the cat. 'What a night, hey! Bloody red Indians, bandits, kidnappings, gunslingers, bodies, the law, straight out of a western.' Cat2 stretched up to rub her face against his chin. Her claws hooked into his chest and thigh. Mace grimaced. 'Eina.' Gently massaged her paws until her needles retracted. He put her aside, stood up. Went to the kitchen, switched on the kettle, turned it off before the water boiled. Back in the lounge poured a two-finger Johnnie Walker Black. Slotted Willard Grant Conspiracy into the sound system. Regard the End. Took a pull at the whisky then thought to chase it with a beer from the fridge. He flipped the cap, sucked back a long slow swallow. Using the remote he skipped the tracks on the disc to Soft Hand. Almost too sexy to listen to. Pure Oumou.

The problem: such racing thoughts he couldn't settle.

Behind them always the sight of Oumou from the spiral staircase. Of her body on the floor covered in blood, gushing blood. Her face turned up at him, stricken.

Mace popped an Ambien, set his cellphone alarm to ring at six-fifteen. Stretched out on a couch in his clothes, the cat curled on his stomach. He drank off the beer in short sips. Finished the whisky in a swallow. Listened to the music. Drifted into a weird world of women: Oumou, Christa, Isabella from the arms trading days, Sheemina February, Dancing Rabbit.

Monday, 25 July

16

SHOOT-OUT AT LUXURY GARDENS LODGE

An American businesswoman was kidnapped, two men shot dead and one wounded in the driveway of an upmarket Gardens self-catering lodge last night.

The men who died at the scene were part of an armed gang that carried out the kidnapping.

Police suspect the latest incident is related to a number of similar attacks on tourists and foreign businesspeople.

Mrs Veronica Dinsmor and her husband, Silas Dinsmor, had only been in the city an hour.

They were due to hold talks with the casino management today. A reciprocal investment deal involving US investment in the casino and local investment in the Dinsmors' US gaming ventures was on the table.

A spokesman for the police said there was no evidence of a syndicate behind the spate of abductions.

Mr Dinsmor pleaded with the men who had taken his wife hostage to show mercy. 'If she is released unharmed because of my appeal,' he said, 'a message will be sent to all international businesspeople trading in this city that despite the current crime wave the African philosophy of ubuntu remains sacrosanct.'

The couple were under the protection of a private security company, Complete Security, when the incident occurred.

Complete Security specialise in the protection of high-profile businesspeople, celebrities, models and movie stars.

In May, one of their clients, German businessman Rudolf Klett, was assassinated in a Complete Security vehicle while being transferred from the airport to his city hotel.

In the same month, the wife of the co-owner of the security company, Mace Bishop, was murdered in the family home. Her attacker died on the scene.

Mace Bishop was also a witness in a murder case a few years ago. During evidence it was alleged by the accused that he had tortured them. No charges were laid against Bishop. One of the accused died in prison, the other was shot dead while trying to escape.

Complete Security could not be reached for comment on last night's kidnapping.

17

Pylon, the newspaper spread across his lap, read the story twice.

SHOOT-OUT AT GARDENS LUXURY LODGE

Couldn't believe it. Talk about hyping it. Reporters! You wouldn't know the difference between a tabloid and a broadsheet, going by the stories. He clucked disapproval. Said aloud, 'Save me Jesus, like what happened was a gun fight.' Couldn't have been more than two shots fired, not counting the own goal. And you couldn't count that, technically had to call that an accident, the one guy shooting himself.

Piece of muckraking journalism that wasn't doing Mace any favours. Not doing the business any favours either. Almighty mess a simple job had turned out to be.

He was about to flip the paper to the sports page when a man stepped into the ward. Said, 'Pylon. Pylon Buso, got shot up did you, buta?'

The voice struck a chord, Pylon sort of recognised it. Looked at the man. Late thirties, from-the-gym trim, short dreads and solid pecs mould, trainers, tracksuit, T-shirt. Rolled up newspaper like a club in his right hand.

'We met one time.' The brother giving him a glimpse of white teeth. Going through the brother's handshake. 'At a funeral.'

The memory coming back dimly. The funeral of the government arms merchant, Mo Siq. A murdered government arms merchant. Coming out of the mosque the voice had said in his ear, 'The old guys all getting iced. Past times are past times. We're the new kids now.' The voice introducing itself. 'My name's Mart Velaze.' Smiling those white teeth in his black face.

The voice saying now. 'Mart Velaze, remember me?'

Pylon moved his head from side to side one movement only, still let lose a jab of pain in his arm. 'I don't recall.'

He did. He'd run a query on the smiley guy. Turned out the smiley guy was an agent trained in the old GDR, a returnee. Bad stuff swirled in his wake. Nothing specific, some hits but no names. A collector. A fixer. A good operator. Careful, discreet, tough. A patriot. Terminating with extreme prejudice unlikely to cause Mart any sleep loss. If that's what the boss said, that's what the boss got. Even if the boss didn't put it in so many words. Mart Velaze absorbed the hidden agenda.

'I read you'd been shot,' he said, brandishing the newspaper. 'Can't be too serious, by how you look.'

'It's not,' said Pylon. 'Flesh stuff.'

'I took a bullet,' said Mart Velaze. 'In the gut. Shredded some intestine which wasn't fun. I didn't like that at all. Weeks 'n weeks before I could move properly.' He clasped one hand on the bed's metal footboard, raised a foot onto the rung, stood there looking down at Pylon. 'Thought I'd say hi.'

'An agent, saying hi.' Pylon forced a laugh.

'My mom's here for kidney stones. So, you know, why not do the rounds? Play the good Samaritan.'

'Save me Jesus!'

'I remember that,' said Mart Velaze. 'The first time we met you used that phrase. Save me Jesus. Unusual, I thought. One of those little sayings we get attached to.'

'What d'you want?' said Pylon.

Mart Velaze pretended hurt, stood back, holding up his hands, still clutching the newspaper. 'Nothing, buta. Just to say hello. Make contact again.'

'This to do with the Dinsmors?'

'The Dinsmors? Oh ja, the Americans. The woman who got kidnapped. No, no. Uh-uh. Purely personal.'

'Your type doesn't do personal. Spooks don't do anything that's not connected to something else. I watch the TV series. I know.'

Mart Velaze laughed. 'It's good, that programme. Better than The Wire. Everybody likes The Wire, but what's it? Ghetto crime and grime. Give me the high stakes. The politics of power. The real deal. I've got a box set of Spooks, one to three.'

Pylon said nothing. Staring at Mart Velaze staring at him. Waited for the agent to say what was on his mind. The no-speaks dragging to a minute. Mart Velaze broke it.

'Good to see you, buta.' But he didn't move. 'We must have a beer sometime, talk about things.'

'Oh yeah,' said Pylon. 'What sort of things?'

'Things you need to know.' He handed Pylon a business card.

Pylon took it. Mart Velaze's name and a telephone number. Nothing else. Then a spy wasn't going to have National Intelligence Agency in an eighteen point branded font splashed across the card.

'Like things have moved on since your day.'

Pylon thinking, spit it out Mart. Enough with the cloak and dagger. Except he didn't get a chance because Treasure duck-walked in, hands under her belly, saying, 'Excuse me, do you mind?' to Mart Velaze. 'This is urgent.' Pointing at Pylon, 'I've got to speak to him.'

'He was just leaving,' said Pylon.

Mart Velaze grinned at Treasure. 'Looks like you're about to explode,' he said.

'I am.'

Mart Velaze backed out the room. 'Congratulations mama when the baby comes.' He pointed the rolled newspaper at Pylon. 'Don't forget the drink, buta. Anytime you can call me.'

Neither Pylon nor Treasure responded. The squeak of Mart Velaze's trainers on the linoleum receding.

'And he's?' Treasure coming round the bed to kiss her husband.

'Search me. Said his mother was in for kidney stones.'

They went through the I'm-okay-how-are-you routine, Treasure adding, 'I'm going downstairs to check into maternity.'

Pylon said, 'What?'

'Yes.'

'Now?'

'The way I feel, yes.'

'You've had contractions?'

'For hours.'

'Jesus, babe.'

'Just get yourself out of here, okay. I'll be downstairs.'

18

Mace, at his office window, still looped on the Stones song, watched the blue Hummer pull into Dunkley Square. Had to be Magnus Oosthuizen would drive a Hummer. What else was a man in the business of weapons going to have for wheels? Not promising. Little about Magnus Oosthuizen was promising, except he'd be good money.

'Hmmmm, hmmm, hmmm, until my darkness goes.'

A big man got out of the Hummer. Hefty in an all-weather bush jacket, grey slacks, grey shoes. Flat hair like a rug but Mace knew it wasn't a rug, it was a style. The Prime Evil style. Once every cop in the country'd had hair like that. Unless it was a mullet. In his left hand, Magnus Oosthuizen held the sort of backpack a day hiker would carry. Caused Mace to smile.

For Mace it'd been a morning of smiles.

First smile. He'd groaned awake to the cellphone's bright chirp after three hours' sleep, dog breath, sour sweat in his clothes that made him gag. Showered, dressed to impress, smacked on Hugo Boss Dark Blue. Over coffee he'd got the charge: that he had Sheemina February in his sights.

Second smile. On time to pick up Christa and Pumla. Treasure spooling on about going to fetch Pylon at the hospital, the fact that he'd need to rest to recover. Perhaps Mace could respect that. Mace saying, 'Can't promise you.' Treasure had leaned back against the door frame, stuck out her huge stomach, patted the bulge. 'This's due to give any hour. I need him more than you. You want help, use your reception girl.' 'Tami?' Treasure'd nodded. From day one,

Treasure'd never liked the idea of the pretty young thing in their office. Would do anything to throw her into deep waters.

Third smile. The two girls got into the station wagon, Pumla at the back, Christa in the front. Pumla leaning over to kiss Mace's cheek, wrinkling her nose at the aftershave. 'Cool perfume.' 'Aftershave,' Mace said. 'Thanks.' Christa belatedly getting in on the act. A peck on his cheek. 'Hello Papa.' Buckling herself in. 'I gave you that cologne. Blue something. This's the first time you've used it.' Mace thought, you are paying attention. That was something.

Fourth smile. He'd walked into the office, Tami was already there. 'Not again, okay?' she'd said. 'Silas Dinsmor's creepy. Tonight one of the boys can do it. But there's something ...' She'd smelt the aftershave. Smiled at Mace, said, 'What's the grand occasion?' He'd returned the flash of teeth. 'No big deal.'

Fifth smile. Mace phoned Captain Gonsalves, told him about the red Golf. Gonsalves didn't know anything about a red Golf. 'Who's the detective?' said Mace. 'Doesn't take a detective,' said Gonsalves. 'Takes common sense from those on the job.' 'Maybe,' said Mace, 'but you've got to have it to start with.' He heard Gonsalves clucking and huffing. Gave him the list of car registrations to check out. 'This'll cost you,' said the captain. 'Another hundred.' Mace put astonishment into a chuckle. 'For the tip-off? That's a bit much.' 'For these others,' said Gonsalves. 'I'm not a skivvy.'

Sixth smile. When he found out that Sheemina February's apartment wasn't connected to an armed response.

Seventh smile. Seeing Magnus Oosthuizen's backpack fall off his shoulder into a rain puddle as the man tried to answer his cellphone.

Mace kept watching as Oosthuizen, phone clamped to his ear, returned to his car. He slung the backpack onto the Hummer's bonnet, took a pad and pen from a pocket to make notes. Mace remembered the man liked long silences on the phone. To enforce his authority. Wondered if he was giving the caller the same treatment. Probably, judging by the way Oosthuizen'd taken to staring at the mountain. That clear sky above it, the colour of Sheemina February's eyes. Nothing like the freshness of the city at the back end of a cold front. Oosthuizen stood still, face tilted upwards. Mace could tell he wasn't talking. Reckoned he wasn't listening either. He was doing silence. Then Oosthuizen banged his fist on the bonnet, closed off his phone. The man did temper too.

Mace turned from the window, headed out of the room at a clip. Calling from the landing, 'Tami, I want you in on this.'

Tami at the bottom of the stairs. 'In on what?'

Mace took the stairs two at a time. 'A meeting right now. Guy's about to knock. Name of Magnus Oosthuizen. Into arms manufacture.'

'And the Dinsmors?'

'Will have to wait.'

'There's something serious ...' – the door intercom buzzed – '... seriously weird.'

Mace waved his hands to stop her. 'Not now, okay. Not now. This first.'

She frowned at him. Thrust a newspaper at him, stabbing the front page.

'You got your name in the paper. Hot-shot publicity.'

Mace groaned. 'Bad?'

'Worse.'

'Hell.'

Mace looked at the headline. A shoot-out, for Chrissakes. At least there was no picture.

The buzzer went again. Impatient Mr Magnus Oosthuizen.

'Get it,' said Mace, folding the newspaper. 'Bring him into the boardroom.'

Tami clutched her hands. 'Yes, baas.'

She pirouetted, made off down the passage to the front door. Mace watched her, gloom in his mood. Could still admire her arse. Stunning. A backside to model jeans with.

He stepped into the boardroom, stood at the window, the light behind him. Heard Tami say, 'This way, please. He's in the boardroom.'

The door opened, Magnus Oosthuizen entered, squinted at Mace, the long table between them.

'That's an old trick,' he said. 'Standing in front of the window. Doesn't wash with me.' He sat down. Said to Tami. 'Coffee. Instant. Hot milk. Two sugars.'

Tami staring at him: like, dude, what's this?

Mace said, 'Thanks, Tami.'

For a moment she hesitated. Mace wondering if she'd lose it. Then went, not closing the door.

'Where's your pellie?' said Oosthuizen, stretching out a leg to push the door shut.

Mace took a seat at the head of the table. 'Pylon was wounded last night.'

'Magtig. There's a thing.'

'A bullet in the upper arm.'

'Didn't say that in the newspaper.'

'No.'

Oosthuizen grinned at him. 'Crap publicity for you, hey? Not the sort of record to give people confidence.'

Mace didn't respond.

'I read it, I thought, hey, why're you going to see these people? This's bad news.' The grin not leaving his blue lips. 'Reassure me, Mr Bishop.'

Mace stood up. 'I don't do that. You want us, that's fine. You don't want us, that's fine too.'

Oosthuizen laughed. 'Ag, sit down, man. Don't get so jumpy. I'm just pulling your leg.'

He drew a file from his backpack. Undid the zip of his bush jacket. Exposed a pink shirt with white stripes, tie the same colour as his Hummer, patterned with yachts.

'Nice 'n warm in here,' he said. 'Under-floor heating, hey. Load shedding's going to make it chilly. Your pellies should've looked after the electricity grid. Done some maintenance. Instead they pay themselves a fortune with the money they save. Bloody darkies.'

Mace let it go. Sat down.

Oosthuizen pushed the point. 'You heard that joke about the new government? Their titles. The Minister of Energy's going to be called the Disempower-munt.' He spluttered a laugh. 'Bloody darkies.'

Mace cocked his eyebrows.

'You can laugh. It's funny, man. A joke.'

'Ha ha,' said Mace.

Oosthuizen opened his file. Arranged the top papers. 'Mr Bishop.' Raised his eyes to meet Mace's. The two men staring at one another. Oosthuizen let it lengthen. 'I can see,' he said, his eyes flicking about the walls at the big photographs of the mud city of Malitia, the tall slender vase mounted in a Perspex box opposite where Mace sat, flared with colour as if it stood in a fire. 'I can see that you have what they call a boutique business. Interesting pictures. Interesting vase. Your wife's no doubt. I heard she was a potter. I heard about what happened.' He cleared his throat. 'Ja, well. You own the property? This house?'

Mace was about to ask him his point but Oosthuizen wasn't waiting.

'Security's a growth business. Lots of small fish in the water. Usually I go for the big ones. More professionalism. Solid training. Discipline. But you come highly recommended. From people all sides of the spectrum. That's impressive. No doubt you have facilities, safe houses. So let me put it on the table.'

Mace held up his hand. 'One moment. For my colleague.'

'Pylon Buso? I thought …'

'Her name's Tami Mogale.'

'The receptionist? Making coffee?'

'My colleague,' said Mace.

Tami came in with a tray of coffees, a plate of chocolate biscuits – Bahlsen's. Instant for Oosthuizen. French roast for herself and Mace. She sat to Mace's right, across from the weapons manufacturer.

Oosthuizen shook his head. Mace could read his mind: despite the references, he was undoubtedly thinking, a Mickey Mouse operation. Too bad he thought that. The weapons man sipped his instant coffee.

'You make a good one,' he said to Tami. Gave her a view of his teeth, discoloured, the gums receding.

She didn't crack a smile.

Another slurp at the coffee, his eye on the biscuits.

'German imports,' said Mace.

Oosthuizen weakened. 'May I?' He tweezered one from the plate between the index and forefinger of his right hand. Something dainty about the movement. Bit into it. Chomped. Through the mouthful said, 'Damn nice. Expensive, hey. Have one, I get them free.'

Mace and Tami declined. Oosthuizen took another. After the first bite said, 'The matter is this.'

Mace interrupted. 'Hokaai. How about you tell us something about you first? There's two sides here, okay, Mr Oosthuizen?'

Took Oosthuizen back a block or two. He popped the rest of the biscuit into his mouth, dusted his hands. Podgy hands, tufts of black hairs on the back of his fingers. Big hands for a big man. Gave Mace the scowl. Mace leaned back in his chair.

'All right,' said Oosthuizen, 'I thought maybe you'd do some homework.'

'What for?'

'To know who you are dealing with.'

'That's what you're going to tell us.' Mace wondering how Oosthuizen'd spin his links to the germ warfare unit.

Oosthuizen considered Mace. 'One person said you were arrogant. Someone else that you were a cold bastard. Cold bastard I like. Stuck-up doesn't work for me.'

Gave Mace smile number seven. 'Not a good opener,' Mace said. Came forward in the chair. 'You want us, you don't want us, Mr Oosthuizen? That's your choice. Then we get ours. On our score you're not doing well.'

'Mine neither,' said Oosthuizen.

For a moment looked like he might close the file. A long pause, staring at his papers. He took another biscuit.

'All right. First I am a businessman. Second an industrialist. By training an engineer. Mechanical. But I've moved on.' First bite at the biscuit. Finished chewing before he continued. 'My company' – he flipped a business card at Mace, Magtech (Pty) Ltd – 'makes weapons systems, the computer part. The software and the hardware. You have to do both or you lose out. My software only works on my hardware. Vice versa, you've got my hardware without my software you'd find a bow and arrow more effective. Understand?' He slotted the rest of the biscuit into his mouth. 'Damn nice. Biscuits and beer, you can't beat the Germans for those.' He finished his mug of instant. 'There any more of that, miss?'

Mace felt Tami stiffen. She said nothing, took out Oosthuizen's mug to refill it.

'So what I'm saying, Mr Bishop, is I have developed a system for the new frigates. Almost home grown. Cheaper than anywhere else, plus it works. You take the Swedes' and the Germans' systems' – he made a fluttering gesture with his hand – 'you'll need to fine tune. At an extra cost, what they call auxiliary expenses. Understand what I'm saying?'

Tami returned, plonked the mug of coffee before Oosthuizen.

'That was quick.' He spooned in two sugars.

'That's what it means,' said Tami, 'instant.'

Magnus Oosthuizen eyed her. Mace could hear his thoughts: watch it, sisi, I'll have your black arse. In the end he sneered. 'Very funny.'

Mace intervened, touched her arm. 'Mr Oosthuizen has a contract to develop the weapons system for our new frigates.'

Tami toasted with her mug. 'Oh wow!'

Mace thought, bloody hell, Tami. Waited for Oosthuizen to rise to the sarcasm.

He didn't. He waved his teaspoon. 'No, no, not a contract. I have tendered. On price Magtech is the best. On technical specifications Magtech is the best. On effectiveness Magtech is the best. We are ahead of the game, Mr Bishop. But in this business ahead is not enough. As you know.' He carefully sipped at his instant coffee. 'In this business you have to watch out. You might be the best man but others can drop you in the shit. Pardon my French. Someone else puts in the right bribes and you are finished. Might as well blow your brains out for all the work you did. Understand me?'

'No,' said Mace.

'No what?'

'I don't understand you.'

Oosthuizen looked at him. 'Come, Mr Bishop, you're not thinking.'

'Think for me. Aloud.'

'Alright. I have the best price, the best system. The men in government want it. The Europeans have a system that is more expensive with some technical drawbacks. They also have money for bribes. The men in government want the bribes.'

'You know that? For a fact?'

'Ah come, Mr Bishop. I don't have to answer that.' He finished his coffee, went on. 'For me this is a dangerous situation. I have a German scientist, Max Roland. He is the man who made my system. In his head is the one small trigger that makes my system work. You can steal my system but if you do not get the small trigger from Max Roland you have nothing.'

Oosthuizen unleashed one of his silences.

Mace would've let it ride, Tami didn't.

'Bit stupid, isn't it? He could have a stroke, a heart attack, get run over by that bus they always talk about.'

Oosthuizen looked at her. Distaste in the purse of his mouth.

'True.'

'What then?'

'Sometimes there is no insurance.'

'You bet on his staying alive?'

'I do.'

Tami snorted.

'I have no option, Ms Mogale. This is a high-stakes business.

Recorded information can be stolen.' Hissing out the Ms, riding the three syllables of her name.

'People can be tortured.'

'Admittedly.' He turned to Mace. 'This is why I have come to you. I need to bring my colleague here. I need to keep him secure while he completes the system.'

Mace stared into his empty coffee mug. A brown stain at the bottom glistening. The future. How exciting! Given what'd happened to the last German he'd babysat. Whacked on the highway coming into the city by a hitman with more luck than savvy. This one'd be a hot target for both the local and the European bounty hunters. Could a proposition be more tantalising? At a time when you've got a partner shot up. A client kidnapped. That client's husband sporting a strange attitude. He was about to say, thank you, Mr Oosthuizen, but no thank you.

When Magnus Oosthuizen said, 'Dollars. US. Cash or off-shore.' Then laid out a payment scheme: so much up front, so much on collection of his colleague, so much for safe delivery, so much per day until the completion of the project.

'In other words when the government signs. Between now and then could be a lot of money for you, Mr Bishop.'

No kidding.

Mace said, 'Who knows where he is?'

'No one. Not even me, exactly. I know the country and the city, that's all.'

Which was good. 'So how do we do this?'

'I will make the arrangements. There are planes every day. There is a flight tomorrow.'

Mace spluttered. 'You've got to be joking! We're talking out of the country?'

'Of course.'

'Then it's too soon. I can't do it that soon.'

Oosthuizen laced his fingers. 'We all say that, Mr Bishop. But as the English say, when push comes to shove we manage miracles.'

Mace thought, given the build-up, undoubtedly had to be good money. Money they needed. But no ways he could take a flight out tomorrow. Thursday, maybe, with a shove. But tomorrow not a chance.

'Who is this man?' said Mace.

'My colleague,' said Oosthuizen, 'you must understand is a scientist. A brilliant man. For ten years he has been living in our country. A few months ago he went home to Germany, a town called Frankfurt in the east, to fix his mother's affairs. His mother was dying. Because our project is almost finished why not take time off? I said, Max, go. With the internet we don't have to be in the same city. He goes off. We are in touch all the time. There are no problems. Nobody in the shadows. I am talking to the government men, they are happy, I am happy. What we are doing is just another job. No cloaks and daggers. His mother takes a long time to die. Two months. I can hear sometimes Max is frustrated. He can see no point to his mother's life any more. Why doesn't she die? Instead of sitting in a chair all day staring at television. She is ill. Cancer. She has twenty-four-hour nursing care. She tells him she wants to die. But for two months she doesn't. Then he phones me to say at last she is gone. I offer condolences. No, Magnus, he says, I am relieved. I am even pleased. I'm not sad. I'm smiling. For two months I thought my life had stopped. Suddenly it is over. I can move on. Today I feel free.'

'He has no other family. Wife? Children?'

'Never married. Plenty of women but no woman. My colleague you must understand is a little different. Some would call him selfish. Personally, I believe he may have helped his mother on. This is a harsh thing to say but I believe it. Max would do that. How do they say it in American: when you come down to the wire. When you come down to the wire, Max is hard core. You understand the meaning of hard core?'

Tami shook her head. 'Sounds buggered up.'

'What happened?' said Mace. 'Afterwards.'

'Two things.' Oosthuizen tapped his file. 'Two weeks ago two burglaries, one here in my premises. The other over there in Germany.'

'Where exactly?'

'My factory and Max's mother's apartment. There were a couple of days in between them but we're not talking about a coincidence. Both times nothing was stolen except probably data off the computer. All neat and tidy.'

'Anything serious?'

'Fortunately not.'

'Which was first?'

'The one in my factory. Another thing.' Oosthuizen stopped. Tweezered up a biscuit. Bit into it. 'Damn nice' – spraying crumbs onto the table. He swept them off with his hand. Finished the biscuit while Mace and Tami watched his chewing, a small muscle in his jaw working like a hamster. Mace thinking how unattractive it was watching someone eat.

'A few days before the burglaries I got a call from Max to tell me he thought he was being followed. Firstly by people in a car on the street and then by a jogger early in the morning. Max goes jogging first thing. He runs marathons. Wherever they organise marathons Max goes to run them. New York, Sydney, London, Tokyo, Timbuktu, if they could organise one. Now he's got company on his morning run. I ask him how he can tell because there're people jogging all day and night. He says, he knows. This is a lady jogger who keeps her distance. But three mornings in a row she's there behind him. It alarms Max. I told him, Max, relax. She's a new kid. Maybe what you should do is change your routine. He didn't listen and then a few days later two men tried to nab him outside his apartment.'

'Like forcefully?' Tami with that expression on her face Mace knew meant I'm not buying this.

'Exactly. This makes Max very nervous. He packs suitcases, and does a runner that night.'

'And this was, when?'

'Two weeks ago.'

Mace looked at Oumou's vase. Elegance, proportion, they'd been her hallmarks. The thing was so beautiful it could make you weep. He was about to ask when Max had last made contact.

Oosthuizen beat him to it, said, 'I got a call from him yesterday. He tells me he's in Sana'a.'

'Yemen? I've been there.'

'Exactly. It is a good place to hide out, and once it was a good place to do business.'

'He can fly in from there.'

'No.'

'What're you scared of?' said Mace. 'Exactly?'

'Everyone.' Oosthuizen palmed his hands flat on the table. The hairs on his knuckles stiff as brushes. 'Look. This deal isn't about three weapons systems for our boats. It is about international sales. The Argentineans, the Chileans, Brazil, the Aussies, the Turks, maybe even the Japs. Probably even licences to European manufacturers. We are talking big bucks, do you understand? Also it is about a small guy, me, putting one on the main manne, the huge arms manufacturers. Do you understand me? The big boys don't like it.' Oosthuizen glanced from Mace to Tami. 'I am not a scared man. Many times before in my life people have tried to kill me.' He magicked up a Colt long barrel from somewhere under his jacket, brandished it. 'Anyone tries it they meet Mister Anaconda.'

'Impressive,' said Mace.

'History,' said Tami. 'That gun's not made anymore.'

Oosthuizen squinted at her, like he hadn't heard right. 'You would know of course?'

Tami nodded.

Oosthuizen sneered. 'It still shoots.' He tucked the gun away. Leaned forward, elbows on the desk, hands up in the style of a blessing. 'So, Mr Bishop, what do you say?'

'Slowly,' said Mace, 'hold on. Another question.'

Oosthuizen lowered his hands. 'Yes?' Dubious.

'Your man, your Max Roland, he feels safe there in Sana'a?'

'Apparently.'

'How long's he been there?'

'Three days at least but probably longer. For a week we were out of touch. But Max is a resourceful man, except now he is getting nervous so I must bring him home.'

'He's a scientist. Scientists don't go on the run.'

'This one does. He is military trained.'

Mace looked at him. Thought: what're you not telling us? Said, 'What're you not telling us?'

Oosthuizen laughed. Embarrassed. Glanced to his left. 'What d'you mean?' Swung back to stare at Mace. 'Max Roland is a weapons specialist. He has a military background. Part of that training required self-protection. Believe me, Mr Bishop, he is a man who understands the stakes in this industry. He knows the risks. Possibly this is even part of what he likes about his career. Some glamour. Some intrigue. Some secrets to tempt the ladies. What more can I tell you about this man? Max Roland likes money. We all like money. He also likes women. All sorts of women, but especially he likes expensive women. Married women, dangerous women whose men occupy positions of power. In government, industry, sport. Especially if the men are powerful, Max will lust for their women. But he is like a bird, he only takes a few bites at the fruit before he goes to the next one. That is Max.'

'Delightful,' said Tami.

Oosthuizen took it. 'If you are shocked you shouldn't be here, miss.'

Mace thought, oh shit. Waited.

'Mogale,' Tami said.

Oosthuizen fully fixed on her. 'What?'

'My surname, Mr Oosthuizen.' The mister italicised. 'Like Mr Bishop. Ms Mogale.'

Mace came in. 'He's been there since before the weekend, that's a long time. A German in Sana'a doesn't exactly blend in with the citizens.'

'Max knows what he's doing.'

'Staying in one place. Doesn't sound like it to me. I'd be moving about if I were him.'

'Probably he is. Because that's where he told me he was doesn't mean that's where he is now. Either way, I need to get him back. Tomorrow. Do I have your help or do I go elsewhere?'

'It's a tough one,' said Mace, wanting to buy time.

'Simple one,' said Oosthuizen. 'Yes or no.'

'Tami?' said Mace.

Tami said, 'You're the boss.'

Mace looked at the vase for help. He couldn't turn it down. Not money like that.

'The best I can do,' he said to Oosthuizen, 'is get one of my staff there tomorrow. Probably. If we can get on the flight.'

'You,' said Oosthuizen. 'The best you can do is get you there tomorrow.'

'Impossible,' said Mace.

'Nothing is impossible, Mr Bishop.'

'Tomorrow is. Three days' time, Thursday, is the best I can do.' Three days to get back Veronica Dinsmor. In three days Pylon would be operative, sort of.

'A compromise. How about Wednesday? I can reassure him. Another day will probably not be so serious.' Oosthuizen shuffled the papers into his file, closed it. Picked the last of the chocolate biscuits off the plate. 'May I?' Without waiting for an answer, crunched into it. Chewed, grinned at Mace. 'Think of the money, Mr Bishop. A stack of crisp greenbacks.'

Mace thought of the money. 'Alright, Wednesday.'

'Excellent.' Oosthuizen beaming at him.

The morning of smiles seeming suddenly less sunny to Mace. His cellphone rang.

'I'll see you out, Mr Oosthuizen,' said Tami.

Mace connected, watching Oosthuizen following Tami's arse as she led him down the passage. Wasn't a man who didn't admire Tami's arse. The voice in his ear, male voice, coloured voice, said,

'Ah, Mr Bishop, I'm an account advisor at the bank. I wonder if you could come in to see me.'

'About?' said Mace, knowing full well.

'Ah, your overdraft's running a little high. And ... there's your bond repayments. You've missed the last one.'

Mace said, 'My wife was murdered.'

An intake of breath. A stuttering apology. 'I'm sorry. Sorry, Mr Bishop, sorry about this but you see ...'

Mace kept out of what it was he should see, let the account advisor stumble on.

'... You see we've got this problem ... If you come in we can maybe work something out. It's just this has happened before, you see. A couple of times. Mr Bishop?'

'It's very difficult for me now,' said Mace.

'Ja, I understand of course,' said the account advisor. 'It's just ... You see it's just that if we could make an appointment it would be better. Then I can tell my boss you're coming in. You see. We could even make it for Thursday. Say in the afternoon.'

'Alright,' said Mace. Heard in his head: 'I see a red door ...'

'Sorry for your grief, Mr Bishop,' said the account advisor. 'Strues.'

Mace thinking, This's all I need – somewhere in his mind Mick singing, '... and I want it painted black.'

19

Veronica Dinsmor hurt. Pain throbbed in her temples. Her face ached. Her shoulders ached. The taste of blood thick in her mouth. She wanted water. Wanted the bathroom. She watched her captors: the tall one, the driver, sitting at the desk opposite her toying with his cellphone; the short one in the van. She had to turn her head to see the minivan, there he was in the front seat listening to the radio. The radio too faint for her to hear it.

She was cold. Shivered. Trembled. Her legs shaking despite the ties, uncontrollably.

She glanced up at the skylights, dull hazy rectangles. Could be eight o'clock, could be eleven o'clock. Could even be the afternoon. In the warehouse a pervading gloom, a grey zone. Grey concrete floor. Grey brick walls. Grey girders. Grey tin roof. A leaden light.

Outside she sensed activity. Distant activity. Engines. Band saw whine. Hammering. Far off, someone calling. Everything too far off.

She wondered if Silas was dead. Had glimpsed the muzzle flash of shots before the short one got her down on the minivan floor. If he was dead, what good was she? The thought ached in her bladder.

'I want the bathroom,' she said, the words loud in her head, the sound a mewling through the gag.

The driver stared at her. Hard eyes, hard face. Not stopping the flip flip flip of his cellphone.

She made the noise again.

He said, 'Stay calm, my lady. Soon, soon, ne.'

Veronica Dinsmor tried a scream. It came out as a long 'neeeeeh.'

The man shook his head.

Nothing for it. She pissed herself. That got his attention.

Got him jumping. Scooting round the desk, voluble in a strange language. Resonant tongue clucks sharp as sticks breaking. He circled her, hit her head with his open palm. Not a hard blow. More out of irritation. But the smack stung. Brought tears to her eyes.

Tears from the pain, and the bladder relief.

'Water,' she said when the man stopped in front of her, shouted his strange language in her face. Uhhh, was the noise she made.

She heard the short one then, the slam of the minivan door.

'This's up to shit. Big time.' Saw him push at the one who'd been the driver. The driver stepping back to get his balance. 'They's dead, my bra. Mors dood. Gone.' The driver grabbing the short one by his jacket, in his face shouting at him.

The short one saying, 'The news. I heard it. Now, now. Shit, man, they's dead.'

The driver pulling the short one out of her sight, behind the minivan. She could still hear him. The fear in his voice. 'Phone her.

This's shit man. This's not the job. Phone her. Tell her I'm gone, my bra, out of here.'

The short one quietened. The murmur of the driver's voice going on. Lecturing. She waited, twisted in the chair towards their voices. They came round the van, stood in front of her. Stared at her.

'Uhhhh,' she groaned. Her sound for water.

'She's pissed herself,' said the short one. 'This's up to shit. So much up to shit.'

The driver spoke in his language. Said in English, 'Enough. We finish what we start.'

20

Silas Dinsmor played silent Injun, staring straight ahead on the drive to the casino.

Back at the hotel had been grim-visaged when Mace picked him up.

First words he said: 'I haven't heard from them.'

Mace, glancing at the mess in the bedroom, thinking now Silas looked more like a man with a kidnapped wife. Agitated. Swallowing a lot. Spider hands on the move: touching his face, brushing over his hair, picking lint off his suit.

Mace said, 'This is what I think it is, they'll be watching. See if you pitch up.'

'And then?'

'Find out what you've got to say.'

'One of them's in on this?'

'Sure.'

End of conversation.

Before they went out the bedroom door the Complete Security guy whispered to Mace. 'Oke's been on that phone for an hour. A US call. Must be earlier than six o' clock there. Talking in Indian.'

Mace told him to hang about the hotel. Watch the comings and goings.

He and Silas Dinsmor got in the Spider, drove off in silence, Mace taking a route through the suburbs, over the Black River into pristine Pinelands, garden estate. Where judges, politicians, spooks bought houses. All the hues of the rainbow nation. Was going to comment on this but didn't. Glanced sideways at the clenched jawline of Silas Dinsmor's big face and kept quiet.

Kept shut up across the back of the industrial estates to the grand casino: a wonderland that could've been Italian or French or anywhere, in fact, but where it was.

No comment from Silas Dinsmor. Not a word crossing the parking lot to the lift, up in the lift to the offices, down the corridor to reception. Mace announcing them. A PA with a red smile ushering them into a boardroom. Nice aspect of the mountain in the window. The boardroom just not high enough up the building to get the full grey sweep of Maitland cemetery.

Silas Dinsmor took a seat in the middle of the table, back to the wall, facing the view. Two women, three men came in, Ms Red Lips following. The woman leading the delegation introduced herself by name and title, legal director. Did the same for her colleagues, names Mace instantly forgot. No problem, only the legal director did the talking.

Opened with: 'We are fully appraised of what happened last night, Mr Dinsmor, and you have our complete support.' Took a seat opposite him. Her hands flat on the table, long well-manicured fingernails clear varnished. Looking him full in the face to express sincerity. 'This is a traumatic, awful situation. Absolutely unacceptable.' She glanced at her colleagues lined either side of her, they nodded. 'Whatever we can do to help, to ease matters … If you would rather not continue until Mrs Dinsmor …' – she hesitated – '… until this matter is resolved, has been resolved, we fully understand.'

Red Lips served tea. Placed a plate of chocolate biscuits in the centre of the table. Not Bahlsen's. Not anywhere like the quality. Mace thought he could downgrade the Bahlsen's when clients called. Go for a local digestive. His cellphone vibrated: Pylon.

The legal director saying, 'Following the report in this morning's newspaper we, the casino, have issued a statement, on behalf of the casino management. A strongly worded position.' The man to her right slid a piece of paper towards Silas Dinsmor. Kept his fingers on it until Silas Dinsmor drew it in. 'We're condemning, in no uncertain terms, this terrorism. That's what we've called it, terrorism. That's what it is. Criminals, thugs, holding society to ransom. This threat is against us all. You'll see there' – she pointed at the press release lying before Silas Dinsmor – 'we're demanding the release of your wife immediately. Before this thing goes any further. I have, also, personally been on to the police, the police commissioner, to express our deep disappointment that this sort of thing can go on. I know him, Mr Dinsmor, the police commissioner, he is as concerned as we are. He tells me, reassures me, they are doing everything they can. Seriously. Everything.'

She stopped. Silas Dinsmor read the press release. Mace glanced round the table, wondered which of the casino people was in on the kidnapping.

'I appreciate this,' said Silas Dinsmor tapping the release.

'It's a gesture.' The legal director leant forward, stretched out a hand as if she were reaching out to touch Silas Dinsmor. 'Our feeling,' she said, 'under the circumstances, is to wait, not take matters any further. This's the advice we're taking. In-house. Our lawyers' opinion. Even the police commissioner.' She withdrew her hand slowly trailing her fingers, like withdrawing a lifeline. 'We've been having,' she said, 'tourists targeted. By syndicates. I'm sure you're aware. But the police tell me, the commissioner tells me, this isn't a random thing. You were both targeted. You and your wife. They wanted you both. This has to be tied to something else, Mr Dinsmor. The only thing we can think of is our business deal.'

A quiet in the room. The low hum of air-conditioning, fluorescent lighting. Mace felt his cellphone vibrate with messages.

'Why would that be?'

The legal director said, 'There is another offer on the table, Mr Dinsmor.'

'Local people?' Silas Dinsmor hunched in his seat.

'Yes.'

'This is how they do business?'

'Mr Dinsmor,' the legal director sighed, 'Mr Dinsmor, let me explain something. This might not seem related, relevant, but we've got to think about it. Last week in a township not twenty kilometres away, fifteen Somali shop owners were attacked by a mob. Five killed, their shops looted, razed to the ground. Their families attacked, two women, girls actually, raped. Those people are living in refugee shelters now. They can't go home. All because they're better businesspeople than the locals. Their prices are lower. The customers are scoring. Paying less for essentials. You'd think they'd be welcome. But no. They're seen as taking away livelihoods. They're not seen as competition, they're seen as invaders. A new sort of colonialism, Mr Dinsmor. Here we call it xenophobia.' She stopped to drink tea. 'It's in the air. You understand what I'm saying.'

'That my wife has been kidnapped to take us out of the equation. Ah, come on.'

'Yes. In fact, that you were both targeted.'

'You people will behave like this?'

'Not us, Mr Dinsmor. Some people in this society. Unfortunately. It's deeply regrettable but it's a fact. Crime is out of hand. So, yes, it is a possibility, yes.' Her head nodding.

'You sit there telling me this. Calmly. Like it's no big deal. You're running a democracy here, ma'am, so I'm informed. A liberal capitalist state. You're encouraging investment, from the brochures I read. I see comments from your finance minister, the director of your reserve bank, cabinet ministers inviting me to do business here. I go to seminars encouraging me to explore an expanding economy. Low inflation. Six per cent growth rate. Excellent banking laws. Nowhere do I hear whispers of banana republic. Sure, I hear tell of crooks and bandits. Crooks and bandits are everywhere. I hear stories of crime. Street muggings. Car hijackings. Which is why I engaged Mr Bishop here, not that it helped much.'

Mace thought, thanks, pal. Felt the heat in his face, on the palms of his hands. The casino people checking him out. But Silas Dinsmor wasn't pausing, headed into a full rant about the accepted principles of doing business. Along the lines practised in the civilised Western world. How this sort of incident gave Africa its image as a basket case. A violent hell-hole of jealous backstabbers. His words.

To which the legal director said, 'We know this is a traumatic time for you …'

Getting no further before Silas Dinsmor snapped, 'Don't patronise me.' His hands balled in fists, those fists not far off pounding the table.

'I didn't mean to … My apologies.' The legal director collecting herself. 'Mr Dinsmor. Mr Dinsmor, it is as likely that we will hear from the kidnappers as yourself. In fact it is more likely that we will be contacted. If this is what we believe it is, and not random. My sense, and that of the police, is that your wife would have been released already if this was random. If this was a tourist hijacking they would have taken your cash, credit cards, electronic gadgets. It would have been over in a few minutes. This is a kidnapping. Believe me, when they call they will demand that our dealings cease.' She paused, eyes on Silas Dinsmor. 'Mr Dinsmor, the casino, under the circumstances, would understand if you withdrew your offer. Obviously, penalty clauses …'

'Never.'

'I'm sorry?'

'The deal stays on the table.' His hands relaxed, his fingers opened. 'I'm not going to back down. We have been in this sort of situation before. Then too, Veronica was kidnapped. We did not back down, we will not do so now.'

The legal director glanced at her colleagues, at Mace, frowning, her mouth slightly open as if to speak. She didn't. Mace's cellphone vibrated on the tabletop, breaking the quiet.

'I'm afraid …' she said, watching the phone shudder twice, its screen light flashing. 'I didn't …' Then: 'I think you need to talk with the police to get their views.'

'I have. All morning. Ma'am, I'm sticking to our proposal.'

21

Max Roland was agitated. The paperback lay open on his lap. He hadn't read for hours. Hadn't tried to. Couldn't concentrate. He chewed qat leaves and maybe that helped and maybe it didn't.

After these limbo days he was antsy. Needing to be on the move again. In transit no longer felt safe. In transit felt in transit: like he was pinned in the middle of a target. Suddenly this place, this hotel was dangerous. By now they had to know where he'd found sanctuary, were waiting for him to make the move.

Yesterday he'd bought a local SIM card, afraid to use the hotel phone again. Today he'd not taken his morning run through the souk, worried that in the tangle of lanes he could be disappeared too easily.

He changed the SIM cards in his cellphone. Toyed with phoning Magnus Oosthuizen. Since breakfast he'd been in his room, gazing out. Watching. Resisting the phone call.

From his window Max Roland's view overlooked a miller's yard. Every day a camel trod a circle round the yard, harnessed by a wooden spindle to a stone mill, grinding flour. For hours. For hours Max Roland watched, mesmerised, this ancient beast perform this ancient task. The miller standing to the side, occasionally flicking a short switch. A fine powder of dust and dry dung rising about the camel's hooves.

Beyond the miller's yard lay a square. From his high vantage, Max Roland could see the front doors of three houses on the square. In the late afternoon, two women would come out to sweep before their properties. Always at the same time. Two black shapeless figures completely covered except for their eyes. He saw a harshness in the forms with only small feet flashing below the hems.

The women would wave to one another. He could see the gestures, had to imagine their voices. The fresh voices of young women. He imagined they were young women. Imagined that beneath their abayas they wore tangas, wonderbras. He'd heard that. That Muslim women were not what they seemed. Especially not the modern ones in the cities. Under those black bags they wore labels: Banana Republic, Diesel, Calvin Klein, low-rise hipster jeans, silk camis. Or only underwear. To tease their men.

Max Roland longed to be among women. To see women in the flesh. Not even in the flesh, but just not hidden in black abayas sweeping silently through the streets. He wanted to hear their voices. See their hair. Their shoulders, their arms, the rhythm of their breasts in a loose top. The press of raised nipples. He shut his eyes. Brought to mind the Sea Point promenade, a trio of young women walking towards him. Their bellies above low-rise jeans. Such a soft, gentle shape a woman's belly. Not a stomach. A belly, rounded, curved. To slide his hand from the belly-button over the rise down the long slope, Max Roland sighed, that was a pleasure. He remembered the trio passing him, their laughter, their gay voices. That'd made him smile. Made him turn round to admire their pert backsides.

He couldn't stay much longer in this city of men. This city of hidden women.

The two sweepers had stopped to talk. Even in the sunlight of the empty square, the black shapes defied his imagination. He could not see the women beneath, could not imagine any part of them. He had to get out of here. Out of this stifling room, this crumbling building, this hot and antique city. Away to a place of women. Where you could hear them, see them. He wanted the smell of a woman on his fingers.

Max Roland phoned Magnus Oosthuizen.

'Get me out,' he said.

Oosthuizen said, 'I'm doing that. It's set for Wednesday.'

'Tomorrow,' said Max Roland.

'I thought you were relaxed about this.'

Max Roland looked at the two women talking in the square. The two black shapes. 'I was.'

'And now?'

'Now I'm not.'

'Something's happened?'

'Nothing's happened. Time's passed. That's what's happened.'

'Wait, Max. Okay, just wait. Only two days.'

The women turned in his direction, seemed to be looking at the hotel. He could see the pillbox opening in their burkas.

Max Roland had been to the square, had stood where they stood now to consider the aspect: a cityscape of buildings none higher than six storeys. Behind them the rise of the old town, the minarets of the Great Mosque just visible. He'd searched out the window of his room. Anyone in the frame would be visible. One pace back they'd disappear into the gloom. He was in the gloom. The women couldn't see him. Yet he withdrew further into the room.

'Two days,' he said. 'In two days' time. That is unacceptable.'

Magnus Oosthuizen pulled one of his silences.

'Two days, Magnus,' said Max Roland. Hissing the words.

'Max,' said Oosthuizen. 'Listen, Max. Hell, man, calm down. Where's this coming from? This is not Max Roland. This is not the man I know.'

'Two days, Magnus.'

'Max, Max, hold on. Okay, hold on. What's the problem?'

Max Roland sat down on the bed. From there he could no longer see the women in the square. He looked out over rooftops and domes and minarets. Looked out to the hazed hills that ringed the city. Two days. He couldn't wait two days.

'I'm organising everything,' Magnus Oosthuizen was saying. 'The trouble's not where you are, the trouble's here. I've got to arrange things. Get us properly protected.'

Max Roland swore in German. 'When I left it wasn't like that. There was no trouble.'

'When you left no one knew what we had. They thought we were cowboys. Now they know what we can do. Things are different, Max. We have what everybody wants. The best weapons system. We have the key to big big money.'

A long silence from Oosthuizen: such quiet Max could hear the miller talking to his camel.

He let out a long sigh of air. Said, 'Ja, gut.' The hotel pension proprietor's saying. From a long time ago.

'Two days, Max. Two days, okay. That's all I ask you. Take a tourist trip. Do something. Two days will pass quickly.'

Max Roland stood up, cut the connection. The women had gone indoors. The square was empty. Two days. He couldn't wait two days. In two days the others might make a move.

22

Sheemina February folded a black negligee under her pillow. Not typical of her, this lingerie. But a cotton shift wouldn't cut it. Placed a rosebud in a vase on the marble top. She closed the curtains, picked up her suitcase on the way out. In the corridor pulled the door closed with her gloved hand, heard the lock click home.

Five minutes later, Sheemina February accelerated the X5 into Victoria Road, headed for the city, Robert Plant and Alison Krauss on the sound system: Gone, gone, gone.

First stop was her hairdresser. 'Wash it out,' she told the stylist. 'Give me back my black. And shorter in the neck, floppy over the forehead.'

'A bit butch isn't it?'

'Butch's working,' said Sheemina February. 'It's a man's world, so we're told.'

'On your head be it.'

Made Sheemina February laugh out loud. 'Nicely put.'

An hour later she was back in her car, not butch at all, very stylish. Got out of the city to the croon of Robert and Alison.

She took a call from Magnus Oosthuizen on the West Coast road heading for the beach cottage that had come her way courtesy of a land deal. A deal she'd scored over Pylon Buso. A deal that'd put people in the ground: her one-time client Obed Chocho, the young couple, the Smits, who'd owned the cottage. A deal made her smile whenever she thought about it. She saw Oosthuizen's name come up, adjusted her Bluetooth. 'Good news, Magnus?'

'Yes and no,' he said.

'Yes, Mace Bishop couldn't resist the money.'

'He will take it on, as you said. In two days' time.'

'Good. So what's the no part?'

Oosthuizen not responding, going into one of his pauses. Sheemina February tapped the steering wheel, thinking, he needed time management on his cellphone account, but kept her cool, waited. Eventually he said, 'Max Roland' – like he'd had to drag the name up from some swamp.

'Tell me.' She saw the sign for the development up ahead, took her foot off the accelerator.

'He phoned me.' Pause. 'A couple of minutes ago.' Pause.

Sheemina February braked, indicated to turn left, the SUV bouncing off the tar onto a gravel road, the road potholed with pools of water.

'He wants me to get him out.'

'Of course.'

'Soonest.'

'You are. Two days isn't long. You said he was tough, Magnus. Trained for this sort of thing.'

'He is.'

'So what's the deal?'

'I don't know. I'm not there. I'm telling you what he told me. He's unhappy.'

'My heart bleeds.' Sheemina February stopped the vehicle at the gate, waited for the security guard to emerge from his Zozo hut, taking his time. When he saw it was her he changed his pace. The guard's sudden acceleration gave her an idea. Maybe it would be better to get Max back asap. She could see advantages opening up. New possibilities. Yes, a change of plan. She smiled to herself. 'So squeeze Mister Bishop.'

'I thought …'

'What?'

'That it was best to keep him out of the country until the end of the week. When we spoke that's what you suggested.'

'Sometimes what we want isn't possible, Magnus. Listen to the Zen masters, go with the flow.' She drove through the gateway, raised a hand in greeting to the guard.

The gravel road became a sand track with a middle hump, redgrass and flat shrubs scraping under the car. She drove slowly across the upland, the track gradually dipping towards the sea, the cottage just visible in the dunes above the shoreline.

In two months, work would begin: a vast tract transformed into a golf estate – greens, fynbos clusters, bunker holes and homes. The cottage become a project manager's office, the birdsong given to the growl and whine of bulldozers. A shame really. But that was progress. In the end the birdsong would be back to bring joy to hundreds of hearts.

Until then she could enjoy the wildness. An hour from the city, close to her apartment, the lair become the web.

Magnus Oosthuizen said, 'Bishop can't move sooner.'

Sheemina February laughed. 'Everybody can move sooner, Magnus, for an enticement. Especially Mr Bishop.'

'I'm paying him a fortune.'

'You haven't paid him anything yet.' She stopped the BMW in a clearing behind the cottage. The sea was wild, pounding against the outer rocks, waves taking spume high up the beach. Farther out, patches of sunlight breaking through the clouds, glistening on the ocean. Maybe, she thought, you'll never have to, but kept this to herself. 'You sort it out, Magnus. It's your boy who's scared.'

That'd give him pause, it did. She stared at the sea, a faint smile on her lips.

'He means a great deal of money to you,' said Oosthuizen.

'To both of us.' She enjoyed reminding him. Enjoyed remembering how much money Max Roland meant. 'So do the right thing, Magnus. Tell me how it goes.'

She disconnected. Connected to Mart Velaze.

'Blue eyes,' he said in greeting.

Sheemina smiled. Mart always trying it on. 'Listen,' she said, 'we need the weapons committee to bring forward Oosthuizen's hearing. How's Friday sound?' She heard Mart suck in air.

'Friday! It wasn't even scheduled for next week.'

'I know.'

'So what's the rush?'

Sheemina stared at the ocean: waves slamming white and high against the rocks. 'Timing,' she said. 'Upping the ante. Getting such a rush going nothing will stop us.'

Mart whistled. 'Sounds very sexy.'

'Can you do it? Shift the committee?'

He clucked his tongue. 'Nothing I can promise.'

'Mart the fixer,' she said. 'You've got a reputation.'

Mart Velaze spluttered a response.

Sheemina February said, 'I'm sure you can.' And hung up. Such an operator Mart Velaze, he'd pull it off. She sat in the X5 enjoying the warmth of the winter sun, listening to the piep of prinias in the thickets. Noisy little birds. There could be worse places to hole up for a day or two. She couldn't see it taking longer than that before she had Mace Bishop where she wanted him.

23

'You didn't ask for advice,' said Mace to Silas Dinsmor, 'and I don't give it. Usually. But this's it anyhow.'

'I don't want it,' said Silas Dinsmor.

'Like I said, here it is anyhow.' Mace and Silas Dinsmor in a casino coffee shop. 'You're making a mistake. Forget the deal. Tell them you can't do business this way. I can get you on the radio this afternoon, you can make it public: the offer's withdrawn, release my wife, we're booked on tomorrow's flight. Outta here. I just want to go home, forget this ever happened. Please let my wife go.' Mace scraped a teaspoon round the cup to gather the espresso froth. Licked it clean. 'That sort of thing. The desperate husband at his wits' end.'

Silas Dinsmor hadn't touched his cappuccino.

'If there was a spy in that meeting, the word's got back already, I'm calling their hand. The way I figure it they're going to make contact now and contact means we've got a dialogue going. Something to work with.'

'You're playing with her life.'

'I told you, we've done it before. You don't know Veronica.'

'I know the scene here. You don't.'

'Can't be any worse than Colombia.'

'Maybe. Maybe not. All I'm saying is the way it happens here, you don't get quarter. Understand one thing, the rage levels are way high. Nobody does anger management. People hit up against argie-bargie they go, to hell with this, bam, bam, shoot their way out. Happens all the time. You saw it last night.'

'My way,' said Silas Dinsmor. 'I thank you for your opinion, Mr Bishop, but this is my call, my hand.' The problem exactly, thought Mace. The gambler gambling.

Silas Dinsmor saying, 'You're my security people. Come down to it, my bodyguard. Contracted for that and that's how we'll continue.' He kept his eyes off Mace while he talked. 'How I'd like this relationship. Businesslike. Don't go Pike Bishop on me. I don't do disloyalty.'

Mace kept his thoughts to himself, what point in telling Silas Dinsmor yet again this wasn't business, this was his wife's safety, her life most likely. Said, 'Okay. We'll stick to that.'

'No offence.'

'None taken.'

Silas Dinsmor pushed the cappuccino into the middle of the table. 'I don't think I've the stomach for that.' He stood. 'I want to take a walk round the place. Get the feel.'

You've got to be joking, thought Mace. Said, 'Not a good idea.'

Silas Dinsmor leant towards him. 'I'm not going to say please.'

Mace stared into the man's eyes, an opaque dullness. Injun eyes. How did some people get to be such arseholes? He pushed back his chair. 'Alright then.' What risk was there to Silas Dinsmor in the casino? Scale of one to ten: down round about one. 'Let's go.' Mace breaking the rules, checking the messages on his phone as they walked.

Four missed calls, four messages.

He got through to his voicemail.

12:11 – Pylon: 'I'm still at the hospital, okay, for some time probably. Treasure's in labour. Bunch of fingers dilated, whatever that means. Nothing doing yet though except the contractions. Here's a strange one: remember at the Mo Siq funeral a smiley NIA type pitched up, called himself Mart Velaze. Then at the Popo Dlamini killing there was a creepy white guy hanging around, NIA written all over him. Well, now black Mart's back on the scene. Dropped in to comfort me. Seems the agency likes keeping a watching brief on us. What's going on we don't know about?'

12:21 – Gonsalves: 'Hey, Mace Bishop, talk to me. Nah! Don't then. Still, pellie, you wanna know about some police work, course you do, we got the name of the tsotsi stole the car. The red Golf. Impressive hey? Soon be talking to the owners. Maybe even take a look at this tsotsi's shack. You wondering how it's done? We're amazing, man.'

12:22 – Tami: 'There's some stuff I found about Dinsmor you need to know. Some more stuff.'

12:46 – Magnus Oosthuizen: 'Very constructive discussion this morning, Mr Bishop. Only thing is we need to tighten up the timeframe. My man's getting edgy. Two days is pushing it. Call me. This's urgent.'

They walked into the banks of slot machines. Mace with his eyes on the patrons. More women than men this time of day. Feeding the coins in, watching the barrels roll. Here and there the clatter of a win. A couple of men with their wives. Tourists. Retirees making the most of their sixties.

He thumbed through to the messages, thinking today of all days Treasure had to pick it. Thinking Mart Velaze, Mart Velaze, hadn't there been a Mart Velaze in the camps? A youngster. A hot kid who was being flagged even then for training in the East. Had to be the same guy. The past resurrecting. Which, Mace knew, was never good news. But it could wait. So could Gonsalves and Oosthuizen. He browsed the messages:

12:09 – A number he didn't recognise. The message consisted of four digits and the words 'Square now.' A security code. Mace grinned. Hadn't even cost him grease money. He saved the sms to his phone's SIM card.

12:27 – Tami: 'Need to talk. Urgently.'

12:53 – Pylon: 'I'm a father. Have been for fifteen minutes.'

12:55 – Pylon: 'It's a boy.'

He had to phone him. The man must be ecstatic, over the moon, bursting with it. A son, too. That'd please Pylon the most. Mace smiled, was about to tell Silas Dinsmor, Pylon's father when he saw them: two women playing blackjack at a far table, the one, the pageboyed one, watching them. Silas Dinsmor saw them too.

'Cute,' he said.

'Very,' said Mace, wondering what it was about the women caught his attention. The way they were dressed? The boots? The white blouses open to a swell of tits? The casual brazenness of them?

Silas Dinsmor chose a roulette table away from the women. Away, but in direct sight of them. Only one punter playing a red combination.

The croupier racked a few low chips from the green. Said, 'Place your bets.'

The punter put down three chips on red variations: two splits and a straight up, took him a good couple of minutes to decide.

'Sir?' said the croupier, looking at Silas Dinsmor.

'No, no.' Silas Dinsmor waved his hand. 'Not this time.'

The croupier nodded, spun the wheel.

Mace kept the women in his side vision. Not difficult, the white blouses blazed like beacons.

With a flick of his wrist, the croupier set the ball circling. Once, twice, third time it dropped down, bounced onto the wheel, ran freely, slotted into black eleven.

The women were both looking their way. Mace could sense it, a change in their posture. He glanced up from the table, caught their eyes. The one dropped her gaze, the other didn't.

'Red-only's gonna kill you,' Silas Dinsmor said to the punter. 'Try two streets. I'd say sixteen and nineteen.'

'And you?' said the punter. 'Let's see you put them down.'

'Too early.'

The punter snorted. Went back to his red variation: a nine-twelve split, seven straight up.

The croupier spun the wheel. The ball slotted twenty-one.

'Yeah, well,' said Silas Dinsmor. 'I should've had money on it.'

The punter grunted. The croupier swept up the chips.

Mace realised the blaze had gone from his side vision. Just the croupier at the blackjack table, laying out cards to a middle-aged couple.

'Where're the girls?' said Silas Dinsmor.

Mace said, 'They've left.'

'Couple of sirens. We couldn't have cut it for them.' Silas Dinsmor laughed.

Mace wondered how he did that with his wife abducted.

24

If they didn't give her water soon she was going to die. Simple as that. Veronica Dinsmor, Dancing Rabbit, tried to plead with her eyes. Stared at the nice one, the one behind the desk, the driver. Please give me water.

'What's it?' he said, taking his feet off the desk. Coming forward to lean on his elbows, looking her straight in the eyes.

She made a high-pitched hum in response. Tried to put desperation into it.

'You come here in winter, what d'you expect, it's cold.' He got up pushed the gas heater closer to her. 'What's her problem?' he said to the short one. 'You think she's cold still?'

Veronica Dinsmor kept staring at him, raising the pitch of her hum. Her throat felt like it would crack. Her tongue was curled back, stuck to the roof of her mouth.

'The heat makes her piss stink,' said the short one.

She hurt from the blows she'd taken earlier. She felt faint. Her sight blurring, the driver's face sliding out of focus.

The driver saying, 'Untie her hands' – fishing a ballpoint and notepad out of the desk drawer. The notepad headed Bob's Auto Spares, fancy scrollwork of cogs and spanners across the top.

Short-arse said, 'Yes, baas.' Got a fierce look for the sarcasm.

When the ties were off Veronica couldn't feel her wrists. Slowly she rubbed one hand over the other. Flexed her fingers, stiff from the cold and reduced circulation. The driver held the paper and pen at her. She took it. Dropped the Bic. The driver picked it up, gave it back to her. She wrote: 'Water. Please. Please.'

'What's it she wants?' said the short one.

'Water.'

The short one backing off, shaking his head. 'Aikona.'

She was looking at the two of them like they were playing a tennis match. Realised that in all this time they'd not used names.

'How can we do that? We undo her mouth she's gonna scream. No ways American.'

'Hey, my brother. Tula.'

She held up her hands for the pad and ballpoint.

'No ways, American. This's not Mr Stupid here.' The short one coming back, stabbing his index finger at his breastbone. 'You see Mr Moegoe, look again, American.'

The driver dropped the pen and paper in her lap.

'I will not scream,' she wrote. 'Take money from my bag. Buy food.' She held up the pad.

The driver took it. Snorted.

'Ja, and nou. What what?'

'The mama's paying for lunch.'

'Of course. Why not?' The short one bending to bring his face level with hers, his words rank and hot, 'Luister, American, you scream, we cut out your tongue. One time, first thing, no problem.' He waggled his tongue at her. 'Strues.'

She nodded. Brought her hand up to her mouth to tear off the duct tape.

The short one grabbed her arm, 'No, American,' he said. 'No shit, I said.'

Again, they fastened the tie around her wrists, though not as tightly, not with her arms behind her back. That was something.

The short one fetched her purse from the van, pulled out two hundred notes.

'Get some pies,' said the driver. 'Big Jacks.'

'Jou moer, my bra,' said the short one. 'Up yours. You go.'

The driver held out his cellphone. 'You gonna talk to her, my brother, if she phones?'

The short one muttering as he walked off.

'Make it a Coke, as well,' said the driver. 'Some more cigarettes.'

The short one gave him the finger.

Veronica heard the factory roller door slide up, felt a cold rush of wind, the door being slammed down again.

The driver clucked, went to sit behind the desk, his eyes on her.

She made the high humming, hoping that he'd remember her note for water.

He shook his head. 'Wait, my lady. He comes back you can have water. But I warn you, you scream I'm gonna hit you one time. Like my brother says, cut out your tongue.'

She sat it out, the time it took the short one to buy food.

Drifting in and out with the thirst. Losing focus. Bringing herself back. Her face hurting. Her jaws aching from the gag. Her throat on fire. Her tongue might have already been cut out, so stiff in her mouth she couldn't feel it. Once she went down, her head flopping forward. The driver shot round the desk, slapped her back to consciousness.

'Come, my lady.' Stinging slaps to her face. 'Come, my lady' – following up with a string of words in his own language. She liked the my lady bit. Even in the fear and thirst liked the my lady.

The short one came back with pies and Cokes.

They warned her again not to scream. She nodded, unable to take her eyes off the cooldrink cans. The driver opened one, stuck a straw in it. He peeled back the duct tape told her, 'Spit out the gag.' She couldn't. Her jaws too stiff. Her tongue not functioning. He had to pull it out. Pushed the straw between her lips, said, 'Suck, my lady.'

She could manage that. Held the can in her bound hands, sucked down the Coke. They watched her. Ate their pies, watching her.

When she could move her tongue she tried to speak. Had to clear her throat a couple of times.

When she could she said, 'Thank you.'

'Alright, my lady,' said the driver, swallowing the last of his pie. Getting up with the duct tape in his hand.

'Wait,' she said, 'wait. I won't scream.'

She watched him pause, staring at her. 'It's our orders.'

The other one, the short one, said, 'Orders is orders.'

'I know,' she said. 'But no one is going to find out.' Glancing from one to the other. Keeping her eyes on the driver. 'Five minutes,' she said. 'Give me five minutes.'

The driver nodded, sat down.

'What're your names?' Veronica looked at the short one then back at the driver. 'It won't hurt to tell me.'

25

He couldn't wait two days. Max Roland sat at the table staring out at the distant square as the darkness came, knew he couldn't wait two days. He stood up, walked to the window. Below, the grind and groan of the camel at the wheel had ceased. The camel stood facing a wall. Did it dream of desert vistas, Max Roland wondered?

He was packed in thirty minutes. Had been living out of his suitcase anyhow, the room not furnished with a cupboard. Had decided to get to the airport, make the booking there. At one a.m. a flight left for Johannesburg. This much he knew, getting the airline schedule among the first things he'd done. He thought about phoning Magnus Oosthuizen, decided that would be best done from the airport. Once he was booked, through customs, waiting to board. He went downstairs.

The men were in the reception room as usual. Chewing qat as usual. The television on, its sound off, the radio wailing Arab pop. They all greeted him, smiling green teeth. For the first time since he'd arrived, he hadn't chewed qat. This was not a time to chew qat. He needed to be alert. Watchful. He waved his hand in greeting, told the man behind the reception desk he was checking out.

'You want a taxi?' the man asked, hand on the telephone.

Max Roland nodded. He glanced at the television while he waited: a wildlife scene that could've been anywhere on the African savannah – wild dogs running down an antelope.

'In five minutes,' said the reception man, printing out Max Roland's bill on a dot-matrix machine.

On screen the buck got clear of the pack, the men groaned. When the lead dog toppled the animal, the men cheered. The buck staggered up, was dragged down by five dogs.

The receptionist made a comment to his friends. Said to Max Roland, 'I tell them it is how do you say, bloody.'

'Bloodthirsty.'

The man smiled. 'Bloodthirsty.' As the dogs fed, the camera zoomed in on the buck's dark eyes.

Max Roland held out his credit card.

'You like Sana'a?' said the receptionist.

'Very old.'

'Good for tourists.' The man tore the credit card slip off the machine, gave it to Max Roland to sign. 'This morning, more tourists. Two men. They come to look. But they tell me not five star.'

Max Roland signed the chit.

'I say speak to my guest. They say who it is my guest? I tell them he is a very nice man.'

'They want to know my name?'

'No. I tell them.'

'They say for them okay but not for the wives. The wives must have the bath in the room.'

The reception man plucked leaves from a qat cutting, stuffed them into his mouth. Chewed hard to mulch them down. 'This is Europeans.' He chewed. 'You are going home?'

Max Roland shook his head. 'To Shibam.'

'It is beautiful city.' The reception man searched among some postcards, pulled out one showing the mud towers of Shibam leaning together. 'Shibam is tall buildings like New York. Mud buildings. Nine floors.' Patting his hands one on the other nine times. 'You go over the desert?'

'Yes.'

The man whistled. 'Very long. Very hot for eight hours.'

'It's okay,' said Max Roland.

In the taxi Max Roland worried about the European men. Didn't sound like tourists, the two men. Sounded more like men searching him out. The Albanians. He directed the taxi driver to the Taj Talha hotel. From there took a walk-through to a back street, another taxi to the airport.

Magnus Oosthuizen, Chin-chin the Chihuahua in a tartan jacket under his arm, could hear John the Malawian gardener talking to Priscilla the maid in the kitchen. John inside to eat a late lunch.

Oosthuizen sat at his dining-room table waiting to be served.

Called out, 'Priscilla, where's my food?'

Got the reply, 'Coming, master.'

She came in with a bowl of pea soup, set it before him. Chin-chin growled, snapped at her hand.

'Little bliksem,' she said.

Oosthuizen laughed, putting the dog onto the chair beside him. 'Good security, hey!'

Priscilla clicked her tongue.

'Don't be like that,' said Oosthuizen. 'It's just a dog.'

His cellphone rang: Max Roland.

'Max,' he said, 'twice in one day. What's happening?'

Max Roland said, 'I shall be in Johannesburg tomorrow morning.'

Oosthuizen blew gently at the steam rising from his soup.

'No, Max. That's too soon. I haven't got the security in place. Stay where you are.'

'I have a ticket for the flight. I am at the airport,' said Max Roland.

'It's too dangerous without the security. Stay there. Right now no one knows where you are.'

'Somebody does.'

Oosthuizen stirred at his soup to cool it. 'Nonsense.' He heard Max Roland laugh.

'Where are you, Magnus?'

'What d'you mean?'

'Where are you now? In your car? At home? At a restaurant? Where?'

'At home.'

'At home. So nice. Where am I? I will tell you. I am in this airport that stinks of sweat. The air-conditioning is kaput. In the waiting lounge the only chairs are plastic. There are people sleeping on the floor. There are some people that have been here for fifteen hours. When the plane leaves I will have been here for five hours. I will want a shower. When the plane goes I still have a long flight.'

Chin-chin pawed at his master's lap, whining.

'You are safer there, Max. Don't take the flight.' Oosthuizen slapped at the dog, hissed, Ssshh, sssh. 'Just another day.' The dog bit his fingers. Oosthuizen yanked his hand away. 'Bliksem! Jou klein donder' – swatted the dog off the chair. Chin-chin skidded squealing across the tiles.

'Stay there, Max. One more night. Tomorrow the security's in place to fetch you. I swear.'

'You're not listening, my friend.'

'Christ, Max, they'll pick you up at customs. Even before that probably. The moment you get off the plane.'

'This has to be risked.'

'It doesn't.' Oosthuizen felt the dog pawing at his leg, then a warmth in his shoe. 'Shit,' he said, 'Chin-chin!' – kicking out. Chin-chin tjanked away. 'The dog's pissed on me.'

He heard Max Roland saying, 'I'm going. Get the security to meet me at the Johannesburg airport.'

'Wait, wait, Max.' Too late. 'Jesus, Chin-chin.' He thumbed through to Sheemina February.

'What is it, Magnus?' she said.

'A lot,' said Magnus Oosthuizen. 'I've got a scientist running scared. The dog has pissed in my shoe. My soup is getting cold.'

He heard Sheemina February's sexy laugh. The kind of laugh he imagined she'd make after orgasm. The laugh she made before she kicked a lover out of her bed. Heard her, 'Poor you.' The sound of waves and wind.

'He's going to be here tomorrow. Customs'll pick him up. They do that it's over. I may as well give the government my system for free.'

'Hey!' said Sheemina February, 'cool it. We're a democracy, Magnus. There're rules and human rights. Maybe this isn't such a bad thing. If your colleague gets stopped, let me know.'

'He thinks they've found him,' said Oosthuizen. 'The people chasing him.'

'I'm sure he does.'

Magnus Oosthuizen caught more sea noise. 'Where're you?'

'In a wild place, Magnus. Wild and isolated. Where someone can scream and no one will hear them.'

'Wonderful.'

'It is actually, yes.' The wind howl stopped, he heard a door close. 'All you've got to do, Magnus, is get hold of Mace Bishop. Tell him he must be in Johannesburg tomorrow morning to meet Max Roland. I've told you before, I'm telling you again, offer him something. Bishop'll move for money. But before that you'd better get the piss out of your shoe. Or you'll get chilblains.' Again he heard her black widow's laugh.

Magnus Oosthuizen sloshed his way to the bathroom. Dropped his shoe and sock in the bath for Priscilla to sort out. Washed his foot with the shower hose, padding back to the dining room in sheepskin slippers. Chin-chin was on the table lapping at his soup. Cocked those big eyes at him. Aren't I cute.

'Ag, ja, doggie,' he said. Shouted, 'Priscilla, bring me more soup.'

26

'What?' said Tami to Mace. 'I must what?'

'Take him around, for a couple of hours.'

Mace and Tami up in Mace's office. Mace anxious to be on the go. Silas Dinsmor downstairs in the boardroom with a cup of coffee and the few Bahlsens Magnus Oosthuizen had left.

'He's an arsehole.'

'Client. Shhhh. Keep it down.'

Tami puffing up her cheeks like a blowfish.

Mace saying, 'Take the gun. Eyes wide open but I don't think there's an issue. No one's after him.'

'I've got to tell you about him.'

Mace held up his hand. 'What?'

'Weird stuff.'

'Two minutes, Tami. One minute. I've got kids waiting, Christa and Pumla. Perverts will snatch them away if I don't get there first. Pylon's had a baby, I've got to go.'

She glared at him. 'I went through his laptop.'

'You what?'

'Checked out his laptop.'

'Jesus, Tami.' Mace closed his eyes. 'Tell me I'm not hearing this?' Looked at her.

'Three months ago he took out major death policies. One on his life, one on her life. Separately for two million dollars each.'

'So? People do this. I've got one.' Remembered, hell, there was one on Oumou's life he hadn't even got round to dealing with. Had to be a couple of hundred thou, would sort the overdraft, the bond repayments. But it felt like bounty. Blood money. He thought about it, he heard Mick Jagger: I see a red door ...

'He's also got a girlfriend.'

'Big deal. Lots of married men've got girlfriends.'

'Mace. Catch a wakeup: two million dollars, a girlfriend, his wife's kidnapped.'

'Three things I've got to say,' said Mace. 'The first thing: they were both kidnapped. The second thing: this's about a business deal. And some men have girlfriends, doesn't mean they want out of their marriage.' Mace flashing on Isabella, feeling heat in his palms. How she'd nibbled his fingertips. Brought her lips down on his. Even after years, even despite Oumou, despite the guilt, raised his lust.

'What if it isn't? What if that's why he's so okay?'

Mace smiled. 'I've got to go, Tami. Take him sightseeing. Probably the sea's too choppy for Robben Island. But the Slave Lodge. The District Six Museum, those'll stir his soul. Show him our valiant struggle.'

'He doesn't want her back. He wants her dead.'

'Too many movies, Tami. Forget the conspiracy theories. Life's not like that. Much more mundane.' He winked. 'Have fun.'

Mace headed down the stairs, two at a time. He looked in on Silas Dinsmor.

'Tami'll be with you for the rest of the afternoon. A ransom call comes through, I'm the first to know, okay? Even before the cops, the embassy, everyone.'

'Mace,' said Silas Dinsmor, biting into a biscuit, 'why haven't they called?'

'They will,' said Mace. 'They're sweating you. Probably till sometime tonight, I reckon.'

Christa and Pumla were waiting outside the school gate. Came rushing to the car as he pulled up.

'Can we go to the hospital, Papa?' Christa even leaning over to kiss his cheek. 'We've got to see him. Pylon says we can.'

Pumla from the back: 'Please, Mace. Please.'

'Sure,' said Mace, 'why not?'

The girls chatting as he headed onto De Waal, sun shafts breaking on Devil's Peak through a sky still grey and threatening.

In the traffic slow-down at Newlands Forest, Christa said to Mace, her body not angled towards him, her head turned slightly in his direction, 'Can I sleep over, Papa?'

'Uh-uh,' said Mace. 'Not tonight. Tomorrow, probably, I'm going to be away overnight. Or the next night, I'm not sure. I want you home with me tonight.'

Noticed Christa pull a droopy lip then think better of it. Considered offering an enticement: maybe a swimming session and a meal out.

'We could do a swim. Hit, I don't know, a Prima afterwards?'

'Ah, not a swim.'

He put out a hand, touched her arm. 'You haven't been for a week, C. You're going to lose fitness. It goes quickly, hey. Then what chances've we got for the island swim?'

'I don't want to do the swim.'

'No!' Mace said nothing past Paradise Motors up to the Bishops Court traffic lights, feeling the blood rush of temper and keeping it tight. Christa could work him up quicker than a street kid hissing for fifty cents.

'You'd be letting her down. Your mother.'

'Maman's dead.'

He could hear the tears in her voice, knew how she felt but couldn't leave it there. 'We're doing it for her memory, C. Because we loved her.' The past tense.

Christa said nothing, stared straight forward, her profile sulky, her eyes liquid.

Brought up an ache in Mace's chest, and anger. He wanted to hug her, he wanted to squeeze the life out of her. The vulnerability of her, the sheer bitter mordancy of her attitude. Always biting at him. He let it go, clenched his fists on the steering wheel.

At the hospital Mace and Pylon went for coffee in the hospital cafe while the girls swooned round Treasure and the baby. Pylon with his arm in a sling, a silly smile on his lips. Couldn't keep the grin down.

Mace said to him, 'Your face's going to hurt tomorrow.'

Pylon smiling. 'Why's that?'

'That grin. Ear to ear, man, it's alarming.'

'Can't help it,' he said. 'Every time I think of the little guy.'

'I know,' said Mace. Remembering newborn Christa lying on Oumou's stomach, sleeping. Couple of hours after the birth, mother and child. The sight had cut him up then, the memory did now. He took a long pull at the thin coffee to ease the choke in his throat, and gagged. The coffee tasted like pulped cardboard. Sent him into a coughing fit.

Pylon said, 'I'd thump you on the back if I could.'

Mace spluttered, wiped tears from his eyes.

'Bloody hell!'

'You can die drinking it.'

'I almost did.'

'I noticed.'

When Mace had his life back he heard Pylon out on the miracles of birth. The wonder of holding a new life in his hands. Some connection he'd felt with the ancestors.

'You don't do that crap,' said Mace. 'Normally.'

'It's what I felt,' said Pylon. 'Like there were a lot of people in the ward.'

'With spears and shields and leopard skins.'

Pylon put on a pained face. 'Hey, I don't need the mockery shit.' Thumbed through on his cellphone to the birth pictures he'd taken.

'You photographed them, the ancestors.'

'Very funny. Like I said, drop the mockery shit.'

'Sorry, okay.' Mace held up his hands in surrender.

'Check this.'

Mace taking the cellphone. On the screen the sort of detail he could have lived without: baby Buso entering the world.

'Amazing.' Pylon smiling in wonderment.

'Amazing,' said Mace, handing back the phone.

'No. Run through them,' said Pylon. 'There's more.'

Mace wondered if Treasure knew about this, how her wounded mate had turned paparazzo.

'Somehow there's got to be a way I can download this. Store them on a computer. Pumla'll know.'

'What for?' said Mace.

'It's history,' said Pylon. 'Family history.'

Mace gave him the phone. 'Congrats. I'll go and see the little guy for real in a moment. No offence: first things first.'

'Business,' said Pylon.

'Business,' said Mace.

Told him there'd been no ransom call, the only development that Gonsalves had got lucky, found a photo of the team on a cellphone belonging to one of the dead gents. Told him Silas Dinsmor was holding to the deal, no matter what the kidnappers wanted. That Tami was babysitting.

'With my gun?'

Mace ignored this, told him about Magnus Oosthuizen. Said, 'This's where it's getting stressed without you.'

'I'm wounded,' said Pylon. 'And on … what's it called, that fathers get? Paternity leave. Sorry for you.'

'To hell with that,' said Mace. 'Wednesday I've got to fetch this dude. From Yemen. That's like ten hours there, door to door. Four hour sit-around. Ten hours back. A knackers run.'

'And the Dinsmor scene?'

'All yours.'

'Crap, Mace. Save me Jesus, how'm I supposed to handle it.'

'With Tami.'

'She's a girl.'

'Who can chop bricks with her hand.'

'No, man. I'm a father now.'

'You've got to do it. We can't drop the Dinsmor. We need the Oosthuizen. That's serious money, given what he needs protecting.'

'Ah, Mace, bra, what're you saying? Treasure won't be easy on this.'

Mace thought, Treasure wasn't easy on many things.

In the ward Mace had to do a double-take. There's Treasure lying on the bed with the new baby in the crook of her arm and Mace saw Oumou. Treasure nothing like his wife had been. Oumou tall, slim, her neck long and beautiful. Treasure stocky, shorter. No ways was she a mama, too modern for that with her jeans, her spaghetti strap tops, but no ramp model either. Oumou came close to that. Had come close to that.

Yet Mace saw Oumou. Christa nestled beside her.

He stopped. The room sliding away, the only sound the sound of his blood. He grasped the metal frame of the bed's foot end. Oumou fading out.

Treasure said, 'It's me, Mace, not a ghost.'

Mace grimaced a smile.

'Though Pylon says we've got the ancestors here too. Quite a party. Meet Hintsa.' She angled the baby for Mace to see its sleeping face. Mace saw Christa.

He bent down to brush Treasure's cheek with a kiss. Said,

'Congratulations.' She smelt of soap and something else antiseptic that he remembered. And the dampness of clay.

Remembered leaning over Oumou like this looking down at mother and daughter through a blur. He straightened up, stepped back to stand beside Christa. She shifted slightly so they weren't touching.

He wanted to say something to her about Oumou, wanted to put his arm around her shoulder, pull her to him. But could feel a tension in her. Her attitude, her rigidity repelling him.

He made a joke about Pylon's smile. Oumou vanished. It was Treasure on the bed. Treasure saying, 'Mace, give us a week to play happy families.'

Mace caught Pylon's eye.

'Don't even think about it,' said Treasure.

'Nothing to think about.' Mace shifted uneasily from foot to foot.

Treasure squinted at him, disbelief writ large in her eyes. 'Good. That's what I like to hear.'

Mace stayed five minutes more. Listened to the girls coochy-cooing, rapt in adoration for the newborn. Heard the lovingness of Pylon and Treasure. Everything distant, until he had to be on the move, couldn't stand still any longer. Backed out saying his goodbyes, reminding Christa that he'd pick her up later about five-thirty, they could do a swim and supper.

In his car in the car park, Mace sat staring at the mountains, the Tokai peak under cloud, veils of rain drifting over the slopes. His hands were shaking. He held them up, let them judder like they belonged to a puppet. Not his hands at all. He gripped the steering wheel.

That'd been Oumou in there on the bed. He'd seen her, clearly. Her smile as he entered the room. Her hand reaching for him. The sheer dazzling beauty of her. He'd smelt her, smelt the warm comfort of clay on her fingers.

'It's your state of mind,' he said aloud. Rested his forehead on the steering wheel between his hands. 'It's in your head. It wasn't her. It wasn't her. It wasn't her.'

It had been. As real as anything was real.

She was dead. She wasn't dead. In the ward she wasn't dead.

He thumped his forehead against the steering wheel. Felt the grief come over him like a blanket damp and smothering and couldn't breathe and the pain in his chest throbbed until he moaned a long elegy of sorrow. In the silence afterwards Mace heard a voice say, 'Are you alright? Excuse me, are you alright?' A tapping on his side window. An old man standing there about to get into the car alongside. A woman in the car saying, 'Leave him, Pa. Come on, we're in a hurry.'

Mace looked up at the man. Could have been looking at death warmed up, his skull right beneath the skin. The man got into the car, slammed the door closed, kept staring at him while the woman reversed out.

'Chrissakes,' said Mace, 'this's all I need.'

With his palsied hand he got out his cellphone, connected to Captain Gonsalves. Having difficulty getting the unlock off.

'About time you got back to me,' said the cop, 'you're gonna miss the fun and games. About half an hour the shit'll hit the fan.'

Mace got the coordinates from the policeman, put foot to the highway. The shaking eased off but he could still feel the blood in his veins. Like it was acid, burning.

Being on the go helped: something to think about, something to anticipate. Also this time of the afternoon, on the highway in the rain with traffic picking up as the early commuters headed home, you had to drive with focus. Motorists lane-hopping, coming up fast on the inside, weaving about like high-speed death wasn't a possibility. Mace swore at those who cut him, those who tailgated, having not too bad a time raving. Even smiled at his excess after he'd given a woman the finger, calling her everything south of stupid bitch.

Beyond the airport the traffic thinned, he wound up the speed to one-forty, reckoning no herdboy would be grazing his cows on the highway shoulders in the wet. The last thing you needed in poor viz was a cow in the lane, chewing the cud, watching you belting down at speed, but Mace was betting against that scenario.

At the R44 off-ramp, he headed up the long slope, went right over the bridge, then right again onto a sand road into shackland between burst bags of garbage. No street names, electricity wires sandbagged across the road, people hurrying through the drizzle. Half a kilometre down, taking it slowly through ruts and holes, he stopped behind two police vans slewed across the gate to a corrugated-iron shack. Gonsalves under an umbrella standing at the shack door chewing tobacco.

'Hey, Meneer Bish,' he said, 'what kept you?' Shot a plug of yellow mush into a puddle. 'Nothing for you here. Nothing here for us either.'

Mace got out of his car, zipped up his anorak, pulled the hoodie over his head, hopping across the rain pools till he bumped into the captain.

Gonsalves said, 'Get your own umbrella.'

Mace took a peek into the shack, smelt paraffin and Lifebuoy soap. 'So what's it?'

'Seems you blotted a contact. Guy was keeping us on the inside, the guy that took the picture.' He held the cellphone towards Mace, a photo of four men on the screen.

'Tough shit.'

'Very, ja. Pissed off some of the makulu bosses. They liked this guy's information. Giving good intelligence about hijacks, the chop shops, all that sorta stuff.'

'Doesn't curl me up with guilt.'

'Didn't think it would.'

'So whose place is this?'

'Chappie called Kortboy who hasn't been home since he drove off with three others last night. According to the neighbour. That house.' Gonsalves waved at a shack across the street. 'Good citizen was outside taking a leak in the rain.'

'And the other one?'

'Not a clue.' The captain picked tobacco strands from his lips. 'All we know's Kortboy's got a family. Well, the way black men have families. A son by a woman lives not far from here. She's with another man now. Says Kortboy has a temper on him, not against giving her a thwack from time to time.'

'Nice.'

'Says too Kortboy doesn't have any interest in his son. Never sees him. How do you figure that one? Here's a father won't have zilch to do with his boy. Unnatural. But that's the SA dad for you, hey.'

Mace wondered about that. Christa wouldn't disagree. Which was why he had to take her for a swim. Talk to her over supper. Tell her what? That losing Oumou was more than he could stand. That he needed her, Christa, to keep him together. That was something to lay on the kid. He sighed.

Gonsalves said, 'What's that for?'

'What?'

'The sigh?'

Mace shrugged. 'Burdens of the world.'

Gonsalves snorted. 'We all got them, pellie. You're nothing special, 'cept for a dead wife.'

'Could be you're right,' said Mace. 'Just remember who's paying your pension top-up.'

'Ooooo, there's a nasty one. Finger jab to the old kidneys.'

Mace bent towards the cop's ear, could smell his stale hair. Whispered: 'Pray for salvation, Gonz. Pylon and me, we're all that's between you and your next job in the marble foyers. With a peak cap. The nightwatch guy chewing tobacco watching security screens of office cleaners vacuuming. The nearest you're going to get to watching a soapie.'

'Know what, Bish?' said Gonsalves. 'You're a complete shit. How's Buso, talking of shits?'

'A father.'

'Tell him congratulations. And his arm?'

'A flesh wound.'

The captain made no comment, looking away through the rain at the cops in the cars waiting for him. 'Time to go.' He edged Mace aside, pulled closed the shack door.

'So what happens here?'

'The neighbour's on our side. Kortboy gets back, he's gonna give us a bell.'

'You could leave a man here.'

'No we couldn't. Manpower shortage.' Captain Gonsalves tiptoed down the path to the cars, still getting his black shoes mucked. Called back, 'Maybe you've got someone.'

'Manpower shortage,' said Mace.

'See what I mean.' The captain got into the first car, started peeling a cigarette even before the driver had turned the ignition.

Mace watched them go. Sirens hee-hawing just to annoy the citizenry.

He looked off at the mountain chain low in the rain haze. The slopes of luxury. Wondered what it would be like opening your door every day on to sand, the rain pissing down, the wind biting your marrow, over there on the mountain slopes you knew warm bodies were turning up the heaters. Kortboy clearly didn't appreciate it.

Mace went across the street to the neighbour, laid two hundred on the man's palm to guarantee that if Kortboy pitched up, the man understood his phone call priorities.

The man said, 'He's a dangerous tsotsi.'

Mace said, 'Let me worry about that.'

The man checking him out. 'That's a nice hoodie, my brother.'

'It's staying on my shoulders,' said Mace.

The man grinned a row of haphazard teeth. 'Doesn't hurt to ask.'

Before he left the township Mace took two calls: the first came in as a stomach punch, a female voice saying, 'I'm a reporter on the Cape Times' – not giving her name. She left a gap there that Mace didn't fill. Then, 'I'm working on the Dinsmor story. Mr Bishop, can you confirm that you've not heard from the kidnappers?'

'That so,' said Mace, ignoring the question. 'Who're you?'

The reporter gave her name, Mace said, 'You wrote that story this morning?'

The woman said she did the crime scene.

'I didn't like it,' said Mace. 'Any more questions, ask the police.'

'I've talked to the police.'

'Then you know everything I know.'

'Mr Bishop,' she said, 'what I don't know is how this happened? How you walked into it?'

'What? Walked into it. Walked into what?'

'The hijack. A security company like yours.'

'You're implying we stuffed up?'

'I'm asking what happened? You're experienced. Ex-mercenaries. Arms dealers.'

'Jesus Christ!' Mace about to lose it. 'Lady, what's your case?'

'I just want to know what happened? How you walked into it, guarding such important clients. With these hijack syndicates part of the scene. Surely you anticipate.'

'Lady,' said Mace. 'We weren't mercenaries. Never ever.'

'I heard …'

'What you heard's not important. What I'm telling you is.'

'So let's put the record straight.'

'It's straight already. We weren't mercenaries.'

'An interview. Okay at your office.'

'You're not listening,' said Mace. 'I said talk to the cops.'

'I've got a quote from the police commissioner that says the security industry is overcharging and careless. He says, quote, The Dinsmor kidnapping should never have happened, unquote. Then he says, quote, There're too many chancers with a gun and smooth talk taking advantage of the situation. When things go wrong, people get hurt. End of quote.'

'That's bullshit.'

'It's what he said. It's what I'm quoting.'

'You can quote what you like. It's bullshit.'

'So what happened?'

'Forget it,' said Mace. 'No comment.'

'You said …'

'I'm ending this, okay. No comment. Goodbye.' Mace disconnected. Bloody reporters. Wasn't a thing you said they didn't twist. He saved her number just in case. He fired the ignition. Half-truths. Insinuations. Suggestions. Outright goddamned lies most of the time. His phone rang again. Mace about to launch with screw you lady I'm not interested, saw Oosthuizen's name on the screen. Thumbed him on.

'Oosthuizen,' said the voice to his hello.

'I know,' said Mace. 'I got your name here on my phone. So what's it?'

'I beg your pardon.'

'Granted. What's it?'

An Oosthuizen silence. Mace put the car into the start of a ten-point turn in the narrow road. Got through three manoeuvres before Oosthuizen spoke.

'There's a ticket at the airport for you. First Joburg flight, oh-six-hundred tomorrow. Gets you there oh-seven-fifty about the same time my colleague arrives. You're on the 10 o'clock back.'

'What's this?' said Mace. 'No, no, no, hokaai, slow down. We agreed two days.'

Another of Oosthuizen's silences, Mace managing to get the car forward back forward back. Then, 'There've been developments.'

'Your problem.'

'I know. It's not what I wanted. But some things you've got no control over. Help me on this one, okay.'

'I told you two days.'

Another waste of airtime. Mace got his car facing out of the township. 'Double rates tomorrow.'

Why, thought Mace, didn't jobs work out in sequence?

'I've got to tell you,' Oosthuizen was saying, 'my colleague thinks he's in danger.'

'Brilliant. You going to tell me who's after him?'

'He might get stopped at passport control, coming in.'

'Then you'll need a lawyer.'

'Oh I've got one,' said Oosthuizen. 'A very good one.' A pause. 'So I can rely on you?'

'Double rates.'

'That is what I said.'

Mace watched the man who wanted his hoodie, standing under a lean-to, smoking, watching him. Wondered what complications the man had in his life? He flicked the windscreen wipers to clear the rain drops. The man grinning his snaggletooth smirk.

'Alright,' he said to Oosthuizen. 'Get the money in my bank upfront.'

'Half,' said Oosthuizen.

The man with the gap-teeth kept wearing the grin, held up two fingers like he was making a phone call. Mace hadn't a clue what was funny.

'Half,' he said to Oosthuizen. What was with the man he had a comeback on everything?

'Excellent,' said Oosthuizen. 'Do you know the writer James Ellroy, Mr Bishop?'

'No,' said Mace.

'You should read more.'

'My daughter does that.'

'Good for her. Ellroy, Mr Bishop, he's the identifier.' Then Mace heard him swear, a Chihuahua yapping in the background.

27

Veronica Dinsmor sensed the day winding down. The skylight a diffused grey, darkening. There'd been sudden sun earlier, shafts that'd lit up the interior, been snuffed as quickly. Then the gradual muting. Less noise from the surrounding streets. No bandsaw whine. No hammering. If she was going to scream, now was the time, before everyone went home.

She sat on the chair in front of the heater, free, untied.

She'd cleaned the blood off her face, doctored the cuts with salve from her medicine bag. Nothing serious but her eye was black. A lot of blood in the white. And she hurt. Her face, her shoulders, her kidneys. A sharp pain that made her wince. She reckoned she'd taken a kick there. Either that or the lack of water was the cause.

They'd let her change into clean clothes.

'Please,' she'd begged.

Kortboy was hesitant.

'It's okay,' said Zuki. 'What's she gonna do?'

'Cause shit.'

'Just a woman, my bra. Nothing to worry about.'

They'd let her sit unbound all afternoon, let her do some yoga to get her circulation back.

She knew their names. The driver was Zuki, the short one Kortboy. She knew their life stories: Zuki the electrician who used to fix illegal connections from the grid until he saw a man fried; Kortboy the window-cleaner who got tired of looking in on rich lives.

She heard they both had children. Zuki a boy and a girl. Kortboy a son. Kids not yet five years old. Kids they didn't see much of. Kortboy's son lived in the township. Zuki's two in the rural areas. 'Better that way,' he said. 'No drugs and crime.'

She told them about her life, gave them a story about an alcoholic father, an abused mother. That her father'd died in jail, that her mother lived on a reservation in a handicap home. Mentally out of it. Didn't remember anything of her life, didn't recognise her own daughter, hadn't done for years.

'D'you know how hard that is?' Veronica said, looking from Zuki to Kortboy, the two men shaking their heads. 'That hurts you when your mother doesn't know you anymore. She doesn't know you were the child she gave birth to.' She reached out a hand to both men: Zuki other side of the desk, Kortboy half-sitting on it.

'I blame it on the white man,' she said. 'They killed us, took our land. When we were down they gave us liquor.'

'You're an Indian?' said Kortboy.

'I am, son. Native American. My name is Dancing Rabbit.'

'We have the same history,' said Zuki.

'Sure do,' said Veronica. She told them about her pregnant daughter. About how she looked forward to being a grandmother. This feeling of the cycle of life: the third generation being born. That they knew the baby would be a girl. How magical that was. She told them about what she and her husband hoped to achieve, so they could leave a legacy. A legacy for people like them. For those who life had mistreated. Why they were in Cape Town. 'We've come to be of help,' she said. 'Create jobs. Spread some wealth.'

She'd been working up to asking about Silas, wanting to put them at ease first. Establish a hierarchy. She had fifteen years at least, more like twenty years on them. She could call them son, draw them in.

'My husband, Silas, he's good at this business,' she said. 'We've built clinics, schools, awarded scholarships. He's a fine man. A man of the people. Our people respect him. Look up to him.' She went from the one to the other with her eyes. Lingering long enough for them to look down. 'Please,' she said. 'Is he alright?'

Zuki nodded.

She sighed a long breath, let her shoulders sag with relief. 'Thanks, son. You don't know how much that means to me.'

Kortboy said, 'Our friends were killed.'

That fell heavily. Zuki getting up to walk off, turn, screaming in his language. Kortboy coming back as loudly.

'I'm sorry,' said Veronica Dinsmor when they'd stopped. Thinking: you're sorry? They hadn't got in on this, their buddies wouldn't be dead. Thinking: stay with them here, keep on their side.

'What worries me,' she said, 'is you boys. What's going to happen to you?' She paused. 'The sort of embassy pressure that'll be on this one ...' She let it tail off. 'You know what I mean.'

Neither Zuki nor Kortboy responding.

'You're the hired help in this, aren't you?' That got their attention. Both men looking at her. 'You're doing this for someone else.' She shifted on the chair to face Zuki. 'The person you phone. You had to kidnap us. Your friends got shot. These people don't even send you food. Don't give you a chance to sleep. Must be nearly twenty-four hours you've been on the job and no back-up. Why's that? Think about it, son. Why's that?' She held a hand out towards Kortboy. 'You too, son. Think about it.'

Veronica let that hang.

Then: 'You've not done this before, I can tell.'

Kortboy exploding. 'Ah, shit, man. This is shit.'

'What happens,' she said, 'what's probably happened is that your masters have asked for a ransom. Silas isn't going to pay that. Not straight off. I know him, he's not that sort of man. He'll do a deal in his own time. So this isn't going to be over quickly. It's going to take days. The three of us in this place for days and days.'

'No,' said Kortboy. 'Forget it.'

'Also,' Veronica pressing on while the two men stared at her, 'as soon as that call's made, the police start working out where it's come from. They can do that. If your person hasn't been clever, hasn't used a public phone, they get him in a couple of hours. Even with public phones they've got ways to do it, the cops.'

Zuki dug out his cellphone, toyed with it.

'Those calls you've made. When they get to the person you're phoning, they're going to get to you. With cellphones they can do that easily. I saw it once on CSI. You get that show here?'

Zuki nodded.

'Another thing: have you asked why you had to do the kidnapping, hmmm? Why you had to take both of us? My husband and me, we should both of us be here now. Then who was going to pay ransom? We're businesspeople, there's no one in this country to pay ransom for us. So then you have to think there was another reason. Someone wanted us out of the way for a while. That's what I reckon. But now it's all messed up.'

'Shit,' said Kortboy. 'This is shit, my bra.' Kortboy beating his fist against the van.

'The best option,' she said, 'is for you to walk out now. Leave me, take the van and get away.'

'She'll kill us,' said Zuki.

'Ah, shit man.' Kortboy giving the van another pummelling. 'Shit man. Shit, shit, shit.'

Zuki spewing a run of language at the short man.

Veronica thinking. Thinking: to make a run for it, bang on the door, scream? Or to sit this out? Sensing a hesitancy in the boys. That's what they were. Boys. Young men in age but boys really.

The boys gone quiet, Zuki's cellphone buzzing an sms. He said to Kortboy, 'Someone's coming.' Holding up the phone for him to see the message.

That decided Veronica. She made for the door, trying to pull it up, banging on it, screaming help me, help me, help me. Kortboy slamming her against the metal, his hand coming hard over her mouth, her head pulled back by the hair. She bit into fingers. Kortboy let go, punched her twice in the temple. Veronica went down.

They tied her to the chair again. Her feet strapped to the legs, her arms tight behind. She bled down her face, long runnels from old cuts reopened.

'Not the gag,' she said, panting, begging, 'not the gag.'

'Fuck you,' said Kortboy.

Zuki shook his head. 'Why, my lady? Why must you do that?'

'American bitch,' said Kortboy. 'Talking shit to us.' He stuffed a cloth in her mouth, wound duct tape round and round her head.

Veronica looked at the men. They'd fetched their guns, laid them on the desk. Zuki back in his chair. Kortboy on a stool. Both of them staring at the gas heater, spluttering on one panel. It gave out. The flame diminishing, dying. The cold settled in.

'Shit,' said Kortboy.

Zuki said nothing.

'Where we going to get gas from now?'

Zuki's phone rang. He answered, didn't say a word. Said to Kortboy. 'There's a guy outside. Open the door.'

'You ill, my bra?' Getting up to do it all the same.

The man ducked under the door as Kortboy hauled it up. Had a silenced pistol in his right hand pointed at the floor. Wore Latex gloves. Over his head a balaclava with holes at the eyes, nose and mouth. Said, 'Howzit, butis.' A pink mouth in the grey wool. 'Bit of a rush here, gents. Sorry about that. At least your shift's over.'

Took out Zuki first with a head shot. A small wop. Zuki's head jerked backwards, tilted to the side, otherwise Zuki didn't even move where he was sitting. Still had his cellphone in his hand. The guns lying on the desk, a short reach away.

Kortboy, behind the shooter, pulling down the garage door, took one in the face as he looked up, a second in the heart. He dropped right there.

Veronica Dinsmor watched. Watched the man swing his pistol arm up and fire at Zuki, continue the movement through half a turn of his body, shoot twice, wop, wop hitting Kortboy. A killer. The way Zuki and Kortboy would never've been killers. The way they didn't even see it coming.

Watching the killer she knew he wasn't going to shoot her. Wouldn't have worn the balaclava for one thing. Would've done her first as she was first in the arc of his shooting.

She could see his teeth at the mouth as if he were smiling.

'Sorry about that,' he said. 'Couldn't be helped really.'

He stepped over to Zuki, eased the cellphone out of his fingers. Went to Kortboy, searched through his pockets until he found the short man's phone. He stood in front of Veronica. Veronica's full attention on him. On the gun he held.

'Not such a great place to hang out. Bloody cold.' He unscrewed the silencer, dropped it into a pocket of his bush jacket, stuck the gun in his belt. From an inside pocket took out a bottle and a syringe in a sealed packet. Waved this in front of her eyes. 'Don't have to worry about HIV.' He tore the packet, fitted the needle to the syringe. Plunged this through the seal on the bottle. 'Nighty, night, Mrs. Well not nighty, night as such. More like sleep tight. When you wake up you're gonna think you're in heaven compared with this place.'

Veronica Dinsmor screamed, came out as a long nnnnnnnn.

'I'll give them one thing,' said the man. 'They do a good gag. Sometimes I've seen gags so useless you can hear people screaming next door. Got you tied down nicely too. So relax, Mrs. Don't worry, be happy.' He clenched the syringe between his teeth, bent down behind her to pop a vein in her arm.

Veronica Dinsmor felt the jab, more a stab. Gave the nnnnnnn scream, the knock-out drug burning into her blood.

'Shoulda done that slowly,' he said, 'sorry for that. Time is tight.' He was blurring in Veronica Dinsmor's vision. He seemed to be holding a camcorder, videoing her. 'Pleasant dreams, Mrs,' she heard. And what might have been a tune he was humming.

28

Mace picked up Christa half an hour late. She was pissed off. Sat in the Spider plugged into her iPod drooping a sullen lip. Mace wanted to belt her one. The last thing he needed was a teenager throwing a sulk.

Going down Edinburgh Drive, grey drizzle, grey light, the cloud low on the mountain, commuter traffic streaming home in the opposite direction, Mace got pissed off himself. The resentment of self-pity. If Oumou was here this wouldn't be happening.

They'd be at home. Christa sprawled in front of the TV doing her homework. The cat curled on the couch. The house warm with cooking. Oumou padding about in his socks, probably still in her pottery overalls, a crusty smear of clay on her face, the smell of clay in her hair.

He'd come in, he'd get their smiles. Light him up like a Roman candle.

Tried to say, I'm doing my best, Christa. I've got serious shit happening right now. There's a kidnapped woman out there. Frightened. Hurt, maybe. Wondering if she's going to live. Terrified moment by moment. There's Pylon wounded, I'm having to handle things alone. There's the bank jumping on my neck. Cut me a little slack, okay. I'm here. I'm thirty minutes late but I'm here. We're together.

It came out as: 'What's your problem, C? Why do we have to live with your selfishness day after day?'

She heard him through the buds in her ears, through the rap of 50 Cent: Just a Lil Bit. Before the tears, snapped back, 'Why aren't you like Pylon?'

'What? What's that?' Mace stretching over to jerk the buds from her ears. 'Listen to me.' Steering with one hand, his left clamped about her wrist, hard.

'You're hurting me.'

'What'd you say?' Squeezing. 'Tell me.'

'Aww. Papa.' Christa jerked her arm out of Mace's grasp. 'Let me go.' A red Chinese bangle around her wrist. The tears starting.

'Christa, what'd you say?'

A sob. 'Nothing.'

'That I'm not like Pylon. You want me to be like him. Uh? That's what you want. Uh? Okay tell me how? Tell me what Pylon does I don't do for you.'

Tears from Christa.

'Come on I'm listening. Now's your chance. Stick it to your papa.'

'Don't …' the tears choking off her words.

'Hit me, C. This's the moment. Stick the daggers in.'

'Papa!' Christa hunched away from him.

The sight of her cowering took the heat out of Mace. The tremble of her shoulders.

'Oh Jesus Christ, Christa, Jesus Christ, I'm sorry.' Reaching out for her, even as she cringed from his touch.

Going up the climb towards Newlands Forest, Mace eased off the road into a parking bay beneath the wet oaks. Killed the engine.

Christa said, 'Don't, Papa. Don't touch me.'

They sat: Christa sniffing; Mace staring at the bright headlights of rush hour. Times like this he hated. Couldn't stand the pain it caused him.

Five minutes. Ten minutes. Fifteen minutes. Neither of them saying a word. Christa put the buds back in her ears.

'Wait,' said Mace. 'Wait.' Taking her hand. 'I'm sorry, okay. I shouldn't have done that.' The words ended there.

Christa sniffed.

Mace leant towards her, reached a hand out to draw her in. For a second he felt resistance, then she yielded. Let him hold her, shifted towards him. He could feel her trembling, held her until the trembling stopped.

She was so slight. Wiry, small-boned, more her mother's build than his. Her head cupped beneath his chin, the smell of her hair in his nostrils, musty like Oumou's would be at the end of the day.

Oumou. He closed his eyes, raised the image of her in a long dress, a loose dress, gliding from the pool deck towards the house. The shape of her body visible against the light. A body he couldn't hold again.

Because of Sheemina February. Tonight he'd be in there, in her apartment, find out what her case was and end this thing. This thing that had gone on for too long.

A flower-seller tapped on his side window, a blur through the condensation. 'Hello my larney, my Mr Gentleman.' Mace wiped the window with his sleeve. 'Buy a bunch, my larney, for your little cherrie there.' The flower-seller soaking wet in a hoodie, the flowers a sad mixture of yellow and red wrapped in plastic. 'My last bunch, my larney, special price for yous.'

Mace waved him away.

Christa, straightened out of her father's embrace, said, 'Buy them, Papa. Why not?'

'Cos he's a bloody drunk.' Wound down his window anyhow.

'Beautiful dahlias, thirty rands, my larney. Jus twenny-five rands, for the beautiful wife, so very young.'

'My daughter,' said Mace, digging out some notes, handing over a twenty and a ten. He took the flowers, water dripped onto his trousers.

'So what, my larney?' said the flower seller. 'I myself like the young ones.' Gave Mace a grin, his tongue where his front teeth should've been.

Mace said, 'Where's my change?'

'Ag, my larney, give a man a small commission. Yous mos the one with the babe.' He winked, backing off, preparing to run if Mace wanted it that way.

Mace's hand on the door handle.

Christa said, 'Papa, let it go.'

'What?'

'We've got the flowers.'

'Lekker, lekker,' shouted the flower seller. 'Nice night, my larney, nice night.'

Christa took the flowers, put them at her feet.

'It's all wet on the floor.'

'It's a leak,' said Mace.

'Can't you fix it?'

Mace turned the ignition. The Spider fired with a bit of throat and smoke. 'Some things you can't fix.' He checked the rearview mirror, took a gap in the evening rush.

Christa said, 'Hey, this isn't a race track.'

Laughter in her voice. The old Christa. Mace gave her a glance, caught her eye, both of them looking quickly away.

She reached over, plugged a bud into his ear. 'Listen to this.'

Mace heard what he hated, the bullet jive of a rapper.

'What's it?'

'50 Cent. He's cool,' said Christa. 'Got these moves. I love him.'

Settled for the nauseating 50 Cent and his chicks all the way to the gym, connected to his daughter by the thin wire of an iPod.

He parked two rows back from the entrance, a car park of high-end silver metal. This time of the late afternoon, Mace preferred: the young looking after their bods, the old looking after their hearts – mortality whichever way you figured it.

Christa opened her door, held out her hand to the drizzle. 'This is so mad,' she said. 'Like what're we doing?'

'Having fun,' said Mace.

Christa came out of the change room wearing her black Speedo and lycra shorts, joined Mace at the pool edge. A couple of swimmers doing laps, an old codger with a wooden board kicking his way up and down. They moved to two free lanes.

'Fancy new outfit,' Mace said.

Christa didn't respond, fitting her hair into her swimming cap.

Mace thought, best to leave the fashion styling alone, young girls and their bodies being what they were: sensitive. Said, 'Long and slow.'

Christa tested the water with her foot, shrugged. 'Whatever.'

'Okay, we'll play it by the clock. See where half an hour gets us.'

They dropped in, kicking off from the wall. Mace let his daughter settle the pace. He'd swum more than she had since Oumou's killing, chances were she wouldn't last half an hour.

Halfway down the length he could feel the rhythm set in, his thoughts blanking, the reptile moving up from the dim recesses of his brain. Swimming he could be alive without thinking. Without feeling. No sensation but the working of his muscles, the bubbles streaming from his mouth.

When Mace broke back to glance at the clock they'd done almost thirty minutes, Christa showing no signs of stopping. Had to be she was training at school on the sly. Not telling him. He powered after her, touched her foot.

She looked round. 'What?'

Mace pointed at the clock. 'Enough.' Panting a bit he realised.

'Race you,' she said. 'To the end and back.'

A length and a half.

Mace said, 'Go.'

She had a metre on him, didn't let him take any of it for the distance. It was Mace at the end heaving for air more than she was.

'See,' she said. 'Who's the slowcoach?'

At the restaurant, Prima's at the Waterfront, the waiter in an orange overall flirted in French with Christa when he brought her Coke.

She came back at him in the same language. Mace reckoned, if a black face could blush it probably did.

'Merde. Excusez-moi, excusez-moi.' The guy almost spilling Mace's beer as he poured it, going into an exchange with Christa, looking like he might cry with happiness.

He turned his French on Mace until Mace held up his hands.

Christa said something, the waiter saying to Mace, 'You look French. Like tourists.'

In winter? Mace thought.

The waiter took their order, told Mace he had a lovely daughter.

'What was that about?' said Mace, sipping the head off his lager.

'He wanted to know where I learnt French. I told him Maman was from Malitia.' She stirred the straw through the ice in her Coke. 'He's from Congo. A refugee. He said his family was killed two years ago. All of them.'

'There's lots of them like that,' said Mace. Raised his glass to Christa. 'Have been for years and years.'

They clinked glasses.

'Santé.'

'Why d'you always say what Maman used to say?'

'Why not? It sounds better than cheers.'

Mace wiped a foam moustache from his upper lip. 'So you've been training,' he said, 'on the quiet?'

'Non.' She shook her head, hair floating about her face. 'You didn't ask me.'

'You didn't tell me, more like it. What else've you been doing you haven't told me?'

'Nothing.' She gave him the cute look: her drink's straw touching her lower lip, the glass of Coke in her left hand, her big brown eyes peering at him through a fringe of hair. 'You're going to teach me to shoot this Saturday, right?'

'That's what I said.' Mace supposing there'd be some time to fit it in when he wasn't dealing with kidnappers and errant scientists and closet arms manufacturers who had Chihuahuas as pets.

'Really?'

'Of course. But first ...'

'What?' Her expression anxious. The cute face gone rigid.

He saw it. Reached for her hand, her fingers not responding to his.

'Relax, C,' he said. 'Tell me about your day. Tell me about school. Tell me what you'd have told Maman.'

'You're not Maman.'

'I'm doing it for her now,' said Mace. He took back his hand, watched Christa's hand scuttle into her lap.

'You're my Dad.'

Mace decided not to push it. 'Tell your Dad then.'

With the straw she stirred her drink into a vortex of melting ice cubes and lemon slice. 'I wrote an essay about why girls should learn to shoot. The teacher failed me.'

Mace frowned. 'She give a reason?'

'She said guns kill. We haven't got a right to kill anyone.'

Mace nodded. 'Your ma would probably have agreed. When we got together she made me stop selling guns for a living. And I did.' He looked at his daughter. Her eyes dull where earlier they'd been alive, quick, flashing. 'This teacher know what happened?'

'Everyone does.' Christa stopped the vortex. 'I don't care what the teacher thinks. A man like that should die. If he were alive I'd shoot him.'

'Yeah,' said Mace, 'so would I.'

The waiter came up with their meals: spaghetti bolognaise for Christa, pesto gnocchi for Mace. The waiter giving his French another workout. Christa all smiles again. As a parting piece the man whipped out a pepper grinder to shower a coarse grind on their food. Bowed off with a bon appétit.

'Sounds a happy chap for a refugee,' said Mace.

Christa didn't respond, absorbed in winding spaghetti onto her fork.

Mace sprinkled a teaspoon of parmesan over his plateful. 'I suppose even refugees have to laugh sometimes.' He forked up two potato pellets, let them melt in his mouth. 'Good, hey?'

Christa sucked up a strand, spraying sauce on to her T-shirt. Nodded furiously. 'Very yummy.'

When they'd eaten, Mace raised the issue of scattering Oumou's ashes. Of having to put if off for a few more weeks, at least until Pylon's wound was healed. He could see Christa's disappointment.

'I need to do it, Papa,' she said. 'It's like Maman's not at peace.'

'I know, C. I know how you feel. I'm the same. Thing is, we don't have to take her back to Malitia. We could scatter her at home. In the garden somewhere. Outside her studio.'

'I suppose.' Christa wiping a piece of bread round her plate. 'It just that ...'

'Just that?'

'I also want to know where she lived. When she was my age.'

'I'm not saying we don't go. In your October holidays there's a window, I'm not saying we don't go then. I'm saying that maybe she should stay with us. Maybe if you ... if we want to put her to rest we do it in the garden. Properly. Make it a ceremony. The two of us alone. Or ask Pylon and Treasure, they were her friends, and Pummie, to be there.'

She looked across at him, those big brown eyes that made his heart ache. Pleading. Confused.

'You want to think about it?'

She nodded, her eyes becoming pools.

In the car going up Molteno Road into a black night, the rain sheeting through the streetlights, the mountain invisible, he said, 'I've got to be gone in the morning by four to catch a plane. Tami's coming over, she'll take you to school.' Hearing Christa suck in breath.

'She's going to sleep at our house?'

'Sure.'

A silence. One streetlight. Two streetlights. Then: 'I don't want her to. I don't like her. I don't want her in our house.'

Mace thought, where's this coming from? Was about to ask, why, what's she ever done to you? – but didn't.

'I can't do it any other way, C. It's one night, okay?'

'You could take me to Pylon's.'

'C. Please, come on. We've had a great evening. Don't spoil it.'

'I didn't. You did. It's your fault.'

'My fault?'

'I can get my things. We can go to Pylon's. Please, Papa. It's not too late.'

Mace sighed. 'Please, C. I've arranged it with Tami. It's no big deal. Leave it.'

Christa slamming shut beside him, he could feel it like a door blown closed.

At home she headed for her room, huffy.

'Don't fall over your lip,' Mace shouted after her. Christ! That a perfectly happy evening could go to hell in a moment.

He flopped onto a couch, noticed Cat2 slipping off to Christa's room, like the two were in league against him. He pulled out his cellphone, put a call through to Silas Dinsmor.

'She's dead,' said the Native American. 'My Dancing Rabbit's dead. I know it.'

Mace hadn't an answer for that. He could hear gunshots in the background. Men shouting. Started to say, 'Until they call we don't know …'

'I can feel it,' said Silas Dinsmor. 'That's what they wanted. It was an assassination. They were going to kill us both.'

'Who?' said Mace.

'Oh, we've got enemies, my friend. At home I've got, we've got enemies, Dancing Rabbit and me. Jealous people. Green-eyed envious sons-of-bitches that resent our success. Want to bring us down into the gutter. Wanna take what we've built up for themselves. There's people would kill us for a dime, for the pleasure of doing it.'

Mace thought, the guy's liquored up. Speaking pure minibar.

'Where's your girl? The beautiful Tami with the tight arse? She's got an arse, my friend. In those jeans. Hey, man, she's got a round arse.'

'She's deployed elsewhere tonight.'

'Deployed. You an army, Mr Pike Bishop?'

'Mace.'

'I got Pike on the telly vision, I got Mace on the telly phone. Bishops rule. Send me Tami, Mr Bishop. She can make it alright.'

Mace's intercom buzzed.

'You've got guests, Mr Bishop. Company for the evening. Oh lucky man.'

'I'm ringing off now,' said Mace.

'Where's Tami?' Silas Dinsmor barely audible.

'Not on duty tonight,' said Mace. 'We've got another guard in the next room. If you get a call, phone me. Any time.'

Mace disconnected, wondering if a call came in an hour would Silas Dinsmor even hear it?

He let in Tami. Gorgeous Tami, smelling of soap and shampoo. You had to agree with Silas Dinsmor about her bum. Mace suspected it was Tami Mogale's bum that most offended Treasure.

'I'm here,' Tami said, sliding a small rucksack off her shoulder, 'though this is not a good idea. I've got a life. I don't want it tied up in yours.'

Mace offered her a drink.

'Scotch,' she said.

While he poured it said, 'Only tonight. An emergency.'

'Like last night was only an emergency.'

'Shit's happening, Tami. You know that.' He clinked glasses with her. 'Christa's in her room throwing a sulk.'

Tami sipped at the drink. 'Because I'm here.'

Mace shook his head. 'Why d'you say that?'

'Because I'm a woman, Mace. I'm not stupid.' She took another hit of the whisky. 'Nice scotch.'

'Glenmorangie.'

'I'm supposed to be impressed?'

He shrugged. 'If you like.'

Tami sat on the couch where he'd been sitting. 'You needed a babysitter you shoulda brought one of the guys in. Left me smoking peace pipes with the Indian. Christa doesn't want another woman in your house, her house. Her mother's house. Wena, Mace, like what're you thinking, dude?' She tapped her head. 'Stop being thick.'

He sat down opposite her. Nights, Oumou had sat there, where Tami was now, he'd sat where he was sitting. Christa curling next to her mother to watch Desperate Housewives. The three of them together with winter howling off Devil's Peak.

You looked at it that way you could see Christa's point. Especially here's this woman in a soft fleecy rollneck staring at him with brown eyes. Brown eyes did it for Mace. Ancient brown eyes.

'Yes,' she said. 'What?'

Mace gulped at his drink, felt the heat.

From her room Christa could hear their voices. She unrolled a tube of tissue that contained the three-blade razor head, took this between her thumb and index finger. Brought it to her eye till the steel blurred.

He could walk in at any moment, her father. Sometimes he'd knock first, sometimes he wouldn't.

She didn't care.

She wore a knee-length cotton nightie, patterned with smileys. In her bathroom, sat on the edge of the bath with her feet in the tub, stared at herself in the wall mirror. Not seeing her image: the dark hair pulled back from her face, her careful eyebrows, her mother's eyes, slightly hooded.

She spoke to herself, said, 'The blood runs like teardrops.' It was what she'd written in her diary the last time.

The blood runs like teardrops.

The Friday slits on her inner thigh were scabbed, not yet healed. On her left thigh, she'd made all the cuts there. The older wounds ghosted in pale lines. Her right thigh was unmarked. She opened her legs and held the blade against her skin, pressed down without cutting. She looked at her hand, her thigh, then at her reflection in the mirror.

She fastened her eyes on her eyes.

Sliced the blade lengthways. Felt the burn, gasped with the pain. The blood came up quickly, dropping off her thigh onto the white porcelain.

Tuesday, 26 July

29

Her car was on the deck. He wanted this done with quickly. Get in, not even bother to wake her up, put a bullet in her head, get out. He had a plane to catch.

So much for his first thoughts of going in easy. Of getting to know her schedule. Now he had the opportunity he wanted it over.

Mace parked the station wagon, Oumou's car, against the kerb. Unwrapped two sticks of spearmint gum. Waited five minutes, chewing like bloody Gonsalves. No traffic, no sign of life anywhere, not even a cat on the prowl. He took the gun from the glove box, the silencer from his jacket pocket. Glanced about: silent dark apartments. A couple of turns he had the can screwed to the pistol's barrel, racked a bullet into the breech. Slipped the safety. Fitted it into a shoulder holster.

Patted his jacket pocket for the reassurance of the pick tool. Simple little rechargeable modified from an electric screwdriver, included a tension wrench. Something Pylon had got Tami to buy off the net. Came with a handy lock-picker's starter kit, extra needles plus a 240V recharger. Very neat. The sort of gadget that would get spies excited.

Mace pulled on a beanie that rolled down into a balaclava. He eased out of the car, pressed the door closed, leaving it unlocked. Didn't want the two-beat neek-neek of the remote waking some light sleeper. That person maybe getting nosey and taking a look-see.

He walked quickly to the apartment block. At least the rain had stopped. The smell of the sea was as strong as before, the waves as loud. Which was good. Although he could have done with some wind noise as well, but the wind was down. Not that a couple of shots from a silenced .22 was likely to wake anyone.

He checked his watch. Four-twenty. From here without traffic would be less than a half-hour run to the airport. In three minutes he could be in and out. Mightn't even take that long.

Mace let himself into the block with the security code he'd been smsed. Pressed the keys with gloved fingers. The door clicked open. He kept his head down going in under the camera, reached up to stick the gloop of chewing gum over the lens.

Mace took the stairwell down to Sheemina February's level. Lights clicked on automatically in the corridor. Amazing that a block like this didn't have proper security. Then again lots of blocks like this didn't have proper security, which was why armed response was a growth industry.

Did have a camera at the end of the corridor but he'd expected that, kept his face down. Two doors: one green, the other red. Black numbers painted large on them. The red door was Sheemina February's. Right underneath the camera.

Mace gave the camera the back of his head, took a look at the door lock: he reckoned a latch bolt attached to the handle, and a single or double cylinder deadbolt. Most people, in Mace's experience, didn't use the deadbolt. Just depended on Sheemina February's levels of paranoia, which given Sheemina February would probably be high. He brought out the lock pick, pressed in a short hook needle, tightened the screw. Occasions like this he was thankful for Pylon's insistence that if you were going to keep the baddies out you had to know how they might get in.

'By throwing a bloody rock through a window,' Mace'd said.

'Not our sort of baddies,' Pylon came back.

So on quiet afternoons they practiced picking locks.

The result: Mace was into Sheemina February's flat in forty-three seconds. Only a locksmith would've bettered him.

He rolled down the balaclava, looked up at the camera before he went inside. In the apartment stood still, let his eyes adjust to the dark. Listened. Fridge hum and sea noise. He pocketed the lock pick, brought out a torch. Found his way over white flokatis to her desk, opened drawers, rifled through accounts, invoices, credit card slips. He flicked the beam over pictures on the walls, stopping at the display case of cut-throat razors mounted above her desk.

One missing.

The one that'd killed Oumou.

Mace tightened his fist around the torch. Wanted to smash the case from the wall. Wanted to scream his rage. Instead he held himself, controlled his breathing.

I see a red door ...

Let out his breath slowly and stepped towards the bedroom, thinking, this is why I'm here. To end it. To end her.

The bedroom door stood slightly ajar, moved easily to the touch, swinging wider. He swept the beam over the bed, expecting her shape, her hair on the pillow. For a moment saw her staring at him with her cold blue eyes. The bed was empty. Mace lowered the torch.

He gave the room a quick check out. Went through her cupboard of clothing, her underwear drawers. Had a feel of a black evening dress, material soft as young skin. Lifted a thong from among her knickers. Not his image of her. Not the sort of underwear he expected. Lacy stuff, yes. Silky stuff, yes. Sexy stuff, yes. Not a thong. Too unsubtle. Almost too obvious. Sheemina February doing aggro knickers wasn't in his understanding of her. Stone cold killer was how he thought of her. But here it was Sheemina February the sex vamp. He flopped back on the bed, found a black negligee beneath the pillow. Held it up. See through. Short. Would hardly cover her crotch. Then saw the photograph in the silver frame on the bedside table. Took a closer look at himself in a Speedo at the gym swimming pool.

Chrissakes.

His guts tightened. He brought the torch up to the photograph. The bitch. Right there in the gym smack in front of him taking pictures like she was invisible. Might have been for all he'd known, standing there dripping wet, not a care in the world: an open target. The bitch looking right at him. Gave him the spine creeps.

Mace put the photograph back on the bedside table. Crushed the negligee into his anorak pocket, launched himself off the bed. He swung the torch beam about the room, no more photographs. She was setting him up. Working him. The bitch. He closed the drawers, shut the cupboard doors, got out of the apartment.

Like she was saying, I expected you.

Mace swallowed a foulness in his mouth.

No way. No way she could be controlling this. He worked through the sequence: estate agent Dave had come up with the gen. To have Sheemina February calling the shots meant she'd gone through Dave. A helluva outside chance. Except, Mace remembered, years back Dave had sold a house for him. A house Sheemina February bought. And trapped him in. Almost had him murdered in.

He had the same feeling about now as he'd had about then.

She'd set him up. Anticipated him. Why else the photograph? She was calling this every step of the way. Making him out the victim, the hunted, the prey.

Mace headed quickly for the door.

Face it. She was way ahead. Stringing him out for the kill. Except he'd get her first.

In the corridor the lights snapped on, he backed inside, listening. Waited until the lights went out before he moved again. The lights came back on. He pulled the door closed behind him, heard the latch bolt click into place. Again he paused. Then moved fast to the stairwell. It was empty. He went up two stairs at a time, slipped into the lobby on the car deck.

Everything as quiet as it'd been five minutes earlier. Still, Mace took it cautiously, sliding his back along the wall to the entrance door. Pressed in the key code. He stepped onto the deck, went quickly to his car. Stuck in the windscreen wipers a long-stemmed rosebud.

Going up Kloof Road through the stone pines, down into the City Bowl, out along De Waal, Devil's Peak rising high and dark against the starred sky, Mace thought of Sheemina February, her sheer cunning. Sheemina February somewhere out there in the vast glow of city lights no doubt smiling to herself.

He'd seen her wiliness from the start. The bedraggled but stunning girl who'd pitched up in the MK camp with the I-walked-from-Cape-Town story. The girl who'd cried that she was telling the truth.

'Believe me. Why won't you believe me?'

Because there was intelligence fingering her as an agent. And the times were paranoid. Everyone who walked in was an agent. Everyone had to prove themselves.

He'd given her a chance. Gone to her one night, said, 'We know about you. Accept it. You're going to die if you don't tell the truth.' She'd reached out, stroked his cheek.

The next morning he and Pylon smashed her hand with a wooden mallet. Her blue eyes on him when he brought down the hammer. No ice in the blue then, only the loneliness of long distances. Like being on the ocean, blue about you, blue above.

At that moment Sheemina February became herself. He'd seen it. Seen the blue harden in her eyes. Even through the tears of pain, she'd set her mind. Even as he smashed her bones. Right then and there she started playing a different game, a game that was manipulating him through her deviousness even now.

Mace came off the dark highway into the airport approach, thinking, this was more reason to kill her. Find her, kill her before she could play out the revenge she'd let lie for decades. Her deadly intent.

What plagued him all the way to the airport was, how she knew he'd go to her apartment? How she got it timed so right? So right to put the rosebud on his car?

He found parking at the back of the car park, hardly an ideal place when you were trying to get someone away in a hurry. The trouble with airport parking, you couldn't get it where you wanted it. These days you often couldn't get it full stop. Had to factor in half an hour just to find a bay. Thousands of bloody cars like half the city had flown elsewhere. Mace shrugged off his anorak, threw it into the boot. Noticed the negligee bulging from the pocket. He let out a long "faaack". The last thing he needed was Christa finding something like that. Also he couldn't remember taking it. The sight of the flimsy material strangely unsettling. As if there were moments in Sheemina February's flat his mind blanked on. 'No ways,' he said aloud. 'No ways' – balling the negligee into his fist. He slammed down the boot. Told himself, cool it, boykie. Just get rid of this thing. On the way to the terminal building Mace dropped Sheemina February's nightwear into a rubbish bin. Kept on walking like it hadn't happened. Mace getting his focus back. He checked in. Was told, 'Have a nice day further, Mr Bishop,' as the attendant circled the boarding time and gate on his pass.

'What do you mean further?' said Mace. 'It hasn't begun nice.'

He checked his watch: 5:15. He'd had what? Four hours' sleep. Less than that. He needed coffee. He got it, only problem it tasted like shit, left a tarry coating on his teeth.

'Have a nice day further, Mr Bishop.'

He phoned estate agent Dave, to hell with it being twenty-five minutes past five on a dark winter morning.

Dave came on sleepy. 'Who's this?'

'Put your glasses on and you'll know,' said Mace.

A pause. 'Mace, my old son, what's the time?'

'Doesn't matter,' said Mace. 'What matters is you told me you had connections. Showed a colleague a picture of Sheemina February and she IDed her. Told you she'd sold her the apartment.'

'Come again? What's this, Mace? What's this you're on about? Christ, my son, it's half past five. I don't wake up for two hours.'

'Dave. Dave,' said Mace. 'Stay with me. A quick answer's all I need. Your friend, the agent, who sold Sheemina February her flat. Did it happen like that? Did you go to her, or did she come to you? Did you ask your friend about Sheemina February or did she give you Sheemina February's address?'

'Jesus, Mace. I'm not with you.'

'Did you ask your friend about Sheemina February or did she give you Sheemina February's address? Simple question, Dave.'

'I dunno. I went to her. How can I remember? It's bloody black as a witch's anus, colder than her tit, you phone to ask stupid questions.'

'Not stupid, Dave. You went to her. Is that right? Is that what happened?'

'Yeah. Sure.' He yawned. 'I'm cutting you now, my son, before I wake up proper.'

'Dave.'

Too late. Mace hit redial but estate agent Dave had switched off his phone. The voicemail voice said he could leave a message. Mace did. 'Think about it, Dave. It's important.'

No sooner disconnected than his cell rang: Oosthuizen.

Mace frowned, said, 'You checking up on me?'

The Oosthuizen pause. Then: 'Mr Bishop, I am a concerned man. In this world concern is ...'

'I don't need your bullshit,' said Mace.

A silence, briefer than usual. 'I am not insulting your professionalism.'

'Could've fooled me.'

'Mr Bishop, please. As I told you I have much at stake. My colleague is a very valuable man. He was being pursued, he went to ground. Now he is on the move again. In less than two hours his passport number will be scanned into a computer. At that point the hunters will pick up the scent again. Do I make myself clear? Do you understand why I am a concerned man?'

'If he's not let through passport control there's not much I can do.'

'Oh they'll let him through, Mr Bishop. Passport control is not the problem. It is what happens afterwards that is.'

Wonderful, thought Mace.

'Good luck, Mr Bishop. There is much resting on your excellent capabilities.'

Mace disconnected before Magnus Oosthuizen could say anything like, 'Have a nice day further.'

All he needed now was bad news from the Dinsmor side to really make it a nice day. He found it in the newspaper under a report headlined 'Kidnapping breakthrough'. Was enough to shoot red flashes across Mace's eyes.

30

KIDNAPPING BREAKTHROUGH

Police are confident that they will soon have tracked down the kidnappers of the American businesswoman, Veronica Dinsmor.

'Our investigations are at a delicate stage,' said a police spokesperson. 'We expect a breakthrough at any time.'

They would not comment further.

Veronica Dinsmor was kidnapped on Sunday evening shortly after arriving in the country. She was abducted during a shootout between her security personnel and the kidnappers at a house in Gardens. Two of the kidnappers were killed and one of the managers of Complete Security, Pylon Buso, was wounded.

Complete Security is owned and run by Mace Bishop and Pylon Buso. Recently a client of theirs was gunned down on the highway while Mr Bishop was transferring him from the airport to the city.

Commenting on the Dinsmor kidnapping, the police commissioner said that although there was no evidence that a syndicate was behind the spate of similar attacks on high-profile people visiting Cape Town, security companies should be particularly vigilant.

'The Dinsmor kidnapping should never have happened,' he said. 'There're too many chancers with a gun and smooth talk taking advantage of the number of important people doing business here or holidaying in the city. When things go wrong, people get hurt.'

Asked to respond to the commissioner's comment, Mr Bishop said, 'That's bullshit.'

In May Mr Bishop's wife was murdered in the family home.

Mr Bishop and his partner founded Complete Security ten years ago after returning to the country with the advent of democracy. According to various sources, both men were active in the armed struggle as weaponry suppliers to MK, the armed wing of the ANC. Mr Bishop denies any links to mercenary organisations.

31

Silas Dinsmor, wearing the hotel bathrobe, opened the door to the room service waiter with his morning coffee.

'You want room service,' the guard from Complete Security had told him, 'you go through me. You need anything, another bog roll, you go through me.'

Silas Dinsmor didn't like the man's attitude. Tried to get Bishop to assign the young black babe with the pretty arse but that didn't happen. Pissed off Silas on account of he was the sucker paying the bill. Got his back up to the extent, Silas Dinsmor thought, screw you, buddy, I'll order my own room service.

And did.

And now there was a package on the tray along with his coffee.

'Where'd that come from?' he asked the waiter.

The waiter said he didn't know.

Silas phoned the reception desk, asked where the package on his tray had come from.

The receptionist said a delivery man dropped it off ten minutes earlier.

Silas said, that was it? A man dropped it off. No receipt, no delivery papers?

That was it, she told him. She'd signed the delivery book, and the bike-man was gone. Hadn't even taken off his helmet.

Silas Dinsmor called Mace Bishop, got his voicemail. Called the babe, Tami Mogale.

'I'm in the traffic,' she told him. 'Taking kids to school.' She also told him that he should've gone through their guy, that they set up these procedures for a reason. That he was to give the package to their guy until she got there. Which would be another twenty minutes or more. What sort of sized package was it anyhow?

Silas Dinsmor said, 'CD size. In a brown padded envelope.'

'That's probably what it is,' said Tami, 'a CD.'

'Or an anthrax bomb. You people do anthrax bombs.'

'Just get it to our guy,' said Tami, 'and sit tight.'

Thirty minutes later she was in Silas Dinsmor's room, the package in one hand, her cellphone in the other clamped to her ear on the line to Pylon.

Pylon saying, 'Shouldn't be a problem, Tami. Open it. I would.'

'You're not here,' she said.

She heard Pylon sigh. 'Ah, save me Jesus, Tami, fetch me if it's that big a deal.'

'Hold on.'

She put the phone on loudspeaker. Said to Silas, 'Okay, I'm going to open it. Or you can wait in the corridor.'

Silas still in the hotel bathrobe, skinny legged and barefoot. Not so much as the faintest definition of a calf muscle, Tami saw. Legs like dowel sticks.

'What if it's coated in anthrax?' he said.

'Why?' she said. 'Why'd that be even vaguely a possibility?'

'It's not,' said Pylon. 'Just open it, Tami.'

Silas Dinsmor moved away two paces but stayed in the room.

Tami opened the package, describing what she was doing. Inside a DVD in a plastic case. She told Pylon this.

'Play it,' said Pylon.

'I'm getting there,' said Tami, 'don't rush me.'

Up on the television screen came a picture of Veronica Dinsmor slumped on a hard-backed chair. Her head flopped forward. A gag across her mouth. Ankles taped together. Hands tied behind her. The focus tightened on her face. A hand came into the frame, tilted her head back. A finger pushed up her eyelid, the camera coming in closer to catch the roll of her eyeball.

'What're you seeing?' said Pylon. 'What's going on there?'

Tami replayed, giving him moment by moment commentary. When she got to the hand coming into the frame, Pylon stopped her.

'What's the colour of the guy's hand?'

'White,' said Tami.

'You're sure?' said Pylon.

'I'm not colour-blind. He's a whitey.'

'Or he's wearing gloves. Surgical gloves.'

A voice said, 'What we want, Mr Silas Dinsmor, is your full cooperation.' The voice computerised.

'What's that?' said Pylon.

Tami went back, replayed it.

'What we're watching now,' she told Pylon, 'is the camera panning away from Mrs Dinsmor to show one, two dead bodies. Shot. Not much blood. Looks like they're in a factory area. Something like that.' Then blackness. 'End of the movie. What you want me to do?'

'Get hold of Mace first,' said Pylon, 'then I'll tell Captain Gonz. Mace must've landed by now.'

32

Mace had. Touchdown five minutes later than scheduled at 07:55 but five minutes wasn't critical to Mace's way of thinking. Max Roland would already have landed. If Max Roland's passport going into the system had woken the watchmen they'd be gathering, wanting to get their man tagged, setting up the pieces for the endgame. Nothing here that could be helped. The fun came later back in Cape Town.

Mace was relaxed about this. He fished out his cellphone as about him in the aircraft went off the happy jingle of the Nokia switch-on. He joined the chorus, the sms buzz letting him know there were two messages.

A voicemail from Captain Gonsalves: 'Meneer Bish, listen up, pellie.' Mace grimacing at the chewing slurps as the cop rearranged the tobacco plug so he could talk. 'Two bodies phoned in. Guess who? Our friends Zuki and Kortboy. No sign of the Dinsmor lady. The plot thickens, meneer.'

Mace checked the time. The call had come in half an hour earlier. Now what? A bit hectic getting rid of the foot soldiers. Spoke of extreme nastiness. You didn't need a sixth sense to work out this was going to end badly.

The message from Tami to call her asap.

Mace waited until he was off the plane, down the escalator out of the arrivals hall, legging it to the international terminal through a stream of tourists. How it must be landing here for the sun and safari jaunts to be told, you want a local flight? Wheel your luggage that-a-way for about a click. Sorry no transfers. Sorry about the building site. Just sorry, hey. We're building you a superstar facility. Welcome, welcome.

The man in the arrivals hall picked out Mace with no trouble. Compared him with a fan of mug shots he held in his hand. Excellent likenesses. Spot-on ID. Even dressed the way he'd been told he'd be dressed: black chinos, grey rollneck, black leather jacket, sunglasses perched on his head, not carrying anything but a cellphone. Walking purposely, not scanning the cluster of drivers holding up name boards. Heading out the door paying more attention to his phone than the situation. Clearly not expecting anything.

The German phoned his colleague in the international hall. Said in English that Herr Bishop was on his way, described his dress. Was told just as well as tricky Max was getting anxious. Looking about him all the time. Toying with his cellphone like he wanted to make a call. They both laughed and disconnected.

The man took the escalator upstairs to the departure terminal, checked in for the ten o'clock Cape Town flight. He went through security, found a cafe that sold stale croissants and piss-poor coffee. A long way from Frankfurt. He broke out two Rennies as a precaution. Talk about getting a taste of what was coming.

Mace outside in the cold air, his breath visible, called Tami.

'What's it?'

'We got to talk,' she said.

'That's why I'm phoning.'

'A DVD came this morning for Dinsmor. Quick delivery, handed in at the reception desk by a biker in a helmet. Reception sent it up to our client with his morning coffee.'

'Bloody marvellous. So much for security.'

'So much. Anyway …' Tami gave Mace a rundown of the visuals and the message.

'Just that? "What we want, Mr Silas Dinsmor, is your full cooperation."'

'That's it.'

Mace said, 'Hang on, let me think.' Gave it some thought dodging through the stream of tourists, keeping his pace at a fast clip. The hijackers were dead. Contact had been made but no ransom. Had to be they were after Dinsmor next. Had to be too there were serious people involved. People who didn't mind killing. 'Okay,' he said, taking a flyer, sounding confident, like Mace Bishop knew exactly how this would play out, 'there's going to be more. Probably sooner than later.' He told her about the message from Gonsalves. 'Don't know how he got onto the bodies but you better get this to him. And watch Dinsmor, Tami. Closely.'

'How'm I supposed to do that and get this to Gonsalves?'

'Your problem.'

'Thanks.'

'Pleasure's all mine. Now I've got to go.'

'There's another thing,' said Tami, 'about Christa.'

Mace groaned. 'If it's her attitude, I apologise.'

'It's that, and something else.'

'So what else?'

'I'm not sure. Something.'

'This's too vague for me, Tami. I do facts not feelings.'

'Something's up with her, Mace. Maybe it's drugs, maybe it's something else.'

'Like grief?'

'Of course grief. But grief plus. I don't know.'

'She's hurting, Tami, that's what. And don't worry, I'm working on it.' He walked into International Arrivals, into a chaos of people. 'Got to go' – disconnected her, scanning the faces for Max Roland. Wasn't this ideal? Wasn't this made for a cock-up.

The Swede saw Mace come in, pause, look round. Not very professional this arrangement, on the other hand he cut Mace Bishop some slack because Max Roland made nobody's life very easy. The Swede folded his newspaper, headed out the door towards the domestic departure terminal.

Mace got an update on the flight from information. Yes, sir, it had landed on time. Yes, sir, the passengers would be through passport control and baggage clearance.

He trawled the coffee shops, searching out the readers. Not many. Spotted the Ellroy from a few paces off, the big white type of the writer's name, the book lying face-up on a cafe table. A fidgety man sitting at the table, playing with his cellphone, watching the world like a scared rabbit.

'Max Roland,' said Mace, introducing himself, 'let's go.'

'You are late,' said Roland, standing, 'soon your people will be here following me.'

Mace checked him out. A fit man, athletic in his movements, early forties, short blond hair, fashionable stubble. Chest hair sticking out of an open-necked shirt. Underdressed for the southern winter. A linen suit might cut it in Europe and Yemen, in Joburg Armani was as good as naked.

'I don't have any people,' said Mace.

'Your government's people. The spooks. The spies. The secret agents. The government men who want my work.' Roland grabbed the handle of his luggage, picked up his book. 'So. We must vanish, Mr Bishop.'

Mace thought, bloody wonderful. Another client who'd be a joy to work with.

'It's a bit of a walk,' he said. 'To departure.'

'That is nothing. I am a runner,' said Roland. 'Marathon man.'

And look what happened to him, Mace didn't say, turning his head to roll his eyes instead.

He led Max Roland to the upper deck, set off at a brisk step towards the domestic terminal, Roland half a pace behind jabbering about getting out of Yemen before he was killed.

'At least here they want me alive,' he said. 'You have a safe house for me?'

'Everything's arranged,' said Mace. 'Even a view of the sea.'

'In Sana'a I had a view of a camel's backside. And you could hear God speak in the mornings.'

'He say anything interesting?' said Mace.

'I do not understand Arabic,' said Roland. Then laughed. 'Ah, a joke, Mr Bishop. You are very funny. Let me tell you a joke.'

Mace's cellphone rang before the joke got underway: Magnus Oosthuizen. Mace wasn't sure if he wouldn't rather hear the joke.

'You have made contact?' said Oosthuizen.

'What kind of language is that?' said Mace. 'Your colleague is standing next to me.'

An Oosthuizen pause. Then: 'No one is following you?'

Mace did a slow 360. 'I'm looking around and no, no one's following us. Why would they? If anyone's interested they'd know we're heading for Cape Town. They'd know the flight. They'd be waiting there.'

'They're interested, Mr Bishop. 'Believe me. And they'll be waiting. So you're going to have to pull the moves. Show us how good you are.' Mace heard high-pitched yapping in the background.

'Give your Chihuahua a kiss,' he said. 'Little dogs need a lot of love.' He disconnected before Magnus Oosthuizen could go into one of his silences, steered Max Roland towards the check-in counters.

His phone rang again: estate agent Dave.

'Dave here,' said the property man. 'Guess what my son, I thought about it, your question. And it all came back, in a proverbial flash, what happened.'

'Not now, Dave,' said Mace. 'Now's not good.'

Dave talking right over his objection. 'What happened was I was sitting in my office when in she walks, this colleague of mine. Haven't seen her in months. Probably a good six months. Actually thought she'd gone to Australia. But there she is, plonks herself down, says, Dave, saw you at the deeds office the other day but didn't get a chance to chat and thought you're the man I need to see. How's your Atlantic seaboard portfolio? After we've had a natter, of course. Turns out she's short of stock, has a client and wants to propose we come to an arrangement. As it happens we can. While we're talking she drops into the convo that the last place she sold was to a rich female lawyer. Jackpot bells go off in my noodle. I say, coloured lady with amazing blue eyes? She says, yes. Major coincidence. But that's how the world ticks over, my old son.'

'Unless it wasn't a coincidence,' said Mace. 'Did your arrangement work out?'

'As it happens, no. Didn't get to square one.'

'Seen her since?'

'Not exactly. Then again we're not kissing pals.'

'So this is it,' said Mace. 'You don't see her for months. You start making some inquiries about Sheemina February at the deeds office, next thing this colleague walks in and offers information about Sheemina February. Helluva coincidence.'

'Way of the world, my son. Happens all the time.'

'When it happens in my life it's not a coincidence.'

'Mind the old ego, my son, could trip you up.'

'So long, Dave,' said Mace, keying him off.

At the check-in counter Mace wheedled two seats on the nine o'clock flight. Wasn't really a duck-and-dive move, more because he wanted to get back to Cape Town chop-chop. Ditch Max Roland for one thing. The scientist was seriously irritating.

As they boarded, he got two more calls. The first from the reporter who'd been at him the previous afternoon, the second from Pylon. He pushed the reporter to voicemail, caught Pylon.

'You heard about the DVD,' Pylon going straight into matters.

'I did.'

'You got the scientist?'

'I have.'

'There's something come up,' said Pylon. 'I'm watching now through my window Mart Velaze depart in a larney X5. Very nice car for an agent to drive. I've just had a bit of a history lesson from Mart about Herr Roland, and what he said may be true and it may not. All the same something we need to consider.'

'I can't now, I'm in the plane.'

'Call me soonest.'

'Quick thing: how're you?'

'Flying high. Drugs and fatherhood. Magic potions.'

Mace switched off his cellphone.

Max Roland said, 'Popular man.'

Mace fastened his safety belt. 'Seems like I can say the same for you.'

33

What Mart Velaze came to tell Pylon was this: Max Roland wasn't kosher.

Tami had just collected Pumla for school with a moody Christa in the passenger seat, wouldn't even smile at Pylon as he waved them off, Pylon thinking Mace had to do something there pronto. The kid wasn't shaping. He swallowed two painkillers with his coffee, called Treasure.

'You can stay another day if you want,' he said, hoping she would. 'No need to rush this.'

'Nonsense. Nobody does. I'm a nurse, Pylon. I can manage. How's your arm?'

'Hurting,' he said. 'In certain positions.'

'Take the muti. You see why I need to be home? Also I have to get out of here. Patients die in hospitals from the viruses, septicaemia, superbugs they haven't even got names for yet.'

'You work in a hospital.'

'My point. I know about it.'

'How's Hintsa?'

'Beautiful. That's another thing. I've been thinking, lying awake here thinking: he's not going to the mountain.'

'What?' said Pylon. 'What mountain?'

'For initiation.'

'Initiation. When did this come up?' Pylon sipping at his coffee listening to hospital noise: a television up too loud, babies squalling. Wondering how Treasure had got to this topic.

'Have you seen the newspaper?'

'Not yet.'

'Eight deaths in the last ten days. Because of this precious initiation ceremony of yours.'

Pylon said, 'Save me Jesus, Treasure. He's two days old. This's not the time to be talking about initiation.'

'I've been thinking about it, even before he was born. And it's out. No ways, no discussion. We can clip his foreskin in a hospital but no initiation.'

'Okay.' Pylon wanting out of this discussion, wanting to say I thought you said hospitals were dangerous places. He didn't. Instead said, 'Okay. When he's old enough we can talk about that.'

'Sitting in the bush doesn't make teenage boys into men. What they think is, fine, I've been to the mountain, I've worn the skins and the white paint, I'm circumcised, now I can drink and sleep around. I'm not into that, Pylon. The primitive stuff doesn't work for me.'

'It's tradition. Our tradition.'

'My point. Initiation's stuck in the past. We have to move on.'

Pylon sighed, but kept the sigh off-phone. 'We'll talk about it later. We've got sixteen, seventeen years to go.'

'Maybe, but that's my line: no time on the mountain with his mates. No old indunas with rusty assegais to butcher him. Every year boys die. Then there's the ones mutilated. For life. So you men can feel like men.' She broke into Xhosa, telling him that it was out of the question. Father and son would have to adjust.

Pylon kept pacifying, careful not to sound like he was humouring her. Treasure caught even a hint of that in his voice she'd go ballistic. When she'd swung off her high horse, he said he'd arrange for a taxi to collect her at eleven.

'I'll be waiting. Tell them that. No African time arrangement. Eleven sharp I'll be waiting.'

He didn't doubt it. No sooner got the taxi lined up than the intercom buzzer went.

'Mart Velaze,' said the voice. 'Something I need to see you about.'

Pylon sighed again. What was his case? Said, 'What's your case? When a spook pops up, there's always something going on.'

A snigger. 'You got it, buta.'

'So what's so desperate seven o'clock in the morning's a good time to disturb me?'

'Max Roland. The man your partner's bringing in.'

'I know who he's bringing in' – Pylon putting some emphasis to the spook phrase.

'So come'n, buta. Hear me out. Won't take five minutes.'

'Go away.'

'Ah, man. This's not the attitude. Focus. Hear what I'm saying: Max Roland isn't Max Roland.'

'That's spook paranoia.'

'Five minutes,' said Mart Velaze. 'It's chilly out here.'

Pylon groaned. Buzzed him in.

'How about a cup of coffee?' said Velaze, crouching at the gas heater to warm his hands. 'I'm freezing.'

Pylon boiled him a cup of instant, Mart Velaze rabbiting on about what a nice cluster development Pylon had moved into. How much better than staying in a township.

'Used to be your mate's, wasn't it?' Not waiting for Pylon to answer. 'Before Mace went larney bourgeois. City Bowl. Chrome and glass. The high-end lifestyle of Mace Bishop. Out there in the red zone, way beyond his means.'

'What d'you want?' said Pylon, giving him the coffee.

'I'm right, hey? That's what I heard. Complete Security not so completely secure in the finance department. Thanks to your buta getting beyond his station.'

'Max Roland,' said Pylon. 'Remember.'

Mart Velaze tasted the coffee, pulled a face. 'Instant's all you've got?' He pointed at the espresso pot on the stove. 'What about one of those?'

'Takes too long,' said Pylon. 'You'd be leaving as it percolated.'

Mart Velaze gave his snigger. 'Don't be like that.'

Pylon looked at him. 'You've got three minutes left.'

'Buta, man. What's with you? I'm doing a favour here, no need for disrespect. Where's the common courtesy?'

'You're in my house nice and warm drinking my coffee before it's light. That's common courtesy, Mart. So what's your story?'

'Are we gonna sit down?'

'Perch on a stool.'

Pylon drew a stool across from him at the breakfast counter. Grimaced as he sat.

'The arm still paining?'

'Talk.'

'Buta, buta, buta. What's with you? Where's the old gun-runner? The arms dealer? The cool brother I used to hear tell of? Swanning round the dark continent in ancient Dakotas and those Russian transports. The Antonovs. Trading ordinance in the hot spots. Man, buta, you and your mlungu mate were legends.' He took a swig of coffee, swallowing hard. 'Now what've we got? Mace and Pylon, muscle-men to the rich and famous, keeping the celebs secure on their surgical safaris. Except these days our heroes are losing people. One client assassinated. Another client kidnapped. Not good for business. Also they're off the moral mountain top sloshing about in the lowland bogs. Taking on whatever scumbag comes wading through the slime.'

Pylon stood up. 'Out.'

'I haven't started, buta.'

The two men doing the hard eyeball.

Snigger, snigger. Mart Velaze took a pull at the coffee, pushed the mug into the middle of the counter top. 'That's awful, Mr Buso.' Pylon reached over, put a grip on Velaze's hand, squeezed. Velaze: 'What? You're going to crush my hand? The Pylon and Mace bust-a-hand special. I don't think so.' He unhooked Pylon's fingers one at a time. 'Listen up, buta. Max Roland's real name is Vasa Babic. Serbian cousin. Nice enough to meet and talk to but, man, he's got a vicious streak.' Mart took a disc and papers out of an inner pocket of his bush jacket, smoothed the papers on the counter. 'You got a laptop handy we could look at some pictures?'

'Do you see a laptop?' said Pylon.

Mart Velaze glanced round the kitchen. 'A computer?'

'In my daughter's room. I don't know if I want you in her room.'

'A DVD player?'

Mart pointed through the archway to the open-plan dining room and lounge. 'Got to have one of those. Even shack dwellers have them.'

'Words will do,' said Pylon, 'I don't need to see pictures.'

'You wouldn't want to miss these. Believe me, your life will be enriched.'

'Your time's up.'

'Look at this, okay. Then I'm outta here.'

'Promise.'

'Scout's honour.' Snigger, snigger.

'Come,' said Pylon taking him through to the lounge.

'Your basic system,' said Mart Velaze slotting the DVD into the player. 'I'd have thought you might be a hi-tech sort of man. Into gadgetry. Anyhow.' He took the remote, pressed play. 'What we've got is three short takes on the mind of Vasa Babic. Ready, buta. Here we go.'

The screen went blue.

'That's sky,' said Mart Velaze. 'Cameraman likes to give us lots of sky. Probably finds it artistic. Soothing.'

The camera drifted left to some puffy clouds, the sort of clouds kiddies would draw, then down to the tops of trees, pulling back for a wider longer perspective of forested hills, grassy meadows in the foreground.

'Very pretty,' said Pylon.

'Wait. Here's the thing coming now. Listen. What's that sound?'

A sloshing noise. Pigs grunting.

'Animals,' said Pylon.

'Pigs to be precise. A farmyard scene. Look.'

A house came up. A double-storey stone building with small windows. Basic but pastoral, set against tall trees.

'Quaint, hey. Rustic. Now hear this.'

Voices. People wailing. Babies crying. A loud voice shouting the same word over and over.

'What's he saying?'

'Shut up.'

A shot, not loud. The cacophony stopped. Then a howl of anguish.

The camera drew back to give more setting to the farmhouse. A tractor, a car up on blocks. The wailing filled the soundtrack. Over this a voice called out a name.

'Where's this?' said Pylon. 'What's this got to do with Max Roland?'

'Patience, Mr Buso. Patience. Hear that name being called? Vasa. Turns out to be the cameraman.'

A clear voice close to the camera mic responded.

'That's our man Vasa.'

'What's he saying?'

'Shoot them.'

The camera rose above the house to focus on a buzzard hovering over the meadows. The soundtrack was switched off. Silence. Just the predator fixed in the sky.

'End of movie one. Arty, hey? Everything off-camera.' The picture blacked out. 'Next one's a little different. Sort of grittier.'

Blue sky again, the camera dropping down fast through a blur of green and brown onto the face of a teenager. Thirteen, fourteen years old. The camera staying tight on her face.

'Pretty girl,' said Mart Velaze.

'She's lying on the ground? Outside.'

'Very observant, Mr Buso. She is. Don't know where though. No soundtrack to this one unfortunately.'

The girl had her eyes open, wild brown eyes all over the place. Her jaw rigid, her mouth drawn wide in what Pylon reckoned had to be a scream. Her head thrashed about until a pair of hands locked her face on to the camera.

'Someone's kneeling at her head to hold her like that,' said Mart Velaze.

The girl shut her eyes, her face screwed up in pain.

'I don't want to see this,' said Pylon.

'Keep with it. Watch her face. See how she bites her lip. Bites so hard it bleeds.'

The girl's teeth went red, blood and saliva welling onto her chin.

'You know how sore that is? Biting your lip. Hurts like buggery.'

The girl was rolled over, her head banging against the ground. The hands clamped again about her head, pressed her left cheek onto the dirt, made her look straight into the camera.

'I don't need this,' said Pylon. 'What's it got to do with Max Roland?'

'Everything. Wait. See that.'

The girl spat, red globules spraying the camera lens.

'Plucky chick. But now.'

The camera angle changed putting the face into profile. The frame shaky, sometimes slipping to show a hand splayed beside the girl's head. The photographer's left hand.

'Takes some doing, hey. Strong fella can support himself on one hand, film her with the other. And shaft her.'

The hand came into view again, Mart Velaze pressed pause.

'There you go. There's what you need. Good an ID as you'll get except fingerprints. See the deformed pinkie: like it forgot to grow. Check out Max Roland's left hand some time. Odd thing, he still plays a mean piano.'

'Where're you going with this?' said Pylon.

'Background,' said Mart Velaze. 'Filling you in.' He fast-forwarded. 'Enough of that, you get the picture. Anyhow I'll leave the disk, you can show Mace.' He stopped when the screen went black. 'Now here you have a different point of view.'

A family came on screen: grandparents and a baby. The grandmother in black holding the baby swaddled in a patterned blanket, the grandfather in jacket and grey trousers. The grandmother unsmiling, the grandfather uneasy as if this might be a joke. The sound on.

'The cameraman is asking them to film him,' said Velaze. 'Here we go, he gives the camera to the granddad, tells him just to hold it straight to his eye. Look who comes into the frame, you wouldn't recognise him yet but that's your client, Max Roland aka Vasa Babic. He asks if he's in focus. The grandfather nods yes and Vasa tells him to hold the camera steady. Handsome guy, your client, hey. No wonder the birds come fluttering to him.'

The face of a thirty-something, wholesome, boyish with floppy blond hair, grinning. Good teeth.

'Now check out the look in Max-Vasa's eyes. Like, where's the laughter gone? We've just got killer eyes there, buta. He's still talking, though.'

Pylon could see it. The man's eyes go dead, his mouth still working, the grin still there but the eyes without any glint to them.

'He's saying, that it's kind of them to film him, that he can send it home to his family.'

A few seconds of this with no one talking, the focus trembling slightly. Then two quick gunshots, the camera sliding off Max Roland, another gunshot, the picture a blur of colour going into black. Another three shots.

Pylon sucked in his breath. 'Save me Jesus.'

'That's your man,' said Mart Velaze. 'Top-class citizen.'

'He shot them. While they were filming him he shot them.'

'How it would seem.'

'No. No. It's bullshit. You're setting something up.'

Mart Velaze looked hurt. 'Cross my heart 'n hope to die. This's on the straight and level. What you see is what you get. That's your man. Now here's the story.'

Mart took the DVD out of the player, slipped it back into its cover, telling Pylon that Vasa Babic was a clever guy, a linguist, spoke five languages, could read another three. Professionally an engineering type at the University of Belgrade. Uber-smart with computers. 'Come that messy business we call the Kosovo War, Mr Babic decides he wants an adventure. Joins the paramilitaries fighting the Albanians.'

Mart Velaze handed Pylon the DVD.

'That building in the first clip, the farmhouse, that was found. A mass grave too. Well, hardly a grave, more a pile of burnt bodies. The farmhouse'd been torched. Shit happens, hey. A lotta shit happens.'

Pylon took the DVD. 'Where'd this come from?'

'Mr Babic's personal collection. Few years ago things started getting hot for him he went on the run. For an IT guy he left a lotta stuff behind. You'd have thought he'd be more careful, more thorough, but maybe not hey when someone's got your name on a piece of paper. Actually Vasa's got his name on a couple of pieces of paper. Some Albanian boykies wanting to cut his dick off, give him the slow burn, the revenge thing. They're the guys made him run. They're the guys he's shit scared of. Actually, they caught him. But Vasa's a clever bugger, what you call resourceful. He got away from the careless bastards. Then there's two others, bounty hunters, a German and a Swede, want to take him to the war crimes people.'

'Bounty hunters?'

Mart Velaze grinned. 'See a financial opportunity there, Mr Buso? You'n old Mace woulda been good bounty hunters. Like in the cowboys, tracking down outlaws. Bastards with money on their heads. Wanted dead or alive. In this case alive. Nothing's changed, you just don't see the posters tacked to lamp posts any more. But there's people still put up money, call it commissions, contract fees, whatever so that other people find it worth their while to bring in the evil ones.'

Mart Velaze gave a mock salute. 'So there you go, I'm done. Au revoir, Mr Buso. Thanks for your time. Thanks for listening.'

Pylon shook his head. 'No, no, no, no. Slowly, my friend.' Put his good hand on Velaze's sleeve.

'Ah, a change in the wind.'

Pylon let go of Mart Velaze. 'That's it? That's all you're going to tell me?'

'What more can there be? I gave you a bunch of dots. Join them.'

'I need more.'

'Like what?'

'Like how do I know he's up for war crimes? Like how'd he get to South Africa? How'd he meet Oosthuizen? And most essentially how d'you know this crap? And why're you interested?'

Mart Velaze rubbed his chin, mock-seriously. Pylon could hear the bristle-scrape.

'Easy answers first. How'd he get to South Africa, why'd he come to South Africa? I don't know. Ask your mate Magnus Oosthuizen. How'd they meet? Rumour only, that it was in the bad old days. Eastern Europe then you could get any shit. And they'd sell it to anybody, didn't matter about your politics. In the woods they're training black guys to be MK guerrillas. Like I was. In the office they're selling SADF generals a rocket system. Who cares? War is money.'

'The war crimes?'

'On the table in your breakfast nook. That's what you call it in clusterland, a breakfast nook? I left the papers there. All yours. Have a read. A bit like the vid, only matter-of-fact. Dispassionate. Gruesome all the same.' He gave a mock bow. 'Gotta dash. Things to do, people to meet.'

'Why?' said Pylon. 'Why'd you tell me?'

Velaze shrugged. 'Like I said, background. And the other thing: shit stinks. Sticks to you 'n stinks. I'm being considerate, buta. I'm the heart-guy reaching out to my comrades, my heroes.'

'Spooks don't do that.'

'Some spooks do.'

'There're questions still, Mart. Like how do you know this about the bounty hunters? Why do you know it? What's the angle here?'

Mart Velaze clapped his hand over his mouth. Whispered, 'State secrets.'

Pylon at his upstairs bedroom window watched Mart Velaze drive off in the smart X5, thinking, all the years in the security business he couldn't remember it being worse. Too much going on. Too much sliding around. Like you're in a car and the road's wet and you're skidding into a highway pile-up at one-twenty and you can't do sweet blow-all to stop. He put through a call to Mace.

34

The Swede called Kalle shot back the cuff of his raincoat, looked at his watch: 9:30. He stared out the plate-glass frontage of the departure hall at the line-up of aircraft below. On the tarmac four turboprops winding up, behind them maintenance hangars. Overhead the burnt white of a winter sky. Better than snow.

The last time he'd stopped in the country had been to collect war spoils. About the same time of year: hazy sunlight and stiletto winds. What was it with war treasures and war crims? South Africa and Brazil, the fences' auction grounds. And the crims, they loved these places to hide away, the vicious ones, the ones with blood on their teeth.

9:35. This wasn't going right. They should have been here already. Take off for the Cape Town flight was at 10:00. He glanced across the passengers gathered at the departure gate, caught his colleague's eye. His colleague Jakob, also wearing a beige raincoat, shook his head, gave a Germanic shrug. The two men sat it out another fifteen minutes until the flight was called, each watching the people hurrying to queue. No Max Roland and his bodyguard, Mace Bishop.

The plan was that Max Roland should recognise them at this point. Let him know that he was a wanted man. He hadn't noticed Jakob in the international arrivals hall because he hadn't been meant to. But here they wanted to surprise him. Remind him it was time for justice.

When most of the passengers had boarded, Kalle and Jakob checked in.

'They were booked on this flight,' said Jakob, 'definitely.' He and Kalle started down the walkway to the plane. 'Perhaps he has taken an earlier flight. Or he will take a later one. But this is no worry, no. Max Roland cannot disappear.'

The cabin attendants welcomed them, directed the two men to their separate seats towards the back of the aircraft.

'This would have been better,' said Jakob as they negotiated the aisle, bumping against people trying to squash major luggage into the overhead lockers. 'Let him know we are not far away.'

Kalle's seat was in the last row. He took off his raincoat, folded it inside out, stowed it. Dropped a book onto his seat. Jakob was a good man to work with. Only problem he talked too much. With relief Kalle picked up his book, sat and buckled up. Leaned his head back, closed his eyes. Heard a voice say in Swedish that he was from Malmo. What a coincidence to have a fellow citizen next to him. Kalle said, 'Hej,' but didn't open his eyes.

35

Magnus Oosthuizen read the piece on the Dinsmor kidnapping in the newspaper, thought having Max Roland in the hands of Mace Bishop did not seem a good idea. He called out to Priscilla in the kitchen for more coffee. 'Strong, hey. Three spoons.' Then he reached for his phone. Before he could key in Sheemina February's number it rang, the name Sheemina February displayed.

'Think of the devil,' he said. 'And there she is.'

'How very biblical, Magnus. And why were you thinking of me?'

'Because I am reading the newspaper. Reading about your man Mace Bishop. A walking disaster it appears. I cannot believe you recommended him.'

Sheemina February laughed. 'He has a little problem but nothing to worry you.'

'It worries me that he is looking after my very important colleague. It should worry you as well.'

'It doesn't, Magnus. Your colleague is in good hands. Really. Now. I have news for you.'

Oosthuizen sat back while Priscilla placed a mug of coffee on his desk blotter. 'Two sugars?' he said to her. She nodded. To Sheemina February he said, 'I am not appeased.' He lifted the mug of coffee, blew at the surface. Let a silence develop.

'Magnus.'

He didn't respond.

'Magnus.'

Oosthuizen sipped at the coffee, the heat scorching his tongue.

'Magnus. Listen to me.'

'I'm listening,' he said.

'Good. Now.'

Oosthuizen called out. 'Priscilla, more sugar, man.' He could hear Chin-chin yapping somewhere. 'And let the dog in, asseblief.' To Sheemina February said, 'What is the matter?'

'Magnus,' she said. 'Focus. Listen to me. The weapons system committee tell me they can hear your presentation tomorrow morning. They want to move on this matter. They want to make a decision.'

'So suddenly.' He spooned sugar into his mug from the bowl Priscilla placed on the desk. 'The dog,' he said to her. 'Please.' Waving her off with his fingers.

'I know,' Sheemina February was saying. 'After all these months, why the urgency now? I don't know. I can't answer that. All I can tell you is that now is the moment.'

'Alright,' said Oosthuizen. He stirred his coffee, not speaking while he tinkled the spoon round and round the mug.

'Magnus,' said Sheemina February. 'Can you make that?'

'Do I have a choice?'

'No. But can you make it?'

Oosthuizen slurped at the instant coffee. Swallowed a mouthful, the hot liquid burning his gullet. He sucked air. 'This is very sudden.'

'I'm doing my best for you here,' said Sheemina February.

'It's not up to me,' said Oosthuizen. 'It depends on Max Roland, if he can finish the programme. And your man, Mace Bishop. If he can keep Max safe.'

Sheemina February sighed. 'Magnus, Magnus, Magnus. Lean on them, Magnus. Your Max Roland and Mace Bishop. This is your moment.'

Magnus Oosthuizen heard Chin-chin skittering across the wooden floors, yelping. He shouted to the dog in Afrikaans 'Come here, come here,' making kissing noises. To Sheemina February he said, 'You can tell the committee I shall be there.'

He thumbed her off as she was saying, 'I already have, Magnus. I already have.'

Oosthuizen reached down for the dog, lifted it onto his lap.

So this woman Sheemina February had the right contacts. Impressive. 'What d'you think, Chin-chin?' he said. 'The gods of fortune are smiling.'

36

Veronica Dinsmor woke with a headache vicious enough to make her groan. She swung her legs out of the bed, sat on the edge, peering at the room. Wooden walls, maps and photographs pinned to them. Interior wooden shutters at the window. A shelf of books, a shelf of shells and old bottles. A pedestal with a reading lamp. Nothing fancy. The linen on the bed white, well washed, worn. An en-suite bathroom opposite her.

She dry-retched, wanted to puke and pee, just wasn't sure in which order.

'Oh God,' she said, rushing to the bowl, thrust her head in, kecked, almost peed herself doing it. White strokes of pain slammed against her temples. When they eased she sat on the loo, a taste of metal in her mouth, putting things together.

Enough light to make it morning.

Birdsong. Seagulls.

Waves.

No gag. No ties around her wrists or ankles.

She remembered the balaclavaed man, the shooting of Zuki and Kortboy. Such a casual shooting. Such hopeless young men.

The man tapping the syringe, the needle going in.

Her stomach knotted, heaved, she spat bile between her legs.

Compared with this, Colombia had been a cakewalk.

Veronica kicked away her underwear, wiped, and flushed the

toilet. Lent over the basin tap to drink water from the palm of her hand. Mouthful after mouthful until it made her giddy. She straightened, steadied herself against the walls.

Above the basin was a window, drawn across it sun-filter curtains patterned with seabirds. She moved aside the curtain, looked out through gratings on scrub and sand, a flat plain sloping upwards to distant hills. Blue sky behind them. An infinite blue of freedom. It made her heart ache, made her think of Silas. Had they demanded ransom? What was Silas thinking? Doing? Where was he? Made her think of her coming granddaughter. Would she ever see her? She gripped the basin, closed her eyes, tried to clear her head.

Useless thoughts. Tormenting thoughts.

She went back to the bedroom, opened the shutters. Gratings on the window, the same view: not a sign of the human world. Veronica Dinsmor, the optimistic Dancing Rabbit, collapsed groaning on the bed. She stank. She could smell herself. With the fear and the sweat her clothes stank worse than she did. She could have wept with despair.

She didn't hear the door open, only looked up at the woman's voice.

'May I suggest you take a shower, then we can talk.' An extremely striking, beautiful woman. 'Oh, yes, there's a hairdryer in the pedestal drawer. Your suitcase is under the bed.' The woman smiled with her lips only, closed the door. Veronica heard the key turn.

After her shower, Veronica, in jeans and a roll-neck jersey, sat on the bed wondering, what now? She ran her tongue over her teeth, no fur, the taste of peppermint toothpaste in her mouth. She could smell coffee, toast. Enough to make her mouth juices run.

She tried the door handle. It was unlocked, the door opened into a short passageway cluttered with bicycles, fishing rods, paddles. To the left another bedroom, to the right an open-plan lounge and kitchen. The woman in an apron at the stove talking on her cellphone, saying goodbye.

'Come through,' she said, beckoning with a gloved hand waving a spatula, 'you must be hungry. I'm Sheemina February, by the way. Excuse the mess. All belongs to the previous owners. Not my style at all.'

Sheemina February watched Veronica Dinsmor come hesitantly into the room. Glance around. If the woman wanted a weapon she had her pick: the metal fire poker, the axe next to the pile of logs, the small anchor propped against the wall, even the eland's jawbone that served as an ornament on the mantelpiece.

'Come. Take a seat.' Sheemina February indicating the table laid for two. 'There's coffee in the Bialetti. Help yourself.'

'Where am I?' said Veronica Dinsmor.

'On holiday.' Sheemina February held up a box of eggs. 'Not far from Cape Town actually. On what we call the west coast. The wild west. From that sand dune' – she indicated with the spatula through the window to the dunes that rose not far from the house – 'you can see the city and the mountain. On a bright day like this, something to behold.' She smiled. 'How do you like your eggs? Sunny side up? Poached? Scrambled?'

'Poached,' said Veronica Dinsmor. 'If you don't mind.'

'Oh, I don't mind. It's why I asked.'

Sheemina February broke four eggs into poaching cups, turned up the gas ring. 'Toast?'

'Thank you.'

Slid two pieces of bread into the electric toaster. The woman sat at the table, taking the place facing the sea. Poured herself a short coffee. No milk. No sugar. A connoisseur, a good sign to Sheemina February. A cool customer.

After she'd swallowed it in an Italian-style single hit Veronica Dinsmor said, 'What's going on?' Like that, as if she hadn't gone through the rough end, been smacked around, seen men shot dead. Very cool.

'Money,' said Sheemina February. 'That's what's going on. It's all that's going on. The only game in town, as they say.'

'How much?'

The toaster popped.

'Can't say, exactly. How long's a piece of string? Thing is this, Veronica, you and Silas are an interesting couple. Bold. Entrepreneurial. Which is good. Except this is our patch and there are certain protocols. So I thought we could talk about your prospects, your portfolio, see how we might work things out to our mutual benefit.' She tested the eggs with the flat of a knife blade. 'Slightly runny or hard?'

'Not hard.'

'Then butter up some toast.'

Sheemina February kept on talking while she dished the eggs, telling Veronica how much she knew of the Dinsmors' American casinos, their plans to invest in the local gaming industry. Help initiate casino developments in the townships, build gambling palaces in the desperate rural areas.

'All of which is good. Laudable.' She sat down opposite the American. 'What I'm not getting is why you thought to cut us out.'

Veronica Dinsmor ate her way through one piece of toast and a poached egg. Saying through a mouthful. 'Sorry. I've got to eat.'

'Be my guest.'

After dabbing at her lips with a paper serviette, Veronica said, 'You weren't cut out. You weren't in it.'

'Here's the problem. We should've been. You should've found out about us. Talked to us.'

'Who're you?'

Sheemina February swallowed a mouthful. Leaned back. Nodding her head, smiling to herself. Who're you? The woman had balls, as she'd been told. She liked that. She could handle a woman with balls.

'More coffee?' Without waiting for an answer emptied the Bialetti into Veronica's cup. 'I'll make another.' While she did, explained she was a lawyer by profession, a director of companies by inclination, companies with mining interests, property developments, also looking to venture into the gaming business with a consortium of black businesspeople. What was known as a black economic empowerment consortium. BEE, for short. If you wanted to see it from a historical perspective, the rightful owners of the country taking back what the settlers had stolen during three hundred years of blah di blah enslavement, degradation, impoverishment, rape, murder, name any horror you like, even genocide.

'Can't be genocide,' said Veronica. 'You're in the majority. More of you native South Africans now than there've ever been. Even with HIV decimations.'

'You know about those?'

'We did our homework.'

'Then why did you overlook us?'

Sheemina February watched Veronica Dinsmor finish her second slice of toast and poached egg. A dribble of yolk oozing from the corner of her mouth, quickly wiped away.

'For us you were a competitor. Seeing as it was an open tender process. The best deal wins.'

'Uh-uh.' Sheemina February brushed her fringe back off her forehead. 'Uh-uh. That's not how it's done. Might look like it but it's not. You're right about the open tender, anyone can submit their proposal. The more the merrier. Some companies are actually encouraged to tender, the big boys, to make everything kosher. They know they're not in with a chance but, hey, they don't want any legal problems, besides it looks good. Looks like a free economy. Except the contract's awarded to the BEE consortium. As I said, simple redress of historical injustices. But …' She gave Veronica two more slices of toast. 'But we're always open to partnerships. International partnerships especially. Which is why we're talking to you.'

Veronica stopped buttering her toast. 'I'm sorry? Did I hear you right? You're talking to me? Like we're having a business meeting here?'

'Yes. That's what this is.'

'You kidnap me. You get armed men to kidnap me.'

'Both of you. You and Silas, it was supposed to be both of you kidnapped.'

'What? Honey, you're way outta line. Way, way, way. I get kidnapped. Tied up. Assaulted. Humiliated. I see men shot. I get drugged and kidnapped again, and you, you, tell me we're having a business meeting now. Like this is ordinary. All this mayhem. This is ordinary!'

'Often.'

'Honey. Sheemina, honey. Do me a favour. Take me back to my husband, let us get on a plane and go home. I have a granddaughter being born in a few months. That is the most important thing to me right now. You can keep the deal. We're outta here. So fast you won't even see our dust.'

Sheemina February bit into her toast, the crunch loud in her head. 'Congratulations. About the granddaughter.' She chewed and swallowed. 'A nice thought that.'

Veronica nodded.

'Thing is,' said Sheemina, 'we don't want to see you flying off. We want to do business with you.'

'You're kidding me. You've got to be kidding me. No ways. No ways ever we're gonna do business with you.'

'There's the money.'

'Young men died.'

'Unfortunately. This happens to hijackers. Violent men lead violent lives and sometimes, more often than not, they die violent deaths. No loss to society.'

Veronica snorted. 'Why? After what you've done to me, what you've put me through, what you're putting me through goddammit, why would Silas and I go into business with you?'

Sheemina February smeared honey over a last finger of toast. 'Money.'

'Oh God! You believe that? You believe greed's the only thing that motivates us?'

'Yes.'

'Miss Sheemina you're so wrong. So completely, just completely off target.' She stared at Sheemina February. 'You think that, you don't know the first thing about us. You ain't got a notion. Let me tell you, when Silas and I got going back home, it wasn't about money, it was about what we could do, the difference we could make in poor people's lives. We came here with the same incentive. Now maybe you don't understand altruism, maybe for all your talk of historical injustice, the first thing you think of in the morning when you wake is money, but Silas and I have other ideals.'

'Ideals that've made you a lot of money.'

'By happenstance.'

'Of course. How silly of me to think otherwise.'

Veronica Dinsmor pushed her chair back from the table. 'I'm going. I'm going to walk out that door and you're not going to stop me.' She stood up.

'I am.'

'What?'

'Going to stop you.'

'You're threatening me?'

'Yes.' Sheemina February brought a small gun out of the pocket of her apron: a stainless steel, double-action North American Arms Guardian .32 loaded with hollow-points.

'You see what I mean?' said Veronica Dinsmor. 'This is what I'm talking about. Your violence. People don't do business like this. People don't go about kidnapping people, killing people, threatening people, pulling out guns.'

'You prefer trust and a handshake?'

'Strangely. I do.'

'Sit down, Veronica. Sit down and listen. Have some more coffee. Hear me out, alright. Hear me out, talk to Silas and then let's see.' Sheemina February dropped the Guardian into the pocket of her apron.

The American sat. 'I don't like guns.'

'You know what Capone said?'

'You're going to tell me.'

'I am.' Sheemina February looked up as if the words were written on the ceiling. 'Now let me get this right. He said, something like, "Sometimes you can get more with a few kind words and a loaded gun than you can with just a few kind words." And you know what I've found?'

Veronica Dinsmor didn't respond.

Sheemina February went right on regardless. 'I've found, most of the time, he's right.'

'When can I talk to Silas?'

'In a moment. Hold tight. There's other stuff to get through first.' Sheemina February topped up both their coffee cups. Began to explain the deal, the whole business plan laid out for a chain of casinos, five in all. Gave her pitch for twenty minutes nonstop. Veronica Dinsmor listening without a question. Listening hard, Sheemina February could tell. The concentration written in her face. All came down to money in the end. The wonder of it. Sheemina could see that, the dollar signs in the Native American's eyes. Dancing Rabbit about to perform a rain dance.

'What's the breakdown?'

'Talk to Silas first. Then we can pow-wow, work out the percentages. What sort of investment you need to make here. What slice you can give us in your US operations.'

'That's a big ask.'

'Negotiable.'

'Let me talk to Silas.'

Sheemina February held out her hand across the table. Veronica Dinsmor hesitated.

'Shake. Trust and a handshake. I'll get Silas to join us.'

'You will?'

'Trust me.'

Sheemina February keeping back the smile from her lips. They shook.

'This is all wrong,' said Veronica.

Sheemina February thought fifty-fifty chance the woman was making this play to keep the game alive. And herself.

37

On the down flight Mace had two hours to think some more about Sheemina February. Nothing that hadn't plagued him on the up flight. Nothing that he could resolve. Like the timing of the estate agent getting hold of Dave. Like Sheemina's car parked on the deck saying one thing, but her flat empty. Like what were the rosebuds about? Like had she really waited all night in the cold for Mace to pitch? Just to leave a rosebud in his windscreen wipers?

Putting herself out like that not really her style. More likely she had a tracker on him. A chilling thought.

Mace went back to the details. Maybe the estate agent chatter was a coincidence, normal shoptalk that wouldn't mean anything in the usual scheme. Her car was on the deck because she was out of town, didn't like leaving it at the airport. The rosebud in the vase was a rosebud in a vase.

You looked at it like that these details meant nothing. You added the rosebud in the wipers into the mix there was a story.

Mace thought about this watching the attendants at the refreshments trolley, five rows away down the aisle. Glanced about. To his right two business colleagues checking pie charts, a young woman in the window-seat laughing at the candid camera video being shown on the overhead screen. Max Roland beside him in the middle seat, other side of him a thirtyish guy scrolling down a spreadsheet on his laptop.

Max Roland flicking through the in-flight magazine. He nudged Mace, holding up a spread of bikini girls on a beach. Summer fashions. The beach could be Camps Bay, Mace believed, with its palms, white sands, the flat turquoise ocean. Water that looked tropical but froze your balls it was that cold.

'Lovely bodies,' said Max Roland. He kissed the pages. 'I was in the Yemen for only five days.' He held up five fingers. 'Five days. My friend, it was eternity. Eternity in another world with no women. Black shapes that show nothing.' He dropped the magazine, drew two parallel lines in the air with his hands. 'Like that. No shape. They could be walking in boxes. The best thing in Johannesburg airport is women, girls.' He drew an air picture of hips, cupped his hands round imaginary breasts. 'That is what I missed. That there are no women to be seen.'

Nice guys, this wanker and Oosthuizen, Mace thought. But what the hell, you didn't have to like them, you just had to take their money. Money for a couple of months, which was even better. And best of all Max Roland didn't seem to be attracting any attention.

Mace ordered rooibos tea from the trolley-dolly. Roland going into his charm shtick.

'Molo, sisi, I like your bracelet' – two strands of plaited elephant hair you could buy in any tourist shop. The woman asked what he wanted to drink.

'Coffee, sisi, black with no white.' Mace saw him wink, the cabin attendant giving him a polite smile. 'Where can I get such a bracelet?'

'Anywhere,' she said, handing him a polystyrene mug of coffee. 'Enjoy your day, sir.'

'Would you be free to show me the shop?'

'Not today,' said the woman, leaning over to give the spreadsheet man a bottle of water.

Max Roland caught her wrist. 'Very nice.'

'Please.'

He released her. 'You have lovely skin.'

The attendant smiled again but Mace saw the irritation in her eyes.

'Enough,' he said to Max Roland. 'Let it go, okay.'

'I am only, how do you say, chaffing her.'

'Sure,' said Mace.

'She is a pretty girl.'

'Enough.'

Max Roland returned to his magazine. Mace picked up on Sheemina

February. One thing she had to know, he was after her. Hunting her. Going to kill her. She goes to ground, then concocts a trap. So the estate agent chatter's a set-up. So the car on the deck's a set-up. Ditto the rosebuds. For why? To let him know that she's one step ahead. Intent on entrapping him. In the process getting him mad. Furious. Irrational. Angry enough to make mistakes.

Okay, Sheemina February, he thought. Let's see how it works tonight.

The Stones coming in: I see a red door ... A door red with Oumou's blood.

Mace closed his eyes. For a moment thought, Jesus, can I get through this? The heaviness of his grief. Christa. The shit with the Dinsmor kidnapping. The bloody newspapers nailing him. Sheemina February. His chest tightened. He wanted to jump up, walk around, get rid of the frustration. Half rose, the seatbelt holding him down.

'You want to pee?' said Max Roland. 'Me too.'

Mace crushed the cup, dregs of tea splashing on to the service tray. He mopped at them with a paper serviette.

The problem with this sort of job, Mace thought, was if the client wanted to pee, you had to go with him. Kindergarten duty.

An hour later the plane taxied to a parking bay, the cabin supremo doing his it's a lovely day in the Mother City number. No one listened, the passengers jostling into the aisle to get on with their lives. Mace flipped open his seatbelt, connected his phone. A voice message from Pylon that they needed to talk about Max Roland. Didn't sound that urgent. Wasn't the sort of conversation Mace was going to have in public anyhow.

He and Max Roland still jammed halfway down the plane waiting to disembark, when Oosthuizen called wanting to know, when were they going to get to the safe house? When could he meet up with Max Roland?

Mace tried to get a word in. 'Slow down ...'

Oosthuizen going into a pause. Then: 'Let me talk to him. Max Roland. Put him on.'

'Not a good idea. Not now.'

To Mace's surprise the man leaving it there. 'Get back to me, Mace Bishop. Soonest, you hear what I'm saying?'

Max Roland, behind Mace in the shuffling queue, said in his ear, 'Magnus does not like to wait. With this project he is very nervous.'

In the bus from the plane to the terminal building, his phone went again: Tami.

'Such a popular man.' Max Roland, flicked back his blond quiff, grinned at Mace.

Mace thought, only so much of this you could put up with. Connected, heard Tami say, 'We don't know where Dinsmor is.'

Mace wondered if he'd got that properly. 'Repeat.' His gorge rising a taste of the airline's omelette and mushrooms breakfast. Not that it had far to rise.

'Dinsmor's gone, Mace. We can't find him.'

Mace thought, shit.

The bus stopped at the arrivals gate.

'I'll phone you,' Mace said. 'Look again. Just find him.'

Max Roland pulled a sad face. 'The popular man gets some bad news.'

My friend, Mace thought, you want me to be nice to you then cut the commentary. Grabbed Roland by the sleeve, herded him amongthe passengers jostling out of the bus.

'Your dog has gone missing? Or your cat?'

'Get your bag,' said Mace.

'Be cool, Mr Bishop, it is the only way in these situations, no?'

Mace got back to Tami, keeping an eye on Max Roland waiting in the crush round the carousel. 'What happened?'

'We're in the breakfast room. He gets a call from America.'

'What time?'

'Now now. Half an hour ago. About twenty to eleven.'

'He told you it was from America?'

'Yes. A call from his office he said.'

'No change in his attitude.'

'Nothing I noticed. Like the guy's agitated obviously. He's got this disturbing DVD playing in his head. We all have. We're not sitting there having a joyous breakfast. But he takes the call and it doesn't seem a big deal. No freeze on his face. He doesn't start tugging at his ponytail. He checked the screen, answered with his name like he always does, said excuse me, and got up from the table, wandered off to the sliding doors and went outside onto the stoep. But like we can see him. Walking around out there, talking on his phone.'

'We. Who's with you? One of the guys?'

'Sure. And the cop, Gonsalves.'

'He's still with you?'

'Hyper pissed off. We've got two cars of cops here searching.'

'Good,' said Mace. 'So go back, Dinsmor's out on the stoep, you're watching him.'

'Sort of. You know, not full-on watching him. Aware that he's out there. You know keeping an eye on him from the table.'

'You're all at the table, sitting down?'

'Yes.'

'Jesus, Tami.'

'What? You'd have done it differently? We're talking, rather Gonsalves is talking, we can see Dinsmor. Gonsalves is looking full at him. Me and our guy, what's his name, haven't got a direct visual, we're a bit side-on but we're aware. It didn't seem to be an issue.'

'You didn't notice a lurker?'

'No one. Anyone had stepped onto that stoep we'd have seen him. No question.'

'Go back again,' said Mace, 'to the phone call. The phone rings, he checks the screen, answers with his name.'

'That's what I said.'

'I know. I'm trying to get this in sequence, get it straight for my own sake, okay.' Mace paused. 'So he takes the call, there's no change in him. Nothing. He's Mr Poker Face.'

'That's right.'

'Then what?'

'Like I said, he listens for a bit.'

'And you're looking at him. And you don't see any emotion.'

'Your Mr Poker Face.'

'He doesn't smile. His jaw doesn't clench. There's nothing in his eyes.'

'He doesn't smile. He doesn't like smiling. He's like, you know, stern.'

'Does he say anything?'

'To who he's talking to he says, hang on. To us he says excuse me.'

'So how'd you know it was his office in America?'

Mace heard Tami take in a breath. 'He said, excuse me, it's my office.'

'He didn't say America?'

'No. I told you that. He didn't say America.'

Mace saw Max Roland lifting his bag from the carousel. 'Got to go, but confirm. The only words he spoke that you heard were: Silas. Hang on. Excuse me, it's my office.'

'Full marks.'

'And outside. How long was he talking outside?'

'He wasn't talking much outside, he was listening mostly.'

'For how long? Thirty seconds? One minute? Two minutes?' A long hum from Tami. 'Come'n, Tami, I've got other stuff happening here.'

'Maybe a minute.'

'Long enough to get you relaxed about the situation.'

Max Roland came up. 'You will fry your brain,' he said.

Mace gritted his teeth. Another quip he'd fry Max Roland.

'Then what, Tami? Then what? What's your take?'

'You're asking me?'

'For Chrissakes, yes.'

'Hey, my opinion counts!'

'Cut it.'

Max Roland glanced at Mace amused at the tone. 'Be cool, Mr Bishop.'

'You want my opinion, here it is. He walked down the steps, got into a car. Poof.'

'You heard a car drive away?'

'There were cars coming and going. It's a hotel, Mace.'

'They've got him,' said Mace.

'The firemen have found your pet,' said Max Roland.

Mace frowned at him. Said to Tami, 'Keep me in the loop' and disconnected. Said to Roland, 'China, don't get my goat.'

'I do not understand.'

'Exactly,' said Mace, heading for the exit, the doors sliding open to reveal a waiting crowd. He did a quick scan, picked up the woman pushing through from the back right away. Young woman in her thirties, bag over her shoulder, conspicuous in a red coat, her eyes on him. Not on Max Roland, on him.

'That woman,' said Max Roland in his ear, 'the red one.'

'Got her already,' said Mace. 'Let's go' – hustling Roland outside towards the parking garage.

The woman in red calling out, 'Mr Bishop, Mr Bishop, one moment.'

Mace didn't pause, didn't look back.

The woman came running past them, turned, a camera in her hand aimed at them.

'How did your client, Mr Dinsmor, go missing?' she said. 'Has there been any contact with his wife?'

Mace lunged for the camera.

'It's on video,' she said, taking a step back.

Didn't stop Mace going for her, wrenching the camera from her hand. People around stopped in surprise but nobody intervened. Only one guy saying, 'Take it easy, pal.' Mace's glare moved him on.

'Who're you?' he said to the woman. Aware of Max Roland to the side, taking this all in, grinning.

'Give that back.' The woman trying to grab his arm. 'I'll charge you.'

Mace shook her off. 'You're the journalist. The one who phoned me. The one writing those articles on the Dinsmors.'

The woman fished in her coat pocket, came up with a business card. Rachel Pringle, crime reporter, Cape Times. 'Now give that back.'

'Uh-uh. Bugger off, Miss Pringle.'

'We're on the Dinsmor story. From what I hear your guys were negligent.'

'According to who?'

'The police.'

'The police were there.' Had to be Captain Gonz had dropped him. So tit for tat.

'Still doesn't look good for your company.'

'Looks worse for the cops.'

Max Roland stepped in. 'I am his new client. He is very good. If you want an interview, I can spare moments for a lovely woman like you.' He held out his hand, palm up. 'Miss?'

Rachel Pringle flipped him a card.

'No,' said Mace snatching it out of Roland's hand. 'Let's go.' Mace shoving Max Roland away from the reporter into the multi-storey.

Rachel Pringle shouted after them. 'You've got my camera. I want it back.'

Mace and Roland half turned. 'Buy another one,' said Mace.

In that moment she snapped them both with her backup digital.

'Goddamned reporters.'

'Nice boobies, probably,' said Roland, 'under that coat. A lady wears a low plunge in winter, the lady's got good melons.' Nattering on all over again about being in a city where all the women wore black tents, you couldn't see flesh, not even a shape of tits pressing against the fabric. Never a cheeky nipple.

Mace wanted to tell the guy, look, shut up. Having to concentrate, check out the parking lot as they pulled away, keep an eye in the rearview at the cars slotting in behind them.

As they drove out of the airport towards the highway, Roland sang the city's praises, the clear sky, the wet smell. On and on about being pleased to be back in the city. What were the chances of getting clothes, books, music from his apartment? He was going to be shut up in a safe house, he needed some of his things.

'Maybe,' said Mace to quieten him. 'Tricky though.' Two cars behind that'd been there from the exit booms.

At the junction Mace took the highway out of the city, Roland getting agitated.

'Where are we going?' he said. 'This is not the road to Oosthuizen.'

'We're not going there,' said Mace. 'We're doing a jolly ride so I can see who's following us.'

'That woman?'

'I don't think so.'

'How does she know you are on the plane?'

'Search me. How do journalists know anything? Someone leaks it.'

'So who did this?'

Good question, Mace thought. For his money had to be Gonz. Maybe the cop'd heard Mace's movements from Tami, wanted to rev him a little. Leaked it to the reporter for some favour. No problem for the reporter to get a flight list. If he could do that sort of thing, no reason why journalists couldn't.

As the highway opened up the two cars behind pulled into the fast lane to overtake. Single men in both, on their cellphones. Some relief to Mace but not entirely. He pushed the car a little faster, went back to the other questions buzzing him. Like maybe Dinsmor hadn't been snatched. Maybe he'd been propositioned. Which meant what? That Dancing Rabbit and her husband were going to end up dead. Or that they'd spring a deal with the kidnappers. He'd have placed money either way.

On a straight stretch of motorway Mace pulled into the yellow line at an emergency phone. A clear view back and front. Across the highway the shacks of Khayelitsha.

'What are you doing?' said Max Roland, squirming in his seat, looking about like he expected wild men to rise from the long grass. 'People get killed when they stop on this highway. Go on. Drive away.'

'Chill,' said Mace, watching the traffic in the rearview mirror. 'A couple of seconds aren't going to get us hijacked.' Amused that the man was frightened. The scornful Max Roland shitting himself.

'There.' Roland pointed at the township fence. 'There are men there. Look. Coming through the fence.'

True enough, on the other side of the highway, six lanes of traffic away, young men were squeezing through the palisade fencing. Mace gave it a quick glance, more concerned with the cars behind them. No one slowed down.

'They're coming,' said Roland. 'Definitely. Those men are coming to us. They are picking up stones. They have sticks. Quickly go.'

'They're probably herd boys,' said Mace, 'looking for their cattle.'

The young men ran down the sand embankment to the edge of the highway, gathered there waiting for a break in the traffic. Four of them. Mace kept his eyes on the cars coming up behind, passing. The woman journalist not in their number, nor anyone else suspicious.

'Oh crap,' said Max Roland, 'they are running.'

Mace saw two of the men, boys really, teenagers, dash across three lanes into the centre island. A blare of hooters from motorists freaking out at the sight of people in their lanes. The boys hurdled the concrete barrier, readied to cross the next three lanes. The oncoming traffic suddenly thin.

'Go,' shouted Max Roland. 'Go. They are taking the gap.'

Mace gave it more time, pretty sure that there'd been no one following them. He heard hooters again, tyres squealing. The other two boys in the centre island now, the first two walking towards them.

'You have a gun,' said Max Roland, opening the cubbyhole, scratching through the contents.

'Relax,' said Mace, dropped the clutch, gently pulled away. The two boys chased after them for a couple of paces. 'Probably wanted to ask if we'd seen their cows.'

'That was a most stupid thing to do,' said Max Roland.

'What's stupid,' said Mace, 'is panicking.' Some triumph in his voice though. This was a score to him that kept Max Roland shut up for most of the trip to the safe house. Before they left the highway, Mace phoned Magnus Oosthuizen, told him, get to the Longbeach Mall, park in the basement, take the elevator to the shopping level and keep walking right out the door. He'd be waiting outside. And to call as he got there.

'That's miles away,' said Oosthuizen.

'Get you out and about,' said Mace. 'Lovely day to see the peninsula.'

An Oosthuizen silence.

'How's Max?'

'Talk to him.' Mace handed the phone to Roland.

He couldn't hear what Oosthuizen said but Roland got loud. 'I have told you I will finish before the deadline. There is nothing to be worried for.'

He listened. Said, 'The deadline is tonight! What is this?'

Then: 'Tomorrow you must make the presentation? Madness. Madness.' Roland running into a torrent of foreign words, harsh, clipped. Eventually he stopped. Said, 'Magnus. Magnus?'

If Oosthuizen was talking, Mace couldn't hear him. Saw Max Roland rub his eyes, nodding, listening. Finally he said, 'Okay. Okay. I will see you later.' He cut the call, gave the phone back to Mace. 'Magnus is crazy. He thinks I am a robot. That all he has to do is click his fingers and I will perform.'

Mace didn't respond, sensed Max Roland's anger and wondered what the story was. Had to be about getting the weapons system completed. Oosthuizen tightening the screws on the scientist. But that was their problem. If it kept Roland shut up for a while then who was he to complain?

Mace cut off the highway, back around the township onto the coast road, False Bay coming up a glassy blue, the mountains bright and stark beneath a sky washed clean. On the narrow road with little traffic ahead he pushed the needle to one-ten up the cliffs, down onto the flats to Strandfontein. The stretch littered with plastic bags, dead dogs, mashed rodents. Slowed for the straight along the beach, the high tide running out metres from the tarmac. Seaweed and shells laced across the road. Ahead Muizenberg mountain yellow in the sunlight.

He took the main road along the seafront through St James, Kalk Bay. Max Roland coming out of his funk.

'This is a nice place for a safe house, Kalk Bay. Good restaurants. The deli. Theresa's. Harbour House. You want cocaine you ask in the harbour. Did you know this?'

'No,' said Mace. 'Thanks for sharing.' The sarcasm not registering with Roland.

'You are not stopping?'

Mace shook his head.

'Such a pity. I could work well in this place. Where is the house?'

'You'll see.' Mace accelerated through the harbour traffic lights round the headland into the Fish Hoek shopping strip.

Max Roland sighing despondently at the motor shops, the fast food joints, the second-hand furniture dealers, the video stores, estate agents, banks. 'So many old people,' he said. 'Like the waiting room for the morgue. You do not have the house here? Tell me that. Please that it is not here.'

'Not far away,' said Mace.

He came at Sun Valley through an estate, Max Roland moaning every kilometre. 'This location is most dreadful. English-style houses, shopping malls and blocks of flats.'

Mace turned into a block opposite the Longbeach Mall. 'Got McDonalds, Ocean Basket, Spur, Mugg & Bean on your doorstep,' he said. 'People we've had here wanted to come back for a holiday.'

They went upstairs to the flat, Max Roland bitching that he expected something better. In the city bowl maybe.

'Listen,' said Mace, 'we're talking safe house, okay. Usually that means a shithole in a small town in the middle of nowhere. Be content.' He opened the door. The place hadn't been aired for a couple of weeks, exhaled a musty breath.

They walked into a small lounge, low ceiling, cream walls of stucco plaster. A brown carpet wall-to-wall. In the centre a two-seater cottage couch and an armchair staring at a television set and DVD player. In a corner a pine table and hard-back chairs.

'People want to come here again for a holiday?'

'Sure,' said Mace. 'Close to amenities.'

Max Roland drew the curtains on the view: over the street an empty car park fronting a facebrick mall. Behind that the Noordhoek mountains.

'Plenty of roads for you to jog,' said Mace. 'You'll love it.' Thinking he could join Dave the estate agent, the spiel he was giving.

Roland flopped onto the couch, looked up at Mace. 'How long must I stay here?'

'Couple of weeks. But you're not a prisoner.'

'That is where you are wrong. Until the contract is paid I am a prisoner. I could be here for a long time.'

'We don't work like that.' Mace stood at the window. A car had pulled into the parking lot, Herbie's Driving School decals on the side panels. The instructor got out, placed red cones on the corners of a parking bay. 'We move you around every two weeks.' Down below, the driving lesson started, the learner reversing slowly towards the cones. 'Gives you some variety, gives us peace of mind. We have four places we use. Five at a pinch.' The learner drove over a cone. The instructor, maybe Herbie himself, clasped his head with both hands, turned his face to the sky.

'Like this?'

'More or less. One of them's a rental. The owner, he's a pensioner, moves out for us. Gives him some welcome bucks every now and then.'

'Mein Gott,' said Max Roland, rolling his eyes.

Magnus Oosthuizen phoned fifteen minutes later. Mace told him again: leave the car in the mall's underground parking, take the elevator up, he'd meet him there. Said to Max Roland, 'I'm taking the key.' Couple of minutes later returned with Oosthuizen carrying Chin-chin the Chihuahua in a tartan coat under one arm, a laptop in a leather case gripped in the other. Mace hadn't figured Oosthuizen for a moffie. Still wasn't sure, Afrikaner men having such a thing for Chihuahuas.

Oosthuizen put the laptop on the table, the dog on the carpet. The two colleagues shook hands. Mace watching, noticed no love lost between them. Out the corner of his eye saw Chin-chin cock his leg at the couch, squirt a yellow marker.

Oosthuizen saying, 'I am glad you are safe, Max. I was worried. You go missing for days. You turn up in Yemen. You don't wait for proper protection. This is crazy behaviour.'

Mace said, 'Your dog's pissed against the couch.'

Roland talking over him. 'You are worried that they would kill me before I had finished the program?'

'Worried about your safety, yes, I was.'

Roland sniggered. 'Ja, Magnus, that is what you say. But the reason is different. Now you can stop the worrying. I am protected here.' He gestured around the room. 'In this ugly dump.'

Mace said again, 'Your dog's pissed against the couch.'

'What?' said Oosthuizen. 'What's that?'

'Your dog has pissed against the couch.' Mace bent down, pointed at the wet stain on the brown fabric. The dog leapt at this hand, needle teeth sinking into his finger. 'Chrissakes.' Mace pulled his hand free. Kicked the tartan bundle under the armchair.

'Don't kick my dog.' Oosthuizen bent to retrieve his pet, making kissing noises, cooing 'Come to papa, liefie.' Master and dog came upright, the Chihuahua licking a long tongue over Oosthuizen's chin.

'I will ask you to show more respect to animals, Mr Bishop,' said Oosthuizen.

'It bloody bit me,' said Mace. 'That means a goddamned tetanus shot. You going to pay for that?' Mace holding up a finger oozing blood from two punctures.

'Love bites.'

'My foot.'

'You should be kind to animals, Mr Bishop, then it won't be a problem.' Oosthuizen turned to Max Roland. Said, 'Max, you need to work.'

'I'm tired now.'

'Rest. Take a sleep. But get the work finished. Tomorrow first thing I need it for the presentation.'

'You said that to me already. On the phone.'

The two men glaring at one another.

'And you said you could do it.'

'I can.'

'So then? We've got to get the contract signed, Max. They'll see me tomorrow morning. I am told they favour us. Now is our opportunity. If they like what I tell them they will sign. The sooner they sign, the sooner we relax, the sooner you go home. Panic over. I can pay off Mr Bishop.'

Mace going, 'Hey, hey, hey, one minute. I thought you wanted our service for an extended period? That was the story.'

'I did,' said Oosthuizen, stroking the dog's head, 'yesterday. But not any more. You have been efficient, Mr Bishop. Professional. The circumstances have changed. As you know, this happens. We live in dynamic times. What I thought might drag out, the government suddenly wants to finalise. This is excellent news and I must seize the opportunity. Carpe diem, not so?' He kissed the top of the dog's head. 'Your services are needed for another day, two days maximum.'

'And that's all you're going to pay for?'

'Of course. What else?'

'We had an agreement. You wanted protection for some time.'

'We talked about that, I will concede.'

'You lied. Right from the start, you lied to me about what you wanted.'

'Come, Mr Bishop, that is a harsh statement. I didn't lie. I had facts at my disposal, I responded to them. The facts changed. Like the weather.'

'Bullshit. You dollied it up, the contract. Came over big time. Bring in your man. Protect him. Gave out it's an extended service, didn't haggle about the fees. I'll see you right, Mr Bishop. Bloody pack of lies. Well, up yours, china. Give me a reason I shouldn't kick you out. Both of you. Right now.'

'I wouldn't do that,' said Oosthuizen. 'Not with the press you're getting.' He gave Mace a thin smile. 'Do the job. Earn the money. Move on.'

Mace took a step towards Oosthuizen. The dog bared its teeth. Snarled.

'Careful, Mr Bishop,' said Oosthuizen. 'Let us keep this professional.'

Mace stopped, caught the smirk on Max Roland's face. 'I'm going.'

'And what about protection?' Oosthuizen still fondling the dog's ears. Chin-chin's rapture drooling on his sleeve. 'That is what I'm paying for.'

'That's what you're getting, pal. I might get angry but I don't break deals.' Mace wagging a finger at him. 'You're lucky I'm doing anything for you.' He walked to the door, opened it. 'Stay put, Roland. One of my staff will be here. Eventually. Till then, you want anything to eat, ask Mr Oosthuizen to get it.' He pointed at the shopping mall. 'All you want's in there.'

38

'I have been to this city before,' said Jakob. 'Also on a job. That time it was to find someone, a witness. For this person I have two addresses: at the first one there is an old lady, at the second one a family. The old lady makes me tea and cake. Very nice banana loaf cake. She doesn't know about my fellow. At the family they don't know about my fellow. He is a witness, I tell them. The mother of the family I am sure is not telling the truth. She knows about my fellow. For two weeks I wait. Sitting in my car in the street in the cold. Nothing. Bah, a dead end.'

The German Jakob and Kalle the Swede in a C-class Merc on the highway into Cape Town, smoke from their cigarillos blueing up the interior, two brown butts already in the ashtray.

'We are lucky it is sunny today. In winter you can be unlucky with the rain. The rain and the wind for days. But it is a nice city to pick up ladies.'

'Fine,' said Kalle.

Jacob gestured ahead at the mountains. 'From here you cannot see the table top properly, only when we get round the Devil's Peak.'

'I know,' said Kalle.

'You have visited here before?'

'Once.'

'When was this?'

'Years ago. Before Mandela.'

'On a collection?'

'No. To fetch some pictures. Art works. Small sketches by Kandinsky from the twenties.'

Jakob said, 'I don't know this artist.'

'Squiggles. Squares. Circles. Not very interesting but worth a lot of money.' Kalle took a long suck on the cigarillo, let the exhale trickle out his nose.

Jakob, at the wheel, glanced sideways. 'I will bet I can tell you this story.'

'It is a Nazi story,' said Kalle.

'Sure. Of course. The grandfather dies and the family find out he is a Nazi. An art thief. The Jews he robbed are holocaust victims. All dead. His family have a bad conscience, they want the pictures returned. But there is no family. So you must take them to a museum.'

'In Berlin.'

'Exactly. This is not the first time I have heard such a story.'

Kalle crushed the butt of the cigarillo in the ashtray.

'I think first we should find the house where Mace Bishop lives,' he said. He opened a map book he'd bought at the airport.

'What is wrong with the GPS?'

'Nothing. I prefer map books. This way we have the whole layout. We can see where we are.'

'I can see where I am when I look out the window.'

Kalle let it go, gave directions that took them on to De Waal Drive up Molteno to the last street beneath the mountain.

'This Mr Bishop has a lot of money,' said Jakob, swinging the car in at the gate. 'Do we see if he is at home?' He cut the engine.

'I think so.'

Kalle got out, buzzed the intercom. He took in the view across the city to the sea. Looked up at the mountain heights.

Jakob joined him, offering a cigarillo. 'Some people live in paradise. Meanwhile I have a flat in Essen with a view of the railway lines.'

Kalle lifted a cigarillo from the box, fitted it to his lips. He pressed the buzzer again.

The two men lit up, stood smoking, watching the cable car ascending.

'We must do that,' said Jakob. 'Go up the mountain. Enjoy some sight-seeing. Even a day in the winelands.'

'When we have found Roland,' said Kalle. 'Then we can relax.'

They finished their cigarillos, ground out the butts on Mace Bishop's cobbled driveway. Calling cards, as Jakob put it.

He rubbed his hands together. In English said, 'As the Yankees say, now we shall brace Mace.'

The two men in macs headed downtown to the offices of Complete Security.

39

THE DINSMOR KIDNAPPING – NEW DEVELOPMENT

Special Correspondent

American businessman Mr Silas Dinsmor disappeared from his Cape Town hotel this morning in what is believed could be a kidnapping.

This follows the violent hijacking of his wife Veronica Dinsmor on Sunday evening shortly after the couple arrived in the Mother City.

There has been no word of her since she was abducted.

In this morning's 'abduction' a police spokesmen said there were no signs of a struggle and that hotel staff were being questioned.

According to a hotel source, Mr Dinsmor was eating breakfast in the dining room with two security personnel from Complete Security and a police detective. While taking a phone call he walked onto the stoep in full view of his bodyguards.

'One minute he was there and the next he was gone,' said the source. 'It doesn't say much for the security company. Or the police.'

The Dinsmors were in the city to support their tender to build casinos in rural areas.

In the earlier attack on the Dinsmors in which Mrs Dinsmor was taken hostage, two kidnappers were shot dead and security operative, Pylon Buso, a co-owner of Complete Security, was wounded.

Attempts to get further comment from the police and Complete Security have been unsuccessful.

Mr Bill Hill, chairman of the newly formed security industry's regulatory authority, said that it was important for clients to 'do their homework' before engaging private security firms.

'Our members are regulated by our code of conduct and audited regularly to ensure they meet the high standards we demand,' he said.

He confirmed that Complete Security was not registered with his association.

The owners of Complete Security, Mr Mace Bishop and Mr Buso, were involved in the arms trade before they ventured into the guarding industry.

40

Mace was hyper.

He'd seen a poster: Another American Kidnapped. He'd bought the newspaper, read the story. Complete Security was head to heel in the crap.

His cellphone rang: the reporter, Rachel Pringle. He pressed it to voicemail. Bloody Chrissakes!

Mace drove to the beach, stared at the sea. For five minutes sat there not moving, hands gripped to the steering wheel. On the passenger seat the front page story screaming at him.

In four days, since Sunday night, everything had changed. Got loose, out of control. He let out a whoosh of breath. This was getting to him. Too much going wrong all at once.

Mace closed his eyes. In the darkness saw the blood pumping out of Oumou, spreading around her, running across the floor to slide about his feet. Her face turned up to him, sad, so sad.

He blinked to refocus: the ocean flat and blue, dotted with kelp gulls. The mountains across the bay ash grey from the summer fires. Seal Island high and clear. Rain was coming. Another cold front.

Christ, thought Mace. Christ, Jesus H.

Then: kill her. Sheemina February. Kill her and stop the nightmare.

He got out of the car, agitated, needing to move. To be in the water swimming, no sound but the bubbles of his breath, the green light around him.

He walked down to the water's edge. A low tide, the sand tracked with plough snails: a pair of them sucking the juice from a dead crab.

What to do?

For the first time realised the kidnapping could take them down, him and Pylon. Collapse the business. The bad press would destroy them. Comments like Hill's nailed tight the coffin lid. Oosthuizen was a sideshow. Unpleasant, unfortunate, a stress they didn't need, but a sideshow. What was killing them was the Dinsmors. This weird situation.

He bent down, plucked the snails from the crab remains, tossed them into the sea. Let the crab have its death.

Godssakes. To be sucked dry by plough snails.

His phone rang: Tami.

'Where're you?'

'At the beach.'

'Oh wonderful. Nice. We've got a hell-on-wheels state of affairs, the boss goes to the beach. You've seen the afternoon newspaper?'

Mace ignored the question. 'Any news?'

'Apart from the bad press. Only that Christa and Pumla need picking up from school. You were supposed to do it.'

'Ah, bloody no.' Mace smacked his head. 'I'd forgotten.'

'Also the newspaper woman's been ringing.'

Tami stopped there, Mace watching a snail sliding towards the dead crab. He flicked it away with the toe of his shoe.

'Can you fetch the girls for me?'

'You're losing it, Mace.'

'Can you?'

'I suppose so.'

'Then you'd best get down to the Longbitch flat. Babysit the Kraut.'

'That's all I need. Europeans have a thing about black women.'

Mace didn't respond.

'I can't wait.'

'Just kick him in the balls, you'll be fine.'

'That gets them going, a bit of S&M.'

'So practice your karate chops. And Tami?'

'Yes.'

'Take the gun.'

'What for?'

'You never know.'

'What're you not telling me?'

'Nothing. It's a babysit, that's all.'

'So then?'

'So just in case.'

'Wonderful.' A pause. Then: 'Mace, you've got to talk to Christa.'

'I do?'

'Yeah, I know. I don't mean that way. She needs help.'

'Ah come on, it's grief. Time, Tami. That's what she needs.'

Again a pause. 'Yeah, sure, alright, whatever. But keep watching her.'

'Thanks for the advice.' An edge in his tone.

'Mace …'

'What?'

'Nothing. Forget it. None of my business.'

'What isn't?' – but she'd disconnected.

Mace looked at the dead crab. A hole in the carapace where a gull had gone in. More snails grooving towards it. He turned away, went back to his car. Some things you couldn't stop.

Mace decided he needed Pylon. The guy had a hole in his arm, a new baby, a post-partum bedonnerd wife, but it didn't matter. Their livelihoods were on the line. He needed Pylon's cool.

Except Pylon wasn't cool when Mace, newspaper in hand, came calling.

'Want to know about Max Roland?' were his first words. Pylon at his front door, blocking Mace's entrance, no intention of inviting him inside. Pylon wearing a tracksuit and slippers, his arm in a sling.

'Yeah,' said Mace. 'Sure.' He moved forward. Stopped when Pylon didn't budge. 'Out here?'

'Shssh.' Pylon keeping his voice low. 'Treasure's asleep.'

Mace whispering back, 'Can we go …' – jerking his thumb at his car. 'Maybe go to the office for a few hours.'

'I can't duck out now.' Pylon rubbing his wounded arm. 'It's urgent though.'

'You didn't say so.'

'I said we had to talk.'

Mace shrugged. 'About what?'

'I told you. About Max bloody Roland. That's what. The guy's a butcher.'

Mace stared at him.

'War-crimes-type butcher. Wanted by the International Criminal Tribunal.'

Mace said, 'Ah come on.'

'I'm not kidding.' Pylon half stepping back into the house. 'I've got footage. Real footage on a DVD.'

'From where?'

'Mart Velaze.'

'Him?'

'Him.'

'And you believe it?'

'Looks bloody real.'

Mace paused, thinking, all the more reason they needed a few hours at the office. 'Just till five. Three hours tops,' he said. 'In that time Treasure's going to be asleep mostly. So's the baby. They wake up, Treasure feeds him, changes his nappy, mother and child go back to sleep. She's not even going to know you're gone.'

'Can't do it.'

Mace stared at his partner. Pylon meeting his eye, then glancing off.

'A big ask, I know. But I'm asking it. We're in shit, you and me.'

'No kidding we're in shit.'

'We've got to find the Dinsmors. Big time. You seen this?' Mace cracked open the newspaper. 'That's the sort of shit we're in.'

Pylon read it, sighed. 'They're killing us. This and Roland. Wait till they get onto Roland. We'll be dead. Might as well close up shop, become night watchmen in the marble foyers. Join Gonz on his pension.' He read the piece again. 'Hill's beating us up because we're not members. I'm going to phone him.'

'And tell him what? That the association's a bunch of arseholes. Government BEE toadies. No more backbone than a slug in a compost heap. Forget it. Don't waste your breath.' Mace shifted from foot to foot. 'Come in for a couple of hours. Help me work the phones. We got to find the Dinsmors.'

'You've got to see the Roland footage.'

'Okay, okay. Can we go?'

Pylon hesitated. 'I can't, Mace, I told you.'

'Can't what?' said Treasure coming up behind Pylon unheard. 'You and Mace going to stand whispering at the door all afternoon? He can come in you know.'

'I can't, Treasure,' said Mace, wondering, what's with the woman and the friendly attitude? 'We've got a bad situation.' He took the newspaper from Pylon, handed it to her.

She read the piece and shrugged, said, 'Where're the girls, Mace?'

The question he'd been waiting for, dreading. 'Tami's bringing them.'

A uh-huh grunt but no comment. She looked at Pylon. 'You're back here by five o'clock, buti. On the nose.'

Pylon got soprano-voiced. 'I'm not going anywhere, babee.'

'I heard. I'm saying you're back by five. I've got the girls here that's fine, they can help. I don't need you drinking beer watching soccer reruns.' She took her matron eyes off Pylon, turned them on Mace. 'You hear: five sharp, he's back.'

In the car heading up the Blue Route to town, Pylon said, 'My mother used to do that. Let me out to play. Yours?'

'No mother,' said Mace.

'That's right. I forgot. You didn't miss anything.'

Mace thought a mother would've been better than a boys' home. Said, 'So what's with the Roland thing?'

'Nasty, nasty, nasty stuff. But you gotta see it first before we decide.'

Mace nodded. 'Fair enough.' Thinking this was going bad faster than fish in summer. Any more shit they'd need trauma counselling. He tried for a change of mood: 'Treasure was unexpected. Coming through that way.'

Pylon laughed. 'Oh yes? You think so? After all these years you still don't know her. There's a price tag, you just couldn't see it. Earlier I almost phoned you to take me away.' He shifted in the seat. 'She gets home from the hospital, puts the baby to sleep and we sit down for a cup of tea. I've made it, one-handed. A parental moment: mom and dad with the baby upstairs. Very sweet. What's on her mind's not so sweet. She's thinking adoption already. Capital A. Also stands for Aids orphans. We've got our baby now, Pylon, I'm told. Now we do our social bit. Can't leave it to whiteys. They're showing us up. I say, How do you know that? When darkies adopt, the kid's the same colour so nobody knows it's adopted. White, it's obvious, that's why they do it. Earns them brownie points. You know what I mean. She's looking at me so hard she doesn't even laugh. Very funny, Pylon, she says. Very funny but it's not a joke, buti. It's up to people like us to show the big boys and girls rolling in money what's their moral responsibility.'

Pylon adjusted his sling to make his arm more comfortable. Grimaced at a lance of pain. 'So when you hear Treasure being nice, what you hear is Treasure writing up a price tag. All I don't know is how big it's going to be.' Pylon jiggled in his seat. 'This car's uncomfortable. We need to get the Merc fixed.'

Mace waved his partner down. 'Uh-uh, no, no. No we don't. Tami got a quote. It's like thousands. Forty grand.'

'And the excess?'

'Seven.'

'That's okay, we can manage that.'

'Sinks our overdraft.'

'It's a business expense. Tax deductible.' Pylon squirmed again. 'You got a spring going to pop through this seat. Where's the Merc now?'

'In a friendly vulture's yard, waiting our instructions.'

'So let's get it done. Save me Jesus, Mace. What you been doing for two days?' Pylon grinning at him.

'Don't start,' said Mace. 'Just don't start.'

They shuffled through the Paradise robots, the traffic thick with moms collecting school kids. A million bucks of SUVs surrounding them. Mace biting his teeth at the thought of Christa without a mom to fetch her. He should've picked her up. A wrong move not doing it.

'I should've made it to the school,' he said, 'to get the girls.'

Pylon didn't respond.

'I've got to organise my day better.'

'Like stop clients being kidnapped.'

'That'd be a start.'

'Tell me about Max Roland.'

'Bit fulla shit. Bit of a prick.'

'But doesn't seem like a killer.'

Mace smiled. 'Who does?' Glanced at Pylon. 'Didn't see him as a situation. Not the way the Dinsmors are.'

'I been thinking about them,' said Pylon. 'I think the call he took was to get him away. And he went. You said the guy's a poker player, a gambler. He's gambling.'

'With his life?'

'Why not? He figures he's got a good hand. You told me they've been in these sort of circumstances before. It's just Texas holdem with an Injun.'

'You reckon?'

'I do. The tricky-dickeys are Max and Magnus.'

'You reckon? You believe that? I don't know.'

'You haven't seen the footage.' Pylon wriggled. 'This spring's right under my bum.' He moved from cheek to cheek. 'Max and Magnus. Not nice people. People we need to keep in our sights. Talking of which where's my gun?'

'Tami's got it.'

'Ah no, Mace. What'd I tell you? One night she could borrow it. Save me Jesus. I want it back. Today. She needs a gun, you give her one of the others. Hear me. To. Day. This. Evening. Latest. I need it.'

'Sure, sure.'

'Not sure sure. I want it back.'

They did the rest of the drive to their office in silence. Mace parked on the square. A scattering of people at the coffee shops, some even outside in the weak sun. Wished he could be at Roxy's for a double espresso and a gruyere croissant. Dab of strawberry jam on the side. His stomach growled. He'd had nothing to eat but plane food. Was about to suggest to Pylon they do this, when he noticed a man sitting on their stoep on the bench they had chained to a heavy-duty eyebolt. Relaxing with a take-away cappuccino.

Pylon groaned. 'You see that man? That's Mart Velaze.'

'What's he want?'

'Guess?'

'Max Roland?'

'Max Roland.'

Mart Velaze stood up, waved. As they approached said, 'This is a cool place. Very classy.'

Pylon introduced him to Mace, the two men shaking hands.

'Pleasure,' said Mart Velaze.

Mace said nothing.

'Don't look round,' said Mart Velaze, 'but you have two guys staking you out. Heavies in rain macs. Sort of macs Europeans wear. They've been sitting in their Merc smoking cigarillos like they're on a film set. What's that old movie?'

Mace unlocked the door.

Mart Velaze clicking his fingers. 'Come on, come on. Casablanca. Bogarde, Dirk Bogarde.'

'How long've they been there?' said Mace, standing back to let Pylon and Mart Velaze inside.

'Before I pitched, and I've been here ten minutes.'

'Bogart,' said Pylon, 'Humphrey.'

'Spot on,' said Mart Velaze. 'Exactly, ha, ha.'

Mace went through to the front room, checked out the two in their Merc. Not exactly being secretive. Sitting quietly in their blue fug staring at the row of semis. He wondered, should he sort them out now, or later?

Heard Pylon saying, 'And why're you here, Mart?' Pylon taking the spook through to the boardroom.

Mace decided leave them for later. They looked settled, not intent on any action. He joined the men in the boardroom.

'Hey, very nice,' Mart Velaze said, taking a look at the pottery exhibit, oohing and aahing. 'I like this. Your wife's, Mace. She was good. Hey, I'm sorry. My condolences. Seriously. That was a bad bad scene. I read about it.'

They sat. Mace and Pylon opposite Mart Velaze, Mart grinning at them.

'Relax, butas. Uncle Mart's here to offer you a deal.'

'About?' said Pylon.

'You seen the footage, Mace?'

Mace shook his head.

'Pity.' Mart looked at Pylon. 'You thought any more on what I let you know this morning?' Mace watched him – the close eyes, the ready smile, the hand loosely holding the polystyrene mug – thinking, an operator. The sort that played all the angles.

'Mace,' he was saying, 'you're up to speed on this?'

Mace inclined his head.

'Excellent.' Mart's eyes breaking contact with them, going up to look out the window at the blue sky over Lion's Head. 'In sum, as outlined in part this morning to Pylon: you guys're looking after two war crims. Oosthuizen, our own death dispenser, and Vasa Babic wanted by the International Criminal Tribunal. Bit kind of low-rent for two strugglistas to be guarding the evil-doers. Not the kind of rep you want in the newspapers. Coming on the back of the kidnapping. Hey, butas?'

'Sounds threatening,' said Pylon.

'It isn't.'

'What's it then?' said Mace, watched the grin spread across Mart Velaze's face.

'It's about a little favour.'

'Oh yeah.'

'Oh yeah.' Mart Velaze leant back tipping the chair onto two legs. Kept his hands on the table for balance. 'I could' – he glanced up at the blue sky again – 'dress it up for you. Talk about patriotism. Doing something for your country. All that kind of crap. But I won't insult you. Thing is this' – he paused, sucked on his lower lip – 'thing is our government doesn't want to make two war criminals rich. This sticks in the minister's craw.' He lifted one hand off the table to pinch the skin on his own throat. 'Now, okay, for you guys guarding them's a job. Maybe you see yourselves like lawyers who defend murderers. Everyone has a right to a defence.' He laughed. 'Nice pun, hey?' Brought the chair forward, both elbows on the tabletop, his hands out towards Mace and Pylon. 'As you know, as you've been told no doubt by the mighty Magnus, he's got the best weapons system for our ships. Undoubtedly. The Europeans are back in the Stone Age. We're talking serious difference in the technology. Like the difference between spears and semi-auto pistols. No question, the minister wants it, their system. For us, and to sell on. To earn foreign exchange to build houses, hospitals, schools. But he also, the minister, wants to buy the European system, because with that comes what is called offset deals. Things they will do for us. Build factories, smelters, power stations. Help us create jobs, put food into hungry stomachs. This is very concerning to the minister.' Mart Velaze made full-on eye contact from Pylon to Mace. 'So now in plain language, in confidence, nothing to do with the minister, nothing to do with government, something you didn't even hear: how about you get it for us? The software.'

Mace kept his eyes on Mart Velaze. The NIA man leaving the proposition hanging there. A smile, raised eyebrows doing the quizzical, come on, guys.

'No,' said Pylon.

'No?' Mart Velaze rode back on his chair. 'Really, no? These are two bad dudes we're talking about. Check out the video again. Two bad dudes who are about to get so rich they're gonna stink of money.' He looked at Mace. 'What do you say, Mr Bishop?'

Mace said, 'The software wouldn't help you.'

'Why's that?'

'It only runs on Oosthuizen's computers. He's locked them together: hardware and software.'

Mart Velaze brushed it aside. 'That's sorted. Ages ago we sorted that. What we couldn't sort was the programme because the programme was in Vasa Babic's head. Except right now it's pouring out of Vasa Babic's head into a computer so that Mr Magnus Oosthuizen can do his presentation to the defence committee tomorrow. All you've gotta do is copy it. Simple. Then we use the budget to buy the European system for the offsets. Sorry Mr Oosthuizen, but your pitch was unsuccessful. Meanwhile, back at the ranch, we've got a home-grown system in our ships and millions pouring in from on-sales. South Africa wins. No fuss.'

'No,' said Pylon.

'Remember,' said Mart Velaze, 'we're talking seriously evil men. Men who have done the worst that men can do. Men who deserve to be punished. Men who will not be punished.' He brought his chair forward, stood up. 'Think about it. Think about what you are condoning, their crimes.'

Mace watched him walk to the boardroom door. Watched him turn to grin at them.

'Poetic justice, butas. Think about it.' He drummed his fingers on the door. 'How about I give you till five?'

'And if we don't?'

'Hey, then you don't. Your conscience. On your head be it. No threats. No smashing hands. You do or you don't. Up to you. Moral integrity's what the philosophers call it.'

'Velaze,' said Mace, getting up from the table, moving towards him. 'Don't try it.'

'What?'

'Breaking into our safe house.'

'Wouldn't dream of it. Cheers, my brothers, think on these things.' He went down the passage ahead of Mace, and out onto the stoep. 'Your surveillance's still there,' he said. 'Probably bounty hunters after Mr Babic. News travels fast.' With that he walked away. Shouted back, 'Till five.'

Mace stayed on the stoep looking at the men in macs. They stared back at him. Eventually got out of their car. Mart Velaze was right, they both looked like 1940s PIs.

'You looking for me, gents?' said Mace as they came in at the gate.

'Ja, good afternoon,' said the shorter of the two, flicking his cigarillo butt into the road. 'We are hoping you can help us. I am Jakob and this is Kalle. Perhaps we can go inside for a minute of your time.'

'Depends.' Mace folded his arms across his chest. The men weren't threatening, if anything looked as if they could do with a few hours' sleep.

Jakob gave a quick laugh. 'Of course.'

The other one, Kalle, holding an A4 envelope, seemed distracted, almost sad.

'We are here about Vasa Babic. The man you know as Max Roland.'

'There's a thing,' said Mace, wondering what Mart Velaze knew about the men made him say they were bounty hunters. 'So much interest in Max Roland.'

'Please,' said Kalle, 'we will not take much of your time.'

'Nothing much we can tell you,' said Mace. 'He's our client. He has our confidentiality.'

Kalle frowned. Jakob nodded. 'Ja, ja, that is no problem. We will do the talking.'

Mace gave it a moment, wondering if Mart Velaze was right about these men. Said, 'You got five minutes' – standing back for them to enter.

In the boardroom said to Pylon, 'Some friends of Max Roland.'

Jakob gave his quick laugh. 'That is a good joke, Mr Bishop.'

Kalle said, 'We will not waste your time.' He took two sheets of paper out of the envelope. 'If you do not know, your client Mr Max Roland is wanted for war crimes in Kosovo. His name is Vasa Babic.' He gave the papers to Mace and Pylon. ICT letterhead, photo of Max Roland, a request for his detention to face various listed charges. Signed Carla Del Ponte, Office of the Prosecutor, International Criminal Tribunal. 'We are private investigators with the power to arrest Mr Roland.' He took two more letters from the envelope. 'This is a job we do for which we are contracted. You will see there our authorisation.'

'Bounty hunters,' said Mace, not looking at the letter.

Jakob snorted. Kalle said, 'Some people call us that, yes. Please remember the people we are seeking are criminals.'

'Somebody else's just mentioned that.'

'I am sorry?' said Kalle.

Mace shook his head. 'Nothing. Thinking aloud.'

Pylon tapped a finger on the two letters. 'They're computer printouts. You could've made them this morning.'

'Please phone the Tribunal,' said Jakob. 'They will confirm our position.' He placed his cellphone in the centre of the table. 'The number is in the contacts. Also on the letters. Otherwise you must have such a facility for international inquiries, yes?'

Mace and Pylon exchanged a glance, enough to say, let's take it for the moment.

'What're you asking?' said Pylon.

'That you take us to him,' said Kalle. 'He must come back to the Hague for his trial.'

Silence. City growl filled the room. Mace looked at Oumou's vase, shifting to face the bounty hunters sitting opposite looking back at him.

He said, 'No can do. We got to get this verified.'

Pylon coming in before Mace'd finished. 'This's South Africa, my friends. We don't do renditions.'

'It is not a kidnapping,' said Jakob, riding back on his chair the way Mart Velaze had done.

'We can get papers from your court but this takes time.' Kalle smoothed down the envelope flap. 'You can keep the letters.' He stood.

Jakob rocked forward, leant halfway across the table. 'Before we can get papers Vasa Babic will disappear again. A lot of people want justice for what Babic did. I ask you to remember them.' He straightened up.

Mace and Pylon got to their feet.

'We know this is a difficult question for you,' said Kalle. 'At five o'clock we will come for your answer.'

'And now?' said Pylon when the German and the Swede had gone.

He and Mace upstairs in Mace's office. Pylon nursing his arm on the couch, Mace at the window staring up at the mountain. A high mackerel sky sliding in from the southern Atlantic: the harbinger of bad weather.

'Dunno,' Mace said, turning into the room. 'Don't bloody know.'

'Perhaps I should phone the security regulators ask them for the ethical line? What the code of conduct says.'

Mace dropped into his desk chair. 'In one afternoon, hey! For shit's sake. Twice in one afternoon we're asked to piss on a client. Steal his software, give him up to the railroad men.'

'He's a crappy individual.'

'I know. I've spent time holding his hand. We're still betraying a client.'

'This's true.'

'And what? You don't see an issue?'

Pylon eased off his shoes, swung his legs onto the couch. The two men staring into the moral wilderness. One minute. Five minutes. Ten minutes before Pylon said, 'Take a look at the footage.'

Mace slotted the DVD into his laptop, got a taste of Vasa Babic doing his thing. As the first images came up said, 'Yup, that's our boykie.' At the end Mace ejected the disc, clipped it back into its case. Sat for a couple of minutes staring at the blank screen. Said, 'Not a nice man.'

'No,' said Pylon. 'Got it in one. You check the deformed pinkie?'

'I did. Makes our decision easier then, do you think?'

'Dunno. Dunno what to make on this one.'

Mace closed down his laptop. 'Perhaps we'd better come at this slowly.'

'We got two hours.'

'Should be time enough.'

'Meaning you've made up your mind?'

Mace fluttered his hand. 'Maybe. Maybe not. You?'

'Maybe. Maybe not.'

They sat in silence until Pylon said, 'One thing to another: you still aiming to take out Sheemina February?'

Mace nodded. 'Probably tonight. If she's home.'

'By yourself?'

'What? I should take back-up? Tami, for instance?'

Pylon smiled. 'No. Me, for instance.'

'Uh-uh, no. Thanks but no thanks. This's my one. I've been in there.'

'You've what?'

'Been in there.'

'Into her place? When?'

'Last night. Early this morning actually.'

'Save me Jesus.' He stared at Mace, shook his head. 'And you don't say anything?'

'I just have.'

'Ai yai yai.' Pylon let out a long sigh. 'My brother, that was not clever.'

'No big deal.'

'No big deal the man says.'

'Look she wasn't there. It was a recce. Now I know the place. The layout.'

'What about the cameras? Have to be cameras.'

'What about them? Guy dressed in black wearing a balaclava. No skin showing. Could be anyone. Woman like Sheemina February's got to be on someone's hit list. Other than mine.'

'It's a bullshit idea.'

'You've got a better plan?'

'Standard traffic-light hit. Why not? What's wrong with that? Works every time, you do it right. We pull up next to her, you give her a cheesy grin to think on when she's dead. Wop, wop. Everyone in the cars about us plugged into iPods, talking on their cells, having sexual fantasies. What're they going to notice? Naathing. Lights change, we drive slowly away. Going to be another couple of minutes before anyone checks why she's not moving. Perfect situation.'

'For a movie.'

'Happens all the time on the Flats, in the townships.'

'Thanks, but no thanks.'

'What's good about it is no residue. Doing it in her flat's just crazy. A fraught condition, full of traps. You're on the CCTV, the cops can tell your body size. Forensic's going to pick up hair, footprints, dirt, fabric threads. All kinds of shit. Maybe someone sees you. Some insomniac staring out his window, someone driving past. There's more worries than walking across a snake pit.'

'I checked it out twice, it's okay, end of story.'

Pylon held up his good hand. 'Just a suggestion.'

Mace said, 'Brings us back to Max Roland. The other thing I meant to mention earlier is Oosthuizen's spun a shit story saying it was going to be a long deal. Now he tells me after he's done the presentation tomorrow we're history.'

'Nice.'

'Bloody nice.'

'So what's stopping us giving up Roland?'

'Professional ethics.'

'Bugger that.'

They stared again into the wilderness.

Mace said, 'One thing nobody's talked is money.'

'My thoughts,' said Pylon. 'They're scoring out of Max Roland but we're supposed to be suckers. Patriotic schmucks.'

'Like you said, bugger that.'

'So for money we'd do it?'

'Makes it worth thinking about.'

Mace's cellphone rang: an undisclosed number.

The voice said, 'Pike, this is Silas Dinsmor.'

41

'This is about Veronica,' the voice'd said to Silas Dinsmor, 'it's a business call between ourselves. Tell them that, your breakfast friends.'

Silas Dinsmor'd said to the cop and the security people, 'Excuse me, it's my office' – getting up from the table.

'That's good,' said the voice. 'Walk away towards the sliding doors, slowly, that's right, now pause. Stop, consider this: anything you do wrong will put a bullet in Veronica's head. Got it? Let me hear that in your words, say: Yeah, that's right, that's the deal.'

'Yeah, that's right, that's the deal.'

'Nice one, Silas.'

'Where are you?'

'No questions. Hear me, I ask the question. Let's go onto the stoep now, what you'd call the porch. Drift over there, like it's no big deal because it ain't – to use your lingo again.'

Silas Dinsmor did as asked, left the door open. Outside, the air chill and damp.

'Good fella, Silas. Listen up: there's a van in the car park, the logo on the panels says International Flowers. What you do now is walk up and down the stoep – porch – twice and you say into your phone: the deal's gotta go down today. That was our arrangement. That's what we agreed. Got it.'

'Yes,' said Silas.

'Okay, say it.'

Silas did.

'Good man,' said the voice. 'On the other matter, the matter of your wife, we're planning to keep our word so we trust you keep yours.'

'Where's she, where's my wife?'

'No questions, Silas. Don't make me repeat myself. It works me up. You'll get the answers in a moment. Now, what we're gonna do is walk you down the stairs and into the van. Go.'

Silas Dinsmor hesitated, looked at the group in the breakfast room. The cop talking, the security man laughing, the woman Tami had been watching him. But she was bent to her food now. And the van would be out of her sight.

'Go.'

'I'm going.'

'Keep walking. Keep thinking of Veronica.'

'You'd better …'

'She's fine, Silas, while you keep walking. See the van, the one with the sliding door open. Get in, close the door.'

Silas Dinsmor obeyed.

'Good man. I'm sorry there isn't a seat. Your pants'll get dirty but it can't be helped. Won't be long now you'll have the lovely Dancing Rabbit in your arms. Au revoir, Silas, been good talking to you.'

Inside the van was dark, dank, smelt of vegetation. No cushions, not even newspaper to sit on. Silas Dinsmor groaned. The Third World was a pain in the butt.

The van pulled off gently, in no hurry to leave the hotel grounds. Silas Dinsmor trying to follow the route, a right, a left, an intersection, the on-ramp to the highway. At first the journey was slow, the stop-start of dense traffic, exhaust fumes making him cough. The commuter crawl eased, the van picked up speed. With the speed came a chill factor. Silas Dinsmor hugged his arms tightly across his chest. He wore only a cotton shirt fastened with the turquoise-inset bolo tie, slacks and a light jacket. He needed a coat. And padding. The metal was hard on his backside, jarred against his spine. Twice he sprawled when the driver braked sharply. Once slid across the corrugated floor as the van cornered fast. 'Hey,' he shouted, dusting grit from his hands. 'Hey, mister, drive carefully.' Banged on the metal panel separating the cab from the pickup box but got no reaction from the driver.

Was this worse than Colombia? Silas Dinsmor reckoned that it probably was. At least in Colombia they had been willing to talk: until now these people hadn't handed out any agendas.

His cellphone rang: a blocked number.

'Silas,' said the voice, Veronica's voice. 'Silas, are you alright?'

'My baby,' he said. 'Dancing Rabbit. What's happening?' – breaking into Choctaw. 'On the video you looked unconscious. Those dead bodies.'

'They're bringing you to me, honey' she said. 'I'm fine. Everything's fine.'

'Talk to me,' he said. 'Talk to me. Are you hurt? On the video you looked hurt. Why don't you speak Choctaw?'

'I'm just so pleased to hear your voice.'

Not the Dancing Rabbit of the Colombia debacle. None of the self-assurance.

'You don't sound fine.'

'I am, I am. Believe me, honey. Everything's going to work out.'

'Then talk Choctaw.'

'They're bringing you to me. It's all been a misunderstanding. Crossed wires.'

'Some crossed wires when people get killed.'

'It's fine. It's fine. Believe me.'

'It doesn't sound fine.'

'I'm with a real lady.'

'I don't like it, Dancing Rabbit, my baby. Not any of it.'

'I'm going now,' said Veronica. 'See you soon.'

The phone disconnected.

Silas Dinsmor would've been less troubled facing a rattlesnake, Stateside. Brought out a cold sweat in his armpits.

An hour out of the city by his cellphone clock, the van slowed, turned onto gravel.

'Open up,' he heard the driver shout. A man said something inaudible. The van started forward, the wheels spinning to take traction. The going rough and potholed, the scrape of vegetation against the chassis. Silas Dinsmor was jerked about, had to jam himself in a corner to keep upright. He kneeled, then rocked back into a crouch, let his thighs cushion the jolts, the downhill slope forcing him to jiggle like a Russian dancer.

The ride ended abruptly, unbalancing him. He was still sprawled when the sliding door opened. A young man grinned at him.

'We's arrived,' he said.

'What're you playing at?' Silas Dinsmor eased himself out of the van. Before him a stone cottage, beyond the sea. 'You didn't need to do that.'

'Gotta stop, you know.'

A woman appeared at the cottage door.

'You can go now,' she called out, dismissing the driver.

He mumbled something, slammed shut the panel door.

'Don't be cheeky,' said the woman, coming towards them across the sand. 'Go on.'

The driver did, accelerating away with a wheelspin.

'Young men can be very tedious,' she said. Reached out to Silas Dinsmor, touched him on the shoulder. 'My name's Sheemina February. Your wife's inside. Come.' She turned back to the cottage. 'I'm sorry about the drive out. Must have been uncomfortable. Normally it's a pleasant drive once you've escaped the city. From the top of the hill back there you can see the mountain. The picture postcard version. On a day like today it's quite spectacular. The clarity of the air. The island too, if the island interests you. Mandela and all that.'

'Where's my wife?' said Silas Dinsmor.

'Inside. I asked her to wait inside. Until the driver had gone.' Sheemina February stood aside. 'Please, go in.'

And there was Dancing Rabbit springing towards him.

Sheemina February watched them clinch.

How sweet. How touching.

She went to stand at the window, facing the sea. The stainless steel .32 lay on the breakfast table where she'd put it out of curiosity: to see if Dancing Rabbit liked guns more than she'd admitted. Smeared low on the horizon was a dark edge that hadn't been there earlier, a cold front pushing in. Tonight it would be wet again. Howling a gale. Nothing more comforting than a storm to Sheemina February's way of thinking.

'We're going,' she heard Silas Dinsmor say.

And turned around. He held the tiny gun pointed at her.

'I'm disappointed,' she said. 'I thought Veronica and I had reached an understanding.'

Silas Dinsmor edged his wife towards the kitchen and the back door.

'I don't know who you are, lady. And I don't care. Guns are not among our business tools. We don't kidnap people. We don't kill people. Good people are our business partners. But I will use this one.'

'I warned you,' said Veronica. 'We are not soft targets.'

'Silas,' said Sheemina February, 'you're holding a gun now. Pointing it at a business partner. A potential business partner. Talk to him Veronica, dissuade him.'

'Like hell, ma'am,' he said. 'We'd sooner do business with George Bush than the likes of you.'

'Sit down, Silas. You and Veronica sit down. I'll make more coffee.' Ignoring the gun still pointed at her, she took the Bialetti to the sink, unscrewed it.

'It's best you let us leave,' said Veronica. 'We'll get out of your life.'

'That's the point, Veronica. I don't want you out of my life. That's what we've been talking about all morning.'

'I'm not joking, ma'am. We're going to walk out now.'

Sheemina February dropped the pot, spun on them. 'And go where, Silas? Tell me. Along the beach? Back up to the road? Where, huh? We're on a wild stretch here, Silas. You wouldn't make it out.' She stared at him, went back to rinsing the coffee pot. 'Know this too, if you don't shoot me dead I'm going to have you back here inside twenty minutes. And you don't look like a shooting man, Silas. So sit down.'

Silas and Veronica Dinsmor moved back.

'Try it,' said Sheemina February, 'if you must.' She heaped spoons of coffee into the Bialetti's basket, screwed the pieces together. 'All you're doing is delaying our discussions. Delaying the time before I call someone to drive you back to your hotel. One way or the other we're going to talk. The best way is here, at this table, with a cup of coffee.' She set the pot on the gas hob, turned up the flame. Watched Silas Dinsmor lose heart, the hand with the gun slowly lowering. She smiled at Veronica. 'Sometimes, Al Capone got it wrong. Now sit and let's parley.'

'Why?' said Silas Dinsmor.

'Why what?' Sheemina February arched her eyebrows. 'Why should we talk?'

'Why, all this? All this violence.'

'A mistake.'

'That's it? A mistake. All this … this bullshit's for nothing?' Silas Dinsmor waving his gun hand around.

'The gun's loaded,' said Sheemina February, 'it's off safety, it's got a sensitive trigger. Best I put it away.' She held out her hand. 'Please.'

'I want to know why.'

'The gun.'

He gave it to her. She slipped on the safety, dropped the tiny Guardian into the pocket of her apron.

'I've explained it to Veronica.'

'Well now explain it to me.'

Veronica sat down where she'd been sitting, pushed a chair out for Silas. Said something in a strange language that Sheemina February didn't catch.

'English,' she said. 'Be polite.' She took a chair opposite them. 'You stepped into a messy situation, Silas. You and Veronica. A local situation you couldn't have known about. You were at risk, as I've told Veronica.

'From you.'

'Not from me. Believe this: I am not your enemy.'

'We had security.'

'Sure, you had security, a joke outfit. Two has-been gun-runners trying to scrape a buck together. Some security. Worst track record in the city. My intention was to secure you both.'

'Through kidnapping!'

Sheemina February nodded. 'I needed to send a message.'

'You did that, ma'am. To me you sent a message that you're mad. Crazy. Loco.' He tapped his forehead.

'A message to others, Silas. Not you. Others. Others who'd have dumped your bodies in the Black River days ago. People who'd still like to do that. Now can we leave this and get onto the serious business?'

'This is serious, lady. Damn serious.'

'Sheemina,' said Sheemina February. 'Not lady or ma'am. Sheemina. That's my name.' She smiled. No mirth in the quick twitch of her lips.

Veronica put her hand on her husband's arm. 'Listen to her, Silas.'

'And forget what we've been through? That she caused it?'

'Put it aside. Please. There's a way out of this.'

'The way out of this is through the door.'

'Silas.'

The coffee percolated, sent a splash out the spout that doused the gas flame. Sheemina February got up. 'Listen to her, Silas,' she said. 'We've discussed the deal. If your wife can see the advantages I'm sure you will.' She poured the coffee, set two mugs before them. 'I'm going outside while you talk.' She took off the apron, put on a long black coat. Transferred the .32 to a coat pocket. 'When you're finished I'll go with whatever decision you make.'

'And one of them's we can walk away?'

'It is.'

'Then that's our option.'

'Hear your wife, Silas. Don't jump to conclusions.'

She left them to it. Went onto the beach to stand in the sun. Felt the winter heat soaking into the black material. He'd fall her way, no doubt of it. Veronica had smelt the money. Silas would too.

She pressed through a call to Magnus Oosthuizen. When he came on she could hear the yapping of his dog in the background. Real moffie's bitch.

'How's your boy, Magnus?' she said. 'All safe and sound?'

'Perfectly,' he said. 'In a pisspot place. A dump. But safe and sound.'

'Better than in the Hague from his point of view. Though if you have to be in jail, that's the place, I'm told. Tribunal cells make Hiltons look cheap.' She held the phone away while the dog yapped, heard Oosthuizen say, 'Go piepie, Chin-chin. Piepie on the grass.' She couldn't imagine what it was that people saw in dogs. The way they talked to them in that weird language. Said, 'Have you been in touch?'

'I have, yes.'

'He'll meet the deadline?'

'No question.'

'He understands the urgency. That there can't be any buggering around. That we – you – need it tonight.'

'Of course.'

'You'll be seeing him?'

'I'm with him.'

'At the moment?'

'At the moment.'

'How sweet,' said Sheemina February. She walked along the tide line, impressed by the sheer body count: two cormorants, a gannet, a blowfish, small lobsters, crabs. Feathers washing in the shallows. As if a grenade had gone off. 'You still there?' she said. Oosthuizen doing one of his silences, except this was on her time.

'I am.'

'I'm checking,' she said, 'because the timing is important. Critical. When it happens I want to know that he's finished. That you will be there tomorrow for the presentation, fully prepared.'

'I will be,' said Oosthuizen. 'I know the scene.'

She disconnected. From where she stood the front of the cottage was obscured by a dune, only the roof visible. She couldn't see the Dinsmors, they couldn't see her. She could see the track leading up the hill and the Dinsmors weren't on it. Nor had she expected they would be. By now Silas would have the hot raw smell of filthy lucre in his nostrils. She smiled. Made some more calls to ensure her plans were in place. By tomorrow Mace Bishop would be closing up shop, taking residence in the gutter. Couldn't happen to a nicer man.

By the time she went back inside the Dinsmors were waiting where she'd left them. Silas Dinsmor with a slump to his shoulders, Veronica leaning forward, her face in her hands. Sheemina February wanted to tell Silas to sit up straight. Show his backbone.

'Well,' she said.

Veronica Dinsmor looked at her, Silas didn't.

'You've got a deal,' he said.

'Excellent,' said Sheemina February, taking off her coat. 'You could look more enthusiastic about it though, Silas.' She draped the coat over the back of a couch.

'Give me one reason.'

'Money. Money's always something to be enthusiastic about.'

'Because you're getting it and I'm not.'

Sheemina February punched up the gas heater.

'It's an investment, Silas, that you're making. Development capital. This is how projects get funded, as you well know. One minute.' She fetched a briefcase from her bedroom, slapped down some papers before the Dinsmors. 'Here's the detail. All you want to know on what's planned with these casinos. CVs of all the major players in the consortium. Reads like a who's who of struggle heroes. These are honourable people, Silas. People who sacrificed themselves during the apartheid years. They suffered. What drives them now is an obsession to build up their country for the benefit of all.' She sat down, her hand on the prospectus. 'Read it. Take your time. But even before you do that I'm asking you to come in with us. Share your expertise. Help us create the v entures, provide jobs, give people some hope where they've got nothing now.

'Look at the photographs, Silas.' She opened the prospectus at the back. 'This one, here. See these scattered huts. Once this was a village, now it's old people and Aids orphans. They live on grants. When they get them. When they're not robbed on payout day.

Mostly the old people drink, we all would out there. Sometimes the children eat cowpats they're so hungry.

'This could change that, Silas. Make them part of the modern world. Show them that someone cared about their lives.' She sat back. Smiled at the Dinsmors. 'End of sermon. You read that, you'll know you've made the right decision. Meanwhile I'll get my office to draw up the contract.'

'Then what?'

'Then the driver will take you back to the city.'

He stared at her. 'I don't believe you.'

'In your place I probably wouldn't either. But these're your options. Once you sign the contract we're partners. We're talking about a lot of money.'

'Five million bucks is a lot of money.'

'Not your investment, Silas. The returns. Go through the figures. Look at the projections. This is not Mickey Mouse, I'd call it big money. Long-term money that'll make five million US seem like small change.'

Silas Dinsmor bowed his head, pinched the bridge of his nose with the thumb and forefinger of his left hand. His wife laid her arm on his shoulder.

'I can't do the transfer today,' he said. 'These things take time.'

'You can set the wheels in motion, Silas. In twenty-four hours it'll all be said and done. When that happens we sign the paperwork and viola.'

He released his nose, white impressions on his skin from the pressure of his fingers.

'Alright.' He took out his cellphone. 'On your word that we'll be released.'

'On my word. You're free agents already.'

'We could run after you've let us go.'

Sheemina February unleashed a wide smile, light striking ice in her blue eyes. 'You could. But you wouldn't get far.'

'Now you're threatening.'

'Not a threat. Reality check for you. This's my city. I know how it works.' Again the smile, the ice glint. 'But I'd rather trust you, Silas. Rather that you learnt to trust me.'

Silas Dinsmor dialled his office, left a message to call him urgently.

'Now all we have to do is wait. But while we're doing that I'll get the contract drawn up,' said Sheemina February. She pressed speed dial to her office. 'And arrange a car for after lunch. I do an excellent moules marinieres with local black mussels. And there's a fine sauvignon blanc in the fridge. It'll be worth waiting for.'

In the afternoon Sheemina February had the Dinsmors taken to Cavendish Mall.

'When the money's in our account, we'll sign the contracts,' she'd said before they left the cottage. 'Till then enjoy Cape Town. See the sights.'

Dancing Rabbit couldn't wait to get into the car. 'Honey,' she'd said before the door closed, 'you might make good mussels but I don't like your way.'

Silas Dinsmor hadn't said anything, only given a brief nod.

At the mall the driver took them to the Vida e Caffè. Said he'd been told to leave them there. Was gone before they could stammer out a response.

Silas ordered two double macchiatos, put through a call to Mace Bishop. 'Pike, this is Silas Dinsmor,' he said.

42

There was Silas Dinsmor and Dancing Rabbit sitting on red seats at a white table at the Vida e Caffè. Dotted about the other tables a mother and baby, three sales reps with laptops displaying Excel sheets, a couple of students, two women in coats and scarves hovering over skinny lattes, the Lindt chocolate squares untouched on the table.

Very clever, Mace thought, to drop them off here. Better than the side of a road, very considerate. Kidnappers with heart. A pissed-off cramp churned its way through his stomach into his mouth, bringing up a bad taste. Like the world and its Chihuahua were jerking his chain.

He saw Dancing Rabbit not looking all that cool about the situation either, her face bruised and cut, washed out with no lipstick, bags beneath her eyes. Staring into the bookshop opposite at some mental horror, the skin furrowed across her forehead, tight.

Silas bright as a starling though. Scoping the scene, spotting Mace and Pylon about the same time they saw him. Stood up with a wide smile to hold out the afternoon paper folded to the story headlined: 'The Dinsmor kidnapping – new development'.

As they approached, said, 'You're being crucified, partners, so now you've got some good news for the morning paper.' Coming over like the last forty-eight hours had been a walk on the beach, or that he hadn't been disappeared for most of the day. Bucko Silas getting a kick out of things.

The two ladies glanced over, bright red lips and pearly teeth.

'What's going on?' said Mace, brushing aside the newspaper, leaning down on the Dinsmors' table.

'Quietly,' said Pylon beside him.

'That's not the attitude, Pike.' Silas Dinsmor dropping the paper as he sat. 'What we want is some concern. Like we meant something to you as clients.' He smiled. 'You want a coffee?'

'What we want,' said Mace, 'is an explanation.'

The mom with her baby also giving them some attention. The mom jiggling the baby, shish, shish. Mace aware of the onlookers but keeping his eyes on Silas Dinsmor.

Pylon said to Dancing Rabbit. 'You alright, Mrs Dinsmor? You need to see a doctor? We can arrange that for you. Or trauma counsellor. The police have them.' His voice low.

'What'd she want to do that for?' said Silas, the American tone loud and clear. 'She's fine. I'm fine. You can get us back to our hotel and we'll call it quits. Go our ways. Forget about this … shall we call it unpleasantness?'

'I'm alright,' said Veronica Dinsmor in a voice so quiet Mace hardly caught it under the noise of the coffee orders.

'Not that easy,' he said to Silas Dinsmor. 'Your wife was kidnapped. You were kidnapped. People are dead. The police've opened a file. They need to talk to you, get an explanation. Which is what we need.'

This stopped the laptop reps and the students.

Pylon said, 'Not here, Mace. Let's go.' Putting his good hand on Mace's shoulder.

Mace shrugged him off.

'I wouldn't say kidnapped,' said Silas Dinsmor. 'More like a private business meeting.'

Veronica Dinsmor nodded her head. 'Please. Please. Can we go to the hotel? If you don't mind.'

'We don't,' said Pylon.

'Captain Gonsalves is going to be at the hotel,' Mace said to Silas. He looked at Veronica, lowered his voice. 'What I'd like to know is why this's suddenly not an issue?'

She was trembling, her eyes liquid.

Mace poked at the newspaper. 'You've read what they're saying about us.'

Pylon coming in. 'Mace, let's go. Leave it, okay.'

Mace keeping at her: 'They're wiping us out. Crucified's got nothing on it. We're dead meat. After this we can close up shop, Mrs Dinsmor. Go twiddle our thumbs. What we don't know is why. Why this's happened with you. So what's going on?' He looked at her, ignoring the teary eyes. 'People've been shot. Pylon's got a hole in his arm. We're being hung out. Because of you two.'

'You shot them.'

Mace nodded. 'I did. Correction: one of them. That's what we do in that situation to save our clients.'

Pylon, bumped against him, said, 'Mace, not here.'

Mace glimpsing the mother dumping the baby into its pram, getting out in a scurry. The ladies open-mouthed, can you believe it, doll! The students watching. But Mace knowing he was too far into the scene to end it.

'We see video footage of you tied up,' he said. 'Two dead bodies.'

One of the sales reps went, 'Oh shit!' loud enough that it got Mace's attention. Mace glared at them only an instant, came back to Veronica Dinsmor.

'This morning your husband disappears on a private business meeting. And then here you are, both of you, having a quiet coffee in a shopping mall. Mr Dinsmor telling us: let's all go home 'n forget about this. Drama's over. And guess what, we don't need you anymore. We're safe and sound in your beautiful city.' Mace hit the table with his fist. 'What's happening here?'

That did it for the reps at the spreadsheet, had them closing down their computers like they had an urgent call schedule to maintain. Only the students and the latte ladies stayed riveted, unfazed, enjoying this. The one woman loosening her scarf to show some cleavage.

Pylon eased up Dancing Rabbit, Silas Dinsmor getting to his feet. Pylon said, 'Mace, let's get out of here. We can do this in the car.'

Mace stepped close to Silas Dinsmor. 'This's been crap from the go. You don't tell us jack shit. You think you're American, you can come in here and change the scene any which way you want. Forget it, pal. It's not like that.'

In the car cutting through the suburb to the hotel, Silas Dinsmor took a softer line.

'We'll give you good press,' he said, leaning forward from the back seat, obscuring Mace's vision in the rearview mirror. 'Talk to reporters, make sure you don't take any of the flak on our score.'

'Bit late for that,' said Mace.

'We can put it right. Straighten out the misunderstandings. Give it good spin.'

'Like what? That your wife wasn't actually kidnapped.'

'She was but I wasn't. You with me? I was AWOL this morning. Guilty as charged. I'll take the rap. My fault, I ducked out of your protection. Foolish. Stupid. Dangerous even.' He leaned back. 'I had my reasons.'

'Which are?' said Pylon, holding on to his damaged arm as Mace swung a tight corner.

'Strategic,' said Silas Dinsmor. 'Like I've said, business-related.' He let it trail into silence.

'Funny goddamned way to do business.'

Mace glanced in the rearview mirror at Veronica Dinsmor, her head turned away from her husband, eyes fixed on the passing houses: palaces set in rhododendron gardens. From the stillness of her she was off in some private zone. And she was supposed to be the tough cookie able to talk Colombian hard men out of a kidnapping. Two days with the locals, she'd taken leave of the planet. Mace tuned back to Silas Dinsmor.

'You better have a story for the cops. Something they can get their heads around.'

'It's not gonna be a story,' said Silas Dinsmor, smoothing a hand over his hair, bunching it around his ponytail. 'It'll be the truth, so help me God.'

At the hotel, Captain Gonsalves ushered them into a conference room he'd set up. Got them seated round a circular table with a silver tray of bottled water in the centre. Mace and Pylon going right to the chairs nearest the door, the two Dinsmors other side of Gonsalves. Once they were seated, the captain coming over officious, reading Silas the sort of riot act that Mace couldn't, not to a client.

Silas apologetic, humble, moving his jaw like he was eating the pie.

At the end Gonsalves returned to his opening riff: 'You're here under our protection, the protection of the South African police, not only the services of Complete Security. In this matter there's gotta be some cooperation. Considering your wife's abducted, you have a video of dead bodies, we are talking about a fraught situation, kidnapping, murder, but you still go walkabout. That's irresponsible behaviour. Out of order. Why's that, Mr Dinsmor?' The captain, hunched forward, taking out a packet of cigarettes that he toyed with, turning it in cartwheels between his thumb and forefinger.

Silas Dinsmor nodded like a toy dog on the rear window of a long-finned Valiant.

'I'd like to hear an explanation.' Gonsalves doing a tap tap tap with his cigarette packet. 'We've got a case opened of kidnapping. We've got four bodies. The sort of thing we can't wish away. So what's happening, Mr Dinsmor? As you Yanks say, what's going down?'

Mace thinking he hadn't seen the captain quite so stung in a long while.

Silas Dinsmor coughed against the back of his hand. 'Captain, I would ask if this can wait.'

There it was. Just as he'd thought. Mace sat back wondering what Gonsalves could say to this. Nothing he could say. They didn't want to talk to him, they didn't have to. As long as they made statements.

'My wife's safe. I'm safe. Another twelve hours isn't going to change anything.'

'Another twelve hours,' said Gonsalves, 'we can close the file. Know what I'm saying?' Looking at Veronica Dinsmor's bowed head. 'Mrs Dinsmor, maybe a description?'

Dancing Rabbit brought up her face, put her wounded eyes on the captain. 'I didn't see him. He wore a hood, a what d'you call it?'

'Balaclava.'

'A balaclava.'

'There was only a male with you all the time. One. The same one?'

'Yes.'

'No one else?'

'No.'

He turned on Silas Dinsmor again. 'Where were you taken, Mr Dinsmor? Who're the people you talked to?'

'Full statements tomorrow,' said Silas Dinsmor, standing up. 'We can help you then, captain.' He shifted his wife's chair. 'We need to rest. Get some perspective.'

And that was it. Mace balled his fists. Would've been a pleasure to smack it straight into Silas Dinsmor's Injun nose. Hear the gristle crunch. Whatever the deal was Dinsmor'd worked out, it was sick. The guy playing a rogue hand. Impossible to even imagine the scene.

'Alright,' said Gonsalves. 'I can only ask for your cooperation.'

'And we'll gladly give it. Tomorrow.' Silas Dinsmor taking his wife's elbow, steering her round the table towards the door.

'A proper statement.'

'Whatever our legal obligations.' To Mace and Pylon he said, 'We appreciate your efforts.'

Mace shrugged. 'Your decision.'

'It is, Mr Bishop. It is.'

The three men standing up while the Dinsmors left, closing the door behind them.

'What you got to tell me, Mr Bish?' said Gonsalves, knocking a cigarette out of the pack.

'Less than he told you. He hasn't said a word, except he walked off this morning on a business arrangement.' Mace dropped back onto his chair. The other two staying on their feet.

'A business arrangement.' The captain stripped the cigarette, spilling the tobacco shreds onto the table.

'Private business meeting, to quote him.'

'He said that, a private business meeting?'

'He did.' Mace watching the process of Gonsalves bending to scoop the tobacco into the palm of his left hand.

'A private business meeting with his wife's kidnappers.'

Pylon came in. 'He didn't say that.'

'Stands to reason, though.' Gonsalves rubbing the tobacco into a ball with the fingers of his right hand. 'Where else'd he be tippy-toeing off to? Comes back like it was no big deal. Everything's hunky. I rescued my wife.' He examined the pellet he'd made – a gobstopper. Broke it down, going through the process again with half the tobacco shreds.

'He didn't say that either.'

'He's got that cockiness. We can't even guess what shit happened.'

Mace said, 'What's your position?'

Gonsalves popped the pellet into his mouth, sucked hard. 'They've gotta give me statements. I can put some questions, maybe they answer them, 'n maybe they don't. Who's gonna push it? We got four dead tsotsis in the morgue, one of them a police informer. Only not inside on this story, inside on another one that's got the commissioner having heart thumpers. Sorry for him. Part from that who cares about four arseholes? Huh? In a scene like ours? Serious Crimes opening murder dockets by the hour. No one. Nobody. I give an update, report the American citizens back safe and sound, I'm gonna be told file the file. Move on. See if there's something that'll give us happy statistics. Show that we're doing a great job.' The captain gave the pellet a vigorous chewing. 'Know what I mean?'

Gonsalves chewed, the click of his teeth audible to Mace above the birdsong coming in from the garden.

'Silly bastard terminating you.'

'You got it,' said Pylon.

Mace got up, went to the window. 'That's our sort of clients.' The gardens yellow in the lowering sun. Winter gardens, all bare branches and leafless shrubs. He looked at his watch: 4:20. 'We've got to move,' he said to Pylon.

Gonsalves kept chewing, facing the two security men. 'Staying in a hotel like this must be something. Only for the rich, hey.' He indicated the door. 'So. Back to the mayhem.'

43

Tami sat on a couch reading You magazine, a story about a Hollywood star wanting to adopt a black baby. A spread of pictures of the celeb and children in the Malawian bush, the celeb and children sitting beside a fire in the dirt, the celeb with children draped around her neck at home among the roses. Tami didn't have a radical opinion on the subject. In Tami's eyes given the chance to be raised by a

Hollywood bimbo was a helluva lot of notches above a Malawian kraal. The way she saw it the baby was a refugee taking shelter in a foreign land. Like the child had escaped.

Max Roland sat at the round table working on his laptop. Focused on it, tap tap tap. Asked her twice to bring him coffee. The first time she did. The second time, she said, 'It's all there, next to the kettle.' Didn't look up from her magazine.

Max Roland said, 'This is a favour I am asking, please.'

Tami didn't budge, pulled out Pylon's gun, waved it at him. 'See this? This is what I do for you. Protection. Not making coffee or sandwiches or going for take-aways. I do killing the baddies that want to cause you injury.'

'You are a cookie,' said Max Roland, the grin across his face pushing his ears back.

'A cookie with a gun.' Tami's heart sinking a level at the sight of Max Roland's wet lips.

He got up, made his own coffee, brought one for her.

'You see I am a modern man' – holding out a sachet of sugar.

'Keep it that way,' said Tami. 'We'll be friends.' She shook her head at the sugar.

'Because you are sweet enough.'

The man standing in front of her so pleased with his witticism. Tami kept the groan to herself.

He went back to work then. For two hours kept at it straight through, didn't say a word. Hummed something that could've been Coldplay's Speed of Sound. Did this a couple of times out of tune, only vaguely like the song but enough there to get it going in Tami's head. Coldplay being a group she fancied.

She put aside the magazine, got up to stare out the window at the closing day. Shadows lengthening across the parking lot. Clouds ridging in from the Atlantic. Another bad front. More rain, more dark days in the grey city. Perhaps it was time to head for Johannesburg. Her friends were there, kept telling her, Jozi's where it's at. The city with the vibe. The city with long bucks. Telling her Jozi was real

Africa, the heart of the continent. The times she'd been there she'd got the sense of fun. Not like Cape Town. Cape Town hadn't been fun. She'd been lonely most of the time, after a relationship that'd gone bad. A hurt she still wasn't over. Though she kept it bottled. Kept it from Mace and Pylon. As if they'd notice. As if they thought of her until they needed something. Men. Maybe a change of scene would swing it. She switched the heater up, suddenly aware of the chill in the room.

Max Roland said, 'When I am finished I would like to have supper with you. Perhaps in the shopping mall there is a restaurant, I am sure.'

'Eating out's not on my list of to-dos.'

'Ah come, doch. It will be okay. Nobody knows I am here even. We can have a beautiful evening.'

A prospect that didn't send tingles of joy racing up and down Tami's spine.

'Come. Just for two hours, nobody will know.' Max Roland absorbed in his work, looking up briefly to catch her eye. 'Please, you do not have to play the ice maiden.'

Tami couldn't see why not.

'Na, ja, phone your Mr Bishop if this is worrying you.'

Tami did. 'When's someone taking over?' she wanted to know.

'Later,' said Mace. 'Can't talk,' said Mace. 'We've got matters to sort out here,' said Mace.

'So've I,' said Tami. 'Later when? The guy wants to eat out.'

'That's okay,' said Mace. 'That's good. I don't have any problems there.'

'I do. Major issues.' Tami her back turned to Max Roland, facing the quick twilight. 'I can't believe what you're saying.'

'Customer service,' said Mace. 'When you're heading out let me know. And where you go. For the record. Get the bill too, hey, it's company business.'

'You're so generous.'

'By nature.'

Tami cut the call.

'You see it is alright.' Max Roland kept his eyes fastened on the screen. 'Your Mr Bishop is a good man I think.'

'Isn't he?' said Tami. 'Has his clients' interests at heart.' If Max Roland so much as brushed against her bum she'd wallop him.

44

Mace said, 'They're going out to eat.'

Mace and Pylon back at Dunkley Square, upstairs in Mace's office. The time a hair to five p.m.

'I gathered. When?'

'In a short while.'

Mace at the window, checking out the square. The sunlight sliding off the paving, waiters taking the cafe tables inside. Quiet Cape Town evening, no sign of the storm supposed to be on its way. He watched a couple of young suits get out of a car, head towards the pub for a toot. Not a bad idea. 'You want a beer?'

'Why not?' Pylon looking unhappy on the couch. 'Officially I'm in the dwang as of about now any rate. A minute or so my phone's gonna chirp.' It did. 'Treasure,' Pylon said, holding the screen towards Mace.

'Good luck,' said Mace, heading downstairs to the fridge. He uncapped two Becks, his phone started jiggling in his pocket. Withheld number. He answered it.

'This's Rachel Pringle, the Cape Times reporter.'

Mace closed his eyes. Opened them on the same world, Rachel Pringle still in his ear. 'We've got no comment. The Dinsmors are safe. You want their story, talk to them.'

'I've got their story. I'm not phoning about the Dinsmors.'

'Then bye bye.' Mace took a swig at his beer.

'Wait. This is about a man called Vasa Babic.'

'Never heard of him.'

'Maybe you know him as Max Roland?'

Mace did an Oosthuizen, letting a silence develop. Then: 'Never heard of him.'

'I think you have, Mr Bishop. This morning, at the airport, I got a photograph of you and Max Roland. You remember? After you took my video camera. I still want it back, okay.'

'Or what?'

'Or nothing. You stole it. Theft is theft.'

'Big deal.'

'This is a big deal. Having a killer as your client is a big deal. Protecting someone wanted by the International Criminal Tribunal is a big deal.'

'I don't know what you're talking about,' said Mace. 'Can we get to the point?'

'The point is,' said Rachel Pringle, 'the passenger list for your flight included a Max Roland. The Max Roland in my photograph looks to me pretty much like Vasa Babic. Google him, there's no shortage of pictures on Flickr. You'll see they're the same man. You'll see Vasa Babic's a killer. Wanted for war crimes in Kosovo.'

'Right, so a man I was with looks like another man. Again, big deal. A case of mistaken identity.'

'We're running a story.'

'I'm sure you are.' Mace thinking, like I really need this. 'With quotes from the security regulator, no doubt.'

'We think it's a serious issue, that this Babic is being protected in Cape Town.'

Mace took a flyer. 'Who tipped you off?'

'I can't tell you.'

'I can probably guess,' said Mace, although he couldn't. He came out of the kitchen, caught the blur of a figure looming in the frosted glass of the front door. The door chimes donged. Punctual Mart Velaze. Mace said, 'So long, Ms Pringle.'

'One minute,' said Rachel Pringle. 'Is Max Roland your client? Are you guarding him?'

'No comment,' said Mace. 'So long, Ms Pringle' – got rid of her. He opened the front door on Mart Velaze.

'What hospitality,' said the spook, nodding at the two beer bottles in Mace's hand. 'Cheers' – making to relieve Mace of a bottle. 'Which one's mine?'

'Neither,' said Mace.

Mart grimaced. 'Don't spoil a perfect moment, buta.'

'I'm not,' said Mace.

Mart Velaze shrugged. 'You gonna invite me in?'

They sat in the boardroom, Mace and Pylon and Mart, Mace relenting, cracking a beer for the man.

'You've thought on my proposition?' said Mart.

Mace nodded.

Pylon said, 'It comes down to money.'

'Always does.' Mart grinned.

'You want something, there's a price tag.'

'I don't think so,' said Mart. He looked from Pylon to Mace. Took a sip of his beer. 'I can't see that scenario at all.'

Mace frowned. 'Meaning?'

Pylon leant back in his chair. 'What're you on about?'

'A simple matter of Treasure Island.'

'Ah for Chrissakes, talk sense.' Mace felt he could cheerfully smash the smirk off Mart Velaze's face. 'Treasure Island? What's this Treasure Island?'

Mart wiped the back of his hand across his mouth. 'Don't be stupid. You know what I mean?'

'I do?'

'Of course you do.'

'Well, pretend I don't.'

Mart glanced at Pylon. 'He means it, doesn't he?'

Pylon didn't respond.

'You know, of course.' Mart keeping his eyes on Pylon.

'Let's hear it from you,' said Mace.

Mart went back to his beer. 'Alright. You want it that way, here it is: sure we're asking you to stitch up a client. But for a reason, like I said before. A good reason. And what've you got to lose? Nothing. Oosthuizen's never gonna know.'

'Never?' said Mace.

'Never. Scout's honour.'

'The word of a spook,' said Pylon.

Mart laughed. 'You must have trust. Listen, guys, the way I understand it, tomorrow afternoon Oosthuizen writes you a cheque says, thank you very much, and off you toddle. What more do you want?'

'Money,' said Pylon.

Mart Velaze looked from Pylon to Mace, back to Pylon. Incredulous. He blew a raspberry. 'You want us to pay you?'

Pylon nodded.

'Hey, butas, no, no, no, you're missing the thing here. This's about the honourable gesture. President and country über alles.' He grinned at them. 'Not so?'

'Not so,' said Pylon.

Mart leaned back, riding the chair 'Again I ask you: think of Treasure Island. Think carefully.'

Mace thumped the table. 'Talk sense, Velaze. Ordinary English.'

Mart came forward, leaning both elbows on the table. 'Alright. One word, Cayman.'

Mace felt his guts crimp, kept poker-faced.

Pylon said, 'What about Cayman?'

Mart glanced from one to the other, sucked on his lower lip. Let it go with a pop. A smile on his mouth, not a hint of it in his eyes. 'Pylon, my friend. You hear that, Mace? What about Cayman? Good old Pylon always in for one last jerk around. Except not today. Today we have to talk straight one time. Okay?' Mart pausing to let them respond; Mace and Pylon staying still as statues. Mart saying, 'Okay. Upfront, no bullshit, we know you've got money there. Mace and Pylon's little nest egg. Undeclared. Untaxed. Illegal. That's okay, not the end of the world, most of the ruling hierarchy right in there with you. Ordinarily as things go, we don't care. Then something happens, a situation develops, new conditions force us to take a position. Know what I mean? Yeah! Yeah! Sure you do.'

'Piss off,' said Mace.

Mart drank a mouthful, his eyes on the ceiling. 'You don't want me to do that. You want to hear me.' Bringing his gaze back onto Mace and Pylon.

'No.' Pylon giving him an uh-uh headshake.

'You do,' said Mart. 'Believe me, you do. Cos if you don't then you're gonna have the Revenue boys and gals round here in a few days. Search and seizure warrants. You name it, they have it. All over your lovely office like ants. Busy ants taking stuff to the nest on Plein Street. Backwards and forwards. Backwards and forwards. Causing the sort of shit you really don't want. Really, really don't want. Get me?'

Mace and Pylon getting him, Mace wanting to smack his beer bottle into Mart Velaze's sneering face.

'All you have to do' – Mart whisked an external hard drive from his jacket pocket – 'is put the dope on here. Simple plug and patience, jack it right into a USB port. About an hour and you're done. No one's gonna be any the wiser. Because no one gets through Mace and Pylon, right? Complete security.' He stood up, gave them a white dazzle. 'Never forgetting that tomorrow Oosthuizen pays you. Money for nothing, hey!' He wagged his finger. 'Just don't be greedy.'

'Bastards,' said Mace.

'Look, Mace,' said Mart, sliding the hard drive across the table until it touched Mace's fingers, 'no need to make a big deal out of this. Do the job and everything goes away.'

'That's a joke,' Mace said. 'More like everything hangs over our heads. Sometime going forward you're back putting the screws on again.'

'Truth,' said Mart, 'it can happen.'

'Will happen,' said Pylon.

'Butas,' said Mart, 'don't worry about it. The future's an unknown place. Focus on this' – he jabbed the hard drive against Mace's hand.

Mace picked it up.

'There's a good man.' Mart finished his beer, put the bottle on the table. 'When you're finished give me a call. Cheers, guys.'

Mace and Pylon sat in the boardroom listening to the city going home. Sat with their own thoughts. Grey thoughts in the greying light.

Mace thinking, Cayman. How to move the money?

Pylon thinking, Cayman. How to move the money?

Pylon said, 'No option, hey?' Looking at Mace through the gloom.

'Seems not,' said Mace. 'One thing though, we'll have to have the offices swept more often, like every week. Christ knows how else they're so up on us.' He put the hard drive into his pocket. 'They're all shits. The bloody lot of them. So does it matter? I reckon not.'

'Me too,' said Pylon.

Mace drained off his beer. 'Should we go?'

They were outside on the darkening square approaching Mace's car when the men appeared. Jakob and Kalle in their macs, smoking cigarillos.

Mr Buso, Mr Bishop, you have not forgotten us?' said Jakob. 'We have this matter to talk about.'

Pylon said, 'Guys, can we do this tomorrow? We're up against something right now.'

'No,' said Kalle. 'That would not be possible. Not at all. We need Vasa Babic tonight.'

Impasse. The four men doing the stand-off.

Ridiculous, thought Mace. Thinking, maybe there was a way through this. Said, 'Okay. You can have him.'

'Mace!' Pylon shaking his head.

'That is what we like to hear.' Jakob dropped his cigarillo butt, squashed it underfoot. 'That is sensible.'

'Mace. No.' Pylon locked a hard grip on Mace's arm. 'This is stupid.'

Mace shook free, said to Pylon, 'Hang on, there's an option here.' To Jakob and Kalle said, 'Tomorrow. We can do it tomorrow afternoon.'

'What is wrong with tonight?' said Kalle.

'A small matter of payment,' said Mace. 'From tomorrow afternoon we are off the job. Get it? No longer our problem. We get paid, you get your man.'

'Where is this?'

'We'll let you know. Be in touch in the morning.' Mace opening his car door. 'Till then.'

The men shook their heads, Jakob taking a hold on the car door. 'How can we trust you? Maybe you will help him to run away.'

'I don't think so,' said Mace, 'Max Roland is not my favourite human being. He deserves his day in court.' Mace held out his hand. 'Shake on it.'

Jakob did. 'We will talk tomorrow,' he said.

'Auf wiedersehen,' said Mace – he and Pylon driving off, the German and the Swede watching.

Pylon said nothing until they were on De Waal Drive above the city. 'You think they'll leave it at that? A handshake deal?'

'Sure,' said Mace, looking in the rearview mirror, 'they're Europeans. Honourable types. Not even following us.'

Pylon snorted. 'They're bounty hunters.'

'Like I said, honourable types.'

Mace humming what Pylon thought could've been a Stones song. Paint It Black maybe, Mace's humming not being easily identifiable. 'You want to know what Treasure told me?' Pylon said, as they drifted across the lanes at Hospital Bend.

'Not really,' said Mace.

'I'll tell you anyhow,' said Pylon, shifting in the seat to get comfortable. 'She said she'd pack a suitcase for me.'

Mace said, 'Shit!'

'Major shit,' said Pylon.

45

Sheemina February, inside Cafe Paradiso at a window table, watched Mart Velaze open the gate, hurry through the outside tables to the door. Only two men with beers braving the cold for the sake of a smoke, Mart pausing to stub his fag in their ashtray. The three laughing.

Mart came in, they greeted with an air kiss. Sheemina letting Mart have privileges.

'What was that?' she said.

Mart signalling a waiter. 'What was what?'

'The joke.'

He looked outside at the two men. 'Addicts anonymous.' Looked back at her. 'What're you having?'

'White wine,' she said. 'A sauvignon.'

'And a beer,' said Mart to the waiter. 'That porra one, Peroni.'

'It's not Portuguese,' said Sheemina. 'It's Italian.'

'Same thing,' said Mart.

She laughed. 'Sometimes,' she said, 'you can be …'

'Yeah? What?'

'Pig-headed.'

'Hardcore's what I prefer.'

'You would.' She raised her eyebrows. 'So?'

'All systems go.'

'Just like that?'

'Just like that.'

'I'm amazed.'

'I'm not. They're shit-scared of losing the money. Fact no one's been done for currency violations hasn't occurred to them. Interesting that, hey? All these people with secret bank accounts in Cayman, Switzerland, Mauritius, you name it, all these people breaking the regulations but nobody ever gets charged. Makes you wonder why? Makes you wonder what's going on in the back rooms of Revenue Services?'

'You're the spy, what is going on?'

'I dunno. Paybacks. Pay-offs. Arrangements. Accommodations.'

'Which is what I'd imagine, despite the squeaky clean image they push.'

The waiter put down her glass of wine, asked Mart if he wanted a glass. Mart said the bottle was fine.

'Revenue is government. Government gets up to dirty tricks.?' Mart snorted. 'E-nuff said.'

Sheemina raised her glass, they clinked.

'Problem here,' she said, 'is Mace thinks he's got away with it.'

'He has,' said Mart. 'Maybe you gotta talk to your little friend Rachel. Put out the word.' He grinned at her. Reached out to run his fingers over her gloved hand. 'Nothing like a bit of publicity.'

'Don't,' said Sheemina. Didn't withdraw her hand.

Mart kept at it. Stroke, stroke, stroke. 'Ms Sheemina February, one tough cookie.'

Sheemina brought the heel of her boot down on his foot. Mart grimaced. Stopped his caresses.

'You ever paid for pussy, Mart?' said Sheemina.

'Never,' he said. 'I can get women.'

'Then maybe you'd better go on the prowl.'

He leered at her. 'Don't you get jags? Ever?'

She smiled at him, took a sip of wine. 'Not for you, buta,' she said.

'For Mace Bishop?'

'Excuse me?'

Mart leaned an elbow on the table, cupped his face in his hand. 'I know you' – wagged a finger playfully. 'Hey, yai yai.'

'You've got to be joking.'

'So why the blush?'

'Coloured chicks don't blush, as you'd put it.'

'From where I'm sitting they do.'

Sheemina February inclined her head. 'Mart Velaze, the great psychologist.'

'Yeah, baby, you got it. What the great psychologist thinks is

you've gotta work out whether you wanna screw him or kill him.'
Mart winked.

'Kill him.'

'The great psychologist's not so sure.'

'Believe me.'

'Oh, I do. I also think you got the hots for him. Lucky ol Mace.'

'Lucky ol Mace is going to find out what it is to die slowly.'

'Tonight?'

'Maybe. Except he's a busy man tonight. Tomorrow night more likely. When he gets all the bad news.'

'An intimate moment.'

Sheemina February's phone rang before she could respond: Oosthuizen. She connected, listened to him telling her that Max Roland had completed the software. When he stopped speaking she let his silence unwind, heard the whining of Chihuahua Chin-chin beneath Oosthuizen's breathing. Mart Velaze gestured at her, who's that? She mouthed: Oosthuizen. Mart blew her a kiss in response.

Eventually Oosthuizen said, 'Are you there?'

'Riveted,' she said.

'Then say something.'

'I'm relieved, Mr Oosthuizen,' she said. 'Now nothing can go wrong.'

'Until I have the laptop in my hands, I'm not sure of that. I'm going to pick it up,' he said.

'Is that wise?'

'Why not?'

'Why not? Because right now it's in a safe house that no one knows of. It is protected. Whereas you, you are not.'

'No problem. I've got Mister Anaconda.'

'Snakes in winter! How original.'

Silence.

'On your head, Mr Oosthuizen,' she said, thumbed him off. To Mart said, 'He's going to fetch the laptop.'

'What? Now?'

'Apparently.'

'That's a bit of a bugger.'

'It is.'

'Be a challenge for our friends.'

'Nothing they can't deal with.'

'Perhaps though …'

'No,' said Sheemina. 'You warn them, they're going to say, set-up. Best to leave it. This's Mace and Pylon we're talking about. They're big boys, let them sort it out.'

Mart's phone rang. He listened, disconnected. Said, 'Seems our Injun pardners are heading out for a bite to eat. Booking's been made at the Cape Malay. How about that?'

'Good choice,' said Sheemina. 'Very tourist. Bobotie and malva pud. Let's hope they enjoy it.'

Mart finished his beer. 'This's all so exciting.'

46

'No, not tomorrow, tonight,' said Silas Dinsmor, his voice tight, not far off shouting. He put his hand over the telephone mouthpiece, twisted his head round to look at his wife, 'Is she stupid or what?'

'Shussh, hon.' Veronica aka Dancing Rabbit rubbed his back. 'Take it easy, she's doing her job.'

'How long's it take to book seats?'

Veronica thinking what she wanted was an end to this nightmare.

'What?' Silas barking into the phone. 'There can't be no seats, there're always empty seats. Every plane you fly in there are empty seats. People don't turn up, there are empty seats.'

Veronica sat on the edge of the bed. She wished it were her own bed. She had this feeling she wouldn't ever lie on her own bed again. Truth? They should've left Africa alone. You couldn't understand Africa. Africa was mad. Crazy lunatic people with crazy lunatic ideas.

Silas shouting, 'Standby isn't good enough. I want a guaranteed seat. Two tickets. Tonight to New York, Atlanta, Washington, Philadelphia I don't care, anywhere Stateside is where we want to go.' Silas doing deep breathing, taking it down a notch. 'Listen, listen to me. Miss. Miss, you listening to me? You with me here? I want two tickets. I am talking emergency. I am saying we have to be on that plane. This is life and death. No joke. Literally life and death.'

'Hon,' said Veronica, 'hon, take it easy.'

'Alright, alright. If we have to go to London we have to go to London. Just get us out of here. Two of us. My wife and me. Dinsmor – spelling it – 'Silas and Veronica' spelling these too. 'For what time is that? Nine-ten's departure. Check-in's at seven.' Silas glanced at his watch. Gave them a little over an hour to get to the airport. On the phone the woman was telling him where to collect the tickets. Silas jotting down a reference number.

Veronica got up, fetched a case from the wardrobe.

'What you doing?' said Silas.

'Packing,' said Veronica. 'We're going aren't we?'

'Not with suitcases. We check out Sheemina February's gonna know in a couple of minutes.'

'We're doing a runner?'

'No other way. This gets back to her, you heard her …' he shaped his fingers like a gun, put them to his head. Said, 'Pow.'

'Don't do that,' said Veronica. 'Don't freak me out.'

Silas walked over to his wife, embraced her. Talked into her hair, 'You've got through this so far, we can get through the rest. We get on to that flight, we get away from here, away from these people. That's the priority. No matter what it takes. That's the major thing. From back home we can settle the hotel bill. Arrange for our luggage to get shipped over. Nothing in it we can't live without for a coupla months.' He felt Veronica nod. 'We're not doing a runner, Vee. We're taking precautions. Now, I'm gonna ask reception to get a taxi, ask them to recommend a restaurant. When the taxi comes we tell him, the airport. That okay?' He stood back from Veronica, his hands on her shoulders. 'Okay. Then I'm gonna phone the lawyers and cancel the deal. Plenty of time to stop the money.'

'What if …?' Veronica leaving the rest unsaid.

'Ain't any what-ifs,' said Silas. 'Maybe Sheemina's checking her balance every hour but even fast-tracked it ain't gonna show up there until tomorrow. Relax, okay. Relax. Deep breaths. Take it slowly. Take a shower. Pack what you need for the flight in a handbag. Then we're outta here. Laughing.'

'I hope so,' said Veronica. 'I hope so.'

'I know so.'

'She's a hard bitch, Silas. Not someone to cross.'

'Exactly. Which is why we're off.'

He went back to the phone. Veronica kicked off her shoes, headed for the bathroom. The trouble with Silas she thought he'd considered all the angles but there were angles he hadn't thought of. That's where Sheemina February would be, in the angles he hadn't thought of. She went back to Silas, waited till he'd finished with reception.

'We go to the restaurant,' she said. 'From the restaurant we get another taxi to the airport.'

'What for?'

'Because that's safer.'

Silas forced a laugh. 'No need. This gets back to Sheemina …'

'It will get back to her.'

'Okay, this gets back to Sheemina February, she hears we're booked in a restaurant, she's gonna leave it.'

'She won't.'

'Even if she doesn't, what's she gonna do? Send someone to check?'

'Yes.'

'No worries. Maybe after fifteen minutes they realise we're not coming. Even if she phones the airport then. Even if she's got a man waiting there, it's gonna be too late. We're gonna be through. Through check-in, through passport control, in the departure lounge. A place not even Sheemina February can reach.'

'Still,' said Veronica.

Silas shook his head. 'We haven't got the time. That's gonna take too long. Delay us.'

Veronica looked at him, Silas pressing through his cellphone contacts for the lawyer's number. Sometimes he didn't get it. Usually the times when things went wrong. 'Play it my way,' she said. 'Please, hon.'

'Okay,' he said, 'whatever.'

She could tell he was humouring her, holding the cellphone to his ear, that smile on his face when he believed he'd scored.

47

The German and the Swede moved quickly to their car. Kalle taking the driving seat; Jakob powering up a laptop. 'Come on, baby, come on' – drumming his fingers next to the touchpad. The screen filled with a map.

'Ja, here we go,' said Jakob, zooming in. 'Where are you? Where are you? Ach, so.' He caught the flashing red dot moving off screen, adjusted the window.

'De Waal Drive,' he said, pointing at the red dot, 'driving quite fast I would say.'

Kalle took Dunkley out of the square, into Hatfield coming up against the lights at Mill. Said, 'Skit, skit, skit' – at the pack of traffic.

'Quickly,' said Jakob, 'they are fading.'

'We cannot move,' said Kalle.

'Maybe they are going towards the airport. That would be a good place. The problem is the split: the airport? Or the south? If they are off the screen we will have to guess.'

Kalle swore, swung the Merc out of the queue of cars into the opposite lane, at the intersection ran the robot into Mill, cars coming up fast behind, hooting.

'Okay, okay,' he said, waving an apologetic hand at the flashing headlights, 'no one is hurt, keep your blood pressure' – the traffic moving at a steady sixty kays into Jutland up the slope onto De Waal. 'Where are they?' he said, accelerating in the fast lane.

'Gone,' said Jakob.

'These bloody things,' said Kalle. He flashed his lights at a slow car ahead, the car's exhaust swirling out blue smoke. 'That car should be off the road. We can die from the exhaust. Do they not know about climate change?' He hooted. Shouted, 'Move over, move over, arsehole. Why do they not move out of the way? In this country nobody understands the fast lane.' He swung the Benz into a gap on the left. 'This is why they have so many accidents. Because you must duck and dive. Crazy, crazy, crazy.' As they drew level with the slow car, Kalle gave the finger. The people in the slow car mouthing at him, slapping him the up-yours fist. He pulled in front of them. 'What is the tracker range?'

'There,' said Jakob. 'There on the bend where the road splits. Ah no, ah no. Gone.'

'Before the split?'

'Not far I would say.'

Jakob lifted two cigarillos from his pack. Hung them on his lips while he dug out a lighter.

'How far is that?'

'The split.' Jakob speaking from the corner of his mouth, the cigarillos bobbing on his lip. 'They have probably passed it.'

'And the tracker range?'

'When there are no mountains, ten kilometres.'

'This city is only mountains.'

Jakob flicked the lighter. Shook it. 'Maybe six, seven kilometres, I don't know.' Flicked the lighter again. Shook it. On the fifth flick getting a flame. He fired the cigarillos, gave one to Kalle, let out a whoosh of exhale against the laptop screen. 'In Berlin they work very well. But not in Rio.'

Kalle clamped his lips round the cigarillo, took a long pull. Breathed out smoke. 'And now, can you see them?'

'No,' said Jakob. 'And we have the split coming up.'

Kalle tailgated into Hospital Bend, keeping to the middle lane. In the four-lane strip, drivers shifting right and left to line up for the split.

'Which way?'

'Airport,' shouted Jakob. Then: 'No, no, the other way. There is the dot. There they are. Near the university.'

'There is too much traffic.' Kalle shouting now, drifted right until the driver alongside braked to let them in. A blare of hooters going off.

Kalle took another drag at the cigarillo. 'Arsehole.'

'On the radar,' said Jakob. 'There are our gentlemen.'

'Good,' said Kalle, 'but we must get closer.'

They tracked the car ahead through Newlands Forest, the Paradise chicane, up Edinburgh, down Wynberg Hill onto the M3, only one car separating them at the end of the highway.

'In the old days,' said Jakob, 'we would have been stuffed.'

'I do not think so.'

'At night! In a place where they have no lights! I think so, yes. We would have been going to the airport. Like fools.'

48

They drove in silence. Pylon uncomfortable, shifting on the seat, Mace thinking about their Cayman money. About bringing it through in suitcases if that was the only way. About how they had to do something or they'd have Mart Velaze rocking up to put the screws on whenever the agency needed a little job done. The sort of insecurity Mace didn't want to live with.

Coming off the highway, Pylon said, 'This is buggered up. We didn't have this kind of trouble selling guns.'

'What d'you mean?' said Mace.

'I mean a coupla days and everything's buggered up. My arm shot to hell. The Dinsmor job down the toilet. This job doing in our heads. Bad press in the papers. And I'm supposed to be having fun being a dad. Save me Jesus!'

'You want me to drop you at home,' said Mace. 'I can do that, no problem.'

'Uh-uh,' said Pylon.

'Not as if this job's a ballbreaker.'

'Maybe not. Thing is, I face Treasure now or in a few hours time makes no difference to her. Makes a lot of difference to me. It's a few hours less of her tongue.'

'Call Tami,' said Mace. 'Tell her to have a slow supper.'

'I'll dial her,' said Pylon, 'then she's all yours. Black chicks prefer whiteys.'

'I'm driving.'

'There's a hands-free. It's no big deal.'

Tami came on, said, 'Wait' – Mace and Pylon getting full volume restaurant noise. When she came on again, the background quieter. 'This's like the deep south,' she hissed. 'The only black people are the waiters. They think I'm some kind of escort.'

'How long've you been there?' said Mace.

'Long enough to feel like shit.'

'How long's that?'

'Ten minutes. We haven't ordered yet.'

'Good,' said Mace. 'Take it slowly, okay. At least two hours.'

'Stuff that,' said Tami. 'You think I'm sitting here for two hours, you're mad.'

Mace let it ride.

'Ah, please, Mace. He's a major prick. Doesn't stop groping me. I slap his hands he thinks that's fun. What's with the two hours anyway?'

'Afterwards,' said Mace. 'Just keep him charmed.'

Tami went off in a string of Xhosa Mace couldn't understand. Pylon could, burst out laughing. Tami giving him a mouthful too.

Pylon saying, 'Hey, sisi, hey sisi, careful sisi.'

'Sisi, your moer,' she said. 'Strues, Mace, you've got black blood, the way you think you can treat women.'

Mace and Pylon protesting to dead air.

'She disconnected.' Pylon gesturing at the cellphone. 'She disconnected. She's staff, staff don't cut us dead.'

Mace brushed it off, accelerating through the slip road onto the Ou Kaapse Weg, Oumou's station wagon powering up the pass. 'What'd she say? Earlier.'

Pylon laughed. 'Lot of stuff about getting the ancestors to chase you into the sea.'

'Me? I'm the one who pays her.'

'We're the ones who pay her.'

They drove in silence to the top of Silvermine, the sandstone catching silver in the headlights, the mountains dark beneath the stars. On the descent Mace said, 'We've got to get that money out of Cayman, even if we sail it in on a yacht.'

Pylon snapped his fingers. 'Now there's an idea. Maybe we could do an asset swap with some rich larney. Maybe you've got an idea there. Yeah, maybe.'

They came off the pass into Sun Valley, approaching the safe house along the main street, then circling the block to stop in the mall's parking lot. Waited in the car five minutes to ensure they hadn't been followed. Mace cracked his door, said, 'Let's do it.'

'I haven't got a gun,' said Pylon. 'Remember.'

'In the glove box,' said Mace.

Pylon took out a small Beretta Tomcat. 'Looks like a toy.'

'Toys don't fire hollow-points,' said Mace.

49

Silas and Veronica Dinsmor waited in the foyer for the taxi. Veronica sitting on an armchair beside the fire, Silas chatting up the receptionist like there was no problem in the world. Veronica with her largest handbag on her lap: their passports, credit cards, cellphone, notebook and pen, comb, packet of tissues, purse with change, glasses case, headache tablets, lipstick, courtesy mints, Silas's turquoise-inset bolo tie that he couldn't leave behind. 'So wear it,' she'd said, but he'd insisted on the silver bolo tie with the jet stone. 'Smarter for a night out,' he'd said, winking at her. Veronica sitting there next to the fire, feeling naked and cold. Dead anxious that somewhere along the path lay a rattlesnake. Heard Silas say, 'So what d'you recommend we eat at this place? You say it's traditional? Real home-cooking?' And the receptionist with her silky black hair and large brown eyes say something Veronica didn't catch, Silas coming back with 'Bowbootay' – or that was how it sounded. Silas again, 'It's a ground beef 'n rice dish. Maylay. With raisins. Sounds dee-licious.' The receptionist flicking back her hair, smiling at him, a hint of white showing between her lips. Silas swinging round, 'You hear that Veronica, the local cuisine' – but not moving from the reception desk.

'I heard,' said Veronica, wondering what was it with Silas he got so overkill in these situations. All have-a-nice-day normality. Talk, talk, talk, talk, talk, talk. To anybody who'd stand still to listen. Mr Jovial. Mr Carefree. Putting out this high-five attitude. A flash of light in the outside darkness caught her eye. Through the window she saw car beams approaching along the driveway. Had to be the taxi. Which put a knot in her stomach, a fist that seemed to push up against her lungs. She glanced at her watch: seven on the dot. Thought: twenty-four hours ago I was tied up in a warehouse. Another twenty-four hours this could be over. Heard Silas say to the receptionist, 'You think that's our taxi?' The young woman say, 'I'm sure it is.' Silas saying, 'See you in a few hours.' Coming towards her, his hand outstretched. 'Let's go, Mrs Dinsmor.'

Veronica stood up, wondered how she managed it her legs felt so wobbly. 'Shouldn't we wait to see?' she said, Silas taking her arm. Saying, 'It's gotta be.' And there in the doorway the taxi driver in a leather jacket and jeans, smiling at them. 'Are you the Dinsmors?' Silas going into overdrive. 'We sure are. Take us to the eatery, Mr Cabbie.' The cabbie offering Silas a business card, stepping back to hold the door open for them. 'Kind of you,' said Silas. 'Polite city, this.' Like she hadn't been kidnapped, seen men shot, like they both hadn't been backed into a corner by a truly evil woman. The cab driver skipping down the steps to the waiting car, opening the back door for them. Felt to Veronica like the leather seats she slid onto might have been the padding in a coffin.

'My way,' she said to Silas after the cab driver had shut them in. 'Restaurant then airport.' Silas nodding, smiling, patting her hand. Patronising. 'Silas, please.' The cab driver slipping into the front seat, turning round to them. 'Okay, folks, the Cape Malay, I believe. Very nice establishment, if I might say so.' Veronica feeling the knot in her stomach harden, painful enough to clench her teeth. Put her hand on Silas's thigh, squeezing. Silas answering, 'They do local food, we're told?' The cab driver firing the engine, saying, 'They do. Not eaten there myself but everyone I've taken there loves it.' Silas covering her hand with his own. 'That right?' 'Absolutely is.' Veronica closing her eyes, leaning back in the seat, thinking, This is going to be alright. This is going to be alright.

'So how far's this restaurant?' Silas wanted to know as the taxi rolled down the driveway.

'Higher up the hill,' said the driver. 'Not far. Not even five minutes. Nice place to stay too, you ever come back here. Great views. Very cosy.' He glanced round. 'You tourists?'

Veronica thinking, Never. We're never coming back here. When we get home we're going nowhere outside America. Hearing Silas say, 'A business trip. You know, thought we'd take advantage and see a new city.' The cab driver saying, 'Great city. Love it.' Silas coming in, 'You born here?' 'Born here, been here all my life. True Capie.' Veronica wondering why was this so much worse than Colombia? People'd got hurt in that shakedown too, but hurt, not killed. Here you got blown away. Somebody snapped their fingers, pow. You're dead. You couldn't talk to people here. You couldn't reach a mutual understanding. Here it was their way or no way. Awful scheming evil people. That woman. Sheemina February. The thought of her: the lipstick, plum red like someone had slashed open her face. The eyes, icy. Blue as winter skies. The black leather glove. She shivered at the thought of the black leather glove. The woman's voice, always her voice cutting in, sarcastic, poisonous, sinking her fangs into your soul. She shuddered. From this deep place heard Silas calling her, 'Veronica, Veronica. This's it.' Heard Silas and the cabbie sorting out the fee.

Then she was outside in the cold night air, the cab driving off. Silas saying, 'Nice young man. The nicest man we've met here.' The two of them walking into the bright foyer, a hostess smiling at her. The knot back in Veronica's stomach, pressing up against her lungs. 'Please, Silas,' she said. 'I'm going to the bathroom.' The hostess pointing. 'It's over there, ma'am. First door.' In the cubicle Veronica got down on her knees, hurled up into the bowl.

50

The German and the Swede followed Mace and Pylon over the mountain, two back in a string of cars held up by a truck – commuters heading home from the city. The speed a slow sixty kays an hour. Kalle tapping his fingers on the steering wheel, impatient. He crushed out his cigarillo in the ashtray. Ahead darkness, distant spots of light. About them the rise of cliffs and slopes. Kalle did not like mountains. He was a Malmo boy. At home on the coastal flatlands. Mountains made him claustrophobic.

'I do not like mountains,' he said, breaking into Jakob rabbiting on about maybe coming to Cape Town for a holiday in the summer.

'What?' Jakob glanced out at the black tops about them. 'These are not mountains. They never have snow on them. Too low.'

'They go up,' said Kalle, 'that is enough.'

'Ah no. If you cannot ski on them they are only hills.'

The train of cars came down into a valley, the road flattening between a shopping mall and the razor-wired walls of a suburb. At an intersection, Mace and Pylon going right.

'We will be behind them,' said Jakob.

'What can I do? They won't see us. We are nothing but bright lights.'

They followed the Opel station wagon past McDonalds into the mall car park, towards a block of flats.

Jakob crouched in the seat when the Opel's tail lights glowed red. Swore. Kalle taking the Merc behind and past the stopped car, pulling into a bay fifty metres away between two SUVs. He killed the engine. In the rearview mirror watched Mace and Pylon sitting in the car.

'What're they waiting for?' said Jakob.

'Being cautious.'

'Them? That is a joke.'

Five minutes passed before they saw Mace and Pylon leave the car, walk towards the block of flats.

'They did not see us.'

'No.'

Jakob closed the laptop. 'So now we find out which flat. You or me?'

'You,' said Kalle. 'I am the driver.'

Jakob pursed his lips. Said, 'It is better when I am the driver. Safer, I think.'

'What is this about my driving?'

Jakob didn't respond, got out of the car.

From the shadows of the entrance gate he watched the two men go into the stairwell, appear on the first floor. Talking happily. No worries. Stupid amateurs to Jakob's way of thinking. They stopped at the third door. The one called Pylon scoping the car park and the entrance, a quick sweep that couldn't have told him anything. The one, Mace, opening the door. If Vasa Babic was in there, he wasn't rushing forward to welcome them. Jakob reckoned Vasa Babic wasn't in residence.

Back in the car he told Kalle his thoughts.

Kalle said, 'They are here for some reason.'

'Which could be any reason.'

'We can wait,' said Kalle. 'What else have we got to do?'

'We could have supper,' said Jakob.

Kalle offered him a cigarillo.

51

Mace and Pylon let themselves into the flat, slipping through the doorway like thieves. Closed the door softly. Stood with their backs against the door, checking out the room: the television on mute, news images flicking across the screen, casting a blue light. Max Roland's laptop on the table among empty coffee mugs. A copy of You magazine on the couch.

Pylon pushed off from the door, said, 'We own this place right? So why do I feel like a tsotsi?'

'Because that's what we are,' said Mace, taking the hard drive from his pocket. 'Criminals stealing intellectual property. And do we care?'

'I guess not.'

'Exactly.' Mace switched on the laptop, plugged in the hard drive, navigating through the pop-ups. A bar appeared on the screen with the legend: copying files, giving a megabyte figure and time – one hour, twenty-two minutes. 'Jesus,' said Mace, 'bloody hour and a half almost. Whizz-bang government technology for you. Fast as a pensioner.'

'You better hope Tami can stay the course,' said Pylon.

'You and me both.'

Pylon eased himself onto the couch so as not to hurt his arm. Picked up the magazine opened at the celebrity spread. 'What shit's this Tami reads?'

'Vital info,' said Mace. 'People in there could be clients one day.'

'I suppose.'

Mace peered at the screen. 'There we go: one per cent downloaded. Clever stuff these NIA boys run around with.' He straightened. 'I'm famished. You fancy fish 'n chips or a burger?'

'Fish's fine,' said Pylon, caught up in the celebrity's adoption of a black child. 'Better take this home for Treasure, get her worked up about rich whiteys buying our children. The new slave-owners.'

Mace didn't know what he was talking about.

In the Ocean Basket Mace's phone rang: Oosthuizen.

'Where's Roland?' he said. 'He's not answering his phone.'

'Chaffing my colleague in a restaurant,' said Mace. 'One of the perks we offer our clients.'

'You're telling me the laptop's not in safekeeping?'

'Where d'you think I am?'

'You're at the safe house?'

'Yeah.'

One of the Oosthuizen silences that Mace let play out until the scientist said, 'I'm coming to collect it.'

'That's not a good idea. You want protection for your product, that's what we're providing.'

'I've changed my mind,' said Oosthuizen. 'I'm the only one I trust. Our arrangement is over.'

'And Roland?'

'You keep him till tomorrow. That's all I'm paying.' He disconnected.

'Salt and vinegar?' said the guy at the counter.

'Yeah,' said Mace, 'lots of it.' Thinking, oh shit.

52

Veronica, sitting with a glass of water on a couch in the foyer, said to Silas and the hostess, 'I'll be alright. Really.' With trembling hand brought the glass to her lips. The hostess said, 'You sure you don't want a Grandpa?' Veronica frowned, questioning. 'A headache powder,' said the hostess. Veronica nodded, smiled wanly. Heard Silas say to the hostess, 'Can you arrange another cab?' The hostess saying, 'Ag shame, sir. What a pity. I'll check the other one hasn't left yet.' When she'd gone Veronica said to Silas, 'Not that one. Another one.' Silas, shooting back his cuff to glance at his watch. 'It's getting tight.' 'Please, Silas.' Silas saying, 'Okay, okay' – looking at the hostess returning, shaking her head. 'I'll get one straight away.'

The taxi took fifteen minutes to arrive. Veronica sitting on the couch with the cold in her bones, the nausea still at the back of her throat, wondering if she'd ever feel normal again. Silas pacing the foyer, checking his watch like he was timing a race. Coming over to whisper to her, 'This's tight now. We're sliding into check-in time. The cab doesn't come soon, we're not gonna make it.' Veronica reached up for his hand. 'Stop, Silas. Sit down for a minute. You're making it worse, hopping about like a crow.'

The hostess came over. 'Everything alright?' Silas told her his wife was feeling worse. 'Ag shamepies,' she said to Veronica, touching Veronica's shoulder with the tips of her fingers. 'The taxi won't be much longer I'm sure.' 'Can you find out?' said Silas. 'My wife's really not well.' The hostess saying, 'Of course, sir.'

Veronica pleaded with Silas, 'Please, hon, you're working me up. Sit. Sit for five minutes.' Patting the couch until Silas perched next to her. She put the glass on a side table, took his hand. 'Hold my hand, hon, please hold my hand.' The two of them sitting holding hands, not talking. Veronica thinking of her pregnant daughter and the coming grandchild. Wondering what it would be like to hold the baby. Her granddaughter. They knew it was a girl. Had seen the scans of the minute creature no longer than her finger. So far away. It all seemed so far away.

The hostess called over from the desk. 'They say he left ten minutes ago. Another five at the most.' Silas said to Veronica, 'It takes about twenty, twenty-five to the airport. This's crazy. We shoulda gone straight there with the other cab.' He stood up, started his pacing again.

We shouldn't have, thought Veronica. This was the right way to do it. The careful way. She watched Silas standing at the door, gazing into the night. Praying, let us get there on time. We have to for the sake of our grandchild.

Silas turned. 'There's a car coming. Can't see if it's a cab.' Peering out. 'Yup, it's a cab.' Veronica watched him stride across the foyer towards her. A huge grin of relief on his face, talking to her in

Choctaw. Telling her it was all going to be alright. He helped her up, returned the glass to the hostess, thanking her for her kindness. The hostess protesting, 'The least we could do, sir.' To Veronica saying, 'Get better quickly, ma'am. We'd love to see you again for supper.' Veronica thinking, no, never, never never. But smiling gratitude for small mercies at the hostess, then looking round to see a man at the door in trainers, jeans, a woollen jacket with the collars zipped up to his chin. Black hair, black eyes. Saying, 'Hello, folks. Taxi for Mr and Mrs Dinsmor.' Silas saying, 'That's us.' The fist tightening in Veronica's stomach for no reason. Every nerve on high alert. The cabbie smiling kindly at her.

In the taxi, the warm, leathery taxi with the Cowboy Junkies playing softly, the cabbie twisted in his seat to look back at them. 'Where to sir, ma'am?' 'The airport,' said Silas. 'Quickly.' The cabbie frowned. 'Rightio, sir, and sir's luggage?' Veronica knowing something was wrong, the way the man had moved behind them down the steps silent as a cat. Athletic. Tense. His eyes everywhere. Reminding her of someone … Someone she couldn't place. And his voice. She'd heard it before, or one like it. That lilt to the accent. The glove around the fist. Heard Silas saying, 'We're not leaving, we're meeting someone.' The cabbie nodding, 'Oh, right. When we get there you'd like me to wait?' He started the car. Silas raising his voice, 'No, that's alright. We'll be fine.' 'No trouble, sir.' Silas keeping on. 'We'll be fine. A business meeting. Could go on a coupla hours.' Veronica saying to Silas in Choctaw, 'Enough. You sound like you're explaining.' Silas responding, 'I am.' The cabbie saying, 'You're native Americans. How cool.' Silas said, 'Please, mister, we're late already.' The cabbie's eyes coming on them in the rearview mirror. 'No trouble, sir. Enjoy the ride.' The music being wound up a notch. 'Your kind of music isn't it, sir.' 'Sure is,' said Silas, although Veronica knew it wasn't at all. She said to Silas in their language, 'I don't like this man.' Silas squeezed her hand.

Veronica stared at the dark suburbs. She had no sense of the city, no idea if they were heading for the airport or in the opposite direction. She could see the mountain rising to their left, a spray of lights below the motorway to the right. She recognised the windmill from the afternoon. She'd seen it not long before they were released at the shopping centre. The windmill on the opposite side of the road now. Was that the way it should be? Was this the direction? At the worry the nausea rose in her throat. Veronica swallowed hard to keep it down, tasted bile. On a tight corner into an underpass, Silas slipped against her, the two of them sprawling into a corner. The cabbie apologising, 'Sorry, folks, sorry, hey. That's a bad one that corner. Very sharp.' Veronica and Silas righting themselves to see an airport sign overhead. Silas nodding upwards. The cabbie said, 'This is Settlers Way we're on now all the way to the airport.' At least they were on the right road. Veronica thinking, Why'm I like this? Why'm I scaring myself? – her vision blurring at the rush of lights on the incoming lanes. But this was a highway. Highway was good.

Until not five minutes later the cabbie took an off-ramp, Veronica, floating in her granddaughter's world, hearing Silas say, 'Where're you going? This isn't the airport.' A huge building like a factory and cooling towers ahead of them. The cabbie replying, 'No, sir, short cut through the back streets.' Silas arguing, 'The highway's fine, the traffic's fast, stay on the highway please.' The cabbie protesting this was better. There were roadworks ahead on the highway, this way they'd miss them. Just this quick detour then back on the highway. 'Promise, no problem.' Silas losing it, shouting, swearing at the cabbie to get back on the motorway. The cabbie driving faster, braking hard, swinging right through a gate onto a track across open ground. The factory complex dead ahead. Silas trying to open the door, the cabbie with a gun out now, waving it about, shouting at them to shut up or he'd shoot. Veronica closed her eyes, knew this was everything she'd dreaded.

The cabbie stopped beside the building, switched off the ignition, switched on the cabin light. Leering back at them. 'Silas and Veronica, aren't we the naughty ones?'

Veronica thought, waste land. Dereliction. A place that was no place. A darkness so intense it was as if the city had vanished. Always there were these sorts of places for these sorts of moments.

'Who are you?' said Silas.

The man grinned, rubbed the muzzle of the gun against his cheek. 'You can call me Mart.'

'I don't wanna call you anything,' said Silas. 'I wanna know what you want?'

'Me? Nothing.' The man Mart kept the grin, letting them get a good look at the gun. 'I'm the hired help. See this?' He showed them a voice recorder. 'This's what they gave me. This means your answers will be your answers. Because they don't trust me to remember your exact words. They think I'll get the details jumbled. Mart the half-wit. What a joker. Memory like a sieve. Why they give me this. This way nobody gets confused. Okay?'

Silas said nothing.

Veronica said, 'In six months we will have a granddaughter.'

'Well isn't that sweet,' said Mart. 'Grandpa and grandma. Congratulations. So here we go grandpa- and grandma-to-be, question one? You ready?'

Veronica said, 'This was all a mistake.'

'I don't know about that,' said Mart. 'All I know are the questions. Well not many questions, actually. Just three. Number one: This morning you agreed a deal?' He held the voice recorder towards them. 'This's where you answer, my friends?'

Silas said, 'We'll speak to Sheemina February. Take us to her.'

'You're gonna speak to her,' said Mart. 'When she plays back what you've got to say. Ne? Sharp, hey, modern technology for you.'

'You do not have to kill us,' said Veronica.

'Phone her,' said Silas.

Mart said, 'Guys, you're not listening. I'm a tolerant sort. Laid back. Happy-go-lucky. No axe to grind. So don't give me uphill. Please. Answer the questions. You can go catch your plane, I can go home, play among the melons.'

Veronica said, 'You're going to shoot us. You're not going to let us go. You shot those men.'

'The question, ma'am. Afterwards we can do the argy-bargy. Promise. But, yeah, you're right, I won't lie to you. I shot those moegoes. Waste of space both of them. No loss to the world. Now we got that outta the way let's do the questions, hey. Make sure we're on the same page here? Know what I mean? That we understand the rules of engagement. We do, don't we?' His eyes flicking between them. 'Course we do. So again: this morning you agreed a deal? What you say to that, grandpa?

'We'll speak to Sheemina February.'

Mart sighed. 'This's not going well, folks. Perhaps what I should do is ask you all the questions. Give you a context you can work in. How's that? Mr Reasonable am I. Question two then: You've got an important meeting tomorrow, will you be there? Question three: You wouldn't be doing a runner, would you?' That's it. Just speak into the mic and we can all go about our business, no harm done.'

Veronica drifting off to that place with her granddaughter, this young girl looking up at her talking child talk, wondering at the world, laughing. The two of them, hand in hand in a place of sunshine. Even from there she could hear Silas arguing, the man ordering them out of the car.

'My name is Dancing Rabbit,' she said.

53

'It is time we went back,' said Max Roland, finishing his coffee. He pulled a face. 'Terrible coffee. Americano is always terrible coffee. Like the Americans, not one thing or another. Not quite water, most certainly not quite coffee.' He pushed the cup away. 'But I am pleased the steak was good. Second to Turkish beef.' He made to stand.

'I haven't finished my wine,' said Tami, pointing at her glass. She lifted the bottle from the cooler. 'And there is still some left' –

poured this into Max Roland's glass. The empty bottle she shoved upside-down into the ice. Flashed Max a grin.

He reached across to take her hand. Tami balling her fingers, like a tortoise drawing in. 'Uh-uh. Don't.'

Max Roland sat back. 'You are a flirt. No?' He raised his glass of wine.

'No.'

'A cockteaser.'

'Bah.' Tami broke into Xhosa.

'What'd you say?' Max Roland amused, taunting her with the glint in his eyes, the glisten on his lips.

'That you think too much of yourself.'

'Of course.'

'You shouldn't.' Tami sipped at her wine, thinking, Mace was gonna pay for this, one way or another. A bonus. Time off. A Mauritius holiday. She could fancy a Mauritius holiday on the beach with blue cocktails. Sexy French boys strutting around. Tax-free.

Max Roland snapped his fingers in front of her face. 'Come back. You have gone away.'

She refocused. Looked at his hand in front of her face, the stumpy little finger like a blob of dough. Gave her the rittles down her spine.

'That is your problem,' Max Roland was saying, 'you go away into your head too much for a young lady. I think you fancy Mr Bishop.'

Tami dropped her mouth. 'Huh?'

'I can see it.'

'That's your fantasy.' She drained her wine, stood up. 'Time to go.'

'But no opportunity for a little, what do you call it, patta patta?'

Tami slapped his cheek. Not hard but the crack sharp enough to make some people stare.

Max Roland rubbed his face. 'Girls are so beautiful when they are angry.'

'All men say that,' said Tami.

'Sit down,' said Max Roland, grinning. 'We have to wait for the bill.'

54

'Oosthuizen's coming here?' said Pylon.

Mace said, 'That's what I said.'

'When?' Pylon with the fish and chips parcel open on his lap picked out two chips from the heap, stuffed them into his mouth.

'Said he was leaving straight away.' Mace at the table also eating from the packet.

'And we've downloaded what?'

'Fifty-five per cent.' Mace leant over his fish and chips to peer at the screen. 'Fifty-six per cent. Gives the time left as forty minutes.'

'Shit,' said Pylon.

'That's what I said. When he phoned.' Mace peeled the batter off his fish, lifted a piece into his mouth.

'Will take him about that to get here.'

'Maybe less this time of evening. Not so much traffic. Forty-seven per cent now. How about that?'

They ate in silence. On the TV a soapie with black diamond types in fast cars, at cocktail parties, in their granite-topped kitchens with all the electronic gewgaws. The diamond types cheating on their partners, everyone making a thing about protected sex.

'I hate that,' said Pylon. 'Aspirational bullshit. You wanna hear Treasure on it.'

'Not really,' said Mace. He finished his fish and chips, balled up the paper. 'Not bad. Just too much batter.'

'Batter's the best part,' said Pylon, waved a greasy finger at the laptop. 'What're we at?'

Mace took a look. 'Going some. Sixty-six per cent.'

'At home,' said Pylon, 'I've gotta put aside the batter or Treasure strips her bearings about cholesterol.'

'Same with Oumou.' Mace stopped there, thinking, was the same with Oumou. The absence of Oumou a sudden pain in his chest. He sighed.

Pylon said, 'You okay?'

Mace stood up. 'Yeah. Still catches me on the turn that stuff.' He held his hand out for Pylon's scrunched-up debris. 'Shrinks call it ambush grief.'

Pylon grimaced. 'Shrinks've got pop raps for everything. What time's left on the download?'

'Thirty minutes. Twenty-nine minutes.'

'And we've got how long before Mr Chihuahua pitches?'

Mace headed for the kitchen to dump the remains. 'About twenty minutes. Twenty-five if we're lucky.'

'Luck's not a factor.' Pylon joined him in the kitchen to wash his hands. 'This's not gonna work out. We'd better think of something.'

'Like what? Head him off at the pass?'

Pylon forced a laugh. 'Be serious.' He wandered back into the lounge, Mace joining him. The two of them watching the download, the minutes dragging by. Eighty-five per cent. Eighty-six per cent. Eighty-seven per cent. . 'Maybe phone him, tell him we'll bring it to his house. Save him the trouble of coming all this way.'

'Not a bad idea.' Mace put through the call. 'Been thinking,' he said when Oosthuizen answered, 'we could drive the laptop through to you. Be safer that way.'

'Nice thought,' said Oosthuizen. 'Too late though. I'm almost there. Fifteen minutes it'll be off your hands.'

Mace disconnected. Said, 'He reckons fifteen minutes.'

'Eighty-eight per cent. Sixteen minutes.'

'Bugger it,' said Mace.

Eighty-nine. Ninety.

Mace said, 'I'm gonna phone him again. Tell him we can't wait, we'll meet him at that shopping centre other side of Ou Kaapse Weg.' He dialled Oosthuizen. The call going to voicemail. 'Shit,' said Mace. 'Shit, shit, shit.'

'There's a dead spot on the mountain,' said Pylon. 'Leave a message. Tell him we're on our way.'

Mace glanced at the download. Ninety-one per cent. He phoned again. 'We're on our way,' he said when the voicemail buzzed, 'meet you outside Jakes at Pollsmoor.'

Ninety-two per cent.

'You think he'll turn round when he gets it?'

Mace shrugged. 'Might at least make him stop to phone us.'

They stood over the laptop watching the bar edge slowly across the graphic. Ten minutes. Five minutes. Ninety-four per cent. Mace's cellphone rang: Oosthuizen.

'You're on your way are you? I don't think so. That's your problem Bishop, you're sloppy, you don't keep strict time. I can hear you're not on the road.'

Ninety-six per cent.

'Fact is I can see your car, that low-rent station wagon you drive. Not the sort of car a security man should be seen in. Want some advice, Bishop, get yourself a Hummer. A serious car. I'm parking next to it.'

An Oosthuizen silence. Into it Mace said, 'Buzz when you get to the gate.' He disconnected. Connected to Tami. To Pylon he said, 'How long d'you think we can keep him waiting?'

Pylon kept his eyes on the loading bar. 'Long enough, probably.'

When Tami came on Mace said, 'We're done shortly. Take the night off.'

'Such kindness,' said Tami.

'And tomorrow.'

Mace heard Tami suck in her breath, say, 'Oh wow, a whole day free.'

55

Jakob dozed, his head rolling off the headrest, jerking back. Kalle listened to the low chatter on the radio. Seemed pensioners had been scammed out of their life's savings. Tales of desperation and tears. Stories Kalle had heard everywhere he'd been, which was most corners of the world. You wanted to see a pirate these days you looked for a guy in a flashy car with a high-end lifestyle. A finance man. A type not far behind Vasa Babic.

A Hummer pulled in beside Mace Bishop's car. In a parking lot of empty places, stops beside Mace Bishop's car? Lone man on the phone backlit against the row of lights. Kalle shifted in his seat for a better view. Could see a small dog at the passenger window. Scrawny dog with bulging eyes wearing a tartan jacket. Its snout trailing a mucus smear across the glass.

The man in the Hummer closed his phone, brought up a pistol. Released the clip, checked it, slid it back into the grip.

Kalle nudged Jakob.

Jakob spluttering, rubbing a hand over the dribble at his lips. 'What? What is it?'

'Over there,' said Kalle. 'The man in the Hummer.'

'Ja.'

'He has a gun.'

'And a dog.'

The man getting out of the Hummer with the dog under his arm, no pistol in sight.

'The gun is in a shoulder holster.'

'This is South Africa,' said Jakob. 'Everybody has a gun.'

They watched the man walk towards the block of flats.

'He is a visitor,' said Jakob, relaxing back into the seat. 'If he was worried he would be looking around. Perhaps he has come to see a girlfriend.'

The man pressed a number on the security keypad at the gate to the flats. Gazed up at the rows of lighted windows, the kitchens and bathrooms of the ordinary citizenry. Walked a few paces off, came back to the keypad.

'He is getting no reply,' said Kalle.

The man jiggled at the handle to the gate. Buzzed again. Dug a cellphone from his jacket pocket.

'Maybe the girlfriend has another boyfriend,' said Jakob.

'No,' said Kalle. They watched him walk to the flat that Mace and Pylon had entered. 'Who is this person?'

Five minutes later the men watched the man with the small

dog leave the flat, nobody seeing him off. Now he carried a laptop.

'Where are our friends?' said Kalle.

Jakob yawned. 'If they are colleagues why would they stand at the door to wave goodbye?'

'If they are colleagues why does he go in with a gun?'

Jakob stifled a second yawn. 'We are colleagues, we both have guns.'

'Still it is strange.'

The two exchanged a glance. Jakob snorted, tapped his head. 'You are being crazy. He didn't shoot them.'

'In this place anything is possible.'

They watched the man come through the gate, carefully closing it behind him. He paused in the shadows beyond the entrance light, scanning the parking lot.

'You see,' said Kalle, 'this time he is more nervous.'

The man hurried to his car.

'This is not a relaxed man.'

'Maybe,' said Jakob. 'Maybe the flat is full of dead bodies but I do not believe it. Vasa Babic cannot be killed so easily.'

They watched the man drive away in his Hummer, the dog in the tartan jacket barking soundlessly.

'Now what to do?' said Jakob.

'We wait and see.'

'And if nothing happens?'

'Then we have a small problem,' said Kalle. He offered Jakob a cigarillo. 'A small problem but nothing that cannot be solved in some way.' The two men lit up.

They smoked in silence. Watched people come out of the mall, hurry through the darkness to their cars. No one so much as glancing at the men in the Benz, dots of fire glowing at their mouths.

'Must be a movie has finished,' said Kalle. 'Perhaps that is where Vasa was? He likes movies.'

'When he is in them.'

After a few minutes, the dribble of people stopped. No Vasa Babic.

'Verdamnt,' said Jakob, stamping his feet to get the circulation going, 'this waiting waiting waiting is crazy.'

'Better than sitting in our winter.'

'Cold is cold.'

'Snow is worse.'

'Ja, okay. But this is Africa. The hot continent.'

'Look.' Kalle pointed at the block of flats. 'Our friends.'

'So they are not shot dead.'

There was Mace and Pylon locking the door of the secure flat, heading along the corridor to the stairs.

'And now?' said Jakob.

Kalle stubbed out his cigarillo. 'We sit still I think.' The men watching Mace and Pylon come out of the shadows at the gate to the flat complex, walk quickly across the car park to the Opel station wagon. 'They are in a rush it seems.' The car's tail lights glowed red, the car pulling off away from them.

Jakob powered on the laptop. 'Let us see which route they take.'

'Good, good,' said Kalle, his eyes following the red dot on the screen as it headed towards the intersection out of the shopping precinct. At the crossroads, the dot turned left.

'Over the mountain again,' said Jakob. 'Back to the big city.' They watched the dot sliding along the Silvermine pass until it faded. When they looked up there was Vasa Babic and a young woman coming out of the mall. Could have been a tourist and his holiday catch.

'Here we go,' said Jakob, opening his door with a soft click, pulling a H&K from a shoulder holster.

Kalle started the Merc. At the catch of the ignition Vasa Babic glanced to his left where the car was edging towards him, grabbing Tami in a tight hug.

Tami shouting, 'Get off me, Max.'

Jakob saying in German, 'Hullo, Vasa, it is time for another little ride' – as Kalle stopped the car next to the struggling couple, popped the boot. 'Let the girl go before she is hurt.'

Vasa laughing. 'The old bounty hunters. Go home old fools. It is pension day soon.'

Both Kalle and Jakob circled the couple, their guns pointing down. The car park deserted. This time of night not even a car guard working his patch.

Tami struggled to free herself. 'Let me go. Let me go' – screamed till her breath ran out.

'Do that again,' said Vasa Babic, holding her tight within the clamp of his arms. 'Shout for help.'

'Another scream in the night,' said Jakob. 'Let her run away, Vasa. There is no need for all this girlie noise.'

Tami heaved for breath, squirmed against Vasa until her arms were free. Gasping, panting.

'This does not have to be difficult,' said Jakob. 'You do not need the girl.'

Tami brought out her gun, swinging it from Jakob to Kalle.

'Ah,' said Jakob. 'That is very brave, miss, but it is unnecessary.'

'So, she is your protection, Vasa,' said Kalle. 'The mass murderer is hiding behind a black girl. This is very amusing.'

'Wrong man,' gasped Tami. 'This's Max Roland.'

'Same thing,' said Jakob. 'Throw away the gun, miss.' Jakob holding up an identity badge. 'We are officers of the International Criminal Tribunal in the Hague. Officers of the court. The man with you is a killer.' Jakob starting forward.

'Stay away. Back.' Tami still heaving for breath.

'We have talked to your boss, miss. He said he would tell you.'

'What? What would he tell me?'

'That we will look after Vasa Babic now.'

'You can release him to us. My colleague has said, we are court officers.'

Vasa Babic and Tami backing away from the men and the car.

'This man has done serious killing, miss. In Kosovo. Innocent women and children. Raping young girls. We have films of him.'

'This man is Max Roland,' said Tami. 'He's a scientist.'

Jakob held up his hand, stop. 'Wait, miss. One moment.' He took a cellphone from his pocket, waved it at her. 'You see this?'

'It's a cell,' said Tami. 'I know what a cellphone looks like. Get real.' Tami fighting for space in Vasa Babic's clasp. 'Give me some air, Max, I can't breathe.' Vasa Babic holding her like a shield.

'Miss,' said Kalle, 'be careful, he is dangerous. Throw away the gun.'

'Miss,' said Jakob, 'I will phone your Mr Mace Bishop, he will tell you what to do, okay? You will listen to him?' He looked at Tami. 'Yes?'

'Yes.'

'Good, miss. I will put the handy on speakerphone. Listen now.' Jakob glancing down at his cellphone to key the connection.

Behind the couple, Kalle with a straight shot into Vasa Babic's back if he wanted Vasa Babic dead. Which he didn't. The deal being: you kill him, that's tough luck on you. This is not the Wild West, wanted dead or alive. No Vasa, no fee. Kalle seeing Vasa Babic drop to the ground pulling the girl down with him, wrenching the gun from her grip. Hearing the girl shout. Jakob shout. Vasa lying beneath the girl twisting to put the gun on him, Kalle. Squeezing off a shot, the bullet zinging into the darkness.

Kalle stumbled, brought his gun up. Fired. Once. Again.

Jakob came in, kicked Vasa's head, kicked his gun hand, the gun skittering across the tarmac. Dragged the girl aside. Kalle putting the boot into Vasa's stomach, the two men hefting him to his feet.

'The girl?'

'Leave the girl.'

The German and the Swede hauling Vasa Babic into the boot of the Merc, slamming closed the lid.

'Let's go, let's go.'

Doors opening in the block of flats, people standing there in their pyjamas.

'The girl.' Jakob looking back at her lying on the tar.

'Forget the girl.' Kalle slipped the gear into drive, pulled away fast in a slither of small stones. 'Phone to get us clearance. We can still make the plane tonight.'

Jakob dialled the Hague. From the boot they could hear Vasa Babic shouting and thumping.

'We should have put him in handcuffs,' said Kalle. 'What a nuisance.'

56

Mace lay on his bed staring at the ceiling, aching with loss. His left hand smoothed the emptiness beneath the duvet as if he could conjure back the life, the body, the warmth. Oumou. He turned on his side to face her pillow. Could imagine her hair on the white linen, her slender neck, her Arabian features. Could almost hear her breathing. Almost an accusation. He slammed his fist into the mattress. Tomorrow night. Flopped back to stare at the ceiling. Tomorrow night, he'd nail Sheemina February.

What'd Mart Velaze said when he gave him the hard drive? 'I hear you know Sheemina February.' That smirk on his dial. The ace spook playing spook games. Keeping him in the corridor, not letting him see into the flat. Had to be a shitty flat in a building like Unitas. Pensioners, Congolese, street-working coloured chicks. Not the sort of place Mace'd figured for Mart Velaze.

'What's it to you?' Mace'd said.

'Cool chick.'

'Like hell.'

'Connected,' said Mart Velaze. 'Like you wouldn't believe. Government, business. A mover and shaker. Not a pie she hasn't fingered in this city. Not a woman you want to mess with, buta.'

'That's supposed to mean something?'

Mart Velaze toyed with the hard drive. 'Nothing much. Thought you might just like to know. Au revoir, buta. Your patriotism is appreciated. Enjoy your dollars.'

'We had an agreement,' said Mace.

'For the time being.' Mart Velaze giving him a camp waggle of his fingers as he closed the door.

Problem there, Mace thought, staring at the ceiling, was that the issue of the Cayman Island money was just that, an issue. Sheemina February knew. Mart Velaze knew. This was going to come back to bite them in the bum. Sheemina February he would deal with but Mart Velaze. Mart Velaze was a problem. He might say he wasn't but he was.

Then there was the bank. The overdraft issue. The bond repayments, or the one he'd skipped. As if years and years of on-the-dot repayments didn't mean a thing! Came down to the nub they'd want a business plan. Proof of an income stream. Trouble was, what income stream? Mace groaned. Jesus! The Oosthuizen contract a stuff-up. The Dinsmors a write-off. A few ongoing guarding jobs more hassle than hallelujah. Nothing on the books to keep the bankers off his back. What could he tell them? Hey, people in suits, take my house. Feel free. Put a father and his daughter on the streets. No worries. Jesus H Christ. Knowing them they'd have the news clippings too. All the crap about the Dinsmors' kidnap. All the lowdown on Max Roland. Vasa Babic. Whoever he was. The complete dissing of Complete Security.

God.

Mace rubbed a hand over his face. Sat up, Cat2 at the end of the bed staring at him. Fat chance of getting to sleep. Sometimes he wished he read so at times like this he could read. He switched the radio on, got the mad snakes that populate the late-night talk shows. Some adder hissing about bringing back the death penalty. String up the murderers, rapists, paedophiles. Way to go, china, Mace said aloud, switched him off.

At the back of the stillness, could hear a rhythmic thump in Christa's room. Couple of days ago it was 50 Cent. At least this he could handle. Beneath that a synthetic whine. Bloody teenage girls. Mace checked the time. Eleven p.m. Why was she still awake? What was she doing? He wanted to shout out, Hey, enough. Let's get some sleep. Knew that no ways in hell he was going to do that.

Mace slipped down into the bed again, buried his head beneath the pillow.

'I see a line of cars hmmm, hmmm, hmmm, hmmm.'

In her room Christa shaved off her hair using Pylon's electric hair clippers. Sat in front of her mirror working at it pass by pass, shearing the cut shorter each time. Sometimes getting the wrong angle, nicking herself in the process. The nicks bleeding as badly as any razor slice. And sore. Nothing like the rush of drawing the blade across her flesh. This was painful, made her flinch each time the teeth chewed her scalp. She ended up with a patchy fuzz, some runnels of blood, drying.

'This is for you, Maman,' Christa said to her image in the mirror.

Wednesday, 27 July

57

The man could hear the rumble of the morning traffic on the highway but he waited until the muezzin called before he moved. In the grey light shoved off the cardboard sheets that covered him, crawled fully clothed out of the sleeping bag, talking nonstop. He was wearing his shoes, old Nikes. He slept in his shoes in case the night got tense. Last night it had, but then the tension had let up and he'd gone back to sleep. He kicked the cardboard into a pile, covering the sleeping bag, talking. He wasn't bothered about other bergies finding them. Five days he'd been using the building he hadn't seen anyone else. He opened the door, looked up, a metal sky over the cooling towers. Still talking, he moved out onto the concrete to take a piss. When the flow came he stopped talking, sprayed the weeds, grinning at the rising steam. As the urine diminished his words welled up. He shook off, jammed his cock into his trousers, his eyes scanning the derelict buildings and the rank yards for signs of the night.

He found them in the long grass beside the track. Stood over them scratching his beard, talking. He walked away, came back, walked away, came back. All the time talking, an endless rush of words that dried his tongue with their intensity, left a crud around his mouth. He crouched beside the couple, his words spraying over them, forming on their clothes like dew. He fingered the material of their jackets, damp from the night, talking, talking.

He removed their shoes first. Then their rings and watches, snapped off the man's necklace. These he put into the pockets of his trousers. He circled the couple, his speech become a stream of invective until he had to stand still, gasping, panting out a word at a time. When he was calmer he unbuckled the man's belt. Examined the trousers but the man had crapped himself, they were useless. He turned to the woman, raising her gently, a nurse with his patient, eased her out of her jacket, careful not to bang her head when he laid her down again. With the man he was less attentive, rolled him over to pull off his fur coat.

He walked down the track across the wasteland, behind him the towers, ahead the traffic backing up on the approach road to the highway. He talked without pause, glancing left and right as he walked. He carried a plastic bag in one hand and a pair of woman's shoes in the other. His coat was too long, wet at the tails where it swept over the dirt. When he reached the commuters in their cars, he turned in the direction they were headed, shambling along the gravel verge as if he'd stepped from an antique age.

58

For Mace the day started badly. The phone woke him from a dream of bats streaming out of a date-palm grove like smoke. He and Oumou in her desert city of Malitia, walking on the old battlements at sunset, watching the bats. Coming towards them a woman ringing a hand bell louder and louder, ringing it in their faces. The woman tearing off her burka. Sheemina February.

He groped for the phone on the bedside table. Pylon.

'Have you seen the paper?'

Mace switched on a light.

'It's still dark. Don't you sleep?'

'Babies don't let you sleep.'

'Hell,' said Mace, 'what time's it? I was having a nightmare.'

'At least you can wake up from a nightmare. What's written here's more difficult to shake off.'

'What time's it, did you say?'

'I didn't. Six-thirty. You want to hear what the bitch's written.'

'That Rachel Pringle?'

'Her exactly. Big photie here of you and Max Roland. Page three. Looks like you're not happy about the picture at all.'

'I wasn't.'

'Other hand, Max's smiling like a celeb. Underneath that it reads, listen to this: "Protection for a wanted man". Save me Jesus, the shit these people write. "Arriving yesterday at Cape Town airport were security operator Mace Bishop with his client the Serbian commander Vasa Babic (also known as Max Roland) wanted by the International Criminal Tribunal in the Hague for crimes of genocide and gross human rights abuses during the war in Kosovo. Babic has been on the run for years and is now being protected in a safe house in Cape Town by the controversial security company, Complete Security.

'"Recently Veronica Dinsmor, an American client of Complete Security, was kidnapped while Bishop and his colleague Pylon Buso were in attendance. Two men were shot dead during the incident. The kidnappers released Mrs Dinsmor unharmed yesterday afternoon. Commenting on the appearance of Vasa Babic in the city, Mr Bill Hill, chairman of the security industry's regulatory authority, said that private security firms had a moral duty to observe international directives. 'This Vasa Babic is a wanted man,' said Mr Hill. 'He stands accused of horrible crimes. By protecting him Complete Security are in violation of our code of practice, they are probably in breach of the law, but more importantly they are behaving unethically.' Mr Hill said that his organisation would look into the irregularities. In the meantime he was referring the matter to the South African Police Services and Interpol.'"

'Shit,' said Mace.

'Yeah, isn't it?' said Pylon. 'But there's more.'

Mace groaned.

'This's worse. Page four story, not very big admittedly. Headline: "SARS brace security company." "Brace" – where d'they think this is? America? Bloody headline writers.'

'Makes me want to cotch,' said Mace.

'Wait'll I read it, you will.'

Pylon cleared his throat. '"Complete Security are under investigation by the South African Revenue Services for failing to declare foreign funds. According to a spokesperson for SARS, the owners of the company, Mace Bishop and Pylon Buso, failed to take advantage of the recent amnesty on foreign exchange holdings. 'We have received information which requires investigation,' the spokesperson said. Bishop and Buso were responsible for sourcing weapons internationally for MK during the years of the armed struggle. See also, 'Protection for a Wanted Man' on page three." Nice, hey?'

'Sick-making,' said Mace. 'Seems we need a talk with Mart Velaze. Perhaps make some things clear to him.'

'My thoughts exactly.'

'Let me get the girls to school first,' said Mace, 'then we'll sort it.'

Mace showered, was in the kitchen cooking porridge oats when Christa came upstairs. He stared at her. His daughter in her school uniform, tie unknotted, bald headed. Actually not so much bald headed as scalped: patches of fuzz hair and scabs. Head like the marabous of Malitia. The storks of death.

'What?' he said, his voice sounding distant. Rasping, hoarse. 'What have you done?'

'Papa,' said Christa. 'Don't.'

'Your hair. Where's your hair?' Mace having flashbacks of the package he and Oumou'd been sent of Christa's hair. After she'd been kidnapped. Her head like now shaved and torn. Shouting, 'Chrissakes, girl, what have you done?' Mace rushing at her, grabbing her by the shoulders. 'Where's your hair? Where's your hair?' Shaking her.

Christa snapped back at him. 'Papa, Papa, you're hurting me. Let go.' Struggled against him.

He pulled back his hand, would have slapped her, would have hurt her, would have … He let his hand flop down.

For a long moment stared at his daughter, his daughter glaring back at him. Tears in her eyes. And something else. Hatred? Anger? Disgust? For an instant, a spark of hurt. His vision blurring. Hearing Christa scream 'Why don't you love me?' Hearing it over and over again. Then she was gone. Out of his grip and gone.

He followed her down the stairs to her room, calling, 'Christa, Christa. Hang on. Please.' Her door slammed in his face. Locked. 'Christa, please. Let me in, C.' Standing there useless, the fury draining out of him. Mace lent his forehead against the door. This early in the morning he felt he'd been awake for hours. 'Please, C. I'm sorry.'

He heard the lock click, opened the door. The shock of her shaved head staggering him again. He wanted to grab her, hug her, wanted to know why. He reached out for her. She stepped back.

'Why, C? Why?'

'Because Maman is dead,' she screamed at him. 'And you don't care.'

Mace went rigid. 'I do, Christa. That's not true. Not true. How can you say that?'

'It is.' She was crying now. Shouting at him through the tears, 'It is, it is, it is.'

He took her hand, drew her to the bed. They sat side by side. Mace put his arm around her shoulders, pulled her closer. The hurt of her words burning in his chest.

'Why, C?'

She sobbed, heaving her grief. Told him through the weeping that a teacher had said some people shaved their heads to show they were in mourning. A cultural tradition. That was why she'd done it. To show she was in mourning for her mother.

'But it's not our culture,' said Mace when she'd quieted. 'We don't do that.' He could hear the phone ringing upstairs. Then it stopped and his cellphone rang. 'What people shave their heads?'

'The Xhosa. Pummie said.'

'Maybe,' said Mace. 'I don't know. We're not Xhosa.' The landline rang again.

Christa pulled away from him. Her face smudged and smeared, raw with misery. 'Maman was someone. She told me stories of her life. Showed me pictures. Of Malitia. Of her family. That's where I belong.'

'You belong here,' said Mace. 'We came here. You've grown up here. Maman wanted to live in this city. She didn't want to live in Malitia anymore. We're Cape Town people.'

'We're no one,' said Christa.

The landline stopped, his cellphone started.

Mace said, 'I've got to answer that.' He pulled her close in a quick hug. 'Come to the kitchen, we'll talk some more.'

Going upstairs he smelt the porridge burning, the kitchen clouded with smoke. He scorched his fingers getting the pot off the hob and under the tap. Had his hand in the water flow when the phone rang again. He snatched up the mobile. Oosthuizen.

'I've been phoning you for five minutes, Mr Bishop. On both phones. That's not good. Doesn't create an on-the-ball impression.'

Mace shook his burnt fingers to ease the pain. Said, 'Far as I recall I don't need to create a good impression with you. Far as I'm concerned you're a write-off, Mr Oosthuizen. An expense. Like a bad debt.'

'Better that, than an impimpi, a rat. That was slimy, Bishop. Underhand. Really low-level stuff.'

'What?'

'Don't give me that, you know what? Max Roland's what. Selling him out's what. How much'd they pay you? A couple of grand? Ten at the most? All because you're pissed off with me. You're scum, Bishop. Shark shit.'

'What the hell're you on about?' Mace thinking, he doesn't know. He doesn't know about the data transfer.

An Oosthuizen silence. Mace didn't let it get anywhere. 'I haven't got all day, arsehole. So bugger off.' He hung up. Christa wearing a beanie in the doorway watching him. 'I burnt the porridge,' Mace said, holding up his red fingers. 'Cornflakes okay?' His cellphone rang: Oosthuizen.

Mace said, 'You don't give up?'

'Right now,' said Oosthuizen, 'Max Roland's in a holding cell at the airport. Awaiting rendition. Snatched out of your hands, Mr Bishop. Hands that I was paying for. Not only that, his picture's in this morning's newspaper with you. Miss Rachel Pringle's gonna love it when I tell her you sold him out.'

Mace saying, 'That's bullshit.' Thinking, Tami?

'Tell it to Miss Pringle. One other thing: I've cancelled the settlement cheque. Not much point in paying you to look after Roland for two days now you've sold him to the head-hunters. Enjoy your life, Mr Bishop.' Oosthuizen's Chihuahua yapping in the background.

Mace put down the phone, said to Christa, 'I'm okay about what you've done. I am. I was shocked that's all.' He took a step towards her. Held out his arms. 'Give me a hug.' She was hesitant but she did. They stood clasped. 'You don't have to wear the beanie,' said Mace. Christa looked up at him. 'Honestly.' He smiled. 'I mean it. Tell you what, this afternoon you can shave my head. We'll both mourn your ma.'

Christa said, 'You promise.'

Mace held her at arms' length. 'Sure.' He kissed her forehead. 'Can you do the cereal, C? I've got to make another call.'

Christa gave him a look that Mace recognised as pure Oumou. When Oumou was reaching the limit, about to give him her version of the riot act. It brought up goosebumps.

Mace phoned Tami, her phone ringing through to voicemail. He left a message, 'I know you've got the day off. And that's still the case but ring me asap.'

Mace got Christa and Pumla to school in the Opel station wagon. Had wanted to take the Spider, except it wouldn't start. Had sat there trying to swing the engine until the battery died. Christa beside him, keeping her eyes averted. Eventually she'd said, 'Papa, it's getting late.' He'd said, 'Once more' – given the battery two minutes to recover then killed it stone dead. No option but the Opel. They changed cars, the Opel firing first time. Mace caught a twitch on Christa's lips. Said, 'I suppose you think that's very funny?' She'd shaken her head but they'd both sniggered.

After dropping the girls, he was heading for Mart Velaze's Unitas pad when Captain Gonsalves rang, redirected him to the cooling towers.

'You maybe wanna get your arse here,' Gonsalves said. 'Take a break from the routine.'

'Why?' said Mace.

'Two stiffs. The Dinsmors. Done execution-style.'

Mace thought, This's all I need. Pulled to the side of the road to make a U-turn. Said to Gonsalves, 'Why're you calling me? They sacked us. You heard them.'

'Thought you might like to know. Sort of after-sales service.'

Mace hooked a turn into a gap in the traffic, causing mayhem and hooters. 'Stupid Americans.'

'All the same,' said Gonsalves. 'Show your concern. Spin some good press outta it. Fella like you needs all the good press he can get. Considering what the Cape Slimes writes about you.'

Mace shot a robot, heard Gonsalves say 'Drive carefully, Mr Bish' – before he keyed him off. Called Pylon.

Pylon coming on with an apology, 'Sorry I missed you when you picked up Pumla: changing a nappy.'

'Very domestic,' said Mace, 'here's what's happening in the big wide world' – laid down the gist of it.

Pylon said, 'Bloody fools. Lucky they sacked us.'

'My thoughts on the nail. Gonsalves thinks we can spin this. Of more concern though is Tami. Ring her, won't you.'

He heard Pylon groan. 'That chick'll just give me lip.'

'She'll love it,' said Mace. 'She'll feel appreciated.'

Mace took the Black River Parkway, dropped onto Settlers Way, came off at Jan Smuts Drive, thinking, this was probably the route the Dinsmors would've been taken. Their last view of Cape Town. Not the best. He turned down the track towards the cooling towers, pulled up behind the cop posse. Gonsalves sauntered towards him, chewing.

Mace got out of the car, hunched into an anorak.

'At least it's not raining,' said the captain, holding out a hand in greeting.

'Can't shake,' said Mace. 'Burnt my fingers.'

Gonsalves looked at the red digits Mace showed him. 'Nasty. Seems you're making a habit of it, burning your fingers.'

Mace zipped up. 'Very funny. Can I check this out?'

Gonsalves didn't move. 'And the great Pylon Buso? Where's he?' Tobacco juice glistening on his lips.

'Changing nappies,' said Mace.

'Even with a crook arm. Whatta daddy.' Gonsalves looked at Mace's car. 'Thought your number was a red Noddy car? Every time I see you you're driving this one. Changes your image. Kinda downgrades you. Not so zooty, I'd say. So where's it, the Spider?'

'Wouldn't start this morning,' said Mace. 'Got a feeling it's had it.'

Gonsalves nodded at the knot of police standing around the bodies. 'Like the Dinsmors.' He spat out a plug of tobacco. 'You wanna take a look?'

'That's why I'm here,' said Mace.

'We're still waiting for the paparazzo to pitch, take his pictures. Wisdom of the sages is that they were probably zapped early like eight, nine o'clock. Doc's over there you wanna talk to her.'

'What for?' said Mace.

Gonsalves shrugged. 'Just being helpful.' He broke out a cigarette, started stripping off the paper. Waved Mace towards the bodies. 'Go on. Take a dekko.'

Mace did. Saw Veronica Dinsmor lying on her side, her face pressed into the weeds. Neat bullet hole in the back of her head. From the angle he couldn't see the exit, had to be near her mouth. He grimaced. Metre off Silas Dinsmor on his stomach. Same sort of bullet hole in the back of his head. Both sans shoes, jackets, coats, jewellery. He turned to Gonsalves. 'What's going on here?'

'You mean the way they're lying about?'

'Yeah.'

'Found first by a bergie,' said Gonsalves. 'In the van over there.' Mace looked over at a patrol van with a man in the cage staring at them, talking. 'Patrol found him wandering along the highway with a pair of shoes in his hand, wearing a sort of furry coat. Had a chat with him. He brought them here.'

'Bergies've taken to robbing corpses?'

'For years now.'

'What's he saying?'

'Lotsa stuff. Doesn't make any sense.' Gonsalves came up close to Mace. 'So what d'you think? About this?'

'Not the foggiest,' said Mace. 'Dunno what these two're about in the first place. Who they're mixed up with. You ask me you've got a long slog here. Professional hit, it looks like.'

'My reckoning as well.'

'Chances are you'll go so far and it'll go dead.'

'Ummmm,' said Gonsalves. 'You think so?' He moulded the tobacco into a pellet, flicked it away. 'Too early for another one. Still, all the same, hey, I'm gonna have to get a statement from you.'

'No problemo.'

Mace checked the time. 'I've got some contact numbers for them, back in the States. You can notify the next of kin.'

'Obliged,' said Gonsalves. 'One thing: they tell you anything about the kidnapping?'

'Nothing they didn't tell you.'

'Weird, hey.'

'No kidding.' Mace watched a car turn in at the track come slowly across the vacant ground towards them. It stopped. A woman got out the passenger side: Rachel Pringle. 'You tell her?' he asked the captain.

Gonsalves shook his head. 'No mileage for me. Don't know who she's paying for the tip-offs.'

'Bloody wonderful.'

She came up and Gonsalves stopped her. 'Crime scene beyond here, lady.'

'Come'n Captain,' she said, 'this isn't even your case.'

Mace watched Gonsalves giving her the heavy frown. 'Doesn't matter whose case it is, you're staying right here,' he said. 'Nobody's gonna be squeezing my balls because of you.'

Rachel Pringle glanced at Mace. 'You can tell me,' she said. 'It's the Americans?'

Mace folded his arms across his chest. More than the cold and damp getting at him.

'Has to be. That's why you're here. That's the information I have.'

'You want to know something?' said Mace.

She cocked her head. 'Tell me.'

'Two things. Number one: we're going to sue about that foreign exchange crap you wrote. Number two: last night, the Dinsmors cancelled their contract with us.'

'You confirming this is the Dinsmors?'

'Not confirming anything, Miss Pringle. Just telling you a point of fact.'

Rachel Pringle brought out her notebook. Flipped pages. 'Here're some points of fact. The Dinsmors're not at their hotel. They went out to eat last night. Except they didn't because Mrs Dinsmor was ill at the restaurant. They called a taxi but the hotel says they never returned. Two last points of fact: they were booked on a London flight. They never checked in.'

Gonsalves cleared his throat.

'So I'm asking, Captain, Mr Bishop, is this the Dinsmors?'

Mace said, 'No comment.'

Gonsalves said, 'You gotta use the channels.'

Rachel Pringle smiled at the two men, Mace thinking sometimes when a real bitch smiled there was nothing lovely in it. 'I'll take that as a positive.' She closed her notebook. 'Thank you, Captain.' To Mace said, 'It might interest you, we're running more on Vasa Babic.'

Mace kept his stare on her until she glanced away. 'So?'

'So, you're guarding him.'

Her eyes back on him again, that smile.

'What's your notebook say?'

'Just that.'

'Then you better make some phone calls.'

Mace loved the uncertainty that flickered on Rachel Pringle's face.

'What d'you mean?'

'You're the ace reporter,' said Mace. 'Work it out.' He started towards his car, Gonsalves walking off with him.

'I still want my camera back,' Rachel Pringle shouted.

Mace muttered, 'Yeah, yeah.' Said to Gonsalves, 'She knows a lot.'

'More'n me,' said the captain. Gonsalves tipping him the nod as Mace was about to drive off. 'Was this worth it or what?'

Mace looked at him, couldn't believe what he was hearing.

'A hundred bucks'll do it.'

'Jesus, Gonz,' said Mace, 'what happened to favours?'

Gonz put his meaty paws on the car door. Leaned down. Gave Mace a blast of tobacco mouth. 'Called intellectual property now, Mr Bish. Carries a monetary value. Ask any lawyer.'

Mace got back on the road to Mart Velaze's wondering what shit the Dinsmors had been dealing in. Rather not what shit, what shits? Casinos were big money. In their murky twilights lurked serious players. They rubbed their hands when the ponytails came to town. The lucky ones got ripped off. The others got a third eye. The eye of eternity, Mace'd heard it called. The trouble with clients, you never knew what you were looking after. You never knew what world you were stepping into. Reminded him of the other wanker, Oosthuizen. And Tami.

Mace got hold of Pylon, filled him in on the Dinsmors.

Pylon's comment: 'Save me Jesus.'

Mace asked about Tami. Pylon told him she wasn't answering. He'd been trying every five minutes, left two messages. The last time got an inbox full response.

Mace said, 'Not good.'

Pylon said, 'Cool it. You gave her the day off. The girl doesn't want to be bothered.'

'Yeah, maybe.' Mace slowing into a tailback along the Parkway. 'When I'm done with Velaze, I'll drop by her place.'

'Because you're concerned?' said Pylon, Mace picking up the bite in his voice.

'Why else?'

'Just wondering? Nothing going on I don't know about? Like her sleepover at your house the other night. Bit kinda close isn't it? For a man in mourning.'

Mace stared at the car in front, an old surfer's combi stuck with stickers, brand decals, a whole way of life. Surfers do it standing up. Just dropping in. Born to surf. Get stoked. Life's a beach – except the beach was scratched out replaced with bitch. Next to that a painted addition, And then you die.

Right on, dude.

Pylon rabbiting away about the process of grief. Some passage of time bullshit. Mace not tuned in until he caught the name Sheemina February.

'What's that? What's with her?'

'That's what I want to know. Sort of thing you gotta get out of your system. Do it or don't. Come to a decision, bru, one way or the other. Know what I'm saying?'

'I told you,' said Mace, hearing the scream of baby Hintsa at full belt in the background. Over that, Treasure shouting for Pylon.

Pylon said, 'Duty calls.'

Mace trying to get in another reminder about Tami but Pylon'd disconnected. He tried her himself. Got the inbox full advice.

Mace sat in traffic a spit short of forty-five minutes crawling through the Koeberg interchange.

'I look inside myself hmmm hmmm hmmm ...'

Hit the redial on Tami five times. No answer. Going into Rugby the traffic eased, Mace put foot when he could, ducking and diving lane to lane.

'It's not easy hmmm hmmm hmmm your whole world is black.'

He swung a left at Boundary to Marine Drive, all the twinkly allure of the Drive at night replaced by a ranch-house suburb, seemingly deserted. The lagoon black and cold.

At the Unitas flats Mace left the car in the parking lot, took a lift to the seventh floor. Wondered how he was going to handle this? Smack Mart in the jaw? Hang his balls over his tonsils? Or find out why he'd lied about SARS? He could hear him, 'Not me, buta. Nothing to do with me. Go speak to Revenue.' Mace reckoned to get in fast when Mart opened the door would be best. Play the rest of it by ear.

He watched the numbers lighting up on the panel. Five, six, seven. The lift stank of antiseptic that he remembered from the previous evening. A camera watching him all the way up. Somewhere on the system, Mace reckoned, there'd be footage of an arsehole puking his guts. Small mercy, though, at least the cleaning staff were still doing their job.

On the seventh floor Mace clipped down the corridor to the flat at the end. Knocked.

Hmmm, hmmm, hmmm, hmmm, hmmm.

Knocked again.

A door opened two doors down. An old man in a tracksuit and slippers came out, taser in his hand. Said, 'No one there.'

'There was last night.'

'Hasn't been anyone there since the woman jumped out the window.'

Mace went over to the old man, got a whiff of burnt toast. The old man giving the taser a blast.

'Good those,' said Mace.

'Dunno,' said the old man. 'You can try it out, if you come too close.'

Mace held up his hands. 'The guy that lives there, what time's he get back from work?'

'No one lives there.'

Mace looked down at the old man's slippers, the old man's big toes popped through the tartan material. 'I was here,' he said. 'last night, nine, nine-thirty, to drop something off.'

The old man sucked at his dental plate. 'I'm telling you. The flat's empty. For four months.'

'I was here.'

'You got the wrong floor.'

'The seventh, right. This's the seventh?'

The old man sucked his teeth. 'That's what it says on the number. Seven one o.' He squinted at Mace. 'You go inside?'

'Not inside, no. We stood at the door. I could see inside: there was furniture. A television.'

'All her furniture's there. Like they think she's gonna come back. I went inside, after she jumped. Place was neat as if she'd just cleaned it. Then she jumped. Nice girl. Always smiling and friendly. About twenty-five probably, with a good job in town, everything hunky-dory. Then she jumped.'

'You sure there's been no one living here?'

He gave Mace the squint again. One eye, Mace noticed, dulled with cataract. 'I'm telling you. The flat's empty. For the last four months. Her parents were here, afterwards. They said they were gonna sell the flat. But they haven't. Won't let anyone come near it. People with more money than sense, you ask me.'

'You got their phone number?'

The old man had it off by heart.

Back in his car Mace dialled. When the call was picked up gave a cock-'n-bull story about wanting to trace their tenant. Was told the flat wasn't rented out. There was no tenant.

Mace thought, nice one, buta.

'I see my red door hmmm, hmmm, hmmm.'

Painted black.

'Mart bloody Velaze,' Mace said to Pylon, 'pulled a blind.'

Mace still in the car park outside the Unitas flats gazing up at the seventh floor window on the end. A long way to fall.

'She's in the Constantiaberg,' said Pylon. 'ICU.'

Mace saying, 'I should've bloody known he'd do that.'

Pylon saying, 'Mace. Mace. You're not hearing me. It's Tami.'

Mace shut up. Ice in his veins.

'She was shot.'

Mace said, 'Fuck.'

He spent the next three hours at the hospital, waiting, thinking, eventually cadging a few minutes to see her. Tami strapped up to machines and bags, unconscious. He held her hand. Stared down at her, not a sign on her face she wasn't just sleeping. Said to her, 'This shouldn't have happened. Stay with us, okay. Stay with us.'

A nurse moved him out, Mace going reluctantly. He collared a doctor in the corridor, asked what were Tami's chances? The doctor gave him the up and down, said, 'Who're you?' 'A friend,' Mace replied. Adding, 'A colleague.' Fifty-fifty, he was told, the doctor's attitude suggesting he thought Mace was responsible for Tami's situation.

Mace thought he was responsible. He bought a coffee in the

downstairs cafe, sat in a corner thinking of what Oosthuizen had said. 'Snatched out of your hands, Mr Bishop.' Wasn't too difficult to work out what went down. The Krauts must've shot her. Mace took a mouthful of the coffee, spat it back into the cup. Only thing for it, find the Krauts.

Mace went looking at the airport. Got Pylon to call up contacts to open doors until a couple of hours later he was standing in Max Roland's cell. Only Max Roland wasn't there any longer. 'D'you believe me now?' said the Interpol man. 'He was taken away.'

'By who? Two men, a German and a Swede?'

'No. Not them. They were cross. Woo yai yai, they were cross. Shouting. Making telephone calls. But what can they do? Nothing. This is South Africa.'

'So who took him?'

'Dunno. State security. NIA. CIA. Big men in black. The sort of people you don't bugger around with.'

'And the European guys?'

'They left.'

'Say where they were going?'

'Probably to get drunk, I should think.'

Mace's phone rang. Christa.

'Where are you, Papa?' she said. 'You should've been here like an hour ago. To fetch us.'

59

Sheemina February pulled her X5 into the Seafarer car park and stopped next to the Hummer. She nodded at Magnus Oosthuizen taking a call in the Hummer, a Chihuahua dancing on his lap. He waved at her, rang off. Change of plan, Mart Velaze had said. Magnus, he'd said. She'd raised her eyebrows. Orders, he'd said, from above. Now she watched Oosthuizen shove the dog aside, come over to her car. No loss really.

'Get in, Magnus,' she said. 'Tell me about it.'

'You haven't heard? I'm surprised.'

'I'm flattered you think I have such good contacts.'

Oosthuizen settled himself. 'Nice view' – gazing at the container ships in the roadstead. The swell breaking around the wreck.

'We're not here for the view, Magnus.'

'Have you brought champagne?'

She inclined her head, said, 'Aah. A celebration.' Saw Oosthuizen's hands were trembling. 'It went alright then?'

'I would say so. Yes, I would say so.'

'Congratulations.'

For twenty minutes Sheemina February listened to Magnus Oosthuizen going on and on about how he'd been applauded, about how the defence committee were blown away by his system, about how it was a done deal just waiting for the signatures. His weapons system, the project he'd ploughed all his capital into, was coming good. After all these years. This was a major triumph. A proud victory against the might of the European arms industry.

She could see the dog in the Hummer smudging its nose against the glass, yapping incessantly.

'Afterwards,' Oosthuizen was saying, 'after my presentation, they couldn't praise me enough. They all wanted to shake my hand. They said I'd pulled off a major coup for the country. I had performed a service. Me! The man they once hated.'

'Magnus,' said Sheemina February.

'The man they wanted to put in prison for God knows what reasons, anything they could think of: anthrax bombs, germ warfare. As if I was an evil man. These same people now fawning at my feet.'

'Magnus.' In front of them a boy was feeding the remains of his hamburger and chips to the seagulls, the birds screeching in to snatch the packet out of his hand. The boy ducking, laughing at the mayhem. It made Sheemina smile.

'Magnus,' she said, 'I'm pleased for you. But there's a thing here: what about Max Roland? His rendition.'

Oosthuizen turned his head to look at her. 'What about him?'

'I know about Max Roland, Magnus. Some things I don't know, but I do know about him.'

Oosthuizen nodded, went silent.

'Whatever he has done, he is your colleague.'

'There is nothing I can do about Max. I have spoken to some people. But their hands are tied. Perhaps as a lawyer, you could intervene.'

'I don't think so.'

'Well then.'

'Well then what?'

'I cannot help Max anymore. What has happened is unfortunate.'

'You could also say convenient.'

Oosthuizen raised a finger at her. 'Look. I won't have that crap. Alright.' He froze into a glare, Sheemina returning it.

'Don't point your finger at me.' She reached out and pushed his hand down. 'I am not one of your minions, Magnus.' She watched Oosthuizen straighten in the seat, stare for long moments at the ocean. 'I know Max Roland is a war criminal,' she said. 'I know his name is Vasa Babic. I know he is wanted by the Tribunal.'

'There is nothing I can do about that.'

'You've kept him hidden for many years. While you were developing the system.'

'There was always a risk.'

'Was there?'

'The Tribunal sent people hunting for him before.'

'But Max was never to be found. Until now. Until this moment when everything is done.'

Oosthuizen spun on her again. 'If you are saying I arranged this, you are mad.'

'Oh, I'm not going that far, I'm not saying that, Magnus. What I'm saying is that you've turned your back on him.'

'His money will always be waiting.'

'Will it? Come now. Let's be real. Max Roland's going down for life. Twenty years at least. That's a long time for you to disappear.

In twenty years, with this deal, you will be very rich. In twenty years, as they say in the cowboys, your trail will be cold.'

Oosthuizen opened the car door. 'I have nothing more to say to you.'

'The truth is the truth, Magnus. Sometimes it is worth facing facts. You used Max Roland and now you're hanging him out.'

'That is how you see it. I see it differently. We were partners, that partnership has come to an end.'

Sheemina February laughed. 'To your advantage.'

'So it would seem.'

'To your advantage, Magnus. You've dumped him, Magnus.'

'You cunt,' said Oosthuizen.

'Oh, really. The dreaded c-word. When you don't know what to say, use the c-word. Very nice. Don't get shirty with me, Magnus. Remember who's been helping you lately. Remember who put you onto Mace Bishop to protect your asset.'

'That arsehole. Don't talk to me about that arsehole. What good was he?'

'He kept them away from Max for long enough. You got your system and you got rid of Max.'

Oosthuizen slammed shut the door, glaring at her through the glass. 'As I've said once so I'll say again: you're a cunt, Ms February.'

'You owe me,' she said, buzzing down the window. 'You owe me commission, Magnus. Don't forget.'

He gave her the finger.

Sheemina watched him get into his Hummer, the Chihuahua yapping with glee. He drove off, spinning the wheels on the gravel, small stones pinging against her car.

Sheemina February took the digital recorder from her jacket pocket, replayed the conversation.

'The truth is the truth, Magnus. Sometimes it is worth facing facts.'

She phoned Mart Velaze. 'All yours,' she said.

60

When they got home, Mace said to Christa, 'I can't deal with this sulking, okay. Put the lip away.' The two of them in the lounge, Mace glaring at her, Christa staring at the floor. 'So I was late, I'm sorry. I've got stuff happening and it's difficult doing it all.'

Christa spun away from him, headed for the staircase, Cat2 following.

'I haven't finished,' said Mace. 'You can't just walk away from this.' A couple of paces and he'd grabbed her arm. 'Listen to me, okay. Just listen to me.' Shaking her.

'Papa,' she pulled loose, 'you're hurting me.'

'Well stand still so I can talk to you.'

Mace watching her turn on the waterworks, tears that made him feel like shit.

'Where were you? Where were you that you couldn't pick us up on time?'

'At the hospital, okay. I was at the hospital. Tami' – Mace seeing the name jolt in Christa's face like he'd smacked her.

She flung down her school bag. 'Tami, Tami, Tami. I hate Tami.'

'She was shot, Christa. She might die.'

'My Maman did die. My Maman is dead. Why don't you cry for my Maman? Why don't you hurt like me?' Christa collapsing on the floor, sobbing.

Mace looked down at her. Thinking, this is awful. This is the last thing I need. He crouched. Put a hand out to touch her shoulder. Christa squirmed off across the floor.

'Don't touch me. Leave me. Go to your girlfriend. You like her more than me.'

Mace pulled his hand back as if his fingers had been scorched again.

'What? What're you saying?'

'You said you were going to shave your head. You said you'd do it this afternoon. So that we can both remember Maman. You said. You said.' The sobs shuddering through her body. 'You lied to me.'

'Christa,' said Mace. 'Christa, listen to me. I said I'd do that. And I will. But not while you're like this. Not while you're …'

'I hate you.'

The words punching into Mace. He jerked back, staggering to his feet. 'You're upset,' he said. 'You don't know what you're saying.'

Christa scrabbled onto her knees. Stared up at him, her face ugly with unhappiness. She snatched up her schoolbag, rushed for the stairs. Mace heard her bedroom door bang closed.

He felt physically sick, as if he could puke. His mouth dry, his hands sticky. He took deep breaths to settle himself. Closed his eyes to see Oumou gazing at him, such sadness in her face. 'Please,' he said to her. 'Please come back.'

'Maybe then I'll fade away hmmm, hmmm, hmmm …'

He opened his eyes on the neatness of his living room. The room he and Christa seldom spent time in anymore. On the coffee table Oumou's vase empty that'd always had flowers. On the sofas the silk cushions she'd bought at the Red Shed market. He swallowed hard, headed for the kitchen. Cat2 at his feet, making her strangled cry.

Mace brewed himself coffee, went outside to stand beside the pool looking down on the city. The sky had cleared, the buildings gleamed in the afternoon light. The view that Oumou couldn't get enough of. The view that the bank could snatch away. On the grass he found shards of the mug he'd hurled against the wall. He'd thought things were bad a few days ago, they were worse now. Far worse.

Mace, in his bedroom, opened the built-in cupboard, pushed aside a rack of Oumou's dresses to get at the gun safe. Keyed in the combination, swung the door open on his own private arsenal. Pistols, revolvers, boxes of ammunition. The gun he was after was a .22 Browning Buckmark that he'd taken off the body of Spitz-the-Trigger after Spitz had killed Oumou. He reckoned it had to be a gun supplied by Sheemina February, so altogether fitting to put it back into the loop by using it to nail her. If ballistics ever got round to an analysis after they'd dug the slug out of her head, they'd get really excited. Because this Browning Buckmark had killed before. Specifically when Mace'd had Spitz shoot the dude Obed Chocho. A nice touch, Mace thought, to recommission it for the killing of Sheemina February.

Nice gun too. Smart black finish. He closed his fist round the grip. Hefted the pistol. Good balance, soft rubber grip firm in his grasp. Curled his finger round the trigger. Known to be one of the best triggers in the business. Pointed the pistol at his reflection in the full-length mirror. The black O of the barrel dead centre of his forehead.

Said out loud, 'Jesus, Mace, what're you doing, putting a gun on yourself?' He lowered his arm. Stood looking at his image in the mirror, the gun at his side. A duster coat and a hat and a good pair of boots, he could join the Wild Bunch. The way he felt, not a bad idea.

He burrowed back in the safe for a cleaning kit and a box of ammunition and the silencer. Took these and the gun through to the kitchen, Cat2 winding about his feet, pestering for food with her wheezy meow. Mace cracked a can of tuna, watched the cat attack the chunks. Thought: Cat2 was another of Sheemina February's victims. Wasn't anyone in his family she hadn't put the black mark on. He picked up the gun, jacked out the cartridge and slipped the shells out of the clip, arranging them in a row on the granite top: rimfire Long Rifle loads. Checked the chamber, one ready and waiting. The way Spitz had left it. He ejected it.

Mace pulled the slide, lifted the slide lock. Among its plus points, the Browning was an easy clean. He took a brush to the breech, ran a bore snake through the barrel. Simple as that. From the box of ammunition, fitted ten rounds into the clip. Not that Mace didn't trust Spitz's stock, just that he trusted his own more. He pushed the clip into the butt. Heard it click home. Screwed the can to the barrel. Ready to rock 'n roll.

All he had to do now was wait.

'Hmmm, hmmm, hmmm, I see a red door and it has been painted black.'

61

The German, Jakob, was driving the hired Benz, this time Kalle squinting at the GPS system. Both of them smoking. Both of them fighting against too many whiskies. A carton of take-away coffees lay on the back seat.

'Turn here,' Kalle said. 'This is the street.'

Deep suburbia: high walls, electric fences, tall trees hiding the street lights.

'This is impossible,' said Kalle. 'The street lights are useless. The houses have no numbers. How do we find number twenty-two? We can ride up and down here all night.'

Jakob crawled the car, made no comment. The headlights snagged a parked Audi – the only car in the street. 'Mr Babic's car maybe?'

'Stop,' said Kalle. 'Let me walk.' He got out, disappeared into the shadows.

Half an hour earlier, a maudlin Jakob and Kalle had been three whiskies down in the hotel bar. Their fourth being served as Kalle's phone rang.

The voice said, 'You want Vasa Babic? He's at this place now' – gave an address that Kalle scrawled on the back of a coaster.

'Who are you?' he said. But the phone was dead, the number withheld.

Kalle swallowed the last of his third scotch. 'Chin-chin,' he said to Jakob, 'we have news of our man.'

Jakob frowned, dubious. 'Someone phones and we trust him.'

'Why not? What else can we do?'

'Get drunk.'

'No,' said Kalle. 'If we do not try this, we will always wonder what we missed.'

Jakob said, 'Ja, okay.' They'd knocked back the fourth whisky, shrugged into their macs.

Now Kalle stepped back into the street, pointing at the Audi and the house behind a high white wall. Jakob waited for his partner to get into the car.

'There it is. Number twenty-two. And the car is very warm. What now?'

'We wait for him to come out.'

'Or we go in and fetch him?'

'We wait.'

Kalle shook his head. 'Wait. Wait. Wait. All we do is wait.'

Jakob drove on fifty metres, U-turned to park the car facing the Audi. The men fired up cigarillos, drank their coffee, listened to a mental health programme on the radio.

'The whole country should be listening to this,' said Jakob.

62

Sheemina February, in Levi's and layers of jerseys, her feet buried in sheepskin slippers, stood on the balcony of her apartment watching the sun slide into the ocean. Looked like an egg yolk, sticky, glistening. Tomorrow when it rose everything would be different.

She thought of Magnus Oosthuizen. A foolish man. Strangely naive, given his deep dark past. They'd played him like a fish.

A cold came off the sea, ached in her battered hand. For the better part of three quarters of an hour she'd stood out there staring over the water, washing her thoughts with sauvignon blanc.

Hard to believe it was almost at an end, her blood feud. Although there was always Pylon. He might want to settle the score. Let him try. He was next on the tick list.

So, Mr Bishop, now was vengeance time.

Sheemina swallowed off the remains of the wine in her glass. Time to put him in a wheelchair. His business reputation ruined. His buried treasure confiscated. The bank after his house. His daughter traumatised. Couldn't have turned out better. She clicked the fingernails of her good hand against the rim, red flashes like her thoughts. Anticipating the moment: the gun shot, the kick along her arm. The blood blossoming on him.

Sheemina February laughed out loud. The blood blossoming

on him. Like plum-red rosebuds. The fear on his face as she came closer, closer, stood over him. Reached down and stroked his cheek.

She shivered. Part excitement, part cold. Cape Town cold. The damp cold that got into your bones, froze you from the inside. She hugged herself, rubbing her arms. Yes, stand over him, reach down, touch him. Mace Bishop at her feet. She closed her eyes: saw him lying wounded, helpless.

She shivered again, shook her head, throwing off the fantasy. Enough. She needed to focus. Get in the zone. Get ready for the big date.

Sheemina February went inside, closed the sliding door on the grey twilight. Phoned Mart.

'Doll,' he said. She flinched, didn't like that, the familiarity, but let it ride. 'You've had second thoughts?'

'To a degree,' she said. 'You still in that cafe?' Could hear chatter and music, Tina Turner belting it out, this time, surprise, surprise, Goldeneye.

'Where else?'

'Good.'

'So what's the deal?'

'I've been thinking,' she said, 'I need a head's-up.'

'I can do that.'

'Discreetly.'

'Aah, doll.' He put on hurt. 'I'm a professional. Nobody sees me.'

'I've heard that before. Famous last words, the spy's epitaph.' She poured a glass of wine, estimated another glass left in the bottle. 'What I want's a warning. The moment Macey-boy arrives, it'd be handy to know that.' She swallowed a mouthful of wine. 'Can do?'

'Was going to anyhow.'

She let that ride too. 'Only, Mart …'

He cut in: 'Discreetly. Ja, I know. I'm an old hand, Sheemina. I can suck eggs.'

'Good.' She paused. Tina Turner telling her a bitter kiss would bring him to his knees. No kidding. 'And you don't come until I call. Got that?'

'Loud and clear.'

'I'm serious, Mart. Doesn't matter if it takes me an hour, two hours, all night, you don't come until I phone. Understand. You come before that I will not be amused.'

'So you'll do what? Shoot me?'

She glanced at the revolver lying beside her laptop. The gun he'd got for her. 'Could happen. Don't try your luck.'

He laughed. She didn't.

'Okay, I'll do that for you.'

'Like now.'

'Yeah,' he said. 'Like when I've finished eating. Boss.'

She ignored the sarcasm. 'Enjoy. I'm cooking risotto. A new recipe with roasted almonds.'

'Lucky Mace.'

'I'm not sure he's going to feel like eating.'

Sheemina cut off Mart going 'Aaaah', Tina Turner triumphant, the target in her sights.

'You and I both,' said Sheemina February.

She settled at her desk, ran a finger lightly over the touch pad of her laptop, brought up the CCTV footage of Mace breaking into her flat. She held her breath. Mace Bishop, the balaclavaed man. Sexy man. Right from those days in the camps she'd felt it, his allure. Well, now he was all hers. She paused the last image where he'd rolled down his beanie into the balaclava that covered his face, then looked up at the camera, like he was looking at her.

She ejected the disc, slotted in the one from her internal surveillance system.

On screen Mace moving into her open-plan lounge by torchlight. Running his fingers along the back of her white sofa, walking over to her desk, opening drawers, rifling through her papers. Moving on. Taking in the empty space in her collection of cut-throat razors. She liked that moment, the moment he realised the missing blade was the one that'd slit his wife's throat. Watched him draw back. Suddenly agitated: glancing left and right, the torch beam all over the place. Then moving off quickly, bumping against the couch, as he headed for her bedroom.

She held her breath. Felt her heart rate rise, an electric tingle twitch the fingers of her broken hand. She crossed her legs, clenched her thigh muscles. Watched the balaclavaed man stroke her dresses, put his hand into her underwear, come out with the satin thong. Hold it up. Rub the material between his thumb and fingers. Smell it. Crush it into his fist. Then find the negligee beneath the pillow.

Sheemina February locked her legs tightly. She tracked back to where the balaclavaed man brought the thong to his face, paused it there. She would get him to do that again. She wondered if he'd bring the negligee. When he lay at her feet would she find it in his pocket?

She'd put money on it.

Standing, she looked round her apartment. Too bright. Solid darkness at the window. Sheemina shivered. Partly from the anticipation of Mace Bishop in her lair, partly from the cold. Turned up the heating, turned down the lights.

7:10 p.m. Three or four hours, she reckoned, before he'd show. He wouldn't move until the good citizens were doped with sleep, the city gone quiet. Until then nothing to do but wait.

63

Vasa Babic, aka Max Roland, closed the door to his flat and smelt the stale air of his long absence. Musty. Listened to the silence. The clock in the entrance hall getting louder and louder. No other sound in the flat. He went through to the kitchen, put the box and the voice recorder on the table, sat down staring at them.

Thought about what the man had promised him:

New identity documentation.

Money. Two hundred thousand US.

An air ticket to a country of his choice.

'And what must I do?' he'd asked.

'Kill Magnus Oosthuizen,' the man had said.

'Or?'

'I call the bounty hunters.'

'Why?' he'd asked.

'Why what?'

'Why must I kill him?'

'Probably because you'd want to.' At that point, the man switching on the recording of Magnus Oosthuizen telling a woman how the defence committee had raved about his weapons system. 'You hear,' said the man, 'your system is top of the pops.'

'Who is the woman?' he'd asked.

Been told: 'His lawyer. Advisor. In your case his moral conscience. Hear this' – Oosthuizen telling the woman that there was nothing do be done about Max Roland. In other words, he was off the radar. How convenient. 'You see what I mean?' the man had said. 'Toast, my friend, is the current expression. He regards you as toast.'

Vasa Babic had made no comment.

The man went on: 'Your partner, Vasa, is not a nice person. Not only for betraying you, for other things as well. Now: do you want your revenge? Or do you want the world to know what you did to little girls in the war?'

He knew the man was setting him up. 'I have no guarantee you will keep your word.'

Again the smile. 'No, you don't. But what are your alternatives?'

The man had driven him to his flat. Given him the voice recorder and the box tied with string. The box on the table. He cut the string. In the box a short-barrel .38 fully loaded. He activated the voice recorder.

Magnus Oosthuizen saying, 'His money will always be waiting.' The woman saying, 'Will it? Come now. Let's be real. Max Roland's going down for life. Twenty years at least. That's a long time for you to disappear. In twenty years, with this deal, you will be very rich. In twenty years, as they say in the cowboys, your trail will be cold.' A car door opening, Oosthuizen saying, 'I have nothing more to say to you.' The woman again: 'The truth is the truth, Magnus. Sometimes it is worth facing facts. You used Max Roland and now you're hanging him out.' Oosthuizen unable to stop: 'That is how you see it. I see it differently. We were partners, that partnership has come to an end.' The woman's laugh. 'To your advantage.' 'So it would seem.'

Vasa Babic sighed. Everybody on his case. Sometimes he wished he could sleep, wake up in another world.

In the bedroom he flopped on the bed, tried to sleep, couldn't sleep. Oosthuizen buzzing his thoughts. He betrayed you, Mr Babic. You used Max Roland and now you're hanging him out. Let's be real. Max Roland's going down for life. We were partners, that partnership has come to an end. Fuck you, Magnus, he said.

Vasa Babic showered, cold water only. He dressed in jeans, a rollneck, a three-quarter-length leather jacket with a pocket big enough for the snub-nose. Shut up the flat. Another place he'd not be coming back to. In the underground parking he popped his car's bonnet, reconnected the battery. Fired the Audi on the turn. Drove out into the evening traffic.

Remembered the man saying, 'When you're done, call me.' The man giving him a cellphone. 'Under names I'm A for aardvark.' The man grinning at him. 'Trust me, my brother, it will be alright.'

Twenty minutes later he drove into Oosthuizen's street, parked outside the high white wall. Sat feeling the gun in his pocket. What was it the woman said on the recorder? The truth is the truth. He got out of the car, pressed his finger long and hard on Magnus Oosthuizen's call pad.

No response.

Vasa Babic looked up at the camera. 'I know you're watching, Magnus. Let me in.'

A crackle at the voicebox. 'I'm pleased to see they released you, Max. Shows what my people in high places can do.'

'Yes, yes. Come on, it is cold out here. Let me in.'

The gate lock clicked open. Vasa Babic pushed at the heavy metal door, thinking, Sometimes, Magnus, metal is not enough protection. He walked up the path to the front door, knocked. Typical Magnus making you wait at the door as well.

The door opened, Magnus Oosthuizen standing there cradling the Chihuahua. The Chihuahua wearing a tartan coat, growling.

'Chin-chin,' said Oosthuizen, 'it's only Max.'

Vasa Babic pushed past Oosthuizen heading for the sideboard in the lounge, poured himself a whisky. Turned to face his business partner. 'So,' he said, 'are we in business?' – watching Oosthuizen sit in a leather lounger, pushing back to bring up the footrest. A man triumphant, arrogant in his success.

'We might be,' said Oosthuizen, the dog bolt-upright in his lap, still grizzling. 'Sit, sit. Let me tell you. But first a toast.'

Toast. The man had said, You are toast, Vasa. To Magnus Oosthuizen you are toast.

Oosthuizen smiling at him, superior, self-satisfied, his glass raised. 'To our system. We are about to pull off a major achievement. We're a hit, Max. We're going to make a lot of money. Ziveli, as you say. To life.'

Vasa Babic ignored him, drank off his whisky. 'I have something you must listen to.' He took out the voice recorder, clicked it on, watched Oosthuizen's face swell red and angry.

Oosthuizen shouting, 'What? What? What is that?'

'You,' said Vasa Babic. 'It is you, talking to your lawyer. But wait there is more.' He pulled out the snubnose. 'Listen' – on the recording Oosthuizen going, 'If you are saying I arranged this, you are mad.' 'But I do,' said Vasa Babic. 'I do say you arranged it.'

'No. Wait.' Oosthuizen coming forward in his chair. 'I am your associate.'

Vasa Babic, aka Max Roland, shot Magnus Oosthuizen Mozambican-style: one to the head, one to the heart, Oosthuizen sprawling back in the lounger. Shot the dog, too, a shot that took off the dog's head, splattered bits over master and furniture. Its body jigging on Oosthuizen's lap, like it didn't know about death.

'Crazy dog,' said Vasa Babic.

He found the laptop in Oosthuizen's study, stacks of US dollars in the open safe. Guessed there had to be maybe a hundred thousand in high denominations. The man A for aardvark had said, a plane ticket to anywhere. Argentina would be good. They'd like a weapons system for their next Falklands war. He laughed out loud. Dialled up the man.

A for aardvark said, 'I need proof, Vasa, okay? Take a photograph of dear Magnus with the cellphone camera. I'm at Blues' Vasa Babic heard Tina Turner singing. 'You know, Camps Bay, the restaurant Blues?'

Vasa Babic said he did.

'In half an hour. Okay. No later.'

Vasa Babic wiped down the whisky bottle, the glass he'd used, the door of the safe. Looked round the room, saw the remains of Oosthuizen's dinner on the dining table. An uneaten chop on the plate. He ate that, realising he hadn't eaten since the previous night with the black chick. Tami. He could do with a Tami.

Vasa Babic left Magnus Oosthuizen's house securely locked. Walked down the path to the gate, stepped onto the pavement, pulling the gate closed. Was making for the Audi when down the street an engine fired, headlights popped on, a big car wheel-spinning towards him.

Vasa Babic dropped the laptop and ran.

64

Sheemina February lay in the bath, topping up with hot water as the temperature cooled.

Before that she'd watched a rerun of Don't Look Now on a movie channel. Buzzed on the love-making and the fear.

Afterwards, slotted Piazzolla into the sound system. Tango-walked to the kitchen, imagined she was staring down Mace Bishop.

She'd cracked another bottle of wine. A pinotage, heavy with chocolate. Drank off two glasses while she browned almond flakes in a frying pan, roasted a handful of croutons, waited for the risotto to soften.

She'd set for two, placed lighted candles either end of the table. In the middle, a single long-stemmed rosebud in a vase. Its colour the deep purple of her lipstick.

When the risotto was cooked, she'd slid the dish into the oven to keep warm. Taken her bath.

10:23 p.m. Not long now.

Wearing the long black dress and high heels, Sheemina February sat down to eat alone. Placed the revolver within reach. Sprinkled croutons and almonds and fine-grated parmesan onto the risotto.

She faced the darkened window, could see herself and the room mirrored there. The two candle flames suspended like holy visitations, her face between them, their flicker glinting in her eyes. Behind her on the granite countertop floated a scattering of tea lights. She raised her glass of wine, toasted her reflection.

'To you.'

Sipped. Said, 'And to your helpless future, Mace Bishop.' Flashed on an image of a man in a wheelchair being pushed by his resentful daughter. The man's hair unkempt, his legs covered by a blanket. His mouth tight, sour. The young woman thin-faced, her beauty blackened by her life.

Sheemina drank again. Set down the glass, toyed with her fork through the risotto. She tasted a mouthful, crunched on the croutons. It was good, she picked up the mushroom flavour in the rice, so earthy, almost truffle-like.

She swallowed without appetite.

'Christa.'

Christa heard her father pause outside her bedroom door.

'Christa.'

She didn't answer, pretended sleep. Before he would've opened the door, come in. But that was before. Everything was changed now.

'If you're awake, I'm going out.'

She lay still, curled with her back towards the door. He hadn't said he was going out. She knew he was going to see Tami.

'Not for long. About an hour.'

Just go then. See her. The words coming loudly into her head as if she'd shouted them.

'I'll set the external alarm.'

She held her breath. The door handle clicked. He was coming in.

'Christa.'

The door handle clicked again. She opened her eyes, expecting to see her father backlit, looming. The door was closed, edged with a thin light.

'Christa, I'm sorry.'

She wanted to scream. Fuck off. Fuck off. Just fuck off. Go to your girlfriend. Ball her fists, howl for him to leave her alone. She thrust her face into the pillow, wrapped it round her ears. Lay there in the blackness, her heart thudding, her blood rushing in her ears.

When she raised her head the house was quiet. She heard the car start, drive away.

Good.

Her hands trembled in anticipation. From her schoolbag she took out the artist's cutting knife she'd stolen from school. Loosened the knob, slid it down the plastic handle until the blade appeared. Gave the blade a couple of centimetres, tightened the knob. She tested the blade against the ball of her thumb, drawing blood instantly.

She sucked at the blood, the iron bitter in her mouth.

She would cut a cross on her inner thigh. A long-armed X. She'd never intersected her cuts before. She wondered how that would feel, the blade snagging as it sliced through the first cut. Would it hurt? With her father gone she could scream. Scream at the clean ecstasy of the pain. The bliss.

In the bathroom Christa pulled down her pyjama bottoms, kicked them away. She sat on the lid of the toilet, spread her legs. With her left hand smoothed out a patch of skin between her thumb and forefinger. Held the knife in her right hand.

Looked down at her skin: soft, brown, laced with faint pale scars. Lightly marked out the cross she'd make. The blade etching harmlessly over her thigh.

Then she cut. Sliced the span between her forefinger and her thumb. And screamed. Sucked in air through tight teeth. And cut again. And screamed.

Mace took the station wagon. Hesitated about the Spider: too obvious, remembered the starting problems. This sort of outing you didn't want starting problems. Also seemed right to have something of Oumou's along for the retribution. He got into the car: smelt clay, as if Oumou had just bought the stuff. As if it were the smell of grief. He placed the gun in the glove box.

As he drove out, Mace thought of Christa: she couldn't have been asleep. She must've heard him saying he was sorry. So why didn't she answer? Why was this desert opening between them? It hurt him, her anger, but what could he do? Everything was smashed. Ruined. The whole world painted black. Because he'd been too slow. Because he hadn't got to Sheemina February first.

As he drove, Mace thought of Oumou: the nearness of her. How he'd glimpse her in a room, the swirl of her clothing. How he caught her scent about the house. Even now, even weeks later, she was there. Sometimes even her voice, sometimes he thought he heard her calling him. The way she did … had done … for a meal, or when she wanted to show him her work. So near. And yet gone. Gone to ash. And pain. And the hollow ache of absence. Because he'd been too slow. Because he hadn't got to Sheemina February first.

She'd be waiting. He knew that. This was what she wanted. What she'd set up. So be it. The matter was in Fate's hands.

He gripped the steering wheel, going too fast down Molteno. Hell with it.

Swung into Camp at the lights, accelerating through the dip, running an orange robot across Kloof to Kloof Nek, up the esses at the circle, swinging through the stone pines in the pitch black towards Camps Bay down below. No streetlights, no cars. On a hairpin felt something bump beneath the car. A cat? A night creature? Flicked his eyes to the rearview mirror: the darkness unrevealing.

Mace stayed focused. Kept his speed, working the gears through the bends. His cell rang, vibrating in his pocket. He ignored it. On Victoria turned right towards Bantry Bay into the cliffs of apartments, the heights of the rich.

He drove past Sheemina February's block: no one about. Most of the windows dark, some lights high up opposite. No bother, Mace felt.

He drove on until he found a place to turn, then came back to park opposite the entrance.

His phone rang again: Pylon. Mace didn't answer. Now was not the time. He worked his fingers into leather gloves, pulled a beanie over his ears. From the glove box took out the .22. Felt that the silencer was tight, released the clip, worked the slide. With the heel of his hand clicked the clip back into place.

'For you Oumou,' he said aloud.

The lyrics in his head: 'I look inside myself …'

She could hear the phone ringing upstairs. For a long time. Then quiet. Then ringing again. But it seemed far off.

Her cellphone rang, vibrating on the bedside table, the ringtone: Don't Cha. She ignored it.

Christa let the blood run over her thigh, drip onto the bathroom tiles. Drop by drop by drop: the splashes small and bright between her feet. Less than she'd expected before the stream coagulated. She felt wonderful. Light. Blissful. The sting of the slash marks prickling at her skin.

She laughed. Drew her big toes through the blood splashes, dabbed them on the tiles until the prints dried.

Then danced, remembering ballet steps from long-ago lessons, a fouetté, a pointe. Whirling, prancing, out of her bedroom, along the passage-way up the staircase into the lounge.

Putting on IAMX – I Like Pretending. The drums coming up behind the rough voice. Are we pretending? Christa shuffle dancing now between the furniture, into the kitchen, round the island, until the song ended. She clicked it to replay. The dancing had started the blood again. She stood one-legged like a stork, staring out at the blackness, the trickles of blood inching down her leg. Chris Corner singing, 'Confirm me into the deathwish …'

Sheemina February's cellphone rang, loud in the stillness of her white lair, vibrating on the coffee table. She jerked away from a far place of heat and dust and pain, to pick up the phone. Mart. The time: 10:36. Earlier than she'd expected.

Mart said, 'Your date's arrived.'

Her blood quickened, thrilled in her stomach, a nausea making her light-headed. She swallowed, fought it down.

'It's no joke.'

'Chill,' he said. 'Keep the ice maiden. It suits you.'

'You're out of sight?'

'He won't see me.'

She caught the irritation in his voice. 'Mart,' she said.

'What?'

'Forget it.'

'What?'

'Not until I call, okay?'

'I got that.'

She glanced round the room: the candles still alight. Her meal half-eaten. The wine bottle on the granite top in the kitchen. Her glass, half filled, on the coffee table. Everything as she wanted it.

'He's parked on the street near the entrance,' said Mart. 'Getting out now. Wearing the same gear as the last time. Like on the footage. The CCTV. Walking towards the foyer door. How's he get in there?'

'He'll have a way.'

'With the bloody code. He's got the bloody code. Some security you're paying for.'

'I appreciate the running commentary,' she said. 'Bye, Mart.' And got rid of him.

The moment.

Sheemina February unstrapped her high heels, left them lying beneath the table. High heels were not the shoes for a gunfight. She picked up the revolver, padded through to her bedroom.

Mace pressed in the security code on the keypad, heard the mechanism click open. He scoffed at the CCTV in the foyer with his gob of chewing gum still stuck over the lens. But he stepped into the corridor, he stepped into showtime. Even so, no worries. All the cops would see when someone got a whiff of Sheemina February's rotting corpse and the whole crime scene thing kicked in, would be a man head down in a beanie. The killer's entrance. The killer's exit.

He moved quickly inside, the foyer light snapped on. The lift doors opened: Mace reflected full-figure in the mirror: beanie, black leather jacket, black leather gloves, black jeans, black trainers. Quite the man in black.

He took the stairway, going down the two flights jauntily, no care in the world. At the door onto Sheemina February's level, he paused. Listened: no movement other side. From somewhere, faintly, the explosions and sirens of a cop show on TV.

He opened the door into the dark passageway, the light clicking on as he entered. Twenty smooth paces past the green door with its large number. The cop drama being played out inside the apartment. He grinned, there'd be the real thing going down inside their neighbour's apartment in the next two, three minutes. And it'd be his gun, on Sheemina February.

Wop.

Wop.

He got to number eight: Sheemina February. Rolled his beanie down into a balaclava, listened with an ear pressed against the door for any sound. Nothing. But he knew she was there. Had to be. Her SUV on the parking deck, her way of telling him she was waiting. Sitting on her white sofa tense, nervous, dry-mouthed, waiting. No doubt with a gun in her hand, but waiting. Better to have surprise on your side. To go in fully loaded.

Mace pressed a short hook needle from the lock pick into the door lock. When it caught, tightened the screws. In less than a minute he was easing the door open, the .22 with the can in his right hand.

He stepped into Sheemina February's apartment, closed the door quietly behind him. Paused there, listening. The sound of the sea suddenly loud. He frowned at the tea lights scattered about the kitchen to his left. Probably ten, fifteen of them giving a liquid hesitant light as if he were under water.

'Mace Bishop,' said a voice above him. The confident voice of Sheemina February, brown, honeyed.

Mace glanced up, in the corner above the door saw a small speaker.

'I'm not going to welcome you. Although I should. You're the first guest I've ever had. How quaint it should be a man with a gun. And what sexy gloves. Snap, Mace. Just like mine.'

She could see him. That was something he hadn't considered, that she'd have the rooms dotted with spy cameras.

'Well. Don't just stand there. Come in. There's wine on the counter, a rather nice pinotage, Diemersfontein. You know the one that tastes like chocolate and roasted coffee beans. Pour yourself a glass.'

Mace scanned the kitchen on his left. The camera could be hidden anywhere: in a downlighter socket, in an alarm sensor.

She read him. 'It's in the alarm sensor,' she said. 'How professional you are. The consummate security consultant, getting the lie of the land.'

The alarm sensor on the wall opposite the door.

'Nice gun, Mace. But then it's what one would expect of an arms dealer.' She sniggered. 'Apologies, former gun-runner. I suggest you put it down on the countertop. Leave it next to the wine cooler when you pour yourself a glass.'

Mace made no move to oblige. Stayed fixed to the spot. She had to be in the bedroom, assuming she was in the flat at all.

'Come on, Mace. Lovely as it is to have you here, we've got matters to settle.'

Take out the sensor, that'd even the situation. Then it was two steps down a short passageway to her bedroom. The door opening onto the bed. On the left the cupboard. On the right a door into the bathroom. Trouble was the moment he opened the bedroom door he was exposed. She could nail him twice before he even saw her.

'Mace, cheri. That's what Oumou called you, didn't she? So French. For an Arab. She was Arab, not so? Or one of those Mali mixed-bloods. Not that I can talk on that score. We had that in common she and I. Mixed blood. You fancy the latte types, Mace? Got a thing for our exotic skins?'

Mace let it ride, the taunt about Oumou tightening his chest. But he didn't move. In his pocket his cellphone vibrated.

'Oh come on, Mace. Say something. Get with the programme. Are you going to keep that balaclava on all the time? It's very macho. Very de rigueur. But entirely unnecessary. Believe me, what you think's going to happen, isn't.'

Christa stared through her image reflected in the plate glass window at the city lights below. Her shaven head, harsh, unforgiving. Her pyjama top riding high on her thighs above the slashed X, dried runnels of blood streaking her leg. She saw neither herself nor the city.

The high had gone, left her abandoned. She wiped a welling of tears from her cheeks, swallowed to ease the nausea in her gut. Bent down, flopped onto the kelim curling herself into a ball, the ache for her mother more painful than the sting of the cuts.

Cat2 found her, nudged a cold nose against Christa's chin. Nudged harder until Christa brushed her away, the cat protesting in her strange strangled sounds.

'No,' said Christa. 'No.' Cat2 swiping out a paw as Christa pushed herself upright, the cat's claws raking her ankle. Christa didn't feel the scratches.

Downstairs in her bedroom, she keyed her father's number into her cellphone. Heard it ring three times then go to voicemail. She thumbed it off without leaving a message.

'Papa,' she said aloud, dropping the phone onto her bed. 'Please, Papa, leave her, come home.'

From upstairs came Chris Corner insistent and mournful. Chris seriously out of it. His voice resounding in Christa's head. Like he was inside.

Christa headed for the bathroom, the artist's cutting knife lying there on the side of the bath. She picked it up, ran the blade under the hot tap.

Behind the IAMX chorus girls she could hear the phone ringing.

Sheemina watched the balaclavaed man on the screen of her small monitor.

What was his case, standing there like a statue?

'Are you going to remain there all night, Mr Bishop? I told you, I'm in the bedroom. You know where it is.'

Mace unmoved.

'I have a present for you, Mace. Want to know what it is?'

She watched him. He was listening. Who would have thought that the man of action would be so inactive.

'It's an exchange really. An exchange for my nightie, the negligee you took last time you were here. Remember, the black silky one.'

Ah, that got a twitch of his shoulders.

'Taking a lady's nightie's not on, don't you think? Bit kinky smelling her underwear like that. What's it with men, this smelling? Going around nosing chairs where a woman's sat. Very animal. What d'you smell, hey, Mace? In my thong. What d'you smell? Besides softener. You can smell a woman? Me? My animal scent? That turn you on, Mace? Give you a twitch in your … What shall we call it? Your manhood?'

No response.

'You're returning the negligee, aren't you? I'm sure you are. Well, you want to know what turns me on? It's you, Mace. You in a Speedo. You look closely at the picture I've got of you, as I've done, oh yes, many times, you can see the head of your prick. Very pretty. So, Mace, what d'you think I've bought you?'

She paused. No reaction from the figure on her monitor.

'I'll tell you, save you the suspense. A new Speedo, Mace. That's what. A little black Speedo. Which, I was hoping, as we girls do, was hoping that you'd model it for me. What do you say? Actually, thinking about it, we could both be models, Mace. How about that? You in your costume, me in my negligee. How'd you like that, Mace? That gets me excited.'

Mace Bishop standing there.

'No. Mace Bishop, the man without feelings. The man who doesn't get worked up even when his victims scream and cry and beg.'

She paused.

'Enough of the sweet talk. Here's the thing, Mace. Here's what I am going to do to you. I am going to put you in a wheelchair for the rest of your life. Make you dependent on everyone. Won't your young daughter like that? How's she doing, Mace? Such a pretty girl so screwed up.'

She watched Mace, the fingers of his free hand balling into a fist.

'Ag shame. There's things I know about your daughter, you don't, Macey boy. Things a father should know if he was paying attention. You've got to watch closely, like me. I watch you both very closely.'

Watched him release his fingers.

Sheemina sat with her back against the wall on the far side of the bed, the smallest target possible, a clear line of sight to the door. The revolver in her lap, both hands wrapped around the grip. The monitor balanced on the bed at eye level. If Mace stepped into the doorway back lit he'd get two bullets: right shoulder to take out his gun arm, slide down, put one in his right thigh. If she hit the knee that'd be good too. This sort of situation, she reckoned, even the great Mace Bishop couldn't react fast enough to get one off. He'd see the muzzle flash but that'd not be useful. If he came in low this could be a challenge, but she didn't see him doing that. He'd push open the door, step in expecting her to be in the bathroom. Expecting she'd use that door as a shield. How wrong he'd be. She smiled. If she could get him to move. Mace Bishop still standing there like some weird sculpture of a thug.

'What I said frighten you, Mace, cheri? Which one the most: the modelling? Or you in a wheelchair? Your future?'

He moved, took off fast. Sheemina brought up the revolver to point at the doorway, rested her elbows on the bed. The man was like a cat, she couldn't hear him.

Mace headed for the sensor, smashed the lens. That evened up the situation.

'Oh very smart, Mr Bishop. Very clever,' came her taunting. In stereo: her voice from the bedroom, its electronic version from the speaker at the door.

She'd be on red alert now, expecting him to come in gun blazing. She'd have the advantage, know where he was while he was shooting in the dark.

He waited. One minute. Two minutes. Checked the time on his watch, the second hand circling slowly.

Mace faced down the short passageway to the bedroom door at the end, slightly ajar. He pictured her in there: probably in the bathroom, the obvious place was in the bathroom. She wouldn't be in the obvious place. She'd be down behind the bed or off left, protected by the door swinging open. That'd be her advantage. Where he'd have positioned himself.

Three minutes.

Amazing she'd let the silence run that long.

Another minute. The only sound the wash and break of the surf, even that was muted.

Mace kept still. Not a chirp out of her. He checked his watch: five minutes. He could wait. See how long it took to break her. He shook his head at the way she'd run her mouth. Not the cool chick she thought she was. Silence would stress her out. Mace let the seconds pass.

At seven minutes he reached over for the bottle of wine, clinked it against the glass as he poured.

Still had the bottle in hand when she said, 'Drinking up some courage, Mace? Not got the balls for this, cheri?'

Mace smiled. Touched his forefinger to his tongue, chalked up one on an invisible board. He faked a cough, feeling the play had swung in his favour. True enough. Sheemina coming in on cue.

'Too heavy for a beer man, is it, the wine? Gun-runners not got the palate for fine wine? Sip it, Mace. That's what you do with wine. Try not to gulp and sluk.'

He set down the glass on the granite countertop, loud enough for her to get the picture.

'Better, isn't it, my way? Another tip. Hold the wine in your mouth before you swallow.'

Mace nodding his head, yeah, yeah.

'How's that? Tasty? Well, at least paraplegics can still drink wine.' She splutter-laughed. 'Through a straw.'

Silence. The loud break of a wave, the hiss of it running onto the rocks. Mace glanced at the red hand on his watch: not quite thirty seconds, she was back at him.

'Come on, big boy. Time we did this.'

Yeah, thought Mace. Time. He grabbed a seat cushion off the leather sofa, surprised at its heaviness, the sofa scraping on the floor at the movement.

'What're you doing?' said Sheemina. 'Rearranging my furniture? I don't need that. It's the way I like it.'

Got to a point, Mace thought, where talk revealed the nerves. At that point you'd lost it. He reckoned Sheemina February was at that point.

Holding the cushion in his left hand, he started down the passageway. Paused outside the bedroom door. Thought, shit, you need to switch off the downlighters. Was as good as catching him in a spotlight the way she'd arranged it.

Mace left the cushion outside the door, walked backwards to the lounge. He tried a couple of switches but none of them worked the passage lights.

Heard Sheemina laugh. 'The switch is in here,' she said. 'Be my guest.'

Mace cursed.

'One of the little design eccentricities. Useful, though, for times like these, don't you think?'

Mace tracked back, lifted the cushion in his left hand. Gripped the .22 in his right. He planted his feet, counted one, two, three, swivelled to the right from his waist to get some momentum going. On three, swung the cushion hard against the door, the door bouncing back, the cushion flying on into the room.

Sheemina's first shot went through the cushion, the lead smacking somewhere high on the wall.

Mace saw the muzzle flash behind the bed. Awkward. Had to step half into the doorway to make his shots, wop, wop, grouping them close together. Knowing he'd missed. That he was wide open.

Sheemina's second shot taking him in the upper arm. The impact staggering him, spinning him against the doorframe.

Mace sucked in air, the Browning falling from his grip, like his arm wasn't his anymore.

Sheemina's third bullet smacked bang into the back of his thigh.

Mace went down, hot pain driving through his body. Again heard Sheemina February's laugh.

'I'd say stick with the day job, Mace. Hitman's not your scene.'

Christa drew the blade up her inner thigh. She'd not cut her right leg before because of the angle. Until now. Until she'd sat on the edge of the bath looking at the smooth unmarked skin, realising if she sliced upwards it would work.

Pricked the blade into her flesh. Not so much as twitching at the cut. Then pulled it sharply opening an angry tear across the softness. The slash beading with blood.

She got the surge. The flash. The hit of happiness. The stinging, the rawness making her laugh out loud.

Upstairs IAMX cranked loud: 'The whole world's insanities.'

Christa sang a beat behind: 'The bleeding hearts …'

'… and tragedies.'

The choir coming in: light voices hopping across the words.

Christa looked at her wrist: the blue lines faintly beneath the skin.

What if …?

What if she cut across them?

'The deathwish.'

He watched the blood spreading.

A dark patch on his black jeans.

Shit, he thought, shit, Mace, you walked into this.

With his good hand he gripped his wounded leg.

Didn't stop the pain or the blood.

If the bullet had holed an artery …

He didn't want to think about that.

About bleeding out. About the next twenty minutes.

He couldn't feel his right shoulder.

He could see his right hand but he couldn't move his fingers.

His gun was an easy reach from his right hand.

If he could slide his fingers there.

If he could …

The pain pulled at his face.

Mace squeezed his eyes shut, thought, bitch.

Said, 'Fuck it.'

Tried to reach the gun with his good hand.

Watched Sheemina February shift it away with her bare foot.

Sheemina on the phone said to her neighbour, 'Mrs Lewis, don't worry. I heard the shots. Four or five, yes. Yes. I've called the police. Yes, they'll send a van. Should we meet them? I don't think so. No, no need for that. What? Maybe someone's wounded? I wouldn't imagine so. I think probably it was just a thug on the road passing by. A gangster. You know how it is these days. Probably firing into the air. Yes, yes. You're right, they shouldn't. It's dangerous. But I wouldn't worry, Mrs Lewis. Leave it to the police. Okay. Okay. Surely, put him on. Mr Lewis! No, Mr Lewis, once one person has reported it that's enough. I don't think you should worry. Alright. Let them handle it. You were watching Miami Blues. Sometimes there's no difference, is there? I mean between that and what you see on the news. I agree, it's confusing. This sort of behaviour? No, I don't think the cop shows influence it. Yes. That's true. Sheer madness. Yes, it's what we've become. A violent nation. Well, not all of us.' She chuckled. 'You wouldn't want to include us in that would you? No, not at all. Night, Mr Lewis. Okay. I'll check my door's locked.'

She keyed off the phone. Said, 'Good to have socially responsible neighbours, don't you think? Concerned people. Most people don't want to know. Too scared they'll get involved in something.' In a single swipe pulled off his balaclava, threw it aside. 'That's better. There's a pretty boy.' She stared down at Mace, Mace half-propped against the wall, clutching his leg with his good hand. His face tight with pain.

'Oh, come on, Mace, be a big boy, you're not going to die.' Sheemina stood back. 'The leg's a nasty one I have to admit. But you're hardly going to bleed to death from that or the shoulder. So grow up.'

She watched him try to grab his gun, inched it away beyond his reach with her foot.

'Besides, pain's useful, it keeps you alive. Now listen, we haven't got too much time.'

She sat down opposite him with her back against the wall.

'Cosy, isn't it? You and me. Together.' She put the gun on him. 'In case you weren't counting, two more left inside so keep calm.' Smiled at him, lowered the weapon. 'Mace, Mace. Take your mind back. Back to those days in the MK camps when you were earning a living by way of smashing people's hands.' She held up her gloved hand. 'Remember doing this? Remember afterwards, when you came to me?'

Mace spat. 'Bullshit.'

'Ah, you're listening.' Sheemina cocked her head. 'Interesting, our position now, isn't it? You know Mace for all your rep – gun-runner, good man in a tough spot, sharpshooter, ace security guy – I got you. Me. Just like that. Wasn't even a major effort. Here you are, the great Mace Bishop, man down having taken lead. Twice to be precise. And I'm not even hurt. Makes a girl wonder how you stayed alive this long.' She looked at him. 'Tongue-tied? Then, the great Mace Bishop never was an orator.' Gave him her purple smile. 'By the way, you approve of the dress, I assume? You seemed to like it when you were here before. On your snoop trip. That's why I'm wearing it. Specially for you.'

Giving him the full-on stare, no smile now.

'Mace, back to that night in the camp when you came to me. Wanting to fuck me.'

'Bullshit.'

'Wanting to fuck me, Mace. I could tell. In your eyes, I could tell. I got to see that look a lot of times, in men's eyes. In Membesh. In Quatro. That's what our heroes did for fun. To pass the time. The big boys. The big boys you see nowadays in their Armani suits. They'd get that look. Come into our cells to pick a woman like they were picking fruit. I'll have that one. You. Collect-a-cunt's what they called it. Nice, hmm? After that recycling thing. Collect-a-can. I can hear them laughing.

'But let's not go there. It's ugly stuff. The sort of stuff can make you want to get even. Makes you fantasise about revenge. My stuff, Mace. Thanks to you.

'That night. I'm lying there naked on the mattress with my broken hand throbbing. Throbbing like I hadn't known pain before. So sharp, so constant, so everywhere in my body death would've been a mercy. I remember thinking that. Thinking please kill me because then I wouldn't be in pain. Pain so bad I couldn't see properly. Everything was blurred. Even you at first. Standing next to me. This white angel with all the blond hair. The devil angel. Staring down at my body, my breasts, my thighs. You remember you crouched down, touched my cheek. Then my nipples. Softly with the tips of your fingers.'

'Fuck you.'

'You wanted to, yes. Running your hand over my breast very lightly, all the way to my stomach. Very gentle was my white angel.'

Mace groaned, tried to shift his position. 'In your dreams.'

'It happened, Mace. That's what you did. You know, I know. That's why you stole my nightie. To remember that night. To take you back. To the smell of pain and fear and sex. The heat. The sweat on my body. Dark stuff, Mace.'

'No.'

'No what?'

'Crap. It's all crap. It's your fantasy.'

'I don't think so. Troubling thing is, Mace, your gentleness. That's what I remember. How gentle you were, for a rapist. Afterwards, the others, they wanted something different.'

'Ah fuck.' Mace grimaced with pain. 'Jesus. Fuck you.'

'Not this time, cheri. Although …' She sighed. 'Another day, another place, who knows? You're a sexy man. You get a certain type of woman horny. Me. Oumou. That American bitch, Isabella. Tami. All the casuals I don't even know about. Testosterone Mace. That was it, you see. Thing is, Mace, you brought a lot of trouble into my life but sometimes I wonder if maybe, if maybe without my broken hand, my Mace-Bishop-smashed-hand, I would've got where I've got. Know what I mean? You gave me credence. Credibility. Sick. So sick. Funny thing is, Mace. Afterwards, in Quatro, I never thought of you again. There wasn't some deep dark vengeance thing in me, I just wanted to survive, to live again. Not until all those years later when I met you with that stutterer, what's his name, Ducky Donald's boy, then I thought about it. When there you were, you and Oumou and little Christa in my city. Then I thought about it. A lot. And you know what? The more you get into it, the revenge thing, the more it becomes its own beast. Takes on a life of its own. That's why they say, you want revenge, buy two coffins. Which is probably true mostly. Except this time it's not. Tough luck.'

She stood, straightened her dress. Glanced down at Mace. 'God you look pathetic. Pain is a smashed hand, Mace. Not two little bullets. Come on, be a man.' She prodded his wounded leg; Mace bit down on a scream.

'Anyhow, before we move to the grand finale, I have a secret for you. Something else you won't appreciate, but what can I do? History is history. Fact is fact. Fact in this instance, Mace cheri, is bashing my hand to pulp didn't get you what you wanted. Didn't get you the truth. Fact is, you know, I was an agent. That hated type, an apartheid spy. How about that? And nobody ever knew for sure. Here's this traitor with a Maced hand waltzing about in their midst and they never knew. I was good. You have to admit, I was good. I'm still good. End result? I got information on all the big players. Both sides. The lowdown. The dirt. Which, I've found, is a misnomer after all. What it's actually is paper. You know, paper in the stock market sense? Like a share that can be converted into money. Hard cash. That's what I got. Come the new country I ditched the whiteys, bedded down with the darkies. Hardly difficult seeing as they'd bedded me already. I snuggled up, got even more paper on them: who got arms deal kickbacks, who got lifestyle changes, which gangster bought presents for which cabinet minister. You know, that sort of thing. Who got farms, cars, houses, holidays, directorships. Whose family ended up with the major contracts. Long and short, who put their pudgy fingers in the state's till. So much of it going on, you keep your eyes open, at some point you're going to score. What can I tell you? In this world, the rich and powerful are the ones with the lowdown. Probably it's always been like that. So there you go, Mace. Story of my life.'

She smiled at him.

'Now, cheri, we get to the hurting part. I'm going to need you to turn over so I've a good shot at your spine.'

Last chance. She was within reach. If he caught her ankle he could bring her down, get her gun. In the tumble things could go any way. Any way was better than her way.

Mace swung at her with his good hand, leaning hard on the leg wound. Pain howled through his body. His fingers grasped her leg. He pulled but his strength was gone.

Sheemina February jerked herself free, stepped back.

'Not a good idea. Either you help me here, Mace, or we're going to have problems.'

'Maybe I can help?' said a voice.

Mace focused through the agony at the shape in the lounge: Mart Velaze.

Sheemina pivoted. 'Mart, I told you. Stay out of it.'

Mart standing there with a gun in his hand. A Ruger, Mace reckoned, .22 with a silencer. The assassin's gun.

'I know,' said Mart, 'but I'm here now.'

'Go,' said Sheemina, waving him away. 'This's my play. This's the way I want it.'

'I don't think so, baby,' said Mart. 'I mean, I got no candle for him' – pointing his gun at Mace, Mace thinking, Jesus the guy's going to shoot me – 'but you need help here. He's a wily bugger, is our friend Mace. Even shot up.'

'Back off, Mart.'

Mace scheming he could try another lunge while she was distracted.

Mart shouting, 'Watch it, he's gonna grab you.'

Mace making his move, swiping his arm through empty air.

Heard Sheemina February laugh. 'Enough now, Mace. Accept your situation.'

'That's Mace's thing,' he heard Mart say, 'not ever giving up.'

The voices coming from a distance.

Saw Sheemina February looking down at him, not hatred in her eyes but amusement, her bright lips parted, a glisten on her teeth.

'Oumou,' he said, the name faint, so faint he wasn't sure he'd said it.

Mace shifted his gaze from Sheemina to Mart. Mart's lips twitching in what could've been a smile, like he was holding back, trying not to grin. Mace squinted. Mart blurring, coming in and out of focus. Becoming a shape Mace wasn't sure was there at all. He blinked. Sweat stinging his eyes, making them water.

'Don't cry, Mace,' said Mart. 'Be a brave cowboy.' Mart raising his gun arm.

Sheemina saying, 'Mart back off. This's my gig.'

Pain tore through Mace blacking his vision. The voices of Sheemina and Mart at the edge of the blackness. Not the words, just the sound of Sheemina strident.

Then Sheemina saying, 'I'm losing patience.'

Mart coming back, 'He's all yours. Forget I'm here.'

Mace snapped on him again. Mart in full clarity: his lips become a grin. His eyes dead brown. His gun arm up. The gun pointing. Mace tried to speak. To say, 'You bastard.' The words in his head, banging in his head: you bastard, you bastard, you bastard. But he couldn't say them loud enough. Could only force a whisper.

'What's that?' Mart saying. 'What're you on about? Speak up, bru.'

'Enough.' Mace seeing Sheemina February bending towards him, bringing her gun in close.

Behind her Mart still in clear vision. Even the tightening of the guy's skin on his knuckle, squeezing the trigger.

The gun firing.

Mace jerked. Saw muzzle smoke. Heard the lead punch home.

Mart putting a single shot smack into Sheemina February's head. From no more than two metres. Sheemina February not even making a whimper.

Mace seeing her folding towards him, like she wanted to kiss him. Her weight warm and dead over his body. 'How sweet,' he heard Mart say. 'Two lovebirds.' Mart suddenly in his face, Mart crouched, whispering at him, 'Don't worry buta, I've called an ambulance, okay. Take this' – folding the fingers of Mace's good hand round the butt of the Ruger – 'it'll look better.' Mart picking up the Browning. 'I'll have that' – backing away.

Mace got the Ruger up enough to squeeze the trigger. A click.

Heard Mart laugh. 'Buta, don't be a moegoe.'

65

Treasure said to Pylon, 'Give them a break. It's half past ten.' She and Pylon and their children playing happy family in the lounge, more worry in Pylon's heart than he'd known ever. Treasure shifted the baby from one boob to the other. With her foot poked at Pumla doing homework on the floor in front of the TV: Don Johnson in white with his gat pointed at the baddies. 'And you young lady, bed.'

Pumla coming back, 'Aah, ma. My homework's not finished.'

'Don't "aah ma" me. Off. Now.'

Pylon saying in Xhosa, 'Why're they not answering any of the phones?'

Pumla saying, 'Can't I …'

'No.' Treasure giving her another prod. 'If you'd watched less TV you'd have finished. Go'n. Upstairs.' Switching to Xhosa to answer Pylon. 'Maybe they're asleep. You considered that?'

'The state they were in? No ways. You saw him, how he left here with Christa. The guy's strung out. Desperate. He could do anything.'

'So's Christa,' said Pumla.

Pylon looked at her. 'What d'you mean? The hair shaving thing?'

She shook her head. 'I can't really …'

Treasure reaching out for her daughter's arm. 'Pumla, can't really what?' Pulling her in. 'What's happening?'

Pumla close to tears. 'It's just …'

Pylon and Treasure staring at her. 'What?'

'I can't tell you. It's a secret.'

'Drugs,' said Treasure. 'Is it drugs?'

Pumla shook her head.

'Something was done to her? She's doing something? Like cellphone sex? There's a video clip on the internet?'

'Save me Jesus,' said Pylon.

'No …' Pumla letting the tears roll.

'Pummie,' said Pylon. 'Please. Something's wrong here. You've got to tell us.'

'She's cutting herself.'

'What?'

'With a blade. On her legs.' Pumla in full flood. 'It's horrible.'

Treasure brushed tears from her daughter's face. 'You've seen the marks?'

'Yes, yes, lots of them. Inside her thigh.' Pumla rubbing the inside of her own thigh. 'Scabby. And some of them still bleed. She likes it. She says it doesn't hurt too much. That you get this like buzz, that you're powerful. That you can do anything. You can make yourself bleed.'

'Wait. Slow down, okay. Slowly.' Pylon standing, cradling his wounded arm. 'When, when did she tell you this?'

'Today. This afternoon.' Pumla collapsed onto the couch beside Treasure. 'It's horrible, horrible, horrible.'

'Tula, sisi' – Treasure snaking an arm round her daughter, the baby grizzling at the movement. 'How long's she been doing this?'

Pumla snivelled, shook her head. 'Not long. Since Oumou was killed.'

'Chrissakes.' Pylon wheeling about the room. 'I'm going. Now. To their house.'

'Pylon.'

'Where're the car keys?'

'Pylon.'

'Where're the car keys? Dammit, where're the car keys?'

'Pylon. You can't drive. You'll have an accident.'

'Where're the car keys?'

'Pylon. Stop it. Stop.'

Pylon stopped, staring at her, his good hand held out. 'We've gotta go there, Treasure. Please.'

She unplugged the child, gave him a sour look. 'Alright. That'll be all of us. Baby and Pumla.'

'It mightn't …' Pylon began, changed his mind. 'Sure. Fine.'

Treasure drove, Pylon in the passenger seat, Pumla in the back plugged into her iPod, beside her the baby strapped in a car seat.

'I could've done this,' said Pylon, 'without bothering everyone.'

'No doubt,' said Treasure. 'Very macho.' She put foot up Paradise Road towards the Rhodes Drive intersection, the light red. Nothing ahead of them, Pylon getting a grip on the armrest in case Treasure had to brake. Fifty metres out the robot went green, he relaxed. 'What I want to know,' Treasure said – winding the speed to a hundred and ten through the forest stretch – 'is what's going on? What's happened? With you and Mace?'

'Nothing,' said Pylon.

'Rubbish.'

'Nothing we can't sort out.'

She glanced at him. 'So it's major.'

Pylon coming back an octave too high. 'No, I wouldn't say that. It's not major. It's not anywheres near major. We've hit some trouble, that's all. Nothing new. We've been there before. We got through it, we can get through it again.'

'Sounded major. The tone of your voices.' Treasure taking the S-bend at the university with some tyre squeal. 'So what's the trouble? Like what kind of trouble're you talking?'

'You know … difficulties. Business issues. Jesus, Treasure, d'you want chapter and verse?'

'Yes. Actually yes.'

'Here? Now?'

'Why not? There's something else you want to do?'

'It's complicated.'

'Naturally.' Treasure keeping the clock at one-ten past the Mill, the wildebeest slopes, into Hospital Bend. 'I'm listening.'

Pylon clucked his tongue, gave her the Reader's Digest version, sans the Cayman boogaloo, bringing the sorry tale to an end as Treasure came off De Waal slowing for the speed camera beneath the stone pines. She didn't say anything when he'd finished. Didn't look at him. Kept her eyes on the road, her hands fastened to the steering wheel. Only on the Molteno rise, saying, 'You'd better sort it, Pylon. For all our sakes.'

She came slowly towards Mace's house.

'And now?'

Pylon lifted a remote, the street gate rolled back. Treasure drove them in.

'Wait here,' he said.

Treasure made a move to open her door. Pylon stopped her.

'Not a good idea.'

She raised her eyebrows but sat tight.

Pylon was out of the car fast, his arm strapped across his chest, juggling keys to the house from his jeans pocket. Realised as he inserted the key his hand was trembling. Realised he was expecting various kinds of horror. Maybe even the typical story: father shoots daughter, commits suicide. The common theme. He paused. Could hear some pop band belting it out.

Pylon unlocked the door, pushed it gently. Despite the music heard the alarm peeping. He shouted: 'Christa! Christa!' Paused. Not expecting Mace around with that racket. 'Christa, it's Pylon. Where're you, sisi?' He closed the door, heading for the alarm pad in the kitchen. Only after punching in the code, noticed the blood spots on the floor.

'Christa!' – hopped down the stairs two at a time to her bedroom, thinking, Fuck it, he hadn't got his gun back. He went through the door with his good shoulder, the door banging back against the wall. 'Christa!'

Christa lying on her bed, the duvet patched with blood. Slashes on her thighs, cuts across her wrist. Veins not arteries.

He found a pulse in her neck. Whispered, 'It's Pylon, sisi. Talk to me. Come on, sisi. Let's have you back with us. You gotta talk to me.' Patting her cheek with his good hand, watching the flicker beneath her eyelids, her eyes popping open. 'There we go.' Smiling at her. 'You gave me a fright there, sisi. Like heart-stopping. Come on, sit up. Hey, Christa' – Pylon drawing her up, hugging her. He could feel her shuddering against his chest, sobbing deeply. He let her drain it out, minute after minute. Only when she'd stilled said, 'Where's Mace?'

Got her sobbing intake of breath, 'W-with Tami.'

'With Tami? At the hospital?'

Christa nodding.

'Not the hospital,' he said. 'Not at this time of night.' Pylon thinking, Sheemina February.

'When did he go out?'

Felt the shake of her head.

'Half an hour ago? Hour ago?'

Caught Christa's 'Not long.'

Too long. What'd Mace said, Bantry Bay? Victoria Road. Estate agent Dave'd given him an address in Bantry Bay.

'I'm gonna find him,' he said to Christa. 'Treasure's here and Pumla. They'll look after you. Okay?'

She nodded, at the movement a smell of sweat coming off her scalp.

66

KOSOVO'S COMMANDER DEATH ARRESTED

Vasa Babic, who was on the run from the International Criminal Tribunal in the Hague, has been apprehended in Cape Town after being spotted at the airport by a Cape Times reporter.

Officers for the Tribunal confirmed that he was arrested last night and is being held in custody pending his rendition to Holland this evening.

It is understood that Vasa Babic has been living in Cape Town for some time under the name Max Roland.

Babic faces charges of crimes against humanity, including murder, rape and torture perpetrated during the war in Kosovo. Because of his alleged brutality he was nicknamed Commander Death.

Americans found shot

The bodies of an American business couple were found in the grounds of the mothballed Athlone power station yesterday. They had been shot execution-style.

The couple, Mr and Mrs Silas and Veronica Dinsmor were part of a BEE consortium planning to develop casinos in the rural areas.

A lawyer for the consortium, Ms Sheemina February said, 'This is a tragedy. Our crime situation is completely out of control. Not only were the Dinsmors going to invest financially but they had useful experience as they have been running casinos in the Native American areas of the United States for two decades.'

Ms February said the casino roll-out would bring jobs to many poverty-stricken areas.

According to a police source, a syndicate might have targeted the Dinsmor couple in an attempt to extort money.

Meanwhile a Youth League spokesman has warned that foreign investment could 'steal' resources.

'Foreigners must watch out,' he said. 'They are stealing our land and our jobs. They are the new colonialists.'

Weapons system awarded to European consortium

The defence committee announced last night that it had awarded the contract for the weapons systems to be installed on the new frigates to a European consortium.

A spokesperson for the committee said that the weapons system was highly sophisticated and was already being used by the German and French navies.

She said that installing a tried and tested system had numerous advantages as there would be no teething problems which often proved expensive and time-consuming to eradicate.

'We expect that our frigates will be fully functional within the next six months,' she said.

Along with the weapons system comes an attractive offset component which will be of benefit to both the manufacturing industry and the labour market as it is expected to create 50,000 new jobs.

The controversial arms deal that led to the acquisition of the frigates was also 'sweetened' with offset opportunities. Few of these components have materialised.

A South African weapons system designed by Magtech was also considered by the defence committee. The spokesperson confirmed that this would have cost less than the system designed by the European consortium but that it was untested and had lacked the offset advantages.

Magtech CEO Magnus Oosthuizen could not be reached for comment.

Shots at luxury apartment

Police and paramedics were called to a Bantry Bay apartment late last night after shots were heard. Police confirmed the incident but could not release any further information.

Tuesday, 2 August

67

Early morning: Captain Gonsalves had a techie run some grainy black-and-white CCTV footage showing a tall man in an anorak, a beanie on his head, face-down, walking towards the camera.

'What you wanna see this for, it's not your case?' said the young techie in front of the computer screen. He twisted round to look at the police captain standing behind him.

'No good reason.' The captain was shredding a cigarette. 'Just sommer for fun. Before it gets lost.'

'Why'd you say that?'

'Just sommer for fun.'

The techie shrugged, turned to the computer.

The man on screen, his back to the camera, neck bent forward, seemed to be working something in his hands.

'He's aware of the camera,' said the young techie.

'It prob'ly sticks out in that corridor. On a metal elbow. You'd have to be blind not to see it, prob'ly.' Captain Gonsalves balled the tobacco from the cigarette into a pellet, popped it into his mouth. 'Lousy picture. Equipment must be old as the ark. In Jewland you'd have thought people could afford better.'

'Look at this.' The techie, pointing at the image. 'Look how quickly he gets in. Forty seconds, I timed it.'

'A pro.' Gonsalves gave the plug a chew. 'You don't even see his equipment.'

'See, he's in.'

The man standing in the doorway rolling the beanie down to become a balaclava covering his face. Closing the door.

'Interesting,' said Gonsalves, eyes on the white flicker of the empty corridor. 'Why'd he do that, d'you think, wear a balaclava?'

'Guy's a thief. Doesn't want to be recognised.'

'He knows the woman in the flat. She knows him. No need for a balaclava. That's weird.'

The techie raised his eyebrows, looked at the captain. 'That true?'

'Yeah,' said Gonsalves.

'Something you're not saying, right?'

Gonsalves laughed. 'There's always something I'm not saying.'

The CCTV footage spooled on, showing the two closed doors of the apartments leading off the corridor. The screen went black.

'The corridor lights must be on a timer,' said the techie. 'Go off after thirty seconds. About ten, twelve minutes later' – he fast-forwarded the tape – 'Check this.'

The light came on again. There's a man in a beanie, head down, stepping into the corridor, walking quickly to Sheemina February's flat. Getting in with a key.

'That guy,' said the techie, 'he doesn't come out. You recognise him?'

'Nah.' Gonsalves sucked at the tobacco pellet.

'The next people on here're the paramedics about fifteen minutes later.'

'That so? No CCTV on the parking deck? Nothing in the foyer?'

'Nothing on the car deck. Camera in the foyer had chewing gum stuck to the lens.'

'Nice. Play it again.'

The young techie did. Gonsalves chewed his tobacco, said, 'That second guy white or black, you think?'

'Probably white I'd guess,' said the young techie.

'You would? Why's that?'

'Way he walks. Hasn't got the floppy's style.'

Gonsalves smiled. 'Watch it, with the race mouth.'

'It's true.'

'Sure. Watch it, that's all.'

'Yes, sir.'

'Captain.'

'Captain.'

'You wanna know what though, he's a darkie.'

'Serious.'

'Ja, man, serious.' Gonsalves swallowed tobacco juice welling in his mouth. 'You sure that second okie never came out?'

'Absolutely, never at all.'

'So what? He's a guardian angel? Flies off. Vanishes like a ghost? A bloody spook.'

The techie shrugged. 'Like you said, before it gets lost.' He glanced at the captain. 'Actually, I heard they're probably gonna shelve it.'

'Who knows, hey? Anything's possible.'

'Swhat I heard. Everything's gotta go to the investigating team. Even this CCTV. That happens, you know, file filed.' He pointed at the ceiling. 'What I heard it's right from the top.'

'You hear a lot,' said Gonsalves.

'When you're a techie,' said the techie, 'nobody sees you. They stand here talking like I'm deaf.' He ejected the tape.

'That's all there is?'

'The total package.'

'Pleased I saw it before it goes upstairs.'

Saturday, 1 October

68

Mace and Christa sat at a table beside the pool, drinking rock shandies. On the table a Hammerli Trailside .22 target pistol, a box of ammunition. The Hammerli a present from Mace to Christa.

Mace'd been amazed at his daughter's reaction to the gun. Like this was better than shoes. Like she couldn't stop touching it, holding it, wanting to know when she could go shooting. He told her first she had to learn the parts, strip it like a pro. Christa'd wasted no time there.

Mace looked at his daughter, thought there was less strain in her face. The shrink beginning to have some effect, perhaps. He leant towards her, floated his hand over the soft fuzz of her hair. She didn't pull away. Three, four weeks ago she would've. Then again four weeks ago he couldn't lift that hand to touch her.

'I like the feel of your short hair,' he said. 'Sometimes it looks like a dirty halo.'

She frowned at him. 'Dirty?'

'You know, it's got this honey tinge, sort of yellowy.'

'Honey would be better than dirty.'

Mace swirled the ice in the last of his drink, took it in a swallow. Said, 'Time to rock 'n roll.' He stood up, grimacing at the pain in his thigh. This reminder of Sheemina February's handiwork, like she was still out for revenge. Of the two wounds, the leg shot proving the slower healer.

Christa shifted Cat2 from her lap, picked up the gun. 'Do we really have to move out of the house, Papa?' she said.

Mace grimaced again, unsure if it was Christa's question or the tear in his muscle.

'Fraid so,' he said. 'The bank's gonna repossess. That means they sell it at any price which'll be lower than I owe them, which'll mean I've got to pay them back the difference.'

'That's like robbery.'

'You said it.' Mace not telling her about Oumou's life insurance policy. The policy he'd hoped would rescue them. Except he'd found that Oumou had cashed it in years before. Probably to get the bank off their backs.

He held back a sigh, watched his daughter clasp the gun in both hands, straighten her arms pointing at a tree. 'I don't want to move. This is our house. Maman's house. It'd be like leaving her.'

Mace thought it just as well they hadn't sprinkled Oumou's ashes in the garden. Hadn't sprinkled Oumou's ashes anywhere yet for that matter. They were still in a vase in his bedroom. But if they'd gone into the garden like they planned, Christa would've been distraught. There'd have been no leaving the house then.

His thoughts flicked on to the diamonds he had stashed. The Cayman money. Funny how Revenue had backed off on that one. Not a peep out of them since the news report. You couldn't help thinking that'd been another of Sheemina February's little games. Then the cops'd backed off the investigation of her death. Like Sheemina February needed a quick burial. As Gonz had put it, 'Aren't you the lucky one, Meneer Bish. Nod, nod, wink, wink. Little pension contribution in order, hey!' Bloody Gonz.

'Papa. Papa.' Christa waving a hand in front of his face. Taking aim at the tree again.

Mace snapped back, said, 'I don't know, C, I'm trying to work something out.'

Pow. Pow. Christa blew off two imaginary shots. 'Come on,' she said, 'let's do the real thing.'

They took the Spider. Christa dubious, Mace saying, 'It's fixed. Listen to it.' He swung the engine and it fired first time. 'See. Sweet as a song.'

They tooled off to the quarry with the top down, the Stones' Aftermath cranked up so loud families in SUVs stared at them. Gave Mace a good feeling. The music, the bright day, his daughter. Suddenly seemed his darkness had gone.

Half an hour later they came off the Blue Route, took Boyes Drive down to Kalk Bay, catching glimpses of the ocean between the trees. Going round the headland into the Glencairn valley, Christa said, 'I don't mind if you see Tami.'

Like that. Out of nowhere. Mace thinking, what? Saying, 'I wasn't seeing her.'

'Well if you want to.'

Mace snatched a glance at his daughter, poker-faced, like her mother, sometimes you couldn't read her. Keeping her eyes on the road. 'She's not working for us anymore.'

Christa said, 'Oh. But if you want to, it's okay.'

'She's gone to Joburg,' said Mace. 'Pity. But there you go, hey.'

Mace parked at the whale-watch point. Popular for a Saturday afternoon, bunch of other cars with people enjoying themselves, old folks and tourists, eating ice creams, watching the sea. Some fishermen on the rocks below. A knot of boogie boarders surfing the reef. Maybe not a bad part of the peninsula to move to when the bank kicked them out of house 'n home. Rent a small condo just off the beach. Good bay for swimming. Something worth thinking about.

He and Christa crossed the road, Mace limping, walked back to the quarry and stood in the huge silence of the pit, gazing up at the raw rock. Some crows on the heights being harried by small birds.

'It's a spooky place,' said Christa.

'I don't know,' said Mace. 'I've been in worse.'

While he was setting up the targets, Pylon rang, invited them for a braai.

'We're shooting a few rounds in the quarry,' said Mace. 'Join us.'

'Ha ha,' said Pylon. Mace got an earful of two crying babies. 'Very funny.'

They disconnected, Mace thinking Pylon and Treasure had to be crazy adopting an Aids orphan. Still, different strokes.

Christa went first. Pulling off the shots one at a time, Mace, the weight on his good leg, standing beside her reading the hits. She was good. Few more outings, probably she'd be better than him. When she'd finished a clip, got her to reload and suggested she run through the cartridge for the thrill of it, fast as she could. Christa braced herself, took a breath, went into it, her grouping spraying out for the last four rounds.

'Not bad,' said Mace.

'I want to shoot pop-ups,' Christa said, a flash in her eyes Mace'd seen before. Had seen in the eyes of Sheemina February. Maybe everyone had it, the killer flash. 'On one of those combat courses.'

'We'll see,' said Mace. 'You're getting there.'

Back at the Spider, Christa got the top down while Mace went to stash the shooting kit in the boot. Lying there was a package tied with string, a long-stemmed rosebud sellotaped to it. Beneath that a hand-written note: 'She was getting a bit hectic.' In the package a Browning Buckmark. Looked like the Browning Buckmark Mace'd taken to shoot Sheemina February.

He did a quick scan of the parking spot. No one watching him. No one paying any attention.

Christa called, 'Come on, Papa, let's go.'

Bloody Mart Velaze. Mace closed the package, the realisation striking home: Velaze plugging her was a State hit because Sheemina February had too much dirt on too many people.

'Papa. Papa.'

Mace smiled to himself. That being the case this thing would disappear. No ways it would see the inside of a court, ever. Like Gonz'd said.

'Let's go. Let's go.'

Bloody Mart Velaze, his guardian angel standing by to ensure he blotted Ms February on their behalf. Bloody Mart Velaze the bloody NIA fixer. An uneasy thought, but what could you do? Mace slammed shut the boot, put on his papa face: all's right with the world.

Except the Spider wouldn't start. Went through the urrr urrr urrr stages, then died.

Christa said, 'I don't believe it.'

Mace gave the battery five minutes, tried again. Nothing doing. He slammed his fist on the steering wheel. Wanted to jump out and kick the car.

Christa said, 'We should've taken Maman's.'

'This car was purring,' said Mace. 'It got us here, no problem. It was going beautifully.'

They sat there gazing at the sea for the hour it took the mechanic to come out. Couldn't even listen to music, the battery was that flat.

The mechanic was huffy. Said, hell, man, he could think of better blerry things to do on a blerry Saturday afternoon. Mace said if he'd fixed it properly the first time this wouldn't have happened.

The mechanic put his head in the engine, came up fifteen minutes later with a diagnosis.

'Ja, hell man,' he said to Mace, the two men standing gazing down at the engine, 'this's a blerry problem. Know what I mean.' He closed the bonnet, wiped his palms on his overalls, looking up at the mountain, anywhere other than at Mace. 'I'd say yous reached the stop street without a rebore. Simple as that. Big bucks this'll cost you, hey.' He rapped his knuckles on the lid. 'Ja, hell man, this old biddy, this' – he shook his head – 'I'd say, hell man, I'd say, ja,' – he folded his arms – 'I'd say the way it is with your car, ag man, short and sweet like a beet, the fucking fucker's fucked, ek se. Finish 'n klaar. Know what I mean. End of story.'

ABOUT THE AUTHOR

Mike Nicol was born in Cape Town, where he still lives. *The Revenge Trilogy*, his first foray into crime fiction, has been greeted with widespread critical acclaim. His previous novels were published by Bloomsbury in the UK, and by Knopf in the USA.